"He was lying there in the dust, peacefully passed out, dressed in one of the fancy cowboy suits that he wore while performing. I could hardly believe it. My Uncle Red, Red Stovall, the soon-to-be-famous singer, rumpled and unshaven, reeking of whiskey, with a small smile on his face, as if he knew a secret that he wasn't ever going to tell..."

Fourteen-year-old Whit Wagoner was going to have to learn that secret—the secret of what it cost to be a hero and what it took to be a man—on an unforgettable journey across America with his legendary Uncle Red.

HONKYTONK MAN

By CLANCY CARLILE

A JOVE BOOK

This Jove book contains the complete
text of the original hardcover edition.
It has been completely reset in a typeface
designed for easy reading, and was printed
from new film.

HONKYTONK MAN

A Jove Book / published by arrangement with
Simon & Schuster, Inc.

PRINTING HISTORY
Simon and Schuster edition / January 1981
Jove edition / December 1982

ISBN: 0-515-07125-0

Jove books are published by Jove Publications, Inc.
200 Madison Avenue, New York, N.Y. 10016.
The words "A JOVE BOOK" and the "J" with sunburst
are trademarks belonging to Jove Publications, Inc.

PRINTED IN THE UNITED STATES OF AMERICA

To the best of friends,
Leonard Gardner and Gina Berriault.

For men must always follow a dream, no matter what. If fortune does not favor the old, it is, perhaps, because they can no longer believe in those chimeras, those mirages of the spirit, which the young go for helter-skelter, so sure of being able to reach them that obstacles fall under their unheeding feet before their existence has been suspected.

> —Henry de Monfried, *Adventures of a Red Sea Smuggler*

We are the music-makers,
And we are the dreamers of dreams.

> —A. O'Shaughnessy

HONKYTONK MAN

1

Uncle Red showed up at our farm one day during a dust storm. It was the first time he had visited us in four years, and it was the first dust storm of the year, and I was the first to see both of them coming.

We were out in the field that day, chopping cotton. The whole family was, except for Grandpa. And I was the first one to see the dust storm coming because I wasn't paying much attention to what I was supposed to be doing. I hated to chop cotton. The only thing I hated more than *chopping* cotton was *picking* it. But chopping was bad enough, because the sun was blazing down and the ground was so hot I could hardly step on it with bare feet. I tried to walk along in the shade of the cotton stalks, but they were so scrawny and far apart they hardly cast enough shade to cool a cricket. And not only were the plants already far apart, we were now having to chop every other plant out because of the drought. Papa said the best we could hope for was to get half the crop in, and if it didn't rain before the end of the month, we would lose it all. Good riddance, I would say, because I hated it. But I knew we had to have it to live. That was how my papa made his living for most of his life, as a cotton farmer, a sharecropper, and that was a hard thing to be in those days, in dust-bowl Oklahoma.

And the dust was another reason I hated chopping cotton.

1

Every time my hoe bit into the fine powdery red dust, it billowed up in little puffs to settle on my sweaty face and turn to mud in the creases and crannies of my neck and under my eyes and in my eyebrows. The gnats that swarmed about my ears and nostrils, incessantly whining, added to my misery, and having to walk barefoot on the hot shadowless ground was torture, too, but the worst thing was the dust. By the middle of the afternoon, when it got so hot that a cricket might leave a cotton stalk and try to hop along in your shadow, a very thin red haze hung over the whole cotton field, and when the heat shimmered through the red dust, the land looked as if it were aflame.

Anyway, I was the first to see the storm coming. Maybe it was the sudden disappearance of the gnats that prompted me to look up, or maybe I began to hear it, a faraway moaning sound, the kind of sound that registers on the senses before it can be heard. But for whatever reason, I suddenly looked up, and there it was on the western horizon: a wall of reddish-brown dust, as high as the sky and wide as the world, moving toward us.

I made a megaphone of my hands and called to Papa across the field. He looked up from his chopping to see what I wanted, but I didn't have to say anything. He saw it. And then the others looked up, too. Mama and my older sister, Margery, were wearing sunbonnets, so I couldn't see their faces, but my older brother's face, beneath the floppy brim of his battered old felt hat, was pinched with a frown very much like Papa's, a look of baffled defeat, like that of a bear that's been bested in a fight by a puny skunk.

Papa was too far away for me to hear his words, but I could see his lips moving, and I could guess what he was mumbling: "Jesus Christ, what next?"

For the last few years we had been plagued by dust storms. Papa hoped each year, as he watched his crops wither and die, that next year would be better, but each year the summer winds brought the dust that ruined us, and now here was another storm, the first one of the year, and surely not the last. So Papa looked up at the sky and cursed his luck. He was the only person I knew who actually talked to his luck, as if his luck, his own personal Luck, was one of the great moving powers of the universe, like Chance and Fate and Evil. And he talked to his Luck in a barely audible mumble, in a tone of weary and grudging forbearance, as if he were sick and tired of waiting for things to get better. "What'd I do to deserve *this?*" he often asked of his Luck, baffled and bitter, like someone who has been punished for something he didn't do.

But he finally shook his head in resentful acceptance of the fact that the dust storm was bearing down on us and that no amount of cursing or complaining would stop it. He signaled for us to go in.

Carrying our hoes, we struck out across the field toward the house, walking fast. It looked as if we would have maybe thirty minutes before the storm hit, and during that time we would have a number of chores to do, such as shutting the animals up in the barn, milking the cows, taking the clothes off the line, locking the chickens in the chicken coop, gathering the eggs, getting plenty of firewood and water into the house— things like that.

As the storm got closer, moving across the prairie landscape from horizon to horizon, a colossal mile-high wall of dust and sand, it blotted out everything in its path except the sun, which burned through the red dust in a deep-red glow, shimmering like the fires inside a furnace. Then I began to hear it, a low rumbling sound, the sound of a distant cannonade, coming closer and closer.

"You! Whit!" Papa yelled at me. "Stop playing with that dog and get that hen and chicks inside."

I was chasing the hen. Tige, our dog, was trying to help but was only scaring the hen and scattering her cheeping chicks, making them harder to catch. I kicked him.

"Get outa here!" I yelled, and he, offended by my lack of gratitude for his help, sauntered on down to the barn to help my older brother, Howard, drive the cows and mules into their stalls.

The wall of dust loomed over us, and soon the first gusts of wind swirled through the yard, flapping my pants against my legs, blowing Papa's hat off. In a spraddle-legged running movement like that of an angry duck, he chased the hat as it rolled tumbling across the yard and finally lodged against the woodshed.

Then it hit. The sound of it, a high-pitched howling noise, and the first showers of sand that stung my face, made me bolt for the house. Margery was at the windmill, trying to pull the chain that would lock the windmill and keep the fan from turning. If left unlocked, the windmill would soon fly apàrt in the high wind, and already the fan was rotating so fast that Margery couldn't pull the stop-chain by herself.

"Help me!" she cried over the sound of the wind and the squeaky clattering of the runaway windmill. Her sunbonnet had blown off and her dark hair blew wildly. Her eyes squinted against the onslaught of stinging sand.

It took both of us to pull the chain and stop the windmill. Then I grabbed a bucket of water and headed for the house. The water sloshed out over my feet and legs as I ran. Margery was directly behind me, also carrying a bucket of water, and directly behind her was Tige. He was the only one of us who seemed to think that all this frantic activity was great fun.

Mama had already gone into the house to help Grandpa stuff pieces of cloth—dishtowels, old shirts and dresses, washrags, things like that—into the cracks around the windows and doors to keep the dust out, a hopeless task. The boards of the house, unpainted, had long ago warped and cracked beneath the harsh summer suns and winter blizzards that blew down across the Great Plains into Oklahoma, and some of the cracks were so big you could see daylight through them. Set in the middle of a cotton field, unprotected by trees, weatherbeaten and wind-buffeted, the house creaked and groaned in the wind like an ungreased wagon.

The rags in the cracks helped a little. They kept most of the bigger grains of sand out of the house. But nothing could keep out the dust, fine as talcum powder, that came in through the cracks to float on the air and settle on the furniture, in our beds, in the food, in the water, making everything gritty to the touch and taste.

Papa came in from the barn cursing. He slapped his dusty hat against his dusty clothes.

"This is it," he announced to everyone. "I'm sick of it. If *this* crop is ruined, I'll tell you right now, we're gonna leave this goddamned place."

After we got all the larger cracks around the windows and doors chinked with rags, there was nothing much left for us to do except hunker down and endure it. We soaked handkerchiefs in water and used them as dust masks. Mama had a hard time making baby sister Penny keep the wet handkerchief over her face.

"How about if we sing something?" I suggested, but nobody

leaped at the idea. During the dust storms last year, when we had been stuck in the house and unable even to listen to our big old battery-powered Philco radio because of the static from the storm, we sometimes passed the hours by singing. Sometimes, though, back before my voice started changing, Mama would ask me to sing a song alone. She had told me that I took after her side of the family because I was the only one among us kids who could really sing. Mama had come from a musical family. Everybody in her family had played an instrument and sung, and her younger brother had even gone on to become a professional singer, a real star—not a big one yet, it was true, but everybody said it was just a matter of time. That was Uncle Red. I always tried to sing like him, and Mama said that as soon as my voice stopped changing, I might even be as good as Uncle Red. At that time, however, I was barely fourteen years old, and the timbre of my once-tenor voice fluctuated, sometimes rapidly, between a squeaky soprano and a gravelly baritone. One day in the cotton field, when I was trying to sing "Wabash Cannonball" as I had heard Roy Acuff do on the Grand Ole Opry, Papa got so tired of hearing me that he said, "Godamighty, you sound like a cross between a screech owl and a bullfrog. Hush that for a while."

"That's all right," Mama said later, trying to console me. "You're still the best singer in the family—or at least you will be again, soon's your voice gets through changing. Till then, though, maybe you'd better go off by yourself when you want to sing."

Maybe that was why nobody took my suggestion that we sing while we waited for the dust storm to end. Still, it was a good idea, because pretty soon, during a brief lull in the storm, I thought I could hear someone in the room humming a few notes of "Swing Low, Sweet Chariot."

It was Grandpa. He was humming into his harmonica, making a sound eerily like the wailing wind, exactly on key with the wind. He sat in a far corner of the room in a rocking chair, holding the harmonica to his mustached mouth with his good right arm. His withered left arm lay uselessly in his lap. He was the only one of us who wasn't holding a wet dust mask to his face. He disdained the dust. He said he had breathed so much of it by now that his lungs had become a mud puddle anyway, so why bother? And from the way he wheezed and gurgled when he breathed, I could believe it. He was Papa's father. About seventy years old, he was, and getting feeble. He didn't do much of anything anymore except sit around the house and play his harmonica and write poems, but in his day he had been a pioneer, a sheepherder, a farmer, a snakehunter and a homesteader. He was always ready to tell any grown-up who would listen about how he had made the Run—talking about the Run as if it had been the most important thing that ever happened in the history of the country: the day the Cherokee Strip had been opened up to white settlers. He loved to tell how thousands and thousands of settlers had scrambled across the starting line and into the Strip to claim homesteads for themselves, and devil take the hindmost. But he had been living with us for over a year now, and he never talked about the Run anymore to Papa and Mama because they had heard about it too many times.

Anyway, as he sat in his rocking chair, blurred by the haze of red dust that hovered in the air, he hummed into his harmonica, accompanying the wind.

> *Swing low, sweet chariot,*
> *Coming for to carry me home . . .*

I began to hum along with him, and soon Mama joined in, too. Mama had a beautiful hill-country voice, and could sing the best harmonies of anyone I had ever heard. It was difficult for us to sing along with Grandpa's playing, though, because he didn't play with a steady beat. He just sort of speeded up or slowed down according to how the wind was blowing at the moment, wailing along with it, and we wailed along with him.

And as we were singing, a gust of wind blew a rag from a crack between the window and the sill, allowing a little jet of dust to spurt into the room. I got up to replace the rag, and, doing so, glanced out the window and thought I saw some strange lights coming down the road toward our house. I wiped the dust from the windowpane and looked again, and, sure enough, there they were, two automobile headlights flickering in the swirling dust, each light with a dust-red nimbus around it, and then the car itself suddenly broke through the dust and I saw what it was: a big beautiful Packard limousine, black as midnight and all shiny with chrome and lacquer. It had white sidewall tires, and carried two spare tires on the fenders, one on each side of the car. It came out of the dust like an apparition, like a spaceship, a chariot of the gods that had suddenly appeared from out of the dusty red sky in answer to our sung invocation to swing low.

"Hey!" I said. "Somebody's coming!"

Everybody fell silent. They all looked at me for a moment, skeptical and a little threatening, as if they suspected me of trying to fool them.

"It's a brand-new car!" I cried, and then I saw what was attached to the car's radiator grill, preceding the car like the bowsprit of a ship: a wide, well-turned, polished and deadly-looking set of longhorns. A glance at the dusty license plate told me that the car was from out of state, but I had never seen one like it before, so I couldn't guess which state it was from.

Mama said, "Company? At a time like *this?*" She hurriedly deposited baby sister Penny on the bed and came to stand beside me at the window, her work-hardened hands moving over her clothes and hair to spruce herself up a little. She was still dressed in her cotton-chopping clothes: a man's frayed and faded blue work shirt, worn over an old gingham dress that had been made from flour sacks, with brogans on her feet. Her hair was braided and coiled into a bun on the back of her head.

"Well, I swear," she said, bemused and suspicious, refusing to let herself hope that the car could possibly be connected with *us*. "Somebody took the wrong road in this storm, is all. But, my my my, just look at that *car*. . . ."

Everybody got up and came to the windows—everybody except Grandpa, that is. He stopped humming into his harmonica, but he didn't get out of his rocking chair. He was an aloof old man, even a little disdainful of our excitement, as if he, who had made the Run into the Cherokee Strip, could hardly be expected to become excited about the mere arrival of an unexpected visitor, however remarkable the means of transport.

But *I* was excited. The car, more beautiful than any I had ever seen before, was exciting enough in itself, but I was really set asparkle when I thought I recognized who was driving it. Before I could cry out, however, I was struck dumb by the realization that the car wasn't going to stop. As it plunged luxuriously toward the old picket fence that enclosed our front yard, it didn't seem to be under the influence of any brakes. It didn't even slow down, in fact, when it hit the picket fence. It just lurched a little, got astraddle the fence and rolled along the length of it. And above the moaning of the wind, I could hear the loud popping of wooden pickets.

And still the car didn't stop. The fence seemed to slow it down a little, but when it hit the small ditch just before the chickenhouse, it lurched leftward, missing the chickenhouse by inches, and rolled on toward the windmill and watertank.

I was the first one out the door, and the others—even Grandpa—followed me out onto the porch to see what was going on, and what was going on was the car. It bounced off a stump near the woodpile, careened around the watertank and struck the windmill. The left front of the car hit one of the windmill stanchions. In an explosion of breaking wood, the stanchion tore away and crashed to the ground. The windmill itself, three-legged now, shuddered and swayed in the wind.

The car came to a bucking stop on the edge of the cotton field, just as the three-legged windmill came crashing down in a mass of splintering supports and cracking timbers. It missed the car by only a few feet.

I was already running. Through the swirls of sand and dust I could see that there was a driver in the car, slumped over the steering wheel. Mama was right behind me when I got to the car and jerked the door open.

It was Uncle Red. He had slumped forward over the steering wheel, leaning against the door, and when I opened the door, he slowly tumbled out. I grabbed for him and broke his fall, but he was too limp for me to hold onto, so he slid on down to the ground. His feet were still in the car. The cowboy boots he wore, made of hand-tooled alligator hide, were splotched with something that appeared to be puke. His cowboy hat was on the floor of the car. So was a smashed bottle of whiskey. The smell was awful.

All the other members of the family gathered around, with mutterings and cries of shock and recognition, and Mama fell on her knees beside Uncle Red, crying, "Hassle, Hassle! What is it? Are you hurt?"

Uncle Red's proper first name was Haskel. That was the name they gave him when he was born, and Mama, his sister, who had been only three years old then, hadn't been able to say Haskel. She had called him Hassle, and it was such a comic way of saying the name that everybody in her family soon started calling him that. But no red-headed boy ever went too long without being called Red, at least by people outside his family, and that was the name that stuck—mainly, I suppose, because he was exactly the kind of person that redheads were thought to be: a prankster with a fiery temper, a hooky player, a hell raiser and finally, of course, a honkytonker.

But now he was lying there in the dust, peacefully passed out, dressed in one of his fancy cowboy suits, the flowery and fringed costume that he wore while performing, and the suit, like his face, looked soiled and slept-in. He had a two-or three-day growth of beard, and there was a small idiotic grin on his face.

"For God's sake," Mama said, cradling his head in her arms. "Is he *dead?*"

"No," Papa said, reaching inside the car to pick up the neck portion of the broken whiskey bottle. "Passed out, is all."

"Oh, Hassle!" Mama cried. "What in the world . . . ?"

The dust swirled around us.

"Well, come on," Papa said. "Let's get him on up to the house."

I could hardly believe it, but there he was. My Uncle Red, Red Stovall, the soon-to-be-famous singer, lying passed out in the dust, rumpled and unshaven, reeking of whiskey, with a small smile on his face, as if he knew a secret that he wasn't ever going to tell.

2

Ever since I could remember, I had heard Mama telling stories about her baby brother, Hassle. He had been the darling of her family, the youngest and most talented of the children, the one that everybody loved and spoiled. I could remember having seen him maybe only four or five times in my life—memories of rare visits to Mama's folks, who lived down near Ardmore. Memories of family reunions, where Uncle Red sang and played his guitar and everybody clapped and asked for more. Everybody was sure that he was going to be a professional musician someday. And it wasn't long after Grandma Stovall's funeral that Uncle Red, the last of the family left living at home, slung his guitar over his shoulder and started down the road.

Years later Mama got a postcard from him that said he had become a member of the Louisiana Hayride, a radio program that was broadcast out of Shreveport every Saturday night. We tried to get the station on our old Philco, but couldn't. We could get the Grand Ole Opry, though, out of Nashville, Tennessee, which was what we listened to every Saturday night. We kept hoping that maybe Uncle Red could someday get on the Grand Ole Opry so we could hear him sing over the radio.

But the next time we heard him sing was in our home in Oklahoma, and he was there in person. He was on his way from Louisiana to Arizona at the time, going West for his

10

health, he said, because a doctor had told him that his lungs wouldn't last another ten years if he didn't lay off the booze and cigarettes and go live in a place where the air was clean and dry. The doctor had scared him by taking him to a place where tubercular patients were dying, and saying, "You see? This's what you're going to be going through in just a few years if you don't start doing what I tell you."

"Scared me a little," Uncle Red confessed. Scared him enough to make him decide to go to Arizona. And he had detoured through Oklahoma so he could visit us. At the time of that first visit, he was driving a Model A Ford coupe that had a rumble seat. It wasn't an old car, but it was considerably banged-up, because Uncle Red was just learning how to drive, and every once in a while, he said, the damned car just seemed to run into something, as if it had a contrary and perverse will of its own.

I was only nine years old when he came to visit us that first time, but I had already listened to enough country singers on the radio—singers like Jimmie Rodgers and Roy Acuff—to know a good one when I heard one, and Uncle Red was a good one. Everybody thought so. He sang in a very special tone of voice, a sort of high lonesome sound, a sound that came to be associated with train whistles and piney woods, with wandering and weariness, with guitars and fiddles played in smoky old barrooms and honkytonks and mountain cabins, with good whiskey and bad women and good women and bad whiskey, with a feeling of loss so profound that it could break hearts. And he was a good guitar picker, too. He played Carter-family-style, mostly: picking with all the fingers of his right hand, making all sorts of little bass runs and treble trills to accompany his high lonesome singing.

"My darling lies asleep in the graveyard," he sang during that first visit to our house, and sometimes I would join him on the chorus. I could sing pretty good harmony then, but my voice was so sharp and penetrating that it sometimes hurt your ears when I hit a high note.

"I swear," Uncle Red said of me then, "this boy could sing tenor to a dog whistle."

I sure hated to see him go. Mama made him promise to write us a postcard every once in a while, but we only got two from him. The first one was mailed from a TB sanitarium in Scottsdale, Arizona. The second one arrived almost two years

later, mailed from Redondo Beach, California. It had a picture
on it, a tinted photograph of an enormous dance hall at night,
with searchlights in front of the place, their beams of light
crossed in the night sky, and along the whole length of the
dance hall's roofline was a sign made of thousands of twinkling
lightbulbs that said *Dream Bowl*. The printed message on the
card described the Dream Bowl as a world-famous ballroom
in Redondo Beach, California. The written message, pencil-
scrawled in an almost illegible handwriting, said, "Dear Sis
and all. Finally played here. Opened for Bob Wills, the headliner. The manager says I could be the headliner here myself
someday soon. Love, Red." There was no return address on
the card.

Mama gave me the card. I kept it on a nail beside my bed,
and every once in a while, maybe just before going to sleep,
I would stare at the picture on the card and wonder—try to
imagine—what it would be like to be Uncle Red and play in
a place like that, the Dream Bowl, appearing on the same bill
with a star like Bob Wills. Maybe someday I would have a
band, too, and would play there. . . .

Almost two years passed from the time we received that
postcard to the time that Uncle Red, dead drunk, came driving
down the road toward our house during the dust storm in his
big beautiful black Packard limousine and crashed it into our
fence and windmill.

We carried him up to the house. Papa and Howard took
him by his arms, Mama and I each took a leg. We put him in
my sister's room. Margery was the only one in the family who
had a room to herself. I and my two brothers and Grandpa all
slept in the same room, with Grandpa and me sharing one bed
and big brother Howard and my little brother Willie sharing
another. Mama and Papa slept in the big bed in the front room.
The only other sleeping room was a small one off the side of
the house—Margery's room—and that's where we put Uncle
Red. He didn't weigh much—probably not more than a hundred
and twenty pounds soaking wet. Hardly more than skin and
bones.

As soon as he was stretched out on the bed, he smacked
his lips a couple of times, as if he had just had a good drink
and began to snore. All of us stood around the bed for a
moment, gawking at him, wondering how he came to be here
and marveling at the beauty of his gaudy performing outfit

the pants and shirt of which were a matching sky-blue color. The shirt had a yoke of darker blue, the same color as the fringes on the sleeves, while the musical notes that were embroidered across his chest and shoulders were a sort of pearl-white and were bordered with sequins. The pants, too, had the embroidered pearl-white and sequin-bordered musical notes on the pockets and down the sides of the legs.

"All right, everybody," Mama finally said, making us quiet down. "Virgil," she said to Papa, "you get him undressed. I'll get some black coffee. Howard, you stoke the fire up and put on a tub of water to heat. Whit, you go down to his car, see what you can find in the way of clean clothes and maybe a toilet kit. The rest of you scoot."

I slipped on an old coat and turned the collar up against the storm before I went out to Uncle Red's car. The sky was becoming redder and redder as the sun, obscured by the swirling dust, edged toward evening. The storm gave the day a sort of eerie significance, and I felt, as I approached the beautiful car, that something significant and irreversible was going to happen when I touched it. I hesitated, my fingers just inches from the door handle, for a long moment, and my heart was pounding when I opened the door and got into the driver's seat. I pulled the heavy and well-oiled door closed, and the sound of the storm was suddenly almost shut out. All I could hear now and then was a faint moaning of the wind, a faraway plaintive sound. There was some dust inside the car, but it must have gotten in while the door was opened, for the car, with all the windows and doors closed, seemed almost airtight and soundproof.

The car reeked of moonshine. And besides the broken bottle, the floor was littered with orange peels and candy wrappers and empty crumpled cigarette packages, and the ashtray was overflowing with cigarette butts. And on the floor amid all this trash was Uncle Red's cowboy hat. I picked it up and tried it on. Didn't fit. Too big. It was a pearl-white Stetson. I left it resting on my ears as I ran my fingers over the luxurious mohair seats and over the highly polished trim on the dark-blue mohair paneling.

Even then, at fourteen years of age, I had an almost reverent appreciation of a beautiful and powerful and well-made machine, and this was the best I had ever seen. The speedometer indicated that the car would do a hundred and ten miles an hour. The fastest I had ever been was about forty-five miles an hour, which was as fast as our old Chevy truck could go, and to think of actually traveling at a hundred and ten miles an hour was enough to make my heart flutter.

The key was in the ignition, in the on position, which meant that the motor had stalled. With a sinking sensation in my stomach, I wondered if the car's collision with the windmill had slammed the radiator back into the fan. I decided to find out.

Papa had taught me how to drive our old Chevy truck, so it wasn't difficult to figure out how to start the Packard. And to my great relief, the engine came alive immediately. It purred, purred without pause, and not one clanking or grinding noise did I hear. I revved the engine up a little. Its purring power vibrated through the car and through my body. I wanted to honk the horn, but I was afraid someone at the house would hear it and think something was wrong—which reminded me of why I had come to the car in the first place, so I shut the engine off and looked around for Uncle Red's clothes and toilet things.

There weren't any. There wasn't a suitcase or a toilet kit in the car. Not even a toothbrush. On the floor of the back seat was a guitar case. I picked it up and put it on the back seat and, after only a moment's hesitation, fumbled it open. Inside was a beautiful big F-hole sunburst Gibson guitar, all lovely with lacquer and inlaid mother-of-pearl. I had seen pictures of such guitars, but had never been near one until now, never before touched one. It was like touching a jewel, cool and glassy-smooth.

Then I saw the bottle. It was in a pocket on the underside of the case lid: an old whiskey bottle with no label on it, filled with a whitish-amber liquid. Moonshine. I knew what it was because Papa had sometimes brought it home in a fruit jar. Mama wouldn't allow the stuff in the house, however, and if she had found it, she would have poured it out. So Papa had hidden the jar in the haystack out behind the barn. Once when he sneaked out to have a drink of it, I watched where he put it, and later I went out to have a taste, trying to find out why grown-ups—especially men—seemed to like it so much. And after one sip, I was more mystified than ever. I could easily understand why Mama called it poison. I wondered if I should tell her about this bottle, but quickly decided against it. I felt vaguely as if I would be betraying her in some way by keeping silent about it, but to do otherwise would be even a greater betrayal of Uncle Red, and I knew I couldn't do that, even if it was for his own good. So I decided to feign complete ignorance of it. I took the guitar, and after checking the trunk to make certain there were no suitcases there, I pulled Uncle Red's hat down over my ears and dashed back to the house.

"Just a guitar?" Mama said, and reached out to snatch the cowboy hat off my head. "Not a stitch of clothes? All the clothes he's got is on his back?" She hung the hat on a nail near the kitchen door.

Papa had finished undressing Uncle Red. The fancy performing suit was piled in a corner of the kitchen.

"Well, he can't wear none of yourn," Mama said, meaning Papa and Grandpa. Uncle Red was probably four or five inches taller than they were. "I guess I'll have to wash these."

We didn't have any dinner that day. No use trying to cook any, with the house full of dust. The food would be so gritty by the time we got it into our mouths that we wouldn't be able to chew it. We had coffee, though, and some dried apricots and some sardines that we ate from the can, passing the can and a fork among us.

Darkness came early. The wind buffeted the house, and the sand that sprayed the windows made sounds like despairing sighs. Talk was sporadic and fragmentary, most of it between Mama and Papa.

"This is the end for us here," he said, gazing out the window, as if he, trancelike, were gazing into a crystal ball. "With the windmill gone . . ."

Fidgeting with embarrassment and guilt, because Uncle Red was her brother, after all, and therefore somehow her responsibility, Mama said, "Maybe he's got the money to fix it. Driving that big car, and all . . ."

Papa shook his head. "He ain't got but two dollars on him, and no checkbook, neither." Pinned by Mama's inquiring gaze, he sheepishly explained that Uncle Red's wallet had accidentally fallen out of his pants and he had looked in it.

"No money?" Mama said, trying not to be accusatory. "But how could he? None at *all?* You're sure?"

"None that I seen. Unless he's got some maybe hidden in the car somewhere."

"And no clothes, 'cept the ones he had on? That's awful

strange, ain't it?" she asked. She was on the big bed, leaning back against the bedstead, nursing baby sister Penny. Little brother Willie was huddled up beside her, sucking his thumb. "You don't maybe think he's . . . ?"

But Papa's thoughts weren't exclusively about Uncle Red. He was worried about the farm. "Wouldn't do any good, anyway, even if we could fix it." He meant the windmill. "The cotton won't stand this." He sighed heavily. "If this storm's as bad as it looks, there won't be nothing to hold us here no more. We best start thinking about moving on to California."

Mama looked as if she wanted to avoid the subject. Preoccupied and puzzled, she said, "He just came from out there, don't you reckon? But with no money and only the clothes on his back? Where's he headed for, I wonder? Oh, I wish to goodness he'd wake up! I'll just cast kittens if I can't find out what's going on!"

"Nashville," Papa said as he lit one of the kerosene lamps.
"Nashville?"

"Probably where he's headed."

Everybody looked at him, waiting for him to explain how he knew *that*. After adjusting the wick in the lamp, he shrugged, sheepish again, and said, "A letter was in his pocket, too. I couldn't help seeing the first few lines, so . . ." He tipped his head, as if to say that he had only done what was natural, after all, something anybody would have done. "It was from somebody in Nashville, wanting him to come and maybe sing on the Grand Ole Opry."

"What?" I said. "The Grand Ole Opry?"

Mama was excited, too. "But why didn't you *tell* us?"

"The letter," Papa said. "Maybe I shouldn't've read it."

"Well, of course you shouldn't've," Mama agreed. "But as long as you did, you might've told us sooner! My Godamighty! The Grand Ole Opry! Oh, if only Mama was alive today." But then she seemed to have second thoughts. With a sidelong look toward Margery's room, she added, "On the other hand, though, maybe it's just as well."

Then we heard Grandpa murmur, "Tennessee"—just that one word, "Tennessee," and then he was silent again. We looked at him. "Maybe I ought to go back," he said after a long pause, as if talking to himself. He had been born there, in Tennessee, but had left when he was a young man, and hadn't been back since.

"Tennessee?" Mama said, astounded. "What on earth for?"

Grandpa didn't answer. And it soon became apparent that he wasn't going on, so we let the remark pass as the dreamy mutterings of an old man in a rocking chair.

I went to bed early. It was obvious that Uncle Red wasn't going to wake up until the next morning, so I figured I might as well crawl into bed and savor my excitement alone. I brushed the dust off the quilts before I got into bed, but there was no escaping the grit. Somehow it had even got through the covers and into the sheets.

Grandpa came to bed at his usual hour, around nine, and he didn't light a lamp. He undressed in the dark, an old man of precise movements who had a place for everything. He brushed off the bottoms of his feet before he got into bed, first one foot and then the other, and then stretched out, pulled his withered left arm across his chest, and tucked the covers under his chin.

"Grandpa?" I said, whispering loudly to be heard above the howling wind. "What'd you mean about maybe going back to Tennessee?"

"Just thinking," he answered, and that was all. He nearly always spoke in a take-it-or-leave-it tone, as if he couldn't be bothered to explain himself. The only time he was ever talkative was on the subject of the Run, but most of the grown-ups I knew had already got tired of the story before I was even born, and he didn't like to talk to kids very much, so I had never heard the story in its entirety. It wasn't that he disliked kids, or had anything against us; he just didn't seem to have any patience with us, no time or words to waste on someone who might not understand or appreciate what he was saying. A man of pure Scotch stock, Grandpa was frugal with everything, including emotions, time, money, words, space. And he looked the part of the dour Scotsman, too, one of those Highlanders whose pictures I had seen in the *National Geographics* at school: gaunt, craggy-faced men with the unblinking eyes of predatory birds.

When Grandpa first came to Oklahoma, he had married an Indian woman, a Cherokee, and their first son was Virgil, my father. I had been told that her name—my grandmother's name—was Tyetha, but I had never known her. She died before I was born. I wasn't even quite sure where she was buried. Grandpa kept a picture of her in a gilt frame on his chest of drawers, a sepia-toned photograph of her when she was maybe twenty years old: a strong, handsome girl, dark and unsmiling. Just the kind of woman for Grandpa. Grandpa was the only one who seemed to have a picture of her.

After a long silence, I said, "Grandpa? You asleep?"

He didn't answer. If he had said yes, as he sometimes did when I asked that question, it would have meant that he didn't want to talk. When he remained silent, however, it meant that he would at least listen if I had something to say.

"Are you ever going to tell me about the Run?" I asked, vaguely fearing that he might go to Tennessee without having told me the story.

He cleared his throat, and when he finally spoke, his voice was as gentle as I had ever heard it. He apparently had been touched by my wanting to know about the Run. It was no doubt a rare request. Still, I was only a boy. . . .

"Someday," he said. "When you're old enough." And after another moment's pause, he added, "Go to sleep."

But I couldn't. Not for a long time. The air was too charged, the events too portentous. I think I realized even then, as I lay awake and listened to the dust storm moaning around the house, that this had been a day of destiny for all of us. I don't know how I knew it, or how I even came to call it destiny, never before having experienced such a day, but somewhere within me, in my flesh and bone, in my blood, was the feeling that this day had marked a turning point, after which nothing would ever be the same again.

3

Sounds woke me twice during the night. The first was the sound of silence, the eerie dead silence that settles over the land after a storm has passed and before the insects that give the night a faint background glow of sound can shake off their layers of dust and bring the world back to life. The dust storm had passed.

The second sound was that of a coughing fit. The ash-fine dust that hung in the air like a haze caused everybody in the house to cough now and then, of course, but such coughs were dry little throat-clearing sounds, while the coughing that woke me up was deep and loud and convulsive. It came from the room where Uncle Red slept.

I heard Mama get out of bed and hurry into Uncle Red's room. After more coughing, muted voices talked, urgent and airy, muffled by walls, and soon footsteps could be heard scurrying to and from the kitchen, while the coughing fit gradually subsided, giving way to longer and longer periods of strangled panting, and then finally lapsed into a blessed and sleepy silence.

I got up at dawn. Nearly everybody did. When the rooster started to crow and the first gray light of day crinkled through the dust-crusted windows, I came awake almost unwillingly, as if in response to some mysterious force that moved gently through the house and waked us one by one. And then we slowly, quietly began to get up and get dressed. Hardly a word passed between us. It was as if some urge—an urge as mysterious and yet as natural as any bodily function—caused us to stumble, bleary-eyed and grimy, out of our beds and fumble into our gritty clothes, and then straggle, one by one, out of the house to see, in the first light of sunup, what damage the storm had done to our world.

A thin haze of red dust still hung in the air, turning the dawn light into a pale reddish glow, and everything was sheathed in the red dust, and the devastation was awful to see. Papa stood at the edge of the cotton field, stunned. Mama stood a little way behind him. The rest of us—Grandpa, Howard, Margery and I, with our dog, Tige, tagging along behind us, as curious and grave as we humans—were scattered across the yard, each of us apart and alone, almost somnambulant in the eerie red glow of the rising sun, gazing at the fields of ruined cotton.

The sand that had blown along the ground in gusts of wind had cut like a scythe through the cotton stalks, topping most of them. The plants that remained standing were shredded and broken.

"Ruined," Papa said in a flat whispery voice to no one in particular—maybe talking to his Luck again. "All ruined. . . ."

Mama sniffled. I was pretty far away from her, but the strange red world was still so quiet that I had no trouble hearing the sniffle, and then I saw that her face was streaked with tears. It wasn't a beautiful face, and never had been, though it had been handsome once. I had seen pictures of her when she was a young woman, radiant, buoyant and strong. Now her face was careworn and pinched, but though she was no longer radiant and buoyant, she was at least still strong.

"Well," she said to Papa, wiping the tears off her face with the back of her hand, "you been wanting us to go out to California. . . ."

Papa nodded. "Shore," he said, looking on the dark side of it, "but we should've gone 'fore this. Now we lost everything."

"I'm sorry," Mama said, her face puckered in her efforts to keep from crying openly. "It was always that . . . it was just that . . ."

It was just that she had never wanted to go to California. She had wanted to stay on the farm and try to make a go of it. "We got kids to raise, Virgil," she would say to Papa. "We can't just go gallivanting off to California. No telling what'd happen to us out there. What if we couldn't find work? What if you got sick and there was no one to take care of us?"

It had all been said before, but now it looked as if there was no choice left. "Well, we can't stay here no longer," Papa said. "We got to go somewheres." But he didn't sound as if he thought living would be any easier, no matter where we went. It pained me to think it, but it was plain to me, even then, that Papa was a defeated man. He was half Indian, and had the dark looks of an Indian, and maybe it was that part of him that seemed so defeated, like the Indian in the painting called *The End of the Trail* that I had once seen on a calendar.

But the hell of it was, Papa seemed to get some strange satisfaction from his defeats, or at least from his ability to foretell them, as if they were ordained and therefore a sort of fulfillment for him.

But not Grandpa. As he stood there in the red glow of the rising sun, staring at the ruined cotton fields with those eyes of a predatory bird, he said, "Wasn't worth much to begin with." It was as if he refused to give the storm the satisfaction of having ruined us.

Papa, however, wasn't going to let anyone minimize his misfortune. He looked around, surveying the damage, and let his eyes linger on the fallen windmill. "And now we won't even have water."

"The tank's full," Mama was quick to say. "It's enough to last us a couple of weeks, and by then..."

While they were talking, I walked over to inspect Uncle Red's car, expecting to feel the same excitement that I had felt yesterday when I first saw it emerging from the dust storm like a chariot emerging from the clouds. What I felt, however, wasn't excitement but a sort of shocked pity. The car looked awful. There were little deposits of dust and sand nestled in every nook and cranny of its body, as if it had been sitting here gathering dust for fifty years. The two tires on the driver's side had gone flat—nail punctures from the wrecked fence, no doubt—and the front fender that had hit the windmill stanchion was bashed in, the headlight was broken, the lovely chrome grill was bent, and the tip of one of the steer horns had been broken off.

And those were only the damages that the car had sustained

yesterday. Now I could see other dents and scrapes received in other accidents, and there were streaks of dried vomit on the passenger's side that stretched from the front window to the back bumper.

"You, Whit," Mama called as she turned back toward the house. "Come on, now. We got lots of work to do."

She was right. Digging out after a dust storm was always a lot of work. We began in the kitchen: swept up the sand, washed all the dishes and pots and pans, ran a damp rag over the cabinets and windowsills. Then Mama made breakfast in the clean kitchen while the rest of us began cleaning the rest of the house, sweeping up sand, dusting pictures and lamps, shaking out quilts and doilies. But we didn't go into Margery's room, because Uncle Red was still asleep. Mama said to let him sleep as long as he wanted to.

"He's sick," she said, and by this I thought she meant that he was hungover, because that was what she always said about Papa when *he* was bedridden with a busthead hangover for a day or two after a moonshine spree. But then she said to Papa in a worried voice, "It's getting worse," and I realized she meant the TB. I didn't know much about TB at that time, except that quite a few people seemed to have it. Nobody I knew had died of it, however, so I hadn't thought about it as being a fatal disease. I thought it was just some unfortunate defect of the body, like Grandpa's withered arm, that a person learned to live with. But having heard that terrible coughing fit last night, and seeing Mama so worried now, I should have realized how sick Uncle Red really was. But I refused to believe it, to consider it, face it—even to hear it.

"Can I go now?" I said. "Is it all right if I go clean up his car?"

"Clean up your plate first," Mama said.

After breakfast, Papa got our old Chevy truck out of the barn and brought it around to the front of the house and used a long rope to pull the Packard limousine back across the little gully, through the chicken yard, and into the area in front of the house where the ground was level enough for me to jack the car up.

After fixing the flats, I dusted the car, took out all the trash and broken glass and went over the interior with a damp cloth. I was even going to wash the outside of it, but Papa said that now, with the windmill gone, we had better not waste any water on the car. I did wash the streaks of dried vomit off it, however, and went over all of it with a damp cloth.

When I went back into the house, I met Mama coming out of Uncle Red's room. She was carrying a washbasin of water in one hand and Papa's razor and shaving mug in the other, with a towel hanging over her forearm.

"He wants to see you," she said, hurrying toward the kitchen, from which came the smells of beans and cornbread cooking.

I didn't know what I expected to find. From the way Mama had said he wanted to see me, in a sort of grave sweet voice, I could easily imagine that Uncle Red was desperately ill, maybe evey dying and had asked to see me one last time before he expired. But what I found was my skinny uncle sitting up in bed, smoking a cigarette and sipping a cup of coffee. His wavy red hair was wild as a haystack, but he was clean-shaven, and his gray-blue eyes, set deep in cavernous sockets, though bloodshot and a little jaundiced, were otherwise lively enough. He winked at me.

"How you doing, Hoss?" He put the cigarette between his lips and shifted the coffee mug to his left hand so he would have his right hand free to shake mine.

I was sort of shy. Usually men didn't offer to shake hands with boys. It was sort of an acknowledgment that you were an equal, and few grown men did that to kids of my age. In fact, I had only shook hands maybe two or three times in my life, and so I didn't know quite how to do it, but Uncle Red had a firm if bony handshake, and he grinned as if he was really glad to see me. It was a sort of lopsided grin, with the cigarette dangling from one corner of his mouth, the insinuating grin of a carnival barker who has seen it all and knows you want to. His was a gaunt face, clawed with fever and fatigue, though still not bad-looking. In fact, he would probably have been considered handsome if his face hadn't been so haggard, so gaunt that it hardly concealed his skull beneath. He was three years younger than Mama, which made him thirty, but he looked older than she did.

He took a long pull off the cigarette and kept the smoke in his throat as he said, "Listen, Hoss, I wanna thank you for fixing up my car like that." Jets of smoke shot from his nostrils and billowed from his mouth so that his voice, caught in the smoke, sounded even more smoky than usual: a deep, resonant voice with a slight nasal edge. "Reckon it was a helluva mess, huh? Still runs, though, huh? Thank God for small favors. Shit, who knows? I might get to Nashville yet."

I made a few halting replies as he spoke, such as "Y'wel-come" and "Oh, sure it's . . .," and then I said, "Nashville? It's true then? You're gonna sing on the Grand Ole Opry?"

He shrugged his bare bony shoulders against the paint-chipped iron bars of the bedstead and flicked the ashes from his cigarette onto the dusty floor. "Who knows? Just an audition for a guest shot." He smiled. "If I ever get there in one piece, that is." Then he coughed. It wasn't a rib-cracking coughing fit like I had heard last night, but it was bad enough. When it was over, his eyes were watery and his voice caught in his throat. "Listen, Hoss, do your ole Uncle Red . . ." He cleared his throat. "One more little favor, will you? My guitar . . . in the car?"

"I brought it in. It's—"

"Bring it here, will you? In the case, I mean."

"Sure," I said, and hastily went into the front room to get it.

The moonshine was what he wanted. He heaved a sigh of relief as he took the bottle from the pocket within the case.

"Damned dust," he murmured. "What we need is a little dust cutter." He tipped the bottle up, his prominent Adam's apple bobbled as he took a long swallow, and then his face twisted into a horrible grimace. "Whooooo-eee, Jay-sus!" he muttered. "You want . . . ?" He held the bottle out to me.

I giggled self-consciously and shook my head. Mama would have had a fit if she caught me taking a drink of whiskey.

"It's all right," he assured me in a recovered but still raspy voice. "Alcohol kills the germs."

"Oh, it ain't that," I hastened to say, hoping to assure him that it wasn't the fear of catching TB that caused me to decline the drink. "It's Mama. If she—"

And as if I had announced her, rather than merely mentioned her, we heard her footsteps approaching. Uncle Red barely had time to cork the bottle and put it back into the guitar case before she came into the room with Uncle Red's clothes. She had washed and ironed his fancy suit, and now she placed it, neatly folded, across the iron bedstead at the foot of the bed.

"Now if you feel like getting up for a while, come have some eggs and biscuits, and we'll get this room cleaned up." She turned to me. "Come on out, now, let him get dressed."

I started to follow her out, but Uncle Red said, "Hoss," and

I turned at the door. He was already reaching for the bottle again. With one eye squinted against the upcurling smoke from the cigarette, he said, "Thanks again, y'hear? And mum's the word on this, huh? No need for Sis to know 'bout it, is there?"

"'Course not," I said, a little hurt that he should think it necessary to ask.

"'Course not," he echoed. He took the cigarette from his mouth and raised the bottle, winked at me over the top of it, and said, "Here's to us ducks, we don't give a quack, do we? If it don't rain, we'll walk."

I left the room smiling, instinctively adopting his seemingly carefree—if not downright careless—attitude, though I was disturbed by it, by what I sensed was his refusal to have any regard for his own life. Driving as he did, drinking as he did, how long could he live? But the question didn't seem to bother *him* much.

And that new name he had given me—Hoss! I wondered where he got *that*. He had a peculiar habit not only of hanging nicknames on people, but of changing the nicknames now and then, according to some whim of his own. For some reason known only to him, for instance, he used to call Mama Goosh, and sometimes he would call Papa Mule. My name was Whitney—Whitney Elmo Wagoner, to be exact—but everybody called me Whit. Everybody except Uncle Red, that is. On his last visit with us, he called me Cotton or Cottontop, because of the color of my hair. It had darkened a little since then, however, and was no longer cottony but more the color and texture of wheat straw. And now, for some reason known only to him, I was Hoss. I didn't really care, though. He could have called me anything, and I wouldn't have cared, just as long as he was smiling when he said it.

I started to go into the kitchen, but when I heard voices on the other side of the door, I stopped to listen. It was Mama and Papa, talking about Uncle Red, and I knew they would stop if I went in, so I put my ear to the door. Mama was saying something about Uncle Red having to leave California in such a hurry that he didn't even pack any clothes or even a toothbrush.

"... couldn't go back to his hotel, 'cause there was somebody looking for him. No, no," she added hastily, "not the law. I got the idea it was maybe some hanky-panky with a gal maybe, or a gal and her pa, you know? With the gal's pa maybe carrying a shotgun or a horsewhip?"

"But why ain't he got no money? If he's driving a big fancy car like that . . ."

Then I heard somebody enter the back door. Papa fell silent, and when it became apparent they weren't going to talk about Uncle Red anymore, I went on into the kitchen. Mama was at the stove, cooking, and Papa was sitting at the table having a cup of coffee. It was Howard who had interrupted their conversation. He was carrying a pail of water in each hand. And as soon as I entered, he gave me a hateful look.

"Why ain't he doing some of this?" he asked.

"He will," Mama said. She mopped her sweaty forehead with her shirtsleeve. "Give him the buckets, and you go bring in some more firewood."

Howard dumped the water into a washtub on the top of the cookstove, then turned and handed me the empty buckets with the slightly haughty look of someone who had just served me right. He was four years older and a lot bigger than I was, and we didn't like each other very much. He had always been a bossy older brother, rigid and authoritarian even then, and it didn't surprise me at all that he grew up to be a career sergeant in the Marine Corps, a professional bully. For now, however, he was satisfied with having maneuvered Mama into giving me the orders and putting me to work carrying water from the watertank to the house so we could take baths later in the day.

I had already made one trip and was pouring water into the washtub when Uncle Red, dressed in his fancy cowboy outfit, with fringes swinging and sequins flashing, finally came into the kitchen. At first everybody greeted him politely, even cheerfully, but before he got to the table, he staggered a little and sniggered with embarrassment, and everyone's cheerfulness was suddenly replaced with surprise and concern—and incredulity, too, because neither Mama nor Papa seemed willing to believe what was obvious to me: that Uncle Red was drunk again—not really soused, of course, but just drunk enough to stagger a little and snigger with a sort of Peck's-bad-boy embarrassment.

Mama grabbed for his elbow and murmured, "Oh, be careful, Hassle." She guided him to the table, where Papa had pulled a chair out for him. "I'll get you some breakfast," Mama said, but he waved her away, saying in a slightly slurred voice that he didn't want anything to eat."

"Just some java, thanks."

"Come on, now, Hassle," Mama chided. "You got to get something in your belly. Look how skinny you are, for God's sake. Mama wouldn't even recognize you if she . . ." But her voice trailed off and died as she slowly began to acknowledge that Uncle Red, limp as a rag, was drunk. She still couldn't quite believe it, though, because she couldn't think how he could have got anything to drink. Then she suddenly looked at me.

I avoided her eyes and hurried back outside as if to get some more water. Having walked barefooted across the hot dust of the yard to the watertank next to the wrecked windmill, I quickly stepped into the puddle of cool mud under the tank's spigot. There were chickens and a runty pig already in the puddle, but the chickens—sorry-looking things with mite-infested feathers—squawked and fled, flapping their scraggly wings in protest. But the runt pig, though startled, didn't leave. He grunted with alarm when the chickens flapped away, but then, seeing that it was only me, he settled back down into the cool mud with a deep grunt of contentment.

When I heard a door slam, I looked up to see Uncle Red and Papa on the front porch. Grandpa had already moved his rocking chair out on the porch, to set and rock and stare, and when Uncle Red came out, he stopped to say a few words to Grandpa and shake his hand; then, with our dog Tige falling in behind, Uncle Red and Papa went on out to the Packard limousine. Uncle Red, wearing his cowboy hat now, was none too steady on his feet, and so he staggered and almost fell backward when he kicked the car's mangled front fender.

"Look at that, would you, Mule?" he said when he recovered his balance. "Don't make cars like they used to, do they? No better'n a goddamn tin can. Ought to trade the damned thing in for a blue-nosed mule."

I was tempted to join them, believing that my obvious interest in the car would excuse my butting in, but after Uncle Red started the motor to make sure it would still run, he and Papa left the car and came toward me, toward the watertank and fallen windmill, and I quickly began filling the buckets from the spigot.

"Goddamn," Uncle Red said, making a noise in his throat that sounded like a muted chuckle, "they don't make windmills like they used to, either, do they?" He idly kicked at one of the fallen timbers, staggered, almost lost his balance. But then in a more sincere tone, in a tone of playful regret, he said, "Listen, Mule, I'm sorry as hell 'bout this."

Papa sounded only grudgingly forgiving. "Well, can't be helped now, I reckon. And it don't matter no way. There's enough water in the tank to last us a couple of weeks, and by then . . ." He tipped his head. "Landlord's been threatening to sell this place to one of them tractor farmers, anyway. Told me this was my last year, and if I didn't bring in a crop this time, he was gonna sell out."

"And you're better off for it, I swear," Uncle Red said. "This damned country! How in hell y'all keep living here is beyond me. Shit, after I get outa here this time, there's just one thing I hope—if I ever see Oklahoma again, it'll be through a long-distance telescope." He clapped his hands and made that sound in his throat again, a sort of chuckling sound. He seemed pretty lighthearted about the whole thing, as if he were trying to find something to say that would cheer up Papa, and that wasn't an easy thing to do.

"Look at it this way, Mule," he cajoled. "I done you a service by knocking this thing down. Now you ain't got no choice but to move, and even Sis'll thank me for it later, when y'all get out to California and start living off the fat of the land."

"Maybe," Papa said doubtfully. "But I don't know how we gonna be able to get there now. Money's all gone. Put the last of it in this crop. Borrowed all we could already. Can't think of no place to steal it, and I can't beg for it. Ain't in me to beg. I'd sit right down here and die 'fore I'd beg for it."

But he was very close to begging at that moment. He was wheedling, anyway. It was sort of shameful when Papa would start that wheedling, trying to get something out of somebody by playing for sympathy. Last winter, for instance, when we went to town to get our government relief handouts every month, Papa always made us three older kids take off our shoes and go stand in the relief line with him, all of us barefooted even when there was sleet on the pavement, because he wanted the government people to see that we had no shoes. He wanted them to feel sorry for us and give us some shoes. We had shoes at home—not perfectly good shoes, it was true, but adequate ones, and none of us had complained. But that was just Papa's way of doing things, playing the helpless and humiliated half-breed who, through no fault of his own, would be forced to accept some shoes for his poor barefooted kids if only the government could see its way clear to . . .

They never did give us any shoes. All we got were some unpleasant memories of standing around on sleet-covered sidewalks barefooted, flushed with shame to see Papa trying to wheedle something out of someone. And that's what he was doing to Uncle Red.

Uncle Red, who was said to be generous to a fault, slapped Papa on the shoulder and said, "Shit, don't worry about it, Mule. I'll get you the money. If you and Sis really wanna go to California, I'll get you the goddamned money. How's that? That suit you?"

But Papa wasn't a balloon to be carried away with hot air. "You?" he said. "But you ain't . . . I mean, have you got any money?"

"Have I got money!" Uncle Red said. "You kidding? I got money ten miles up a bull's ass." He pulled his wallet from his hip pocket and opened it with a flourish. "Oh," he said then, with a reflective lift of his eyebrows. "Looks like I'm a little short at the moment. But, hell, don't let that stop you from making arrangements to go. I said I'd get it for you, and I'll do it, too, don't you worry none."

We heard a car coming, a Model T Ford. You could tell it was a Model T by the peculiar putt-putt-putt sound it made. It was the Butz family, our neighbors, coming down the road toward our house with a long cloud of dust trailing behind the open car. Mr. Butz, a stringbean man with a straw hat, was driving. His wife, the fattest woman I had ever seen, sat on the passenger's side of the front seat. She weighed so much that the car listed to her side like a crippled ship. Between them sat their only son, a boy of about five, and in the back seat were the three Butz daughters, all of them replicas of the mother.

Papa and Uncle Red went up to the front yard to meet them. I left the buckets at the watertank and followed. Mama and sister Margery came out of the house and stood on the front porch, Mama drying her hands on her apron, waiting for the Butzes to get down and come in the house. For a moment, all of us were engulfed in the cloud of dust that the Model T pulled along in its wake. All the Butzes looked sour and dispirited until they saw Uncle Red.

"Light down and come in," Papa said as he waved the dust way from his face.

"Can't, Virgil," said Mr. Butz, adjusting the spark lever on the Model T's steering column so that the engine would idle smoothly. Little jets of steam escaped, hissing and gurgling, from under the radiator cap. "We on our way to town. Gonna send a telegram to my cousin out in California, see if there's any work out there."

"You're leaving?" Mama said. She and Margery were on their way out to the car, fanning away the dust.

Mr. Butz nodded emphatically. "If there's work out there, we sho gonna leave. I hear there's...they say there's a..." But his attention faltered. Like everyone else in the car, he could no longer resist openly staring at the Packard limousine—or, more precisely, alternating his gaze between the Packard and Uncle Red. But the three Butz daughters couldn't take their eyes off Uncle Red. Squeezed into the back seat, the three girls, in nearly identical print smocks and powdered all over with red dust, ogled Uncle Red as if he were someone who had just stepped out of a dream, or from off the pages of a movie magazine.

Mama was at the side of the car now, standing next to Mrs. Butz. "Oh, shoot, you got to get out for a spell," she said, "and tell us..." But her voice faded when she saw the direction of Mrs. Butz's gaze, so she introduced Uncle Red to them.

"Sho," Mr. Butz said. "I heard of you. You're that sanger."

"Well, I declare!" Mrs. Butz said. Her eyes almost disappeared into the folds of flesh on her face as she grinned.

"That yo car?" Mr. Butz asked. "Ain't that something, now! Been banged up a bit, though, ain't it? California! See that, Ma? He's from California! You coming to the Grange Hall meeting tonight?"

"Meeting?" Papa said.

"Sho. People getting together, talking about forming a caravan and going on out to California. You folks oughta come," he said, "and bring Red here with you. You just come from out there, didn't you?" Mr. Butz asked Uncle Red. "Maybe you'd come on down to the Grange Hall tonight and tell us what it's like...." Then he noticed the windmill. "Hey, wha happened? Storm blow it down?"

"Ain't it awful?" Mama said quickly, before anyone could blurt out the truth. "First time we ever had a wind strong enough to blow down a windmill, I reckon." Mama wasn't the type t tell an outright lie, but she could be cleverly misleading whe she needed to. "But what's this about a meeting?"

"Everybody's going," Mr. Butz said. "The storm wiped us all out, looks like. The Tanners and the McCalls—you 'member Joe McCall? He took over the Maddox place last year when Maddox left for California, and now Joe's leaving, too. We're all meeting at the Grange Hall in Roscoe tonight."

The three Butz daughters suddenly giggled, and not only were their voices in harmony, but in a sort of counterpoint, too, which caused their *hee-hees* to sound like a musical composition, a sort of madrigal of giggles.

"I declare!" said Mrs. Butz, and turned to give her daughters a look of reproach. "What's the matter with you girls, anyway?"

Uncle Red had winked at them, that's what. And when they giggled, he smiled, which caused them to giggle some more. It was fascinating to see the effect he had on people, especially on women. Mama had once said that Uncle Red was a mover and a shaker, a man who had the capacity to excite people, to delight them, and that was obviously true. With nothing more than a wink and a sly smile, he had transformed the three dusty and dispirited Butz daughters into mounds of flesh-jiggling delight, and after they said goodbye and were driving out of the yard, he doffed his hat in a courtly bow to the backward-looking girls, which sent them into another chorus of their giggling madrigal.

"Always did have a weakness for fat women," Uncle Red said ruefully as he stood and watched the Model T dissolve in a cloud of dust.

"Hassle," Mama said.

"Well, it's true," he said. "Never had one, though. Not a really fat one, I mean."

"Hush that," Mama said with mock-maternal severity. She put her arm through his and guided him back toward the house. "If you're feeling so feisty, why'n't you come on in the house and sing us a song? Seems like ages since I heard you sing."

Uncle Red didn't seem eager to do that at first, but as they were going into the house, Mama pleaded, "Oh, come on, just one," and Uncle Red grinned and said, "Well, I tell you what. I'll play a song, but only if you'll do us a little dance. I know you still got them old tap-dancing shoes of yourn hid away somewhere. Put 'em on, we'll do it."

Mama seemed shocked by the idea. And she wasn't the only one. Her shock seemed half-pretended, however, while mine was genuine. It was the first time I had ever heard anything about Mama being able to tap dance.

"Oh, don't be silly, Hassle," she said. "I ain't danced a lick in years. Probably forgot how by now."

"Well, I bet you can still do it," he said joshingly, and then turned to me. "Hoss, fetch me my guitar, will you?"

I didn't have to be told twice. I dashed into his room and brought his guitar back, and everybody was settling down in the front room, hoping to hear Uncle Red sing. Hoping to see Mama dance, too, though that looked as if it wasn't going to happen.

"No, Hassle, I told you, I can't—"

"Come on," Uncle Red chided. "Where you keep them old taps?" He strapped his guitar on and sat down in a straight-back chair. I sat down on the floor near him.

Mama seemed to weaken a little, as if considering the idea, and then Papa, who had taken a seat on the woodbox by the stove, said in a slightly goading voice, "They're in that old box under the bed. But I bet you she won't do it." He seemed to like the idea of her dancing, but that was Papa's way: he couldn't encourage, he could only challenge.

And that's what finally caused Mama to make up her mind. "All right," she said to Uncle Red. "I'll make a fool of myself, but I got a condition, too. I'll do it only if you play that song you wrote that time—what was it? 'The Guitar Picker and his Dancing Sister'?"

"That old thing? Hell, that was 'bout the first song I ever wrote. Got maybe twenty verses to it. Oh, well, I'll see can I remember a couple of 'em. Go on, then, get your shoes on, we'll do it."

While Uncle Red was tuning his guitar, Mama got down on her knees and dug into an old storage box that had been secreted under the bed. She brought out a pair of tap-dancing shoes—pink shoes, cracked and curled and faded with age and disuse. It was the first time I had ever seen them. She hugged them to her and bolted for the kitchen, closing the door behind her.

Uncle Red began the song without her. For a moment he couldn't remember how it went, but after he stumbled through the first few lines, the words began to come easily. He sort of talk-sang the song, not even trying to sound good, and he mugged a little as he sang.

Down in Oklahoma where the wild wind blows
Lived a little boy who picked his nose,
But then he got a guitar, and that was when
That little boy learned to pick and grin.
Yeah, he'd pick....

And then Uncle Red picked out a solo on the guitar, playing in a bouncy, chicken-picking style, plucking strings with just about every finger on his right hand, while the fingers on his left hand scurried up and down the frets so fast that they sometimes became a blur. Then he sang another verse.

Yeah, he got his first guitar when he was ten,
He got him a learning book, and then
He'd sit out behind the barn all day,
Blowing on his fingers and trying to play.
And he'd pick....

This time, though, when he played the solo on the guitar, he did it in a comically inept way, as if he were just learning how to play, hitting sour notes and missing the beat and all that. And it was during this solo that Grandpa pulled out his harmonica and started to play along with Uncle Red.

"Hey, that's it, Mr. Wagoner!" Uncle Red said encouragingly, still playing, and then he shouted toward the kitchen, "You ready, Goosh?" There was no answer from the kitchen, and Uncle Red went on to the third verse.

But it wasn't very long till he got pretty good,
Playing that guitar like the book said he should,
And then pretty soon he got the chance
To play his guitar while his sister danced.
Yeah, he'd play....

Again Uncle Red started a guitar solo, but then he added in his singing voice,

And she'd dance....

And that was when Mama came dancing out of the kitchen. Blushing furiously, she made an entrance into the room as if

who continued to stare silently at the pink shoes. "Boy howdy, there wasn't a church social or a corn-husking where we didn't knock 'em dead, me picking and her dancing. Ain't that right, Goosh?"

But instead of answering, Mama suddenly got up and left the room. She went back into the kitchen, carrying her pink shoes.

"And you, Mr. Wagoner," Uncle Red said, laying his guitar aside and turning to Grandpa. "Damned if I don't think I'll hire you for my band. You play that thing like you know what you was doing."

I got up and went into the kitchen to see if Mama was all right. Uncle Red was obviously through playing, anyway, and I was a little worried by the way Mama looked when she left the room. I expected to find her in the kitchen putting on her brogans, but she wasn't there. She had stepped out on the back porch. Dangling the pink dancing shoes in her hands, she stood barefooted on the porch and seemed to be gazing absently out across the back yard toward the ruined cotton fields beyond. She didn't look at me when I came out, and I had to sort of lean forward over the edge of the porch to get a look at her face.

"What's the matter, Mama?" I asked when I saw the tears in her eyes.

"Nothing," she said in a mind-your-own-business tone.

After a long pause, I said, "Then why're you crying?"

"I'm not crying."

I didn't want to contradict her, but neither did I want to pretend to believe her and walk away, so I just kept standing there, gazing at her, and pretty soon she held the cracked and faded pink shoes up and looked at them again, and then in a dreamy, abstracted way, she said, "It's just that . . . while I was dancing, I remembered what it was like to be young again. I was only sixteen when I bought these." Sighing, she lifted her eyes once more toward the yard and the fields. "Who would've thought then that life would be so *hard?*"

I had an impulse to try to comfort her in some way, but I didn't know what to do or say, and she didn't give me any signal, so I just stood there in silence, gazing at her careworn face with mingled sympathy and amazement. She had been happy once. That's what she was telling me, and for some reason, that seemed as strange to me as it did to think that she had once been a tap-dancer—strange to think that she had once been young and happy and full of laughter. I had never seen her that way.

She sighed again, this time in an effort to compose herself, and then said, "Well! Best not to think about it, I guess." And still without meeting my eyes, she turned and went back into the house to put the pink shoes back into the box under her bed.

Uncle Red was standing near Papa now, trying to roll a cigarette with Papa's Bull Durham tobacco. He was still joshing Grandpa about joining his band. Papa was watching Uncle Red's labored and inept attempt to roll the cigarette, smiling a little as though he was certain Uncle Red would fail, and Uncle Red was sure enough having a hard time. The tobacco kept dribbling out of one end of the lumpy, wet cigarette, and the paper wouldn't stay glued.

As Mama put her shoes away, she said, "If we're going to that Grange Hall meeting, we best start getting ready. But if we go, you'll come along, won't you, Hassle? I'm not going 'less you do."

"Sure," he said, lighting his cigarette. "But I'm not gonna make any speeches." His cigarette fell apart, the fire and tobacco spilled out, leaving him with a loose wet cigarette paper hanging limply from his lips. "Looks like I'm gonna have to go to town and get some cigarettes, anyway, so I'll drive y'all to the meeting in my car."

4

The car lurched across the culvert and almost went into the ditch as we careened onto the dirt road leading toward Roscoe.

"Hassle!" Mama cried. "Don't drive so blamed fast! We got plenty of time."

She was in the back of the car with Papa and the kids—all the kids except me, that is. I was riding in the front seat between Uncle Red and Grandpa. All of us—even Grandpa—were dressed in our best Sunday clothes, with shoes. We had spent most of the afternoon taking washtub baths, cleaning and cutting nails on fingers and toes, trimming hair, primping. We had eaten a quick supper of cornbread and warmed-over beans, and then climbed into the Packard limousine and started for town. And it had become quickly apparent that Uncle Red was in no condition to drive. He was, in fact, scaring the daylights out of all of us before we had gone a mile.

Uncle Red wasn't a good driver. That was the simple truth of the matter. Not only did he misjudge distances and angles, but he seemed to have no feel for the car. He was always grinding the gears, or lugging the engine, or slipping the clutch. And of course, being half-drunk didn't help either. He had evidently been tippling the moonshine all afternoon, and now, as he drove down the dusty road toward town, the car lurched and skidded but stayed on the road, no doubt the same way

37

Uncle Red, had he been walking, would have staggered and swayed but stayed on his feet.

But the final fright came when another one of his hand-rolled cigarettes fell apart and the fire dropped down between his legs. He whooped and jerked his ass off the seat, his body suddenly becoming straight and stiff as a board, which caused his foot to slam down on the accelerator pedal, sending the car plunging headlong down the road.

"Be careful!" Mama cried.

"Get that thing! Get that thing!" Uncle Red shouted.

I reached under him to brush the burning tobacco off the seat, and while I was doing it, Uncle Red jerked his stiffened leg off the accelerator and jammed it down on the brake pedal, which locked all four wheels and sent the car into a sideways skid in the dirt and gravel.

"Careful!" Mama cried again, and sister Margery, occupying one of the jump seats, was beginning to cry when I yelled, "Okay!" and Uncle Red sat back down and jerked his foot off the brake pedal just as the car came to a skidding stop sideways in the middle of the road. But Uncle Red didn't depress the clutch when he stopped, and since the car was still in high gear, the engine stalled. A good thing it did, too, or the car would have leaped forward and landed nose down in the ditch on the other side of the road.

"Godamighty," Papa murmured from the back seat.

"Hassle!" Mama snapped, angry now, cuddling the squawling baby. "Hassle, damn you, what're you trying to do, kill us all? Can't you drive no better'n that?"

Uncle Red chuckled. "Well, I guess if I could, I would. I can most of the time, but I'm not at my best when I got a live cigarette under my ass."

"You been drinking, that's what it is," Mama said. It was very unusual for her to be so angry. When she got mad, though, she could be awfully blunt and bossy, at least to us kids and to Uncle Red. I never heard her speak to Papa or Grandpa like that, though. "Why don't you let someone else drive?"

Grandpa, who was sitting in the front seat with me, cleared his throat with an emphatic "Hummph!" to indicate that he thoroughly agreed with Mama. He kept his eyes straight ahead, however, staring at the cloud of dust that had been pulled along in our wake and that now blew past the stalled car.

"I suppose you could do better?" Uncle Red asked, and fo

the first time I heard a note of defensive hostility in his voice, the resentful sound of a little brother being badgered by an older sister.

"I'm sure any of us could," Mama said. "Even Whit could. Even he could drive better'n *that*."

It was true that I hadn't had much experience driving. Papa had taught me how to drive our old Chevy truck, and on a couple of occasions, when he took a load of cotton to town, he had let me drive all the way there and back. And though that was hardly enough experience to qualify me as a good driver, it still hurt my feelings that Mama used me as the standard of incompetence below which even Uncle Red fell.

Still, it did have a good effect. Uncle Red looked at me challengingly and said, "That true, Hoss? You think you can drive better'n *I* can? Better'n your ole Uncle Red?"

I didn't know what to say to that, so I said, "I don't know."

He obviously hadn't expected me to take him seriously, but I did, and so he said with a vaguely challenging chuckle, "Wanna try?"

"Oh, come on, Hassle," Mama chided. "Let somebody drive who knows how."

He ignored her, waiting for me to answer. "Well?" Everybody else waited with bated breath to hear what I would say. I knew they all wanted—expected—me to turn the offer down, and I knew they would be mad at me if I didn't, but I didn't.

"Sure," I said.

"*Can* you?" he said.

After a slight hesitation, I nodded. "I think so."

Uncle Red seemed pleased by my impudence. "Well, by God, jump over here, then, and let's see what you can do."

"Oh, boy," Howard groaned in a tone of sepulchral despair, and Grandpa said, "Hummph!" and Mama said, "Now, Hassle, why'n't you let Virgil drive? Or even Howard. He can—"

Uncle Red threw up his hands. "Nope. The decision's been made. Hoss says he thinks he can drive this here car as good as me, and, by God, I, for one, think he can do it. Come on over here, Hoss." He helped me to climb over his bony legs to exchange places on the front seat.

I was petrified. I thought I knew pretty well how to drive the car, but the realization that I had suddenly been given the *chance* to do it was overwhelming.

"Okay, start'er up," Uncle Red said.

I had to sit on the edge of the seat so I could reach the pedals on the floor and see over the top of the enormous steering wheel. The end of the hood looked a mile away. My God, it was a big car! And for a little while it would be mine to control. . . .

"Yeah, that's it," Uncle Red said cheerfully, "put it in low. Yeah, that's low. Now, the thing is, you got to let out on the clutch real slow, see, while you're—"

"I know," I said.

The car started moving all right, and I got it turned straight in the road, headed toward town. I had broken out in a cold sweat and my heart was pounding wildly, not only from fear, but from excitement, too, for when I got the car moving smoothly down the dusty road, I realized I was experiencing one of the most thrilling moments of my life.

It was the *power* of the thing. The power and the luxury of it! The car seemed to float, as if it were on water, rather than on a deeply rutted caliche road. And instead of wrestling with the steering wheel, as I'd had to do on our old truck, I could have steered the Packard with one finger. And all I had to do was touch the accelerator pedal with my foot and the enormous engine would purr and the front end of the car would lift up a little, as if it were going to take off like an airplane. But I made sure I didn't go too fast. I knew everybody was already scared of my driving and I didn't want to give them any cause to be.

"Hey, you doing real good," Uncle Red said when we had gone a few miles down the road without a mishap or even a blunder. "Ain't he, folks?" But nobody was willing to express what might turn out to be a premature opinion. Still, they had relaxed a little by now. They were no longer waiting breathlessly to see if they were going to get out of this alive. And as I gained confidence in my handling of the car, my own fears slowly subsided, giving way to a sort of sublime wonder, a thrill that suffused my whole body, a feeling that seemed to tingle in my every cell, from the tips of my toes to the very tips of the hairs on my head.

There was no traffic on the road until we got closer to Roscoe, and by then I had enough confidence in myself to keep from panicking when I passed a car or a wagon coming from the opposite direction. And of course I didn't drive fast enough to overtake any cars that were going in our direction. As we got nearer to town, though, we began to come up behind a few wagons that carried our neighbors toward the Grange Hall. And the mules that pulled the wagons were so slow that I had to pass them. It was something to see the faces of the people in the wagons when they saw who it was in the big black Packard limousine.

To get to the Grange Hall, we had to go through town, which was hardly more than two rows of dusty old buildings, most of them false-fronted and tin-roofed, divided by a two-lane blacktop highway. There were a few dwellings behind the main buildings on both sides of the highway, houses without numbers on streets without names.

The railroad tracks and the train depot and the municipal water tower were on the north side of the town, the poorer side, where the Indians and Negroes and a few Mexicans lived in paint-peeled houses and tar-paper shacks. Loud music blared from the houses and shacks, snotty-nosed and half-naked kids played in old wrecked automobiles, and mangy dogs prowled the area.

But there were a few bright spots in the town. There was a barber shop, for instance, with its candy-striped pole, and a dry-goods emporium. And best of all was the town's movie theater. It was there, in the theater, on Saturday afternoons and nights, that I first learned of faraway places. There that I learned of people like Hitler and of places like China. There that I saw the Buck Jones and Gene Autry westerns, the Flash Gordon serials, the monster movies. There that I worshiped my heroes. There that dreams began.

Anyway, I turtled along Main Street as slowly as I could without having to change gears, giving everybody in the car a chance to wave hello to friends and neighbors along the way. It also gave people time to gawk at *us*. Heads turned when they saw us coming, elbows dug into ribs to call attention to us, eyes widened and jaws went slack with amazement as the big Packard glided smoothly and quietly through town.

"Hello, Bertha!" Mama called out the open window, waving to her friend Bertha Higgins, who was so surprised to see us poor folks riding along in a rich man's car that she couldn't return Mama's greeting until we were already past her. And when some stuck-up kids I knew saw me driving the car, I swelled up with a rare and luxurious pride.

Still, I felt an acute sense of relief when I finally turned the car into the graveled parking lot at the Grange Hall and brought it to a smooth stop among the numerous cars and trucks and wagons already parked there.

"Well, damn it all, Hoss," Uncle Red said when I switched off the ignition, "I gotta hand it to you, boy. When it comes to driving, you're slicker'n snot on a brass doorknob."

"Hassle," Mama said in a tone of amused revulsion.

"Well, it's true," he insisted. "Think I'll hire him as my chauffeur."

Small knots of people were gathering here and there in the parking lot, gossiping, maybe sharing nips from bottles of bootleg whiskey or moonshine, and some were making their way into the lighted Grange Hall. But most everybody stopped what they were doing and turned to stare at the Packard when we drove in. Among the gawkers were the Butz family, who, having arrived before us, now made their way toward us as if to demonstrate to everybody that they were friends of ours— of Uncle Red's, actually, because that's who everyone began to stare at when he got out of the car.

I stayed in the car for a while after everyone else had got out. I wanted to be left alone for a few minutes to savor the experience I'd just had, to savor the copper-penny taste of excitement that lingered in the back of my mouth.

5

Though Uncle Red had said he didn't want to make any speeches at the meeting, it didn't take much encouragement from the audience to make him change his mind. He obviously loved being the center of attention, and it was marvelous to see what he could do to get and hold that attention. To the degree that singing and performing are different, I learned that evening that Uncle Red was not only a singer, he was a performer too. He could spellbind an audience without singing a note.

It helped, of course, that the man who spoke to them first had left them feeling condemned. He—a beefy man named Dobbs—had warned them that they had better not go to California. He had once owned the Texaco service station in Roscoe, but like a fool, he said, he had let himself be persuaded that California was the Promised Land, so he sold his service station and headed West. Joined the thousands of others who were fleeing the dust bowl in unplanned caravans of old jalopies and trucks loaded down with household belongings and filled with hungry-eyed people looking for a better life.

"Ha!" Mr. Dobbs said with a Calvinistic scorn, and struck the lectern with the palm of a big grease-begrimed hand. "Don't you believe it!" He was standing behind a lectern, on a dais at the far end of the hall. "Once I seen one of them printed circulars that said three hundred workers was needed at a fruit-

and-vegetable cannery in Modesto, no experience necessary. Well, let me tell you, they had three hundred jobs there to fill, all right," he continued, passionate and defensive, "but you know what they'd done? They'd sent out hundreds of them circulars. And you know how many people showed up for them three hundred jobs? Over four thousand!" He paused to let that figure have its effect.

There were *tisk-tisks* from the audience, and a few mutters of outrage and disgust, but most of the listeners were merely restless and inattentive, and that was about how things stood when Mr. Dobbs finished his bitter speech and relinquished the lectern.

Then the man in charge of the meeting asked Uncle Red if he, having just come from California, would please come forward and tell them what *he* knew about the situation out there.

Uncle Red, sitting beside Mama in the seat directly in front of me, held up his hands in a gesture of demure refusal, but the man on the dais clapped his hands a couple of times, a polite but encouraging applause, and the audience quickly joined in, so Uncle Red, with a shrug and a smile, hitched up his fancy pants and went down the aisle to the dais. He glittered when he walked.

"Folks," he said, tipping his cowboy hat back on his head and wiping his palm across his sweaty brow, "as some of you know, I'm an entertainer. Oh, I done a little cotton and prune picking out there, when I got hungry, but that was a few years ago, and I tell you the truth, I don't know what things are like out there now. I've heard a lot 'bout how the Okies are getting treated by the big landowners out there, and it's just about like Mr. Dobbs says it is. Fact is, I hear there's some counties out there that actually have vigilantes to drive the Okies out after all the harvesting's been done and the big landowners don't need 'em anymore.

"Sure, that sort a thing is happening. *But . . .*" Here he paused, held up one finger, and in a voice that conveyed a sort of mischievous challenge, he added, "But what I say is, so what? When the alternative is staying here in *this* hellhole, I say whatta you got to lose? Our grandparents, now, they was pioneers who headed West in covered wagons, and what they had to face—wild Indians, mountain lions and bears, starvation, loneliness—why, I don't know what all!—but, hell, they didn't let that turn 'em back, did they?"

"Hell, no!" Grandpa interjected from his place in the audience, surprising all of us with the force of his assertion.

"Hell, no!" Uncle Red repeated. "And there's a man who can tell you. Mr. Wagoner there, when he first come to Oklahoma, he had to fight Indians and claim jumpers and bushwhackers and rattlesnakes and no telling what all, trying to find his fortune." He smiled. "It was his misfortune—and ours, too, I reckon—that it all turned to dust, but, hell, there's still places in this country where a man can make a stake and maybe, by God, get rich. And it's just across them deserts, for people who got enough guts to still be pioneers—*pioneers*," he repeated in a sort of chant, beginning to use hand claps to punctuate his words. "Not a bunch of rag-tag, self-pitying refugees from a dust bowl who tuck their tails betweeen their legs and give up at the first sign of trouble! Let's hear you say it, are y'all pioneers or not?" He leaned forward across the lectern with his right hand cupped behind his ear, as if straining to hear a sound from far away.

And what he heard was what he expected to hear: a sudden rush of assent, a garbled outpouring of words and phrases from an audience that had suddenly come to life again: "That's it!... You tell 'em, cowboy!... That's right, brother!.... Amen!"

"Sure, there's some bad times waiting for you out there," Uncle Red went on, "but there's some good times, too, and the things you always wanted. Big green valleys with rivers running through 'em."

"Amen!" said an old man in the back row, and some woman down front—Mrs. Butz?—cried, "Tell us about it, Red!" and I realized then that Uncle Red had complete control over the audience. I would remember this scene, years and years later, as the first time I was privileged to see a master audience manipulator in action. Without singing or playing a note, but only with talk and a sort of evangelistic fervor, Uncle Red proceeded to transform this crowd of dispirited and fearful refugees into a band of eager pioneers.

"No more dust and drought!" he said, and clapped his hands.

"That's right!"

"No more howling blizzards to blow through the cracks in your walls! No more leaky roofs and squeaky floors and stinking outhouses! No more worms in your cornmeal! No more weevils in your flour!"

"That's right, brother! . . . You tell em, Red!"

He had begun to strut back and forth on the dais, clapping his hands, gesturing wildly, smiling and winking. He worked the audience up into a jubilant mood by dangling before their eyes a vision of what they could get in the Promised Land: " . . . big shiny cars and tractors and inside toilets that flush. Hell, they got more water going down their toilets out there than you got going down your rivers!"

Laughter flowed from the audience, and shouts of "Amen! . . . We're ready! . . . Hallelujah!"

"Out there they got steam heat and hardwood floors and plaster walls and electric lights and . . . *telephones* . . . and drive-in places where you can eat without getting outa your cars . . . *movie theatres* . . . dance palaces . . . *beauty parlors* . . ."

By the time he finished, he had nearly everyone stamping his feet and clapping his hands and shouting, as if he were a preacher and they were his glory-bound congregation. It beat anything I had ever seen, the way he had turned the audience around.

And there was no telling how long he would have kept it up, he seemed to be enjoying himself so much; but suddenly, in the middle of a word, he broke into a coughing fit. It was such an explosive sound that everyone suddenly fell silent.

Uncle Red quickly jerked a handkerchief from his back pocket and covered his mouth, muffling the craggy sounds that racked his chest and caused him to bend over as if in a deep bow. He held up his other hand as a sign that we shouldn't be alarmed, he would be all right. He quickly suppressed the cough, and then said to the audience, "It's okay, folks. Just this damned Oklahoma dust sticking in my craw. What I need is a bottle of medicinal moonshine. Who's the bootlegger in the crowd?"

This brought a burst of laughter from the audience, and as Uncle Red hopped off the dais, everybody clapped for him, and kept clapping as he made his way up the aisle. A few people got up to pat him on the shoulders as he passed, thanking him for his talk, and it looked for a moment as if his path would be blocked by the enthusiastic well-wishers. But then a man in a dusty fedora stepped forward and took Uncle Red by the arm, whispered something in his ear, and ushered him up the aisle and out of the hall.

I followed. As we were going outside, I noticed that the man in the fedora had a pint bottle in his hip pocket, and when we got outside, he pulled the bottle from his pocket. They had stopped just inside the perimeter of the light from the bulb over the hall's entrance door. I stopped a few feet from them, sort of hanging around, and they didn't pay any attention to me. The night air was hot and dusty and alive with the sounds of bugs swarming around the light over the entrance.

"Here," the man said, handing Uncle Red the bottle. "I know how it is."

I couldn't see the man's expression because his gaunt face was hidden in the shadows of the fedora's turned-down brim, but his voice was sympathetic in a matter-of-fact sort of way— sympathetic without being pitying.

"That right?" Uncle Red said, uncorking the bottle.

"I got it, too," the man said.

"Ah," Uncle Red said, and it was hard to tell whether the sound was meant to express his understanding of the man's words, or his appreciation of the man's whiskey.

I expected Mama to come out of the hall at any second to see if Uncle Red was all right, and I was worried that she would catch him drinking the whiskey. But she didn't. In fact, nobody came out of the hall right away. Everyone had been so fired up by Uncle Red's speech that they stayed inside the hall to mingle and talk and maybe make plans for going to California. And among the many voices inside the hall, I could hear Mr. Dobbs's, loud with contempt, telling everyone that they were foolish to believe what Uncle Red had told them.

After Uncle Red took a second drink from the bottle, he said, "You selling it?"

The man's smile was apologetic rather than amused. "No. Bootlegger's other side of town. If you wanna buy a bottle, I'll show you."

Uncle Red handed the uncorked bottle back to the man and confessed with a forced chuckle, "Afraid I'll have to wait a day or two for that. Temporarily on the shorts."

The man's smile was one of good-natured skepticism, as if he didn't really believe Uncle Red's story, but was willing to pretend that he did and let Uncle Red take advantage of him. It was as if he had exempted Uncle Red from the normal rules of conduct. "Keep it," he said, and handed the bottle back to Uncle Red.

Uncle Red pretended to be surprised, as if the gift had been totally unexpected. "Well, by God," he said, his voice strong with friendly admiration for the man's generosity. "Appreciate it."

He had time for one more sip from the bottle before Mr. Dobbs came out of the hall. A big man in bib overalls and a railroad engineer's cap, Mr. Dobbs, with his wife and a few kids in tow, started out across the parking lot, but suddenly, as if on an irresistible impulse, Mr. Dobbs turned sharply away from his family, signaling them to stay where they were. He approached Uncle Red.

"Leroy," his wife said in a hushed voice that was both deferential and demanding.

"Wait," he said without turning to look at her. He didn't seem menacing or even angry as he approached Uncle Red, but I found myself instinctively edging closer to them, acting under a sort of protective impulse, even though Mr. Dobbs's demeanor wasn't at all threatening. Indeed, while he was obviously upset and puzzled, he was also clearly a little intimidated by Uncle Red.

"'Scuse me," he said. "I'd just like to know . . ."

"Yes?" Uncle Red said.

"I was just wondering *why*—why you told them people that stuff? If you just got back from out there, you know what it's like."

Uncle Red seemed a little discomfited by the concern and sincerity in Mr. Dobbs's voice. He probably would have been on surer ground if Mr. Dobbs had been truculent or combative. Anyway, he took another quick sip of whiskey before he plunged the cork back into the bottle, and when he finally spoke, he didn't raise his voice, but he looked around as if appealing to an invisible audience. "I'm an entertainer, mister. A singer. And you know what I sing? I sing the songs that people wanna hear. Same thing when I talk, I tell people what they wanna hear."

"But . . ." Mr. Dobbs broke off, baffled. He shook his head and started to turn away, but as if determined to make one last effort to understand, he said, "But it's not true, what you told them. And what're they gonna do when they find out?"

"You ain't accusing me of lying, are you, mister?" Uncle Red looked directly into Mr. Dobbs's eyes for the first time, leaning forward in a slightly threatening attitude.

"No," Mr. Dobbs was quick to say. "I don't recollect that you actually told any *lies*. But you can't deny you misled them people, can you? You gave them the wrong impression. You—"

"You know what I gave 'em?" Uncle Red interrupted, speaking once again as if to some invisible audience gathered around him in the yard. "I'll tell you. I gave 'em what they needed— something more important than facts and figures and hard-luck stories. I gave 'em something to keep 'em going when everything else fails. I gave 'em a dream."

"One that'll turn into a nightmare," Mr. Dobbs said, openly exasperated now.

Uncle Red made a snorting sound of irony and contempt, glancing around at everything and nothing. "A nightmare? What d'you think *this* is?"

Mr. Dobbs sighed, and his wife, evidently alarmed by the increasing intensity of their voices, called in an inflectionless voice, "Leroy," as if merely reminding him that his family was there waiting and then he abruptly turned and left without another word.

I wasn't even sure that Uncle Red was aware of my presence until he turned to me. Holding out the whiskey bottle, he said, "Here y'go, Hoss. Put this in the glove compartment of the car, will you? Don't let your Mama know about it." He winked. "I'm going back inside, see if I get a chance to pinch that fat woman's ass."

So I was left there, bottle in hand, to watch as he and the man in the fedora, with an air of easy camaraderie, went back into the Grange Hall. Although I felt vaguely as if I had been left out of something, I was glad enough to have something to do for Uncle Red, so I took the whiskey back to the car. I didn't put it in the glove compartment, however. I had tasted moonshine before, but never real store-bought whiskey, and I figured if Uncle Red liked it so much, there must be something to it, and this was my chance to find out what.

He had said that alcohol would kill the germs, though that didn't keep me from being slightly afraid of getting TB. There was even a deeper and more disturbing fear, however, that kept me holding the bottle at arm's length and staring at it for a long time even after I had taken the cork out. It was a nebulous fear, a fear such as I had only experienced in dreams, the fear and horror of the forbidden, of darkness, of being lost and forsaken and maybe even mad. I had seen Papa drunk a few times, and each time he had either become a mean bully or a maudlin self-pitying fool. It was Mama who always caught the brunt of his bullying or his blubbering self-pity, of course, and on at least one occasion he had beat her. He had caught her pouring his moonshine out, and they'd had a terrible row while we kids, terrified, huddled in our rooms, and the next day Mama had a black eye. But she had always stayed with him, no matter how drunk and despicable he became. She always tried to cajole him into sobriety and nursed him through his hangovers.

It was Mama who was the stable one in our family, the one who tried to instill in us a sense of order and cleanliness, of light and decency, good manners, religion. It was true that I often resented the dull and tedious demands that her world made on me, such as doing my school homework every day, and being forced to attend church on Sunday, when all I really wanted to do was go fishing or hunting. Even so, it had never before occurred to me that I might one day be tempted to leave her world altogether and plunge into a world of darkness and excitement, of intoxication and wild adventures and sin—Uncle Red's world. Not until I sat in his car that night in the Grange Hall parking lot and summoned up enough courage to take a drink of his whiskey did I ever suspect that I might someday voluntarily leave Mama's world to follow Uncle Red's footsteps.

But I did. I finally took that drink. I tipped the bottle up and took a big swallow. I had once seen a fire-eater in a carnival and, amazed, had wondered how it felt to have a mouthful of fire. Now I knew. It took my breath away like a blow to the belly. It burned its way into my guts like some fiery molten metal. Tears flooded my eyes, and I gagged, fighting to get my breath, and I thought for a moment that I might pass out from the shock of it.

But that didn't stop me. I was nothing if not determined, and I was determined that now, while I had the chance, I was going to find out what whiskey did to men—to Papa and Uncle Red—that made them want to drink it. And as soon as I began to recover from the fiery shock of the first drink, I began to feel a warm glow emanating out from the scalding heat in my throat and stomach, and with it came a strange feeling of expansiveness, of well-being, of power.

So I screwed up my courage once again and took another

swallow. And this time the shock wasn't nearly so harsh. It still tasted absolutely awful, of course, but again there was that suffusion of warmth, of well-being, of strange dark powers. . . .

I don't remember much after that. Everything sort of went topsy-turvy, and I got the impression that I was in the back seat and Mama was saying, "Where'd this boy get aholt of any liquor?" And I remember Uncle Red saying, "Stole it, I reckon," and then the car was moving. Papa was driving. I was in the back seat with Mama when I began to throw up. Margery and Howard made sounds of disgust and Mama told Papa to stop the car and then I was out on the side of the road, puking into the weeds, and Mama was there to put a cooling hand on my brow and hold my head as I heaved everything out of my stomach.

She didn't scold me. She let me rest my head on her lap for the rest of the ride home, and when we got there, I had to throw up some more, even though there was nothing left in my stomach. Mama stayed with me in the yard after everybody else had gone into the house. She told me to stick my finger down my throat, and I did, but the only thing that came out was bile and long strings of saliva.

She put me to bed and bathed my face with a cold washcloth. I kept moaning, "Oh, God," and promising I would never do it again, and Mama stayed with me until I fell into a deep black sleep. I had never loved her so much as I did then, especially because she comforted me without reproaches, sympathized without scolding, and I knew then that I never again wanted to leave childhood. Never wanted another drink of whiskey. The dark adventures of adulthood weren't for me. To hell with them, where they belonged. And in my ignorance, I thought I might actually have some choice in the matter. Little did I realize that it was already too late. Little did I know that there was no turning back now, this side of death.

6

What a terrible hangover I had the next day! And when Mama finally got around to asking me where I got the liquor, I told her I had watched one of the men come out of the Grange Hall to take a drink from a bottle that he had hid in a bush. She believed me, because that was how the men always did their drinking at the Grange Hall socials. But though the lie saved Uncle Red from censure, it added another sin to the already galling burden of guilt that I had somehow seemed to acquire since Uncle Red's arrival.

Uncle Red seemed to appreciate my willingness to lie about the whiskey, though he didn't mention it outright. He came into my room to see me that morning.

"Well, Hoss," he drawled with a small grin on his gaunt face, "how you doing?" He sat down on the side of my bed and rolled himself a cigarette out of Papa's Bull Durham, a flimsy and falling-apart cigarette. After he struck a match across the sole of his boot and puffed the cigarette to get it going, he offered it to me.

"Want a puff?"

I made a sound like vomiting.

"Oh, well, I thought maybe you was addicted to all the vices. Glad to see you ain't a smoker, anyway. But you sure one helluva drinker, ain't you? I never seen anybody put it away like you did last night. Probably take you more'n ten minutes to get drunk as a skunk and twice as smelly."

He joshed me for a little while like that, but then his cigarette came unrolled and the tobacco spilled onto the floor. As he stamped the fire out, he said, "Well, you hurry up and get over that headache, you hear? Me and Virgil's going into town, and he's gonna drive, but I already told him that you was gonna be my regular chauffeur, soon's you're up and about." He winked at me and turned to go.

"Uncle Red? While you're gone, could I . . . I mean, if I ain't too sick after a while, could I maybe play your guitar?"

"You take good care of it," he warned.

"I will. I promise," I said, so excited by the prospect of playing his guitar that I sat up in bed; then felt a sudden pain in the back of my head as if someone had hit me with a mall. I groaned and lowered myself gently back down onto the pillow as Uncle Red chuckled and went out.

Mama kept bringing in cool wet washcloths to lay on my forehead, so my headache was nearly gone by noon, and I couldn't wait to get up and play Uncle Red's guitar. He had showed me a few chords when he had come to visit us the first time, and thought I had forgotten them, but they came back to me soon enough, and I sat in the front room and played the beautiful guitar all afternoon. A couple of strings were out of tune, but I didn't let that stop me. And after about an hour of constant strumming, the tips of my fingers on my left hand were nearly as sore as boils. But I didn't let that stop me, either. Even Howard couldn't stop me. When he came in from hauling water to the barn and saw that I had recovered enough to be out of bed, he told me to come and help him with the water.

"Howie," Mama said, "don't be so bossy, now. Just because he's singing don't mean he's not sick."

"He sounds sick, all right," Howard said.

At first Grandpa took out his harmonica and tried to play along with me, but he couldn't stand the strings being out of tune, and I didn't know how to tune them, so he soon gave up trying to accompany me. I stopped playing only when my fingers got so sore I could no longer fret the strings.

Papa and Uncle Red didn't come home for supper. Mama told me they were out trying to rustle up some money some-where, but it became apparent, when they finally got home, that they had also been out getting some bootleg liquor. It was about ten o'clock, and I was in bed, but I woke up as soon as I heard their voices in the kitchen. Papa sounded as if he'd had a few drinks, and Mama sounded upset, and Uncle Red sounded as carefree as the duck that didn't give a quack.

They hadn't succeeded in getting any money. They had gone to loan companies and banks and tried to get a loan on the Packard limousine, but since Uncle Red didn't have the ownership papers, he couldn't borrow any money on it. So now what were they going to do? Uncle Red needed money to get to Nashville, and Papa needed enough to get us out to California. Papa sounded almost morbidly pessimistic when he said that he could sell all the livestock and all our farm machinery, of course, but altogether it probably wouldn't fetch over two hundred dollars, the market being the way it was, with everybody trying to sell out at once, and that wouldn't be enough to take us to California and keep us in grub till we found some work.

"Well, I'll match that," Uncle Red said.

I heard Mama start to protest, but Uncle Red said that he was going to give them the two hundred, by God, and that was that. The only trouble was, he didn't know just where to get it at the moment. He could probably get it once he got to Nashville, he said, but since he didn't even have enough money to get *there* . . .

That was when Grandpa's voice entered into the discussion. "I was born in Tennessee," he said. "Cainsville. Just north of Murfreesboro. Know where that is?"

"No, sir," Uncle Red said. "Never been to Tennessee before."

"I was born there," Grandpa said again. "Came out to Oklahoma when I was eighteen, riding an old mule, and—"

"Pass the beans," Papa said, interrupting Grandpa before he could get started telling Uncle Red about the Run. Papa didn't mean to be rude, it was just that he had heard the story too many times while he was a boy living in Grandpa's house, and now that Grandpa was living in *his* house, he'd be damned if he was going to sit around and listen to it again. So he always found some way to divert Grandpa's attention whenever Grandpa mentioned anything about the Run.

But then Grandpa said, "Well, the fact is, I might be able to help you out a little. I could give you maybe thirty dollars," and that got everyone's attention.

"Sure, sure," Uncle Red said, as if he thought Grandpa was just being polite. "But you'll need that, help get you to California."

"I ain't going to California," Grandpa said, and there wasn't another sound from the kitchen until Grandpa cleared his throat and added, "Too old for that. I been thinking. I ain't got that much longer to live, and I don't want to die and be buried out there, or in this place, either. Been thinking, I want to go home."

"Home?" Mama said. "Why, Grandpa Wagoner, your home's with us."

"I mean Tennessee," he said. "Ain't been back there in forty-five years. But that's where I was born, and that's where I want to die and be buried."

To hear Grandpa talk so calmly about dying and being buried evidently startled everyone around the table as much as it did me. I realized that he was an old man, of course, as old as the hills, but to me, in my youth, in my ignorance, he, like the hills, had always been there, and always would be—eroded and barren, maybe, but indestructible. And now, to lie there in my darkened room, in the lumpy bed that I shared with him, and hear him talk of dying and being buried caused me to feel very strange and alone.

"But . . . but . . ." I heard Mama stammer, and then fall silent, reluctant to broach the subject, though she finally blurted it out, "What about Tyetha? Don't you want to be buried with her?"

"She's buried with her people," he answered, as if that explained something.

I had never seen Grandma Wagoner before she died—had never even seen her grave. I had, of course, heard the story of *how* she had died, though it wasn't entirely from Grandpa that I'd heard it. It had usually been told in family circles when Grandpa wasn't present. It was presumably something he didn't much want to talk about, and I could easily understand why. It gave me goosebumps every time I thought about it, imagined it. Papa sometimes mentioned it when he was drunk and feeling sorry for himself, and a couple of times I had overheard Mama telling some of her kinfolks about it, and I had imagined the rest of it in all its nightmarish details.

It had happened the year I was born. Grandpa and Grandma, already old and with all their children grown up and gone off on their own, had found that they were no longer able to do the backbreaking work on the sharecropper farm they had over in eastern Oklahoma. So they left the farm and hired themselves out as sheepherders on a big ranch down in Muskogee County.

It was in the dead of winter when they moved into the small, one-room sheepherder's cabin on the ranch. The first thing Grandpa did was to cut some wood and get a fire roaring in the fireplace, while Grandma—an old woman, half blind, with most of her teeth gone, with skin as wrinkled and brown as a walnut—dusted and cleaned the cabin and unpacked her pots and pans. And that night, before crawling bone-weary into their old four-poster bed, Grandma raked some of the old dead ashes from under the grate in the fireplace and threw some more logs on the fire. The cabin was drafty and she didn't want Grandpa to get chilled during the night for fear that it would aggravate his rheumatism.

Grandpa said later that the cabin had probably been built by Indians, since there was a hole in the hearth through which you could rake the dead ashes from the fireplace. That was the way Indians built fireplaces, he said, so they could clean it without carrying the ashes outside. You simply lifted the plug from the hole—the plug being a loose rock or brick—and raked the dead ashes through the hole into a pit beneath the cabin. In the spring, the ashes would be hauled from the pit and used as fertilizer in the garden.

But after Grandma finished raking the ashes from under the grate, she neglected to put the plug back into the hole—an oversight that was to cost her her life.

As the night wore on, the fire burned low, leaving the cabin so chilly that Grandpa woke up. It was then that he smelled something, he said, a faint and very peculiar odor—a musky odor—that he couldn't quite place. It reminded him of snakes, he said, but he knew it couldn't be that. Snakes, being cold-blooded creatures, had to hibernate during cold spells. He had sometimes seen them—rattlesnakes—in their winter dens, their sluggish bodies entwined in huge masses in order to keep from freezing. So he dismissed the idea of snakes.

But he couldn't ignore the chill. It was getting into his bones. So he started to get up and put some more wood on the fire. Grandma, however, who slept on the outside of the bed because she was always the first one up in the morning, told him to stay put. She would do it.

Dressed in an old cotton nightgown, she got up and started

for the fireplace without lighting a lamp, and she was maybe halfway across the room before she stepped on something that suddenly came alive under her foot. She felt something like needles rake the side of her leg. She cried out and jumped away, only to step on another squiggling something, and to receive another wound. She fell forward on her hands and knees, cried out again in pain and terror, and by then the whole cabin had come alive with a storm of terrible thrashing and rattling sounds, the sound of a dry cornfield being swirled by a gale-force wind.

At the sound of her first cry, Grandpa jerked upright in bed, but amid Grandma's cries of horror and pain, she had managed to warn him to stay.

"Snakes!" she cried. "Stay! Snakes! Don't get—" And her words were cut off by another cry.

Grandpa had been paralyzed with confusion for a moment, completely unable to fathom what was happening, but he heeded her warning and, against every impulse of his body, did not rush to help her. Instead, he frantically grabbed his trousers from the bedpost (he still had two good arms then, he hadn't as yet received the wound that would leave his arm withered and useless) and dug into his pockets until he found a match. Fumbling and cursing, he finally succeeded in lighting the kerosene lamp beside their bed. Then he saw what was happening: Grandma on the floor, writhing in a mass of thrashing and striking rattlesnakes. The floor seemed to be covered with snakes, all of them alarmed and shivering their rattles, and those nearest to Grandma, as she wallowed among them, struck out at her, again and again, at her arms and legs and buttocks and shoulders.

Grandpa leaped up in the bed and stood with his back against the wall for a moment, petrified, helpless, knowing that if he rushed to save Grandma, he too would be struck and killed. What could he do? He said later that he didn't even know when the idea occurred to him, but only that he suddenly found himself jerking the quilts off the bed and throwing them like nets across the rattlesnakes on the floor. In that way he made a path to Grandma, walking over the quilts that covered the squiggling rattlesnakes, and through which they couldn't strike him.

He pulled Grandma onto the quilts. With his bare hands, he grabbed and flung the last two snakes away from her and dragged her back to the bed. She was hysterical by now, out of her mind with pain and horror, and Grandpa knew that she was beyond help. Her nightgown had been slashed and bloodied by the strikes, and there were fang wounds on her face and neck, so there was nothing he could do to save her.

That's when all his fear and horror turned to rage. He found himself roaring his fury and beating his fists against the wall, and then he turned on the snakes. He grabbed one of the quilts. Using it like a whip, he drove the rattling and hissing snakes away from the bed. The snakes struck at the flailing quilt, leaping from their coiled positions like springs. Their fangs got caught in the quilt now and then and they were flung about the cabin as if propelled from a slingshot, thumping against the walls and furniture, banging into pots and pans in a pandemonium of hellish sounds.

He beat a pathway through them to the doorway of the cabin, then dashed outside and got a hoe, whirled and rushed back into the cabin, and then the slaughter began. He brought the hoe down on them, one by one, and cut their heads off, all the while roaring like the wounded and frenzied beast that he had become. The next day he counted them: thirty-two in all, and one of them was over six feet long. Each one with its head cut off. They thrashed and convulsed as they died, their blood spewing out until the floor was awash with it and the walls and the furniture and Grandpa's feet and the legs of his underwear were splattered with it, their cold and clammy blood.

Thirty-two of them. They had been in the ashpit beneath the cabin, using it as a hibernating den, and when Grandma raked the dead but still-warm ashes through the hole in the hearth, the ashes had fallen onto the snakes and warmed them to life. They had followed the source of the heat, each one slithering up through the hole in the hearth to bask in the warmth of the cabin.

After the frenzy of killing was over, Grandpa went back to the bed to try to comfort Grandma, who was already swelling up like a balloon. She was in a coma by then, and she never regained consciousness. She took her last breath just as the sun was coming up, and the last feeble glint of light went out of her eyes.

Grandpa hitched up the team of mules and put Grandma's swollen body in the wagon and took her back to her people, the Cherokees, and buried her there on the old Cherokee India reservation. He buried her, and then returned to the sheep-herder's cabin, and after that the rattlesnake killing really began.

He started by killing every rattlesnake on the ranch. Later he extended his killing territory to include most of Muskogee County. In the wintertime, he hunted out their dens. He could smell them. He never forgot the peculiar musky odor he had smelled that night in the cabin, and when he smelled it again near a rocky outcropping or a cave, he would start searching, tossing aside rocks and debris, until he found the writhing mass of snake bodies. Then he would pour kerosene over them and strike a match and say, "You want to get warm, do you, fellers? Well, here you are," and drop the match on them. The fire would roar upward, and he would stand there, fiercely gloating, as the snakes sizzled in their dens.

If, however, he found them in a hole, where the oxygen would be used up and the fire would go out before it reached the ball of entwined snakes, he would use dynamite. He would shove a stick of it far down into the hole, light the fuse, and then stand back. When the dynamite exploded, dirt and bloody bits of rattlesnakes rained down all around him.

In the summertime, when the snakes were scattered singly over the hot dry rocky grassland, Grandpa found a unique way to slush them out without any danger to himself. He cut two pieces of stovepipe and slipped them over his legs, so that the tops reached just below his knees, and the bottoms rested on the instep of his boots. Thus armored, he would stride noisily across the land, carrying a sharp hoe, and the rattlesnakes would strike at him and hit the stovepipes—*whang!*—and bounce off. Then he would chop their heads off.

This went on for years, and it became known all over eastern Oklahoma that if you wanted your land cleared of rattlesnakes, get in touch with old man Wagoner, the snakehunter. And finally, after his thirst for revenge had been slaked and his mad fury began to abate, he started skinning the snakes and selling the skins to people who made belts and cowboy boots out of them. Some he captured alive and sold to zoological laboratories. He kept some captive and milked them for their venom, which he sold to hospitals and medical laboratories.

But his luck finally ran out, and one of the snakes bit him. He had his snakebite kit with him, so the bite wasn't fatal, but his arm swelled up to twice its normal size, and then, once the poison was gone, the arm shriveled to skin and bone and the useless fingers curled up like a bird's claw.

He knew then that his snake-hunting days were over. Well, he was getting too old for it anyway, he said. He was no longer alert enough, angry enough. He was tired.

That's when he came to live with us, a couple of years ago, and the only piece of furniture he had brought with him was his old rocking chair. He put the rocker out on the front porch and eased himself down into it, and there he stayed for hours at a time, the withered left hand cradled in his lap, his hawkish eyes steady and fierce as he stared at everything and nothing. Or sometimes he would sit there and write poetry. I thought at first that he was a famous poet because he'd had some of his poems published in newspapers like the Muskogee *Sentinel*. And if any grown-up showed any interest, he would willingly take from his wallet tattered and yellowed pieces of creased newsprint on which were printed some of his poems. But he was with his poems as he was with his story of the Run: he didn't share them with kids. It wasn't that he was mean or cruel to kids, but just indifferent, like a crippled old bear who refuses to play with frolicsome cubs.

However, he did quote me one of his poems once. He had been living with us for three or four months then, and one day I went out hunting with my slingshot. The weapon wasn't accurate enough to be dangerous to anything except windows and balky mules, but I sometimes went hunting with it, and one day I happened to hit a meadowlark. It was a very exciting moment for me when I saw the bird topple off the fence and fall dead into the weeds. It was the first time I had ever killed any game with my slingshot.

"Look!" I cried triumphantly when I reached the front porch, where Grandpa sat idly rocking in his chair.

But Grandpa only gazed at the dead bird in my outstretched hand and said in a small dry voice,

> *"Don't kill the birds, the pretty birds*
> *That flutter from tree to tree.*
> *'Tis God that sends them in the spring,*
> *To sing for you and me."*

I couldn't have been more shocked if he had struck me. I looked down at the bird in my hand, the pretty fluffy yellow breasted bird that God had sent to sing for me, and suddenly I felt awful. Just terrible. It had been the meadowlark's lovely song that had first attracted my murderous attention to it, and the shot that had killed the bird had silenced the lovely song in midnote.

After that I could never have eaten the bird, as I had intended doing. Not even if I had been starving. I took it out behind the barn and dug a small grave and gave it a good Christian burial. Even put a cross made from twigs at the head of its grave. Then, on my knees, I asked God to forgive me for having killed this pretty bird that He had sent to sing for me.

As I knelt over the small grave, however, I began to suffer my first confusion and doubts about the infallibility of grown-ups and the wisdom of God's order. Why, I wondered, was it bad for me to kill a bird if it wasn't bad for Grandpa to burn, blow up and hack to death more rattlesnakes than probably anybody who ever lived?

"Grandpa?" I said as I sidled up to the porch.

"Ummm?"

"Grandpa. If God sent the birds, didn't he send the rattle-snakes, too?"

Then Grandpa really *looked* at me for the first time since he had come to live with us. His head turned very slowly in my direction, the eyes unmoving in their sockets, and fixed me with a stare that had all the cold ferocity of a hawk eyeing its prey. I thought he was going to pounce on me. But after a moment of dreadful tension, I saw the ferocity fade from his eyes and I thought I even saw a slight smile play at the corners of his mouth, though I couldn't be sure because of the drooping frontiersman's mustache that covered his upper lip. Then he said in his dry, matter-of-fact way, "Wasn't a bird that tempted Adam and Eve and got 'em throwed out of the Garden. Was the Devil, in the disguise of a snake. I was doing the Lord's work, boy. You did the Devil's."

Well, after that I wished I hadn't said anything at all. I could have bit my tongue off. It was bad enough to bear the guilt of having killed the pretty bird; it was even worse to learn that I had been the instrument of the Devil. I threw my slingshot away, and that night, as Grandpa was getting undressed for bed, I asked him if he would teach me to hunt snakes. All he said was, "Go to sleep, boy," and I did.

7

Uncle Red didn't show up for breakfast the next morning. When I asked Mama if I should save him some of the scrambled eggs and gravy, she said, "He's not coming to the table. He's feeling poorly this morning, and don't you go bothering him, either, y'hear? Let him rest."

"What's the matter with him?" I asked, sopping the last of the gravy from my plate. Now that I was fully recovered from the hangover, I felt famished, as if I wanted to make up for the food and growth I had missed out on yesterday.

"What's the matter with him!" Mama mocked.

I assumed, then, that it was the TB that kept Uncle Red in bed. But how could I be expected to know that? I knew next to nothing about TB. I knew enough about Mama, though, to see that she was awfully touchy today. In fact, everybody seemed a little out of tune, and it wasn't hard to guess the cause. It had been agreed that we—all except Grandpa, that is—were moving to California, but nobody seemed at all sure *when* we would go, let alone *how* we would go, so nobody was sure of what should be done to prepare for the trip. Everyone seemed to be waiting for Fate to give us a sign, show us the way. But finally Papa and Howard went out to work on our old Chevy truck, to see if maybe they could fix it up good enough to drive it to California, while Mama and Margery started bringing up from the cellar and packing away all the jars of food that we wouldn't be needing between now and the time we left. And as soon as I finished feeding the chickens and doing my other regular chores, I went to help Mama and Margery. The first thing I did, though, was break a jar of tomatoes, so Mama told me to never mind.

"Just go away," she said. "Go and see what's wrong with Penny. Make yourself useful, can't you?"

And even though Mama had meant it as a humiliation to punish me for breaking the tomatoes, I didn't mind taking care of Penny, since I would be in the same room with Uncle Red's guitar. I was itching to play it again, and I did, too, as soon as I lulled Penny to sleep by jouncing her up and down on the bed a little to make it seem like a cradle. Then, very gingerly, maybe like a novitiate handling a holy relic, I got Uncle Red's guitar out of its case. It was still a little out of tune, one or two strings were, but I was so enraptured by the power to pluck sounds from the strings that I didn't let a random sour note stop me. But Uncle Red couldn't stand it.

"Goddammit," he yelled from his room, "either tune that thing or stop playing it!"

After that, I couldn't have tuned the guitar even if I had known how, so stunned was I by the sound of his voice. He was mad. It was the first time I had ever heard him use that tone of voice to anyone, and the fact that he had used it to *me*, who idolized him, was even more stunning.

After I recovered a little, I stammered, "I . . . I don't know how."

"Bring it in here!" he yelled.

I took the guitar into the room, where he lay on top of the covers in the rumpled bed, dressed only in his shorts. I hardly knew what to expect, but he looked awful. It was easy to forget how cadaverously skinny he was, how sunken were his chest and cheeks and eyes. And he was sweating now, big drops of sweat on his forehead, as if he had just run a race, and he was as pale as whey. And for some reason, his unruly hair seemed a little redder today, as if all the blood in his face had gone into it.

"Gimme that," he barked as he swung his bony legs over the side of the bed and snatched the guitar out of my hands. "I'm gonna show you how to tune the goddamn thing, and you better pay attention. I won't show you twice, and you're not to play it 'less you can tune it. That clear?"

He waited for an answer from me, but I was still too stunned to say anything. I couldn't believe what I was seeing and hearing. This wasn't the Uncle Red that I knew. There had been no winks, no nicknames, no jocularity at all. This man was mean and petty, vindictive, maybe even cruel, and the Uncle Red that I knew had never been like that.

"Well, what's the matter with you?" he demanded. "Close your mouth, for Christ's sake, you're catching flies."

I closed my mouth, but I was still too dumbfounded to pay any attention when he began showing me how to tune the guitar by pushing the bottom E string down at the fifth fret and then striking the . . .

"Say, are you getting any of this?" he demanded.

I tried to shrug. "Well," I murmured, "I . . . I . . . uh . . ."

"And just what the hell're you looking at me like that for? Something peculiar 'bout the way I look?"

Almost shuffling now, I said, "It's just that I've never . . . seen you like this."

He flared like a struck match. "There's a lotta things you ain't seen, kid," he snapped, but the flame of his anger seemed to gutter out quickly, leaving him with a frown of self-disgust. "Go on," he said then, "get outta here! I'm tired a you staring like that, your mouth hanging open. You think I'm some kinda freak or something?"

I tried to protest that, no, I didn't think he was a freak, but he waved me away. He didn't want to listen to me anymore. He slammed the guitar down against the wall and fell back on his rumpled bed. And that was the most puzzling and painful thing about it all, the way he treated his guitar, slamming it against the wall like that. I knew then, for sure, that Uncle Red had a mean and vicious streak in him. I figured that if he would hurt his guitar, he would hurt anybody or anything, and that caused me to be afraid of him for the first time.

"Go on," he said. "Beat it."

I backed out of the room as if afraid to turn my back on him, and then, with my eyes already awash with tears, I hurried through the kitchen and out onto the back porch. I sat down on the porch and hugged one of the posts and kicked fitfully at the dust with my bare toes. I was sniffling when our old dog Tige came out from under the porch and licked my foot and then pushed his cold nose under my hand and nudged it, the way he always did when he wanted to be petted.

"Get away from me," I said, just like Uncle Red had said it. But at least I knew why *I* was angry and mean; I didn't know why Uncle Red was. What had I done? Surely he wasn't really mad because I played the guitar a little out of tune, was he? No, of course not. At any other time he would have joked about it, or at least softened his criticism with a wink or a smile.

"It ain't your fault," Mama said. She had been in the kitchen and apparently overheard what Uncle Red had said to me. After I had been on the porch for a couple of minutes she came out and sat down beside me. "It's the sickness that makes him like that. When people have it, they sometimes get like that."

I wanted to believe it was true, of course, because I didn't want to believe that I had been the cause of his anger, or that his anger and meanness were a part of his character, rather than symptoms of his sickness.

"Anyway, it's not your fault, so don't think it. And it's not his fault, either. You can't blame him, no more'n you could blame a cripple man for hobbling, or a drunk person for throwing up," she added pointedly. "You understand?"

I nodded. I realized she was right, and her explanation helped soothe my hurt feelings. But I couldn't explain to her that it was more than just hurt feelings that had brought me to tears. There was something else, a sorrow more profound, a feeling of disillusionment and loss that I couldn't name or understand. But Mama apparently divined that, too, because what she said next made me realize what was bothering me most of all.

"He's only human," she said.

That was it. Only human. Until then I had believed—wanted to believe, anyway—that Uncle Red was more than just human. Until then I had believed that he was some sort of demigod—someone who, no matter what he did, could do no wrong.

"He likes you a lot, you know," Mama said. "Sometimes I think he likes you best of all of us."

That brought a new rush of tears to my eyes. At the same time, however, there was something in her voice that caused me to fight back the tears, something that urged me to compose myself, and then I suddenly realized what it was: for the first time in my life, Mama was talking to me as if I were a grown-up.

"Now, come on," she said in a spirited way as she got to

her feet. "I'm going to cook him something to eat, and I want you to take it in to him."

I gave her a terrified look. "But what if he ... ?" I started to say something childish, but caught myself in time and changed the question. "What if he don't want it?"

"You tell him he better eat it, or I'll come in there and shove it down his throat."

She cooked him a big breakfast of eggs and flapjacks, and I took the plate into his room on a tray. He glowered at me for a moment when I first entered, but when he saw that I wasn't going to shrink from him as if he were some sort of monster, he switched his feverish eyes to the food. And true to my suspicion, he turned up his nose and said he didn't want any. But I told him what Mama had said, and he sort of sighed, not so much with resignation as relief.

"Oh, well," he said, "I reckon I'd better try."

I had already turned to leave when he said, "Listen, Hoss . . ." He sighed again. "Don't pay me no mind when I'm like this, y'hear? Goddamned fever. When it comes on like this, I'm liable to get as snappish as a pair of sheepshears."

I shrugged and mumbled something about its being all right.

He took a bite of the flapjacks and mumbled with his mouth full, "Get it. I'll tell you how to tune it."

I would rather not have tried to do it just then, so afraid was I of incurring his displeasure again, but I knew that the surest way to incur it was to decline his offer, so I took the guitar and sat down on a chair next to his bed, and, gritting my teeth, tried to do what he told me. He took a deep breath, as if summoning up all his reserves of patience, and then began his instructions.

It didn't take long, though, for his fevered temper to flare up again. It happened when he told me to hit the A string open, and then snapped, "The A string, goddammit, the A string!" He realized then that I didn't know one string from another. So he took another deep breath and proceeded to teach me the names of the different strings.

Actually, once I got the hang of it, tuning the guitar didn't seem too hard. He made me untune and retune it a few times, then began teaching me chords. This went on for maybe an hour and I had become very excited about it ("Settle down, Hoss," he said to me at one point, "you're as nervous as a whore in church") by the time Mama came into the room to get Uncle Red's tray.

"How y'all doing in here?" she asked with a smile, pleased to see that Uncle Red and I had made up. "Learning anything?"

"He's a natural," Uncle Red announced.

I couldn't tell whether or not he was merely joshing her, but it sure made me feel good to hear him say it. Every minute that I held that beautiful guitar in my hands made me hope more and more that maybe I really could be a guitar picker someday, just like Uncle Red.

"Well, hadn't you ought to stop for a while?" Mama suggested to me. "Let Hassle get some rest?"

"I'll throw him out in a minute," Uncle Red said, lighting another cigarette, and after Mama had gone, he said, "Hoss, there's something I want you to do for me." He paused for a moment to let the silence imbue his words with significance, and then said, "I got to find some way to get some more money. There's a honkytonk just outside of Roscoe. I'm gonna go there tonight, play a few tunes, pass the hat, and I'd like you to come along to drive, 'case I get drunk."

I was too excited to speak for a moment, and then I said, "Damn come a-tooting, I will," because it sounded like the way he himself might have said it. "But . . ." And here my big grin wilted. "Mama might not . . . I mean, she'll probably say Papa ought to do it."

With a silencing gesture, he said, "Never mind. Sis ain't gonna let Virgil get within a mile of a honkytonk. Don't worry, I'll take care of that. But there's something else. Y'all got any gunny sacks 'round here?"

"Sure. In the barn. Lots of 'em."

"We'll need about ten. And a pair of wire cutters and a board about six feet long. Now, I want you to get them things and put 'em in the car without letting Sis see you do it, y'hear? And don't say a word to nobody."

Totally mystified, wondering what in the world he could be up to now, I said, "Well, sure. But how could I do all that without being seen?"

"For Christ's sake," he snapped, "use your head. We won't be leaving till around nine. Do it after dark."

It was dark by the time the family sat down to supper that evening. While we were eating, Mama scolded me for cramming my mouth full, but I was in a hurry to finish before anybody else did. Then I excused myself, saying I had to go to the outhouse, and Uncle Red, who had got up to join us for supper, winked at me across the table.

I went out to the barn and got the things he said he wanted. I put them in the car without anybody seeing me, feeling sneaky and sort of scared all the while, not to mention mystified. Try as I might, I couldn't figure out what in the world he could possibly want with those things.

Just before we left, Mama came into my room, where I was getting into a clean pair of bib overalls and my old brogans. She said, "Whit, listen to me for a moment. The only reason we're letting you go is, I want you to keep him out of trouble, if you can. Don't let him drive while he's drinking, and— listen, now—you have to promise me you won't drink anymore yourself, y'hear? You have to promise me that, or I won't let you go."

That was a promise I didn't mind making at all.

"And, Whit? Promise me you won't hang out in that honky-tonk, either. You stay in the car. Promise?"

That was a harder promise to make, since I was looking forward to hearing Uncle Red sing. But I knew she wouldn't let me go unless I promised, so I did.

8

Driving at night was a little different from driving in the daytime, but with Uncle Red giving me instructions, I soon got the hang of it. It helped that ours was the only car on the road except for a couple of old jalopies we met coming back from town, and all I had to remember was to stay on the right side of the road and dim my headlights—or headlight, I should say. And I had remembered to bring a couple of pillows, one to sit on and one to put behind my back, so I could sit up close enough to reach the foot pedals and see over the hood of the car.

The honkytonk we went to was called the Pair-a-Dice Cafe. It was on the highway outside of town a couple of miles, a sort of roadhouse surrounded by cotton fields. There was a graveled parking lot in front that was filled with dusty cars and pickups, and on the roof of the old barnlike building was a neon sign in the shape of a pair of dice with three dots that blinked on and off.

"Wait here," Uncle Red told me after I had parked the car in front of the place. "I'll go in, see if it's okay. If I give you the high sign, bring my guitar in."

"But I promised Mama I wouldn't . . ." I faltered, feeling childish all of a sudden, and Uncle Red, getting out of the car, said in the tone of someone dispensing manly advice, "Promises

69

made to women are made under duress, so they don't have to
be kept."

At the time I didn't know what "duress" meant, but I knew
what *he* meant, and I couldn't believe he was serious. With
him, the way he was always bantering, it was never easy to
know when he was serious and when he wasn't.

Anyway, I stayed in the car and watched the people going
in and out of the place, the good-time Charlies in cowboy boots
and Saturday-night suits, the women in their bright flimsy
Montgomery Ward dresses, laughing and talking in boozy
abandon. Music from phonograph records drifted, faint and
timorous, from the interior, and in the brief silent moments
between records I could hear the night sounds from the blighted
cotton fields beyond the building, the almost orchestrated hum
and chirp of katydids and crickets.

In about twenty minutes, Uncle Red appeared in the doorway and signaled to me. I got his guitar from the trunk and
carried it inside with dread and excitement. This was a world
I had never seen before. Smoky and dim, tense with unnamable
menace and dark promise, loud with laughter and music, rank
with smells of fried foods and bootleg whiskey, with the acrid
odors of spittoons and perfumed flesh. There were tables and
a counter as in a regular cafe, but only a few of the customers
were eating. Most of them had soft-drink bottles and coffee
cups in front of them, and it was easy to assume that the cups
and bottles contained more than just coffee or cola.

The creaky, boot-scarred wooden floor was littered with
cigarette butts, and the clapboard walls—once a light lemon
color, apparently—had long since turned to a sort of sun yellow, splotched with stains from hurled bottles. The only bright
new thing in the room was a twinkling jukebox, from which
blared an old-time fiddle tune, "Under the Double Eagle."

I recognized one of the customers. It was the man in the
fedora, the one who had given Uncle Red the whiskey at the
Grange Hall. He sat among the men at the counter, slim and
quiet and slightly sinister, the fedora tipped back on his head
and a cigarette dangling from one corner of his thin dark mouth.

In the rear of the room was a bandstand with a chicken-
wire screen in front of it. There were a couple of microphones
on the bandstand, but no musical instruments. Uncle Red was
standing nearby, talking to a blond-headed woman.

"Well, looky *here*," the blonde said in a strident voice when

I handed Uncle Red the guitar case. Beneath her fluffy apron she wore a tight red dress, and her huge bosom bulged against the confines of the dress as though about to spill over the low-cut top like the filling from a squeezed pastry. And from her direction drifted a cloud of cloying lilac perfume. "What's this, Red? Got y'self a helper?"

"That's my nephew. Name's Whit," and it was the first time I could remember hearing him use my name. Until then I wasn't even sure he knew it. "This here's Lulu. She owns the joint."

"Your *nephew!* Well, ain't he something, now? Sure is cute, ain't he?"

"Yeah," Uncle Red said, "and he got it all from me."

"Well, hell, Red, you shoulda kept some for y'self."

There was a burst of laughter from some people nearby. Uncle Red laughed too. I blushed.

"Well, I like 'em young, and that's a fact, but not *that* young," Lulu cackled, and then said to me, "Hon, how 'bout if I give you a nickel and you call me up in a couple of years?"

There was another burst of laughter, and then Uncle Red said, "How 'bout that, Hoss? Lulu's a cherry picker. You ripe for plucking?"

"*Plucking!*" Lulu said. "Come on, Red, you can talk plainer'n *that.*"

I could feel my heart beating and the blood burning in my cheeks and ears. I tried to swagger it off and think of something snappy to say, but I was tongue-tied by the storm of mingled embarrassment, excitement and fear that raged within me.

Lulu took a nickel from the coins that jingled in her apron pocket. "Here you are, hon. You can spend it now if you want to, but you gotta promise you'll gimme a call in a couple of years, y'hear?"

I held back, unsure of what to do.

"Go ahead and take it," Uncle Red said, nudging me with his elbow. "'Member what I told you 'bout promises made to women?"

I took the nickel. I even managed to mumble, "Thank you," and Lulu suggested I go buy myself a soda pop, which I did. The nickel never saw the inside of my pocket. I asked the man behind the counter—a big man in a dirty apron, with tattoos on his hairy forearms—for a Nehi orange. I took the soda pop and went to stand by the front door, as if ready to bolt from the place at any second, and I sipped the cold, tangy beverage with deliberate slowness. I kept remembering that I had promised Mama I would stay outside the honkytonk, but I figured I was justified in staying inside until I finished the soda pop, at least, so that I could leave the empty bottle behind, and that's why I drank it so slowly. I thought maybe I could make it last long enough for me to hear Uncle Red sing a couple of songs.

It wasn't easy, but I did it, and when the tattooed waiter turned the jukebox off and Uncle Red shambled up onto the stage, I forgot about everything else. I even forgot about my soda pop, so entranced was I with his presence. On the small stage, behind the chicken wire that shielded musicians from flying bottles, resplendent in his fringed and sequined suit, he strummed his guitar a few times and tuned a couple of strings, totally at ease, maybe even a little arrogant in the way he slouched over the microphones. His first song, called "Honkytonk Heaven," was one of his own, but he didn't bother to introduce it. In fact, he didn't even introduce himself. The audience was so noisy and rowdy that he apparently felt it would be futile to try to get their attention by talking, so he just started singing.

> *If there's a heaven for honkytonk men,*
> *That's where I'm gonna meet all my friends.*
> *We paid our dues,*
> *And so when we die*
> *We'll all get together*
> *In that barroom in the sky.*

And, my God, how that man could sing! For a little while, though, it seemed that I was one of the few persons in the room who thought so. Most of the customers just kept right on talking and laughing. At first I was baffled by their rudeness, and then I felt myself becoming outraged. I wanted to shush them, and I was afraid Uncle Red might get mad and stop singing. But he didn't. He just kept on singing, self-assured and confident to the point of carelessness.

> *There'll be jukebox angels*
> *Singing hillbilly songs*
> *In Honkytonk Heaven*
> *For boys who've gone wrong."*

But by the end of the first verse, something began to happen. The conversations around the room began to subside, one by one, into a sort of surprised hush. At first, there was a quality of skepticism in the gathering silence, as if the listeners couldn't believe that Uncle Red was as good as he sounded, as if they simply couldn't believe that here, in a cockroachy little honkytonk on the edge of a cotton field in Oklahoma, they were hearing a voice that was as good as any they had ever heard in their lives. It took them a little while to accept it, to realize what was happening, and then the surprised and skeptical quality of the silence turned to wonder and gratitude. From that moment on, the hard-bitten and boisterous audience was in the palm of Uncle Red's hand, raptly silent.

> *"There'll be pretty young barmaids,*
> *And free drinks for the band,*
> *And, oh, that'll be Heaven*
> *For a honkytonk man."*

When he finished that first song, the audience exploded with loud applause and shouts of appreciation. I sat my soda pop down so I could clap with the rest of them, and once again I felt my chest swelling with pride and wonder, with an excitement so intense that I simply couldn't contain myself. I *had* to share it with someone, and there was a kindly-looking man sitting alone at a table nearby, a clodhopper type in bib overalls, who was smiling broadly and clapping wildly for Uncle Red, and it was to him that I turned and cried, "That's my uncle! That's my uncle!"

The man obviously shared my enthusiasm, but he didn't know quite how to respond to my declaration. He said something like, "Oh, yeah? Well, he's shore a good un, ain't he?" And by then I had got hold of myself. Slightly abashed at my forwardness, I nodded and smiled and turned my attention back to Uncle Red, who, when the applause began to wane, finally introduced himself.

"Howdy," he said into the microphone, and the last of the scattered shouts and whistles quickly died away. "I'm Red Stovall. I'm here to sing a few songs and pass the hat. If you all got any requests, just holler. And if any of you feel like dancing, why, by God, get up and go to it."

And without allowing time for the audience's enthusiasm to cool, he began singing a rollicking old hoedown called "Ida

Red," and the driving force of it brought many of the customers to their feet. They began dancing. Whooping and clapping their hands in rhythm, they sashayed out onto the dance area in front of the bandstand and began doing the Okie stomp. It was a wild and formless frolic, a sort of cross between an Irish jig and an Indian war dance, and though most of the dancers were couples, a partner wasn't really necessary. The clodhopper sitting at the table near me didn't have a partner, but he didn't let that stop him. He got up and danced by himself. With the blissful look of someone who isn't very bright, he whirled and whooped his way through the other dancers, his scruffy brogans slapping the floor with the rhythmic precision of a woodcock's mating thump.

The applause and cheers and whistles that followed the song were as wild as the dance had been. Everybody was having a great time, and so was I—at least I was until Uncle Red started his third song, a song that the clodhopper himself requested. Sweating and panting from the exertion of his dance, the clodhopper waited for the applause to die down, and then he asked Uncle Red if he could play "Mother, Queen of my Heart."

That brought a burst of laughter from a few people, and the clodhopper looked around with a goofy grin, as if he not only expected ridicule, but welcomed it. But Uncle Red didn't laugh. "Sure can," he said, and struck the first chord.

It was a Jimmie Rodgers song, a waltztime tearjerker, and ordinarily I would have loved it. Under the circumstances, however, it proved to be a very unfortunate choice of songs for me. It was about a son whose dying mother calls him to her bedside and asks him to promise that he will never start drinking and gambling. The son promises, of course, but he doesn't keep the promise. He becomes a lowdown gambler, and

> "One night I bet all my money,
> Nothing was left to be seen,
> But all I needed to break them
> Was one card, and that was a queen...."

Very few people danced now. Most of the audience listened intently as Uncle Red sang, and the clodhopper, with a moon-calf expression on his face listened most intently of all. He had returned to his table near me, and now sat staring at Uncle Red like a weepy child listening to a sad bedtime story.

"The cards were dealt all 'round the table,
And each took a card on the draw.
I drew the card that would beat them,
I turned it and here's what I saw—

"I saw my mother's picture,
And somehow she seemed to say,
'Son, you have broken your promise,'
So I threw the cards away."

I had long since finished my soda pop, so I put the empty bottle on the counter and was on my way out the door as Uncle Red was singing the last verse.

"My winnings I gave to a newsboy,
I knew I'd been wrong from the start,
Now I'll never forget that promise,
To Mother, the queen of my heart."

I skulked guiltily out to the parking lot and crawled into the back seat of the Packard, pushing the board aside so I could lie down. Uncle Red's voice, amplified through the micro-phones, was still audible, so I lay in the deep mohair comfort of the car's back seat and listened to him, hearing his voice drift dolefully out across the dusty land to mingle and fade into the sounds of the myriad insects that sang their own songs in the moonlit darkness of the ruined cotton fields. He sang all sorts of songs, but none of them quite got to me the way "Mother, Queen of my Heart" had, at least not until he sang "Hobo Bill's Last Ride," a song about a dying hobo who is taking his last ride on a train. That was a tearjerker, too, and as he sang it, I heard, from somewhere far away, thin and muted, the lonesome whistle of a train as it hurtled through the night. And I knew—hadn't I seen it often enough?—that the train would be carrying many hobos, mostly men but sometimes women, too, and even kids, who, homeless and hungry, dreamed of someday finding the pastures of plenty. And it wasn't hard for me to imagine that among the hobos on that train there would be one who was taking his last ride, and the thought of it overwhelmed me with a terrible sense of loss and loneliness and waste, of wasted lives in a wasted land, and my heart went out to that dying hobo, and I cried.

Afterward, wrung out and exhausted, I closed my eyes and

drifted into a sort of trance somewhere between sleeping and waking. At no time, however, did I ever stop hearing—not listening to, but just hearing—Uncle Red sing. It was only when he stopped singing once, right in the middle of a song, that I began to listen again, realizing that something was wrong. Then I began to hear the sounds of a ruckus coming from inside the honkytonk. It didn't occur to me that Uncle Red might be involved in it until I heard his voice, hostile and loud, say over the loudspeaker, "Mister, if everything about you was as big as your mouth, you wouldn't have to work for a living."

The voice that followed that insult brought me fully awake. There were more shouts and sounds of overturning chairs, of bottles breaking. It frightened me to think that Uncle Red might be involved in a fight. Hell, he was so skinny and weak, it would probably take only one solid blow to kill him. I had no idea what I could do about it, but I knew I would have to do something, so I jumped out of the car and hurried toward the front door.

Before I got there, however, the door flew open and there was a crowd of people gathered at the threshold. In the front of the crowd was Uncle Red. Close to him, with his arms pinned behind him by the burly tattooed waiter, was a drunk man who tugged against the waiter's restraining grasp like a maddened bulldog tugging against a leash. There was a woman next to the angry drunk who kept touching his shoulder and saying in a plaintive, placating voice, "Now, Dub. Behave y'self, now, Dub."

And the waiter who was holding Dub kept saying, "Not in here! Outside if you wanna fight! Y'hear? Outside!"

Dub was a heavy man with a beer belly bulging over his belt. His shirttail was hanging out and his hair was in wild disarray, as if he had already been in a scuffle. Glowering at Uncle Red with drunken ferocity, Dub said in a loud challenging voice, "Awright! Come on outside, you sonofabitch! Come on! I'm gonna stomp a mudhole in your ass and then walk it dry!" To the waiter who was holding him, he snapped "Turn me loose! Goddammit, I'll . . ."

"Dub, now!" the woman said. "He didn't mean to . . ."

And Uncle Red, who was standing there just as cool as you please, even with a little mirthless grin on his face, bowed and made an elaborate gesture toward the door. "After you, Alphonse," he said.

It was crazy. This Dub was about twice as big as Uncle Red and a hundred times meaner, a mean drunk if ever I saw one, and he would probably break Uncle Red's neck with one punch.

The man in the fedora was standing just behind Uncle Red. He was silent and grim-faced, but the surging crowd behind him was noisy and excited at the prospect of seeing a fight.

"Lemme go!" Dub said, jerking against the waiter's grasp, and the waiter once again said, "All right, but you go on outside." He gave Dub a little shove toward the door when he released him, and Dub, accepting Uncle Red's invitation to precede him, started outside.

That was his mistake. As he turned his back on Uncle Red and stepped over the threshold, Uncle Red drew back his fist, taking careful aim, and then let fly with a real haymaker right into the base of Dub's skull.

Dub pitched face forward as if he had been picked up and heaved over the front steps. He landed on his face in the gravel. The woman—presumably Dub's wife—cried out and dashed down the steps to fall on her knees beside him.

"Well, that's that," Uncle Red said as if congratulating himself on a job well done. He turned and started to make his way back through the crowd, but the man in the fedora touched his arm lightly and nodded toward Dub.

To the surprise of everyone, Dub was making heroic efforts to get up. As the distraught woman hovered over him and wailed his name, Dub wallowed over on his back. He sat up, looked around with glazed eyes, as if trying to figure out where he was, and when he caught sight of Uncle Red standing on the top step, he cursed with renewed fury and tried to push himself to his feet, only to stumble backward and fall heavily on his butt in the gravel. No sooner had he fallen, however, than he was trying to get up again. Shaking his head and bellowing like a goaded bull, he got to his knees and then pushed himself to his feet. He stood there for a few seconds, swaying unsteadily, as his wife caught at his arm, saying, "Dub! Don't, now, Dub!" But he flung her aside, never taking his eyes off Uncle Red, and then seemed to throw his body forward so that his wobbly legs would have to run to catch up and prevent him from falling face forward.

It was a charge. Nothing less. With that bellow of a tormented bull, he charged Uncle Red, and Uncle Red was waiting for him. When Dub got within striking range, Uncle Red's cowboy boot flashed upward, and the pointed toe caught Dub under the chin.

I could hear the sickening *pop* of bone breaking as Dub's head snapped backward. His body stiffened and he pitched backward, striking the ground with such force that he bounced once before coming to a quivering rest.

The woman cried out again, and again dropped to her knees beside him. This time, however, there was more than just fear and pleading in her voice. This time there was horror, too, because Dub's jaw was hanging grotesquely open and askew from his face.

"Now let's go on back in," Uncle Red said. "That loudmouth won't be bothering us no more."

And now the small grin on his face had changed from one of smug defiance to one of triumph. He made his way back through the crowd, which opened for him the way the Red Sea must have opened for Moses, and then closed in behind him, following him back inside the honkytonk. The man in the fedora, however, remained standing in the doorway for a while longer, and another man, a big bald-headed man, hurried out to where Dub lay sprawled in the gravel.

Dub's wife, whose hysteria had diminished to a sort of sing-song lament, looked up at the bald-headed man and said, "Look! Look what he done, Clyde. His jaw! Look what he done!"

Clyde was apparently Dub's friend. He stood over Dub for a moment, his fists clenching and unclenching with gathering rage, and then he muttered, "I'll kill 'im. I'll kill the sonofa-bitch!"

"Look at his jaw! It's broken! Oh, Dub . . ."

It took a moment longer for Clyde to work up enough rage to turn on his heels and start back into the Pair-a-Dice. But he found that the man in the fedora now had his right hand sunk deep into his pocket, while his left hand was raised in a gesture of a policeman stopping traffic.

"Stay right there, friend," he said, his voice tense and cold.

"Get outa my way," Clyde said threateningly, but he didn't try to shove the man aside.

"Don't try it."

Clyde glanced at the man's right hand clenched deep in his pocket, and he knew—and I knew, too, as sure as I knew anything—that there was a knife in the pocket, and that the man in the fedora would use it if he had to.

"Now, you just put your friend in his car and take him on down to the clinic in Tallapoosa," said the man in the fedora. "If you try to make any trouble, you'll be needing a doctor, too, before it's over with. Hear?"

Clyde hesitated for a moment, indecisive, assessing his danger, and then suddenly snorted with a sort of face-saving contempt, and then went back to Dub, who had begun to come around a little. Under the sorrowing ministrations of his wife, he stirred, groaned, tried to say something, couldn't. As his wife and Clyde helped him to sit up, a small stream of blood dribbled out of his mouth and down his chin.

The man in the fedora remained in the doorway and watched as Clyde and the woman tugged and pulled Dub to his feet. Clyde put one of Dub's arms around his shoulders and, with the woman supporting him on the other side, half-walked and half-hauled Dub to a car.

After they roared out of the parking lot, the only ones remaining outside the Pair-a-Dice were the man in the fedora and I. We looked at each other. The brim of the fedora hid his eyes in deep shadow, but I knew he was looking at me, and it seemed that there was something about him—a look of cool and dark depthlessness—that somehow made him seem to be a strangely fated being, a sort of personified prophecy of something I didn't understand. Then he turned and went back into the building.

It took a few more seconds for me to recover, and even then I moved back to the car like a sleepwalker. I crawled into the back seat and lay down again, pressing against the seat as if trying to hide from something. And it wasn't until Uncle Red started singing again that I could even begin to understand why the violence I had witnessed had shocked me so much: it had been *fun.* That was it: *fun.* I had seen fights before, of course—had even been in a few myself at school—but they had always been the results of uncontainable rage and frustration and fear. Never until I saw Uncle Red there in the doorway, with that small grin on his face just before he hit the man in the back of the head, had I seen anyone who seemed to *enjoy* fighting.

And what about that? What about his having hit the man in the back of the head like that, when the man least expected it, and then, still with that small grin on his face, kicking him under the chin with such force and viciousness that he broke his jaw? Of course, I couldn't have expected Uncle Red to fight the man fairly. Given the differences in their health and physiques, it would no doubt have been Uncle Red who ended up with a broken jaw, or worse. Still, even though I was thankful it wasn't Uncle Red who had been hurt, it bothered me to think that he had actually *enjoyed* hurting the other man.

And not only him. The crowd had enjoyed it, too. When Uncle Red began playing again—mostly fast, up-tempo tunes, what he called shitkickers—the crowd really whooped it up. They clapped their hands and stamped their feet and hollered. It was as if the fight had been a cathartic for them, as if the increase in their drunken revelry had been purchased at the expense of poor Dub's pain.

Well, there was no use me trying to figure it out. Whatever else Uncle Red was, he was still the best singer I had ever heard, and he had proved that tonight. He could move people, no matter what he sang, and that was all there was to it, and that was everything.

I didn't realize that I had fallen asleep until I heard—and felt—the lid of the car trunk open and close. Then Uncle Red was shaking me.

"Wake up, Hoss. Time to go."

"What? What time is it?"

"Time to go."

I stumbled out to stretch my legs and rub the sleep from my eyes. Other cars in the parking lot were starting up, the engines racing, headlights flashing on, others pulling out onto the two-lane blacktop. Uncle Red was talking to somebody as he got into the car on the passenger's side, and when I got into the driver's seat, I saw that it was Lulu. She was bending over and talking to Uncle Red through the opened window. She seemed to expect—hope—that Uncle Red would kiss her.

"Sure you gotta go?" she pleaded in her strident voice. "I got a room out back. The boy could sleep in the car, couldn't he?"

"Love to, honey, but I got some business to do yet," Uncle Red said in his bantering tone, his words slightly slurred. He smelled harshly of whiskey and tobacco. "But I'll be back tomorrow night."

"Promise?" she said, holding her face close to his. "You promise me, now, Red?"

"Hell, yes, I promise," he said, and then to me, "Come on, Hoss, let's get this show on the road. Bye, honey. Keep it hot for me, now, y'hear?"

Lulu stood and watched as I pulled the car into the stream of traffic leaving the parking lot, and I wondered, once we were on the blacktop headed back toward Roscoe, if it had only been polite evasion, or had Uncle Red really meant it when he told her he had some business to take care of tonight. I was thinking of those gunny sacks and that board in the back of the car.

"Sure 'nuff have," he said in response to my timid inquiry. He had pulled a pint of whiskey from his hip pocket.

"What is it we gonna do?" I asked, though I was uncertain I wanted to hear the answer.

"Gonna steal some chickens," he answered.

"Gonna *what?*"

"Steal some chickens." He uncorked the bottle, tipped it up for a long swig, and then banged the cork back into the bottle with the palm of his hand. "There's a chicken farm li'l ways outside of town, on the way to your house. That's where we going."

I was appalled. "Old man Vogel's chicken farm? Are you kidding? That's the meanest old man around here. Soon's he hears a squawk from a chicken, he'll come after us with a shotgun."

"Ain't gonna be no squawks from any chickens *I* steal," Uncle Red boasted. "Hoss, you may not know it, but you have the honor to be assosh . . ." He tried two or three times to say the word, and finally got it out. ". . . associated with the slickest chicken plucker this side of the Mississippi," only he said it "Miz-slippy." He was drunk again. "Boy howdy, I can pluck a chicken 'fore that fucker can cluck." He had a hard time saying that too.

The boast didn't reassure me in the least. I was frightened by the mere thought of trying to steal old man Vogel's chickens because it was rumored that he kept his shotgun loaded with rock salt for just such occasions. And, anyway, even if we succeeded in stealing some chickens, what was Uncle Red going to do with them?

"Gonna sell 'em," he said. "Jack Wade—fella back there that give me the whiskey at the Grange Hall other night? He—"

"The man in the fedora?"

"Thass 'im. Jack Wade. Owns a little processing plant over near Tallapoosa. Said he'd buy all the chickens and such like as we could bring 'im, and he don't ask no embarrassing questions 'bout who owns 'em. Know what I mean? Thass why he was out to the Grange Hall other night. Offering to buy stock and stuff like that from people heading for California."

So that's what he was, a skinner. That's what they called men like him, this Jack Wade, and there was always at least one of them at meetings where people got together to talk about going out West. They—the skinners—bought stock and farm implements and things like that at a few cents on the dollar and then hauled them somewhere else—into another state, maybe—and resold them for a hefty profit.

As we traveled down the dark highway, with bugs splattering against the windshield, I tried hard to think of some argument against exposing ourselves to old man Vogel's rock-salt shotgun. "But why d'you have to steal chickens? Didn't you make any money tonight?"

"Twenty-two dollars—not bad for singing a few songs and having a good time, hey?"

"Well, wouldn't that, and the money Grandpa's gonna give you, be enough to get you to Nashville?"

"Naw," he said. "That's chicken feed"—which I thought was an unfortunate choice of words, under the circumstances.

"Sure seems like a lot to me," I said.

"Hell, out in California, me and my band sometimes made two-three hundred dollars a night."

And with that I was more than impressed. I was awed. "Really? *That* much? My God . . ."

Pleased with my reaction, he said, "Hell, once I get on the Grand Ole Opry, I'll be a star, might make that much by myself."

"Gol-*lee*," I murmured, glancing at him with open-mouthed wonder, for I had no doubt that he was going to do everything he said.

He winked. "Stick with me, Hoss," he said, opening the whiskey bottle again, "and you'll be shitting in high cotton."

9

"Turn off the lights," he said.

We were approaching old man Vogel's chicken farm. The caliche road shone in the dim moonlight, so I didn't need the headlight to see where I was going. When we got to the high chicken-wire fence that enclosed Vogel's place, Uncle Red told me to pull over and stop. Beyond the fence were the oak and blackjack trees, in which roosted the chickens we were going to steal—that we hoped we were going to steal, that is, because I had no confidence at all that we were going to succeed.

"Bring the board," Uncle Red said in a whisper. He got the wire cutters from the glove compartment, replacing them with his bottle of whiskey, and then we got out and sneaked up to the fence. We were hidden from view of the Vogel house by the trees, and it must have been about three o'clock in the morning, so there were no cars on the road, which meant that we were in no danger of being seen for the moment. I knew, however, that as soon as those chickens started squawking, all hell was going to break loose.

Uncle Red, still humming a little tune, as nonchalant as you please, snipped away at the strands in the chicken wire until he had opened a hole in the fence big enough for us to duck through. Then he took the board from me and whispered,

"What's the matter with you? You shaking like a dog shitting peach pits."

"If Mama knew what we was doing..." But the thought was too fearful to complete.

"Well, she won't know 'less you tell her, and what she don't know won't hurt her—or you, either," he said. "Come on."

I followed him as he staggered through the hole in the fence. When we got under the first tree, we could see the roosting chickens on the limbs as thick as fleas on a dog's ear.

"Now when I lower 'em down," Uncle Red said, whispering still, "you grab 'em by the beak and the legs at the same time, and run 'em back to the car. Put 'em in them gunny sacks, then hightail it back here, quick as you can, y'hear? And 'member, now, grab 'em by the beak so they can't squawk."

"Okay," I said, but I was wondering how he was going to keep them from squawking as he got them out of the trees.

I found out soon enough. And it was the darnedest thing I had ever seen. He just pushed one end of the board up under a sleeping chicken's breast, put a little pressure on it, and that chicken made a sleepy little pauuuuuk-puck-puck sound and stepped right up on the end of that board. Uncle Red then lowered the board, with the chicken on the end of it still sleeping, and I grabbed it by the beak and legs at the same time, and ran for the car. The chicken came awake, of course, as soon as I grabbed it, but all it could do then was flap its wings a little and that didn't disturb any of the other chickens.

I shoved it into one of the gunny sacks and tied the mouth of the sack, and even though the chicken then started squawking its fool head off, none of the other chickens could hear it. I ran back to Uncle Red. Up went the board, down came another sleeping chicken, and back to the car I ran.

It was fun. I had to admit, as soon as I saw how slick it all was, that this kind of chicken stealing was more fun than Christmas morning. I worked up a sweat running back and forth between the trees and the car, and by that time I was so excited I could hardly suppress a giggle.

It probably took no more than thirty minutes for all the gunny sacks to be filled with plump chickens. And once there were two or more chickens in a sack, they sort of settled down and stopped squawking, except for a protesting cry of discomfort now and then from one of the chickens on the bottom.

"The sacks're full," I said to Uncle Red in a panting whisper.

"How many we got?"

"Don't know. Maybe forty or fifty. Enough. Let's get outa here."

"One more," he said.

But all the chickens were gone from the lower limbs now, so Uncle Red had to reach up as high as he could, even going up on the tips of his toes, to get another chicken off the higher limbs. And that's when it happened. He staggered, almost fell, and the board, on top of which perched a big red rooster, slid down along the limb, knocking into the other chickens, and suddenly chickens started toppling out of that tree all around us. Each one hit the ground shrieking and flapping its wings, and the alarm immediately spread to the chickens in the other trees, who must have thought a big coon or fox was after them. They panicked. I had never heard such a godawful racket in my life. They dropped like ripe fruit from a shaken tree, *plop plop plop*, and hit the ground running. But they didn't know where to run to, so they just ran in circles, all the while shrieking with a crack-brain hysteria.

"Holy shit!" Uncle Red said.

"Come on!" I cried. "Let's get out a here!"

And by then I could hear dogs barking. As I started to run, I glanced in the direction of old man Vogel's house and saw a light flick on.

"Run for it!" Uncle Red said.

And now I could hear the dogs coming. They had been released, and were coming through the trees toward us like demons from hell.

"Hurry!" I cried, and shot ahead of Uncle Red so fast that I was maybe twenty feet ahead when I ducked through the hole in the fence. By then I could hear the distant voice of old man Vogel yelling, "Hey! What the hell's going on out there?"

Scared half to death, I reached the car just in time to turn and see Uncle Red hit the fence. He had been running with his body bent forward so he would go through the hole, but he must have forgot where the hole was. He hit the chicken wire head first. The fence bulged outward under the force of his charge, then snapped back, tossing Uncle Red on his butt, his cowboy hat jammed down on his head.

The dogs—two vicious black dogs, growling and barking as if they were prepared to tangle with a bear—were closing in on him, and in the distance, coming through the trees in a white nightgown, was old man Vogel, yelling, "Stop, thief! Stop, or I'll blow your ass off!"

Uncle Red scrambled through the hole in the fence just as the dogs were coming up behind him. I ran around and jumped into the car and started the engine and reached across to open the door for Uncle Red, who was kicking at the snapping and snarling dogs.

"Holy shit!" he yelled. "Get away! Get away! Holy shit!"

When he finally jumped into the car, the rear wheels were already spinning in the dirt, and I had hit second gear before Uncle Red got the door closed, and was already in high gear when I heard the shotgun fire. The rock salt spattered pinging against the back of the car, but we were too far away for it to do any damage.

"Whooo-eee!" Uncle Red shouted. He was panting like a man who had just run two or three miles. "Goddamn, we made it, Hoss! We made it!" He laughed as he tugged the hat off his head and fixed the crease in its crown.

My heart was pounding so hard I could hardly breathe, but when Uncle Red laughed, I felt myself smiling a little, and when he said, "Whooo-eee! Boy, I thought them dogs was gonna make hamburger of my ass," I heard myself sort of chuckle—a nervous chuckle of relief, to be sure, but a chuckle nevertheless.

The chickens in the sacks in the back seat had burst into a flurry of squawks and cackles when we first roared away from the farm, but by the time we had gone a few miles, they had begun to settle down again. Uncle Red, once he had caught his breath, took the whiskey bottle from the glove compartment and had a swig; then, with only a slight hesitation, offered the bottle to me. I smiled and shook my head, and he said, "Just as well. You got some driving to do. Let's head on out for Tallapoosa."

By the time we got through Roscoe, Uncle Red had begun to sing—softly at first, and then louder and louder as the whiskey got lower. Without even trying to sound good, he bellowed,

> *"When I die, take my saddle from the wall,*
> *Put it on my pony, lead him from the stall."*

"Come on, Hoss," he said—almost shouted. "Help me out." I joined in, timidly at first, but when I saw that he wasn'

going to be bothered by my alternating soprano and baritone,
I began to bellow the song almost as loudly as he.

> *"Tie my bones to his back, head him toward the west,*
> *And we'll ride the prairies that we love the best.*
> *Ride around . . ."*

At some point along the way, I realized that I had never
felt so good, so elated, so alive in all my life. With wild
abandon, we raced down the empty highway in the limousine,
both of us singing at the top of our lungs, while Uncle Red,
using the whiskey bottle for a baton, conducted.

> *"Ride around, little dogies,*
> *Ride around slow,*
> *For old Fiery and Snuffy*
> *Are raring to go. . . ."*

In a way, though, it was too bad that we got so wrapped
up in our singing. We might have been able to prevent the
sudden explosion of squawks and flapping wings that occurred
in the back seat when we were about halfway to Tallapoosa.
Evidently I had been careless when I tied up one of the gunny
sacks, for all of a sudden about ten chickens burst loose. They
erupted in a horrible pandemonium of squawky cries and ear-
piercing cackles, and were suddenly everywhere—on our heads,
on the back of the seats, banging against the windows and
windshield. Uncle Red ducked and batted them away, yelling,
"Shoo! Shoo! Goddamn!"

I tried to steer the car with one hand while slapping the
hysterical chickens away from me, ducking their flapping wings,
and for a brief moment one old hen perched precariously on
the steering wheel, her tailfeathers in my face.

So there we were, careening down the highway from one
side to the other, with Uncle Red yelling, "Stop the car! Shoo!
Holy shit! Stop the car!"

I was trying to bring the car to a stop, but I could only get
brief glimpses of the road between the flopping and flapping
chickens, and then suddenly the car stopped without any help
from me. There was a sickening *whunk* when it hit and flattened
a metal signpost, then both wheels on the the right side skidded
into the ditch, and the car dragged along on high center for a
few feet before it came to a metal-grinding stop.

The door on Uncle Red's side flew open and he fell out into the ditch, followed by about a half-dozen chickens. The interior overhead light came on, so I could see Uncle Red lying there on his back, head down in the ditch, with his feet still on the running board. And for a moment a rooster stood on his chest. The rooster, in his confusion and hysteria, must have mistaken the car's overhead light for a sudden sunrise, for he suddenly flapped his wings and crowed. It was a very strident and uncertain *cockle-doodle-doo,* which was sharply cut off somewhere between the *doodle* and the *doo* when Uncle Red violently knocked him off his chest.

"You all right?" I asked.

"Don't know," he said. He didn't sound as if he were injured, but he didn't make any move to get up right away. Panting heavily, he stayed there for a few moments in the weeds, as if he were contemplating the stars.

There were still four or five chickens left in the back seat. They made weak, exhausted efforts to plunge through the closed windows now and then, but mainly they just perched on the back seat, or on the chicken-filled gunny sacks on the floor. The car was littered with feathers and big blobs of chickenshit here and there.

I slid over and looked down at Uncle Red. "Need a hand?"

"Sure," he said. "I could do with a little applause right now." After floundering around a little in the dusty weeds, he finally caught hold of the door and pulled himself up. He dusted the seat of his pants and then walked around to the front of the car, assessing our predicament.

"We gonna be able to get this thing outa here?"

"I don't know," I said. "I think it's on high center."

"Start 'er up, see what you can do."

The engine started up again readily enough, but when I put it in gear and tried to drive back onto the pavement, the rear wheels spun and squeaked in the dirt and on the blacktop. The car didn't budge.

"Turn it off," he said after he got down on his knees and looked under the car. "It's stuck tighter'n a big-dicked dog."

I killed the engine and turned off the headlight, then go out to inspect the damage by moonlight. There was a dent in the middle of the front bumper, and the right section of th steer horns had been broken off. But the real worry was wha damage might have been done to the underside of the car.

"Well, there ain't doodley shit we can do about it tonight," Uncle Red said. He looked both ways up and down the dark highway. "Have to wait till morning, see if somebody comes along that can pull us out. Meanwhile, might as well get some sleep."

He crawled into the back seat, using the uphill door so the gunny sacks full of chickens wouldn't fall out. He rolled the window down and shooed the remaining chickens out of the car. Cursing softly, he used the newly emptied gunny sack to wipe the blobs of chickenshit off the seat.

"Didn't tie that one sack too good, did you, Hoss?" He checked the other sacks to make certain they were tied securely; then he stretched out on the seat, his feet propped up on the windowsill, and went to sleep.

10

I woke up. I thought I had heard the sound of something coming down the highway. The sun was already coming up. I hadn't realized that I had been asleep. It seemed only a few minutes ago that I had been lying there on the front seat, worrying and fretting about everything—particularly about the possibility of a sheriff's car coming along and finding us with all those stolen chickens—and the next minute the sun was coming up, and I was hearing a sound coming down the highway. It was a team of mules pulling an old wagon, approaching us from behind.

"Uncle Red?"

He was still snoring away, his cowboy hat pulled down over his face. I had to repeat his name a couple of times before he came awake. We were both so sore and sleepy that we had to struggle to get ourselves out of the car when the old black man on the creaky wagon halted the mules to see if we needed help.

Uncle Red offered the old man a dollar if he would pull us out of the ditch, and the old man was glad enough to do it. He looked scarecrow-poor, ragged, and hungry, and his wagon was empty. He took a piece of trace chain from under the wagon seat, tied it onto the bent front bumper of the car, and then ran it through a stanchion hole in the back of the wagonbed. I got into the car and Uncle Red got behind to push, and with the old black man slapping the mules with the reins and ho

lering, "Hum up, mules! Hum up, theah," the car began to
groan and screech as it inched forward, then finally broke loose.

While Uncle Red and the old black man unhooked the wagon,
I crawled under the car to see what damage had been done and
discovered that the oil pan had been bent a little and that a few
drops of oil were leaking out of a hole about the size of a
pinhead. That wasn't a fatal injury, but I knew that from now
on I would have to keep a sharp eye on the oil gauge to make
sure that the oil didn't all leak out and ruin the engine.

In addition to the agreed-upon dollar, Uncle Red gave the
old black man a couple of chickens, which made him grin with
delight. Then we were off again, zooming down the highway
toward Tallapoosa.

Jack Wade, the man in the fedora, had given Uncle Red a
map showing how to get to his place, which was an old dairy
farm on a county road just outside of town. The front yard was
filled with old cars and all sorts of farm machinery—cultiva-
tors, plows, planters, tractors—while the barnyard pens behind
the house bulged with mules, cows, pigs and chickens. A whole
pack of growling dogs kept us in the car until Jack Wade came
out of the house and called them off.

We had forty-two live ones left (three were dead at the
bottom of the sacks), and Jack Wade gave us thirty cents apiece
for them. That was a nickel apiece more than he usually gave
for chickens, but he did it, he said, because he liked Uncle
Red. And that was obviously true. They were as alike as two
stringbeans on a vine: stoop-shouldered, long-legged, shambling men with skeletal faces and fevered eyes. Uncle Red,
though, was expansive with his gestures and expressions, quick
to smile or curse, while Jack Wade had the mirthless look and
composure of a cobra.

After he had given Uncle Red the twelve dollars and sixty
cents, he invited him into the house for a drink. Much to my
surprise, Uncle Red declined.

"I better get this boy here on home 'fore his mama has the
cops out looking for us."

I was glad to hear that, of course, knowing that Mama would
be worried out of her mind by now, wondering what had happened to us. As it turned out, though, Uncle Red had a couple
more things he wanted to do before we headed back home.

"Gotta get myself some duds," he said as we were on
our way back to Tallapoosa. "Can't wear this getup all the time.

First, though, let's get the car filled with gas, and then get us some breakfast. I'm hungry as a bitch wolf with ten sucking pups."

I was hungry, too—famished, in fact—so he didn't get any argument from me. Also, I'd never eaten a regular meal in a cafe, and the prospect excited me. Made me feel grown-up. On a couple of occasions in my life I'd had the inexpressible pleasure of going into a cafe in Roscoe on a Saturday afternoon and buying a big juicy ten-cent hamburger, but before Uncle Red and I had breakfast in Tallapoosa that morning, I had never gone into a cafe and sat down at a table and ordered a man-sized meal from a menu.

"Ham and eggs," Uncle Red told the fat waitress. "Heavy on the hash browns, eggs over easy, and keep the coffee coming."

When the waitress looked at me, her pencil poised over the order pad, I said, "Me, too," and Uncle Red winked at me across the table because the waitress was fat and he was making pinching motions near her buttocks while she wasn't looking.

I dug into the ham and eggs with gusto. Uncle Red, however, after a hearty beginning, soon slowed down, left his fork hanging indecisively over the unfinished food for a moment, then pushed his plate away.

"Goddamned eyes're bigger'n my stomach," he mumbled. He had just picked up his cup of coffee when he was suddenly convulsed with an explosive coughing fit. He slammed the cup down on the table and grabbed for his handkerchief. The short, racking coughs exploded from his mouth, muffled finally by the handkerchief. He jumped up and staggered toward the toilet in the rear of the cafe. All the other customers were looking at him.

The fat waitress came over to wipe up the spilled coffee. Casting a suspicious glance toward the toilet, she asked me if he was all right. I told her, "Yeah, sure. Just a bad cold, is all." She grunted skeptically and poured more coffee into his cup. She refilled my cup, too, though I didn't feel much like finishing my breakfast. I felt guilty, sitting there gorging myself while the muffled sounds of Uncle Red's lung-tearing cough continued to come from the toilet.

When he came out, he was pale and trembling and very irritable. He stopped at the table and pulled some money from his pocket. "You go ahead, finish your breakfast," he said, dropping a five-dollar bill on the table. "I'll get the check and the tip. That's your share of the chicken money. Go buy your-self something. Meet you back at the car in about an hour."

"Can't I come with you?"

"No. I'm gonna buy myself some clothes, maybe get a drink somewhere. You finish your breakfast."

He paid the check and left me there, staring at the money that he had flung down on the table. Five whole dollars! I had never had so much money at one time before in my whole life. I was rich. Who would have thought that stealing chickens could be so profitable? I shoved the bill into my pocket, took a deep breath, and tried to steady my nerves, and finished my breakfast by sopping up the last of the egg yolks with a piece of jelly-smeared toast. When I left the cafe, I had a toothpick stuck jauntily in my mouth, my belly was full to popping, and I had a five-dollar bill in my pocket. The world was mine.

I dawdled along the dusty streets for a while, gazing into store windows and wondering what I should buy with my money, marveling at the possibilities. It was all idle fantasy, though, until I arrived at the store toward which I had been headed, willy-nilly, all the while: a music store, the only one in town—in the whole county, as far as I knew, and maybe the only one in the whole state. I had never been in it before, never having had enough money to buy anything. But now I had five dollars, and the store had guitars for sale.

"This here's the cheapest one we carry," said the unctuous little salesman with a challenging smirk. "Five ninety-eight."

My heart sank. It was a lovely guitar—not nearly so lovely as Uncle Red's, of course, but it was new and shiny and had all its strings. The salesman was impressed when he saw that I could tune it and play chords on it.

"Say, now, you're pretty good, kid. What d'you say? Want it?"

"Sure, but . . . but five dollars is all I got."

He took the guitar back. "Almost enough, but not quite. Tell you what, I'll put it back, but I won't let anybody else have it, and when you get the other ninety-eight cents . . ."

Crestfallen, I left the store to stroll along the dusty streets back toward the car, wondering if I should ask Uncle Red for one more dollar. It seemed a monstrously ungrateful thing for me to do, after he had already given me five, but I wanted the guitar so much I probably would have done it if Uncle Red hadn't been arrested.

The car was parked on Main Street among many other cars,

all headed into the curb, and Uncle Red was already in it when I approached. I saw him sitting on the passenger's side in the front seat, tippling on a bottle. And at the same instant, I also saw a dusty sheriff's car pull up and stop directly behind the Packard, blocking it in. I slowed my pace. I watched the two deputies get out of the car. Uncle Red apparently didn't see them until they were approaching him, one on each side of the car; then he made a hurried, bumbling attempt to hide the bottle under the front seat.

The deputy who stepped up to the window on the passenger's side, a jowly man with a belly that bulged over his pistol belt, said something to Uncle Red. I was too far away to hear what it was, but Uncle Red, as if following orders, got out of the car. He was still wearing his cowboy hat, but was no longer dressed in his fancy performing suit. He had bought himself a new pair of khaki pants and shirt. The pants appeared to be three or four inches too short for him.

I had slowed my pace to a dawdle, pretending to be win-dowshopping, and then stopped directly in front of the car and, gazing into the window of a hardware store, watched their reflections in the glass. The beer-bellied deputy spurted a long stream of tobacco juice onto the hot dusty street and said, "Got a call last night"—*spit-tooey*—"'bout a car like this un here. Man over Roscoe claimed somebody in a limo-zeen stole some of his chickens." The deputy had a slow way of talking, con-descending, even a little contemptuous, as if he considered it beneath his dignity but still his duty to bother with a chicken thief. "Of course, I didn't believe 'im. I says to myself, now, I says, what would a man in a late-model limo-zeen be doing stealing *chickens?* And, anyway, I says to myself, I ain't never seen no late-model limo-zeen 'round these here parts. But then me and Jim-Bob here, we was driving down the street, and I says to Jim-Bob, I says, God-durn, Jim-Bob, would you just look at that big ole car there, come all the way from California. I'll bet you, I says, I'll just bet you that's the feller that stole them chickens over Roscoe last night. Ain't that what I said, Jim-Bob?"

The other deputy, a younger man with buck teeth and little ferretlike eyes, had come around from the other side of the car to stand on one side of Uncle Red, as if to block his escape route should Uncle Red decide to make a run for it. Nodding, smiling, enjoying himself, he said, "That's it, Snuffy. That's what you said, all right."

Snuffy peeked inside the car, opened the back door, and picked a feather off the floor. "And just looky here, would you? That a chicken feather, or ain't it?"

"Looks like a chicken feather to me," Jim-Bob said.

"And that stuff on the back seat there, what you reckon that stuff is, Jim-Bob?"

"Looks like chickenshit to me, Snuffy."

"Think so?"

"I'd swear it. I seen enough chickenshit in my life to know."

Uncle Red had noticed me by now, but since he didn't give me any signal, I supposed I was doing the right thing by acting like a stranger. And by now a few passersby had begun to stop on the sidewalk to watch the scene, which made it easier for me to be inconspicuous.

Uncle Red seemed sort of disdainfully amused by the whole thing. At one point he reached up to scratch the back of his head; in doing so, he pushed his hat so far forward that he had to tip his head backward to see from under the brim. And his lips were slightly curled with the same small cocky grin that he'd had on his face last night at the Pair-a-Dice when he hit the man in the back of the head. I hoped to God he wasn't thinking about hitting one of the deputies. Was he capable of doing such a crazy thing? Well, almost: he might as well have slapped the deputy called Jim-Bob when he said to him in a low, disdainful voice, "Seen enough to know, huh? And when'd you last see any chickenshit, Jim-Bob? When you shaved this morning?"

Jim-Bob flushed with fury. He made a quick, automatic move toward his pistol. My heart almost stopped. I whirled to gawk in horror and dismay as Jim-Bob's hand twitched on the butt of the pistol.

"Jim-Bob," Snuffy warned. He, too, had reacted with anger at Uncle Red's remark, but now he sighed, trying to regain his air of playful sarcasm. "Smart-ass, huh?" He squirted another long stream of tobacco juice onto the street. The spittle landed close enough to Uncle Red's boots to splatter a little on them. Uncle Red slowly looked down at his boots, but he didn't do anything else, thank God.

Wiping some spittle from his chin, Snuffy said, "Reckon what you'd find, Jim-Bob, if you was to reach down under the front seat there, feel around a little?"

Jim-Bob reached under the seat and brought out the bottle of whiskey.

"My my my," Snuffy said. "Whatta we got here? Bootleg whiskey, shore's I'm born. Well, looks like we'll just have to take you down to the courthouse, see if you can explain how these here things come to be in your car."

Uncle Red shrugged. "Ain't my car."

Snuffy reacted with spurious surprise. "Oh! Not your car! Hear that, Jim-Bob? Ain't his car. He was sitting here waiting for the owner to get back."

Uncle Red had folded his arms across his scrawny chest, and now, with his head still tipped backward at a cocky angle so that he was looking down his nose at them, he said, "That's right."

Snuffy quit pretending to be amused. "That case, I reckon you wouldn't have the keys, would you?"

"Sure ain't," Uncle Red said. "Hell, Sheriff, I can't even drive."

With a knowing glance at the car, Snuffy said, "I can believe that, all right." Then in a flat, businesslike tone, he said to Jim-Bob, "Frisk 'im and cuff 'im."

Like a teased dog suddenly unleashed, Jim-Bob grabbed Uncle Red by the back of the collar, spun him around and slammed him against the car. "Put your hands on the car," he snapped. "Spread your legs."

Uncle Red didn't do it fast enough to suit him, so Jim-Bob kicked his legs apart. I felt an impulse to step forward and give the deputies the keys to the car, wanting to mollify them and keep them from hurting or provoking Uncle Red any more. And Uncle Red must have sensed the impulse in me, for he suddenly gave me a warning glance, which caused me to hang back. I tried to seem just another spectator in the small crowd that had gathered on the sidewalk to watch, but I felt certain that my gape-mouthed expression made me stand out in the crowd, and all the deputies had to do was glance at me and they would take me to jail, too, and then what would I do? I was afraid that I already had one foot in prison or reform school, but even more than that I was afraid for Uncle Red—afraid his cocky attitude was going to goad the deputies beyond endurance. And I was right.

After Jim-Bob had finished frisking Uncle Red, he said, "No keys. Here's his wallet."

That was when Uncle Red, still with that insolent little grin on his face, looked back over his shoulder and said to Jim-

Bob, "That give you a thrill, groping a man's crotch like that?"

Exploding with fury, Jim-Bob grabbed for his pistol again, and this time he drew it. He shoved the muzzle under Uncle Red's nose. "You sonofabitch!" he spluttered, his whole body trembling.

And now the grin was gone from Uncle Red's lips. I stood there amid the startled spectators on the sidewalk, petrified, almost wetting my pants with fright, praying that Uncle Red would realize how much danger he was in. Maybe now he would shut up.

But he didn't. The grin was gone now, true, but there was an even greater contempt in his voice—the scathing contempt of absolute indifference—as he stared at the deputy over the big black barrel of the pistol and said, "Boom boom, big man."

A cry caught in my throat and came out as a squeak. I thought Uncle Red was dead now for sure. I would have run to the deputy and begged for Uncle Red's life, but I could neither move nor speak—immobilized not only with fear and dread, but with amazement, too, wondering why in God's name Uncle Red kept provoking the man. What was he trying to do, get himself killed? It certainly seemed so. It seemed as if he couldn't care less whether or not Jim-Bob pulled the trigger.

Maybe that was what saved him. Jim-Bob seemed disconcerted for a moment, his anger stymied by Uncle Red's incredible indifference as they continued to stare at each other over the barrel of the pistol. Jim-Bob was the first to blink.

Snuffy said, "Jim-Bob." His tone one of slight admonition. "Put it away. Put the cuffs on 'im. We'll see if he's such a smartass when we get him down to jail. See how he likes being locked up in a cell with fifty filthy hoboes."

"Yeah. We'll see," said Jim-Bob, trying to cover a baffled retreat with a snarl. After he slipped the pistol back into its holster, he pulled a pair of handcuffs from the back of his belt and snapped one manacle onto Uncle Red's right wrist. And it could only be called unnecessary force, the way he jerked Uncle Red's arms behind his back and snapped the other manacle onto his other wrist.

"We'll come back and get the car," Snuffy said.

"Somebody might drive it away," Uncle Red said.

"Your partner, you mean? Sure," Snuffy said, "and he might get surprised, too, if he finds somebody here waiting for him, huh?"

They shoved Uncle Red into the back seat of the patrol car. Snuffy got in beside him. Jim-Bob went around to the driver's seat.

After the car pulled away, the small crowd of spectators around me, sighing and muttering and shaking their heads at the disgraceful ways of the world, began to break up, and I waited for all of them to leave before I dashed for the car. I knew what I had to do—Uncle Red had told me—and that was the only thing that kept me from falling apart. I knew I had to get the car out of there before another patrol car arrived. However, I didn't know what I was going to do with it. Instinct told me to drive it to a hiding place somewhere, and that's what I did. I backed it out of the parking place, almost hitting a passing truck, and then, rattled by the truck driver's furious honking, I drove around the first corner I came to so fast that the tires squealed and the car lurched into the oncoming lane, almost sideswiping another car before I got it straightened out again and headed down a back street. I turned left and then right again, onto an unpaved street that led into one of the poorer residential sections of town. Instead of sidewalks and streetlamps, the street was bordered with dusty trees and bushes, with trash-strewn vacant lots and tar-paper shacks.

I kept looking for a place to park the car, and finally found what looked like a good spot under a canopy of pecan trees. I was pretty sure the cops wouldn't find the car there. But that was about the only thing I was pretty sure of.

Under the trees, I didn't get out of the car for a long time. I just sat there, fighting back tears of panic and bewilderment, wondering what I was going to do now. Uncle Red was in jail, I was a criminal on the lam, my folks were no doubt worried sick waiting for us at home, and I couldn't do anything except sit there and ask myself again and again: What the hell am I going to do *now?*

11

What I did, I did purely by instinct. Thinking was useless. I couldn't think of a single thing to do. As for *feeling*, all I felt like doing was crying—just sitting there, lost and confused, in the dusty shade of those enormous pecan trees, and crying. But that would have been just as useless as thinking, of course, so I decided simply to start moving and see what happened. Simply let myself be guided by instinct, or whatever it is that causes you to move when you've been thrown in over your head and don't know how to swim.

I locked the car and left it there and headed back to town along the hot dusty unpaved streets, walking along as if in a dream, hardly noticing the dogs—mangy, scrawny and mean—that came out of the yards to bark at me, paying no attention to the rowdy kids who, high in the mulberry tree, taunted me and pelted me with mulberries as I passed beneath them. I simply went on without even being conscious of where I was going.

I ended up at the county courthouse. It was a shabby old brick building on a corner in the center of town. I loitered around on the hot sidewalks in front of the building for a little while, wondering what to do next. I couldn't just walk in and say, "Please let my Unce Red out of jail." They would only have thrown me in with him. And yet that was the only thing could think to do.

Then I heard the voices. I heard singing—men singing. I thought at first it was coming from a radio somewhere, but soon I recognized one of the voices, the loudest and best voice among them: Uncle Red's. I followed the sound to a back alley that ran alongside the courthouse. After glancing furtively around to make certain nobody was watching me, I went up the alley to the rear of the courthouse. The singing was coming from a small barred window about ten feet off the ground, the only window in the otherwise solid brick facade of the courthouse's rear wall. And it was Uncle Red, all right. The other voices, with uncertain harmonies, were joined with his as they sang,

> *"There's a long, long trail a-winding*
> *Into the land of my dreams,*
> *Where the nightingale is singing . . ."*

Directly behind the courthouse was a small parking area for the sheriff's patrol cars. A few patrol cars were there now, and one of them was parked next to the courthouse wall directly below the barred window.

Without thinking about it, without giving myself time to become cowardly, I climbed up onto the roof of the patrol car parked under the window. It was just high enough for me to peek in the window—which was really more of a ventilation opening than a window. Set in a thick steel frame, the window was maybe four feet long but only seven or eight inches high— too small for a man's body to slip through, even if the thick steel bars were sawed away. It opened onto the corridor that ran between the jail cells, and what I saw made me catch my breath. Not only the cells but the corridor itself was jammed with prisoners. The beer-bellied deputy had mentioned that he was going to put Uncle Red in jail with fifty filthy hoboes, and he hadn't been kidding. The floors of the cells and the corridors were littered with small thin mattresses and clothes and trash, and nearly every foot of space was occupied by ragged, dirty men in all sorts of positions and postures, talking, singing, smoking, resting. The cops had apparently rousted a whole trainload of hoboes, and I remembered hearing stories about the county work farm—how every now and then, when the farm's labor supply had to be replenished, the Tallapoosa cops would make a sweep of all the freight trains passing through town. They would arrest the hoboes, charge them with vagrancy, and send them up to the county work farm for two months at hard labor. No wonder Tallapoosa was said to be such a hell town for hoboes. . . .

I couldn't see Uncle Red. His voice seemed to be coming from directly below the window. I called to him in a forceful whisper, but he didn't hear me until a few of the hoboes looked up, drawing attention to me, and then I said his name again. The singing stopped. Uncle Red had been lying on a pallet against the wall in the crowded corridor directly below the window, and when he jumped up his face was only a few feet from mine.

"Hoss!" he exclaimed in a loud whisper of surprise and delight. "Goddammit, Hoss, it's you!" Then a quick shadow of anxiety flickered across his face. "Did they get the car?"

"No. I got it hid. Listen, what . . . what should I do?"

There had been a stir of excitement among the hoboes when they saw me, but none of them said anything to give me away. Uncle Red glanced over his shoulder toward the other end of the corridor, and then said in a harsh undertone, "Looky here, Hoss. They gonna try to send me up to some damn county work farm, but if they do, I sure as hell ain't gonna stay there. Can you bring me some hacksaw blades? And some money?"

"I got . . ." I started to reach into my pocket for the five dollars he had given me, but just then there was a disturbance at the other end of the corridor, and a few of the hoboes gave us harsh warning hisses.

"Get down!" Uncle Red said.

I ducked below the window, hugging the side of the building. I heard a loud voice in the jail calling someone's name. And then, worse luck, I heard voices and footsteps coming up the alley beside the courthouse. Two men were approaching, walking fast. I jumped down off the patrol car and hid behind some garbage cans, just in time. The two men came around the corner of the courthouse, talking and laughing, and I recognized their voices as those of Snuffy and Jim-Bob. Car doors slammed, a car backed out of the parking area and roared away.

They had taken the patrol car I had been standing on. Now I had no way to talk to Uncle Red again. Not that it really mattered, because what was there left to say? They were going to send him to the county work farm, and I knew, as well as I knew anything, that Uncle Red would never survive it. So my task was clear and simple. I had to save his life. I had to

get him out of that jail—not just bring him some hacksaw
blades once he was at the work farm, but get him out now,
today, before he got sent to the farm.

But how? The only jailbreaks I had ever seen had been in
movies, and had been accomplished with guns. But then I
recalled one movie—a Buck Jones movie, it was—in which
some men on horseback had broken a pal out of jail by tying
their lassoes around the bars of the jail window and pulling the
window out.

I went to the nearest hardware store and bought forty feet
of the strongest hemp rope I could get. It cost me just over
two dollars, which meant that it would probably be a long,
long time before I would get the money to buy that guitar, but
I didn't begrudge it. I had to save Uncle Red's life. I didn't
know where I was going to get the courage to do it, but I
thought I would just go through the motions and hope the
courage would be there when I needed it.

After going back to the cafe where we'd had breakfast and
buying myself a big juicy hamburger and a soda pop for lunch
(another fifteen cents gone from my money), I walked back to
the car with the coil of rope over my shoulder. There was
nothing I could do during daylight, so I lay down on the back
seat and slept fitfully till dark. Then, screwing up my determination, I backed the car out of its hiding place and drove
cautiously back to town, hoping—praying, really—that the
sheriff's deputies wouldn't spot the car and arrest me before I
even got started. For that reason, I didn't drive into the alley
at the side of the courthouse, but drove in from the other end.

The parking area behind the courthouse was dimly lit by
one naked bulb that hung near the entrance of the back door.
And I noticed with a sort of despair that the patrol car that I
had stood on earlier was once again parked next to the courthouse wall directly under the barred window—despair, because
now I would have no excuse for not trying. Now I had to go
through with the plan, even though I didn't think I had the
courage to do it. Even so, I got the car turned around and
headed away from the courthouse. I backed it up until I was
close enough for the rope to reach the barred window and yet
still give me a straight run forward. Then I took a deep breath
and hauled the coil of rope out of the car.

If a man can live on borrowed time, why might not a boy
act on borrowed courage? That, at least, was what I seemed
to be doing: borrowing courage, drawing on some source of

determination and audacity that I hadn't as yet even acquired, a manhood that I hadn't as yet known. But I got the job done. I tied one end of the rope to the car's trailer hitch, then strung the rope across the hoods of the parked patrol cars and again climbed upon the car parked next to the wall.

Inside, the hoboes were drinking coffee from paper cups and eating what seemed to be bologna sandwiches. They didn't notice me as I tied the end of the rope around one of the steel bars. Then I called Uncle Red once more in a loud whisper, and he came up like a jack-in-the-box from his place in the corridor beneath the window.

"Hoss!" he whispered with puzzled delight. "What're you doing here again?"

"Get ready," I said.

"What? What d'you mean?"

"Get ready," I repeated. "I'll be waiting," and with that I jumped off the patrol car and ran up the alley to the Packard. "Oh, my God," I moaned as I put the car in low gear and revved up the engine. Then I took off like the proverbial bat out of hell. The tires squealed horribly, spewing gravel like a scattergun, the tires caught, and the car leaped forward. The rope had about ten feet of slack in it, and when that ran out, the car seemed to hesitate for a fraction of a second, and then I heard a horrendous roar behind me. I glanced into the rearview mirror just in time to see the bars come out of the wall as if they had been hit on the other side by a gigantic battering ram, as if they were blown outward by an explosion, bringing with them a hail of bricks and mortar and a cloud of dust.

The car had lurched forward again, but I slammed my foot down on the brake, shoved my head out of the car window, and waited to see Uncle Red come through the ragged, gaping hole in the jailhouse wall. But he wasn't the first one out. Nor the second. Nor the third. It was those hoboes. They had begun clambering through the gaping hole, one and two at a time, like alarmed bats from the mouth of a cave, fighting at each other to get out, running off in all directions. I thought I saw Uncle Red's cowboy hat bobble up over the opening a couple of times, but evidently the hoboes, in their scramble to escape, kept pulling him back, pushing him aside. Then the alarm went off. It sent a shiver of horror up my spine, that terribly high-pitched clangor, as if it had reached out and laid physical hold of me.

"Uncle Red!" I yelled at the top of my voice. "Uncle Red!

Hurry! Hurry!" And I kept yelling even though I knew he couldn't hear me above that ear-piercing alarm bell.

Finally one of the hoboes must have given him a hand, for he suddenly came through the hole as if he had been thrown.

"Here, Uncle Red! Hurry!" I called as he darted, bent over, around the patrol cars. I reached across and opened the door, and he piled into the car.

"Get outa here!" he yelled, but by then the car was already moving. His door closed with a bang as the car lurched forward. As we pulled away, there was a sudden series of explosions. At first I thought they were gunshots, but what happened was, the long heavy steel bars tied onto the end of the rope had jerked forward with the car and were dragged across the hoods of every one of the parked patrol cars, shattering their windshields.

"Holy shit!" Uncle Red cried, wild-eyed, turning to see what was happening.

My first impulse was to stop and untie the rope from the trailer hitch, but Uncle Red shouted, "Don't stop!"

"But I—"

"They'll be on us in a minute like a duck on a June bug! Go!"

"But what about—"

"It'll break loose! Go on! Go!"

So we got out of there in a hurry, dragging the bars after us down the dark alley. The car squealed around the corner on two wheels, and the bars came around the corner after us. With split-second shifts of my eyes from the street to the rearview mirror, I got a glimpse of the bars as they cut the corner behind us and, like a giant scythe, sheared off a mailbox, tumbling it high into the air. The impact with the mailbox flung the bars across the street, and every time the bars struck the pavement in their wildly careening, bouncing flight, they sent up long sprays of flying sparks.

"Whoooo-eee!" Uncle Red yelled.

I had never before seen him so wildly excited. He laughed, he yelled, he beat the back of the seat with his hands, stamped on the floorboards with his boots.

"Whooooooo-eeeee! Pour it on, Hoss! Pour it on!"

I turned at the first corner I came to and headed toward the highway, and when the bars came around the corner after us, sending up another shower of sparks, the rope wrapped itself around a streetlamp, and again it felt as if the car had struck some invisible impediment for that split second before the rope broke, freeing us from the bars. The Packard lunged forward with terrific power. It took only a few seconds for us to reach the highway, and we were on our way home.

"Goddamn, you did it!" Uncle Red cried triumphantly. "You did it, Hoss, you did it!"

I was in a state of shock. Adrenaline had been pumping into my veins so furiously that I was numb to every sensation except desperation and fear. My hands were cold and clammy, my legs were trembling.

As the miles between us and Tallapoosa rapidly increased, my shock began to wear off a little—only to be replaced with a growing recognition of the enormity of what I had done. But there was one thing that made it all worthwhile, and that was Uncle Red's new and almost unbounded admiration for me. After his guffaws and whoops had subsided, he shook his head a couple of times like a man trying to regain his senses after being knocked for a loop, and then, reaching across to slap me heartily on the shoulder, he said, "By God, Hoss, you're a man after my own heart."

It was a common phrase, sure, but he had called me a man, and I knew he meant it, and that meant more than anything in the world to me.

But suddenly the *huh huh huh* sounds of his chuckling changed timbre, became phlegm-rattling sounds, and then I realized that he was coughing. And the first few coughs were like a trickle through a dam that finally burst and the trickle became a torrent of deep, body-racking coughs. He fumbled frantically for his handkerchief.

"Should I stop?"

Bent forward on the seat with his face buried in the handkerchief, convulsively coughing, he waved his left hand back and forth at me, and then gave me the sign to go on. The coughing fit lasted maybe three or four minutes, and during the last part of it he seemed as if he could hardly get his breath and would suffocate.

I was about to stop anyway, even if there was nothing more I could do for him than to pat him on the back, but then the fit reached a climax, and Uncle Red spat into the handkerchief. After that the coughing fit subsided, leaving him as spent as a man who has just finished a long and arduous footrace, his breathing rapid and shallow.

"God*damn*," he moaned in an undertone of outrage. He

took the handkerchief from his mouth and stared at it. In the light from the instrument panel, I could see a dark spot on the handkerchief, the object of his long and angrily brooding stare. Blood. He kept staring at it, and then said once more, "God-damn," though his tone was now edging away from outrage and into despair, a sort of musing despair. "Those sonsa-bitches," he said. "Took my whiskey and my wallet. You got any money left?"

"Two dollars and forty-some cents."

He straightened up and leaned back in the seat, crumpling the handkerchief up in his fist. "Well, it's too late to get any-thing now anyway, I guess."

I assumed he meant whiskey. I said, "Maybe if you . . . if you'd just rest up for a couple of days? Mama said if you'd just rest . . ." My words trailed off and died. I felt as silly as someone offering advice to a man who was about to be hanged.

"No," he said, and sighed. His breathing was becoming more regular. "No rest for the wicked. We might've got away clean, but if we didn't this car'll be hotter'n a two-dollar pistol. Have to leave here tomorrow, the latest."

I wasn't prepared for that news. He was right, of course, but that didn't make the thought of his leaving any easier. After what we had been through together during the last couple of days, it didn't seem real that I could just say goodbye to him and go back to being who I was before he came.

"Fact is," he murmured, "we ought to get off this highway soon's we can, just in case. Any way to get to your house without going through Roscoe?"

A new twinge of panic made me search my memory for an alternate route home, and it didn't take long for me to figure one out. There was an old unpaved farm road that intersected with the highway a couple of miles farther on. I remembered that it went by the Woodsall farm, and that we could get to the Woodsall farm from our house without going through Ros-coe, so we could also do it from where we were.

By the time I turned off onto the dusty road that led from the highway through miles of ruined cotton fields, the atmo-sphere in the car had become one of heavy, oppressive silence. Uncle Red, who, only a few miles back, had been in a mood of hilarious excitement, was now sunk into a terrible and brood-ing despair. He roused himself only once, when we were near-ing home and I asked him how we were going to explain our long absence to Mama and Papa. He said, "Tell 'em . . . oh, shit, tell 'em the car broke down, we had to stay in Tallapoosa to get it fixed. Oil pump. Tell 'em the oil pump went out."

Another lie. I should have been getting used to them by now, and after what Uncle Red and I had done in the last twenty-four hours, there was obviously no way we could ever tell Mama the truth. But it still bothered me, because every lie was like a brick in a wall that seemed to be going up between Mama and me, shutting me away forever from her trust and comfort. But there was nothing I could do about it.

All the kerosene lamps seemed to be burning behind the drawn windowshades, and when we pulled into the yard, every-body—even Grandpa—came out on the porch to see us. But only Mama came all the way out to the car. She was trying to be angry and stern when she demanded to know where in double-damn tarnation we had been, but her relief and gladness at seeing us again almost overwhelmed her, so she vacillated wildly for a moment, not knowing whether to hug us or hit us. As soon as Uncle Red told the lie about the oil pump, however, her anger evaporated—not so much because of the lie, perhaps, but because of the way Uncle Red looked when he said it. He had gotten out of the car by then and was walking toward the house like a pale and trembling invalid, like an old man on his last legs.

Mama clutched his arm to steady him. "What is it, Hassle? You all right?"

"Yeah, sure. Just a little spell, is all." But his tone was one of peevish martyrdom, which had the effect of causing the others on the front porch to exchange sheepish glances, as if they had been accused of something and believed themselves guilty of it—guilty of being in good health, maybe, while he was obviously suffering and on a downhill run toward death. And it was this, more than the lie about the oil pump, that silenced the questions and reproaches that they had stored up for us.

Mama had kept some dinner warm for us. I ate ravenously, as usual, and, also as usual, Uncle Red just picked at his plate. He sat hunched over the table, still in his dark mood, with wispy strands of his red hair clinging to the sweat on his fore-head, and talked to Mama and Papa and Grandpa about leaving for Nashville the first thing in the morning. He silenced Mama's protests with a petulant wave of his hand. She was sitting with us at the table, as were Papa and Grandpa, though they had already eaten. The kids had been sent to bed.

"Got no choice. Time's running short. Only thing is . . ." He took a small bite of turnip greens and wallowed them around in his mouth for a moment before visibly forcing himself to swallow them. "Thing is, I ain't been able to raise that money yet."

Papa grunted as if he had expected that, and Mama said, "Oh, don't worry 'bout that, Hassle, we—"

"Fact is," he added, cutting Mama off. "Fact is, I had to spend nearly every penny I had on that damned water pump."

"Oil pump," I quickly corrected.

"Oil pump," he said.

"Don't talk with your mouth full," Mama said to me.

Uncle Red turned to Grandpa. "But if you sure enough want to go with me, that thirty dollars of yourn'll get us to Tulsa, and there's a feller there owes me some money—enough to get us on to Nashville, maybe." He fell silent for a moment, slightly panting, as if all this talk was tiring him out. Then he took a deep breath and said to Mama, "When I get the money for singing on the Opry, I'll send it back here to y'all, so you can go on out to California."

Again Mama told him not to worry about it. "We been talking about it, and we figured we'd sell our stock and things and go on out to Bud and Dora's. I reckon they won't mind us staying with them for a little while, till Virgil can maybe find some work, and . . . and . . . well, we'll see." She didn't seem optimistic about it, though, and Papa, of course, was downright glum.

She was talking about Uncle Bud, Papa's younger brother, and his wife Dora, who had a farm out in the panhandle in Cimarron County.

"That case, I'll send the money to you out there," Uncle Red said.

They talked for a while longer, Mama protesting that Uncle Red shouldn't worry about sending any money, Papa grunting dolefully as if he expected Uncle Red not to worry about it. And then, when I finished eating, Uncle Red said to me, "Hoss, why'n't you go on to bed now? I wanna talk to Sis and Virgil alone for a minute. Okay?"

Something was up. I knew it. I had no idea what it was but I knew Uncle Red wouldn't send me away unless it wa me he was going to talk about, and what could he possibly say about me that he didn't want me to hear? My nettled curiosity made me reluctant to leave, but Mama backed him up.

"Go on," she said. "Time you was in bed anyway."

Thinking quickly, I said, "I got to go to the outhouse first," and was gone out the back door before they could tell that I was lying. Instead of going to the outhouse, I ducked under the kitchen window so I could hear what they would say. Tige came out from under the house to lick my hand and see what I was doing, but I shoved him away, tense and irritable with growing curiosity, anxious to catch every word that was said in the kitchen.

As soon as he judged that I was out of hearing range, Uncle Red said, "Well what I was thinking about . . . I was wondering if you'd maybe let the boy go with me to Nashville."

My heart did a flip-flop. Nashville! He wanted me to go to Nashville with him! I couldn't believe my ears. I had never allowed myself to think about it before, but if someone had asked me what I wanted to do more than anything else in the world, I would have said that I wanted to go to Nashville with Uncle Red. And now he was asking Mama and Papa if I could! Above the loud pounding of my heart, I strained to hear what they would answer. To judge by their long silence, however, they were apparently as stunned by the idea as I was.

"Fact is," Uncle Red said after a long pause, "I need a driver, and he's a good un. Handles the car as good as anybody I ever seen. But I wouldn't take him just for that. The boy's got talent. I could learn him to play the guitar, and he might make a singer someday, maybe a damned good one." After another pause, he added, "Well, it's up to you all. He might make a musician even if you take him to California with you, but he ain't likely to get anybody better'n me to learn him. Well, talk it over, if you want to. Let me know in the morning. Right now, I'm gonna go lay down 'fore I fall down."

As soon as I heard him leave the kitchen, I dashed to the back door and went in. I figured I could tell by looking at their faces what the decision was likely to be, and hoped that I could maybe influence them in case it appeared as though the decision might go against me.

They gave me sheepish, sour looks, the same kind of looks we kids would have gotten if it had been near Christmas and had to be told that there would be no presents this year because there was no money to buy any.

"Go to bed now," Mama said.

"Oh, please," I begged. "Please let me go with him."

"So you was sneaking around listening," Papa said with sour satisfaction, as if I had once again confirmed his low opinion of me.

"Please," I said, on the verge of tears now. "You heard him, he said I was talented, didn't he? Said he'd teach me how to play the guitar and sing, and I could... I could... Oh, Mama, I want a chance to *be* somebody. I don't want to be a... a damned cotton picker all my life!" And even as I said it, I knew I was going too far. I couldn't help it, though. I was desperate.

"Ah," Papa said. "So mister smarty-pants don't want to be no *damned cotton picker* all his life, huh? What's good enough for your papa ain't good enough for you, huh? It's come the time when you start looking down your nose at your papa, has it? Well, if it hadn't been for me and your mama picking cotton all these years, working our fingers to the bone for you kids, where in hell you think you'd be now, mister big-britches?"

"Oh, it ain't like that, Papa," I pleaded. "I just want a chance to *be* somebody."

"Go to bed this minute," Mama ordered.

"He said he would—"

"Go to bed!" Mama yelled, and slammed her spoon down on the table. Then, as if surprised by her own anger, she added in a gentler tone, "We'll talk about it in the morning. But if I hear one more word out of a you—just *one* more—then you won't go at all, and that's final."

I sulked off to bed. I hadn't intended to hurt their feelings, but they just seemed to have no idea how much it meant to me, this once chance in a lifetime to go to Nashville with Uncle Red. They knew how much I hated picking cotton, all right—that much had been obvious from the first day I had ever been taken into a cotton field and shown how to pick the stuff. It was hard for me to remember how old I was then—five, I thought—but it certainly wasn't hard to remember how much I hated it. That day—a blustery cold day in December—marked the first time in my life that I refused—absolutely refused—to do something I had been told to do. It had happened when Howard and Margery and I went into the field to pick the few scraps of cotton that had been missed during the two previous pickings. Ordinarily, such scraps weren't even worth gathering and were left to rot in the fields, but Christmas was coming soon, and Mama told us that there would be no money for Christmas presents unless we gathered the scraps and took them to town and sold them.

Papa had gone off somewhere in search of work, but Mama, who was then about seven months pregnant with my younger brother, Willie, said she would come down to the field and help us as soon as she finished with the household chores. So off we went, Howard and Margery and I, with cotton sacks slung over our shoulders. I thought at first that it was going to be quite a lark, and I felt a sort of heady pride in being able to help Mama get enough money for us each to have a present in our stockings and—who knew?—maybe even an apple and an orange or two, when we woke up Christmas morning.

But that soon changed. As soon as I bent over between the two rows of brown leafless cotton stalks and began to snatch at the scraps of cotton that lay on the ground or dangled from the prickly bolls, I realized that this wasn't going to be any fun at all. Far from it. Gusts of cold wind blew across the field, rattling the dead brown cotton stalks, and my fingers soon grew so cold I could hardly move them, though not so cold that I couldn't feel the sharp stinging pricks of the cotton bolls.

Since I had to stop every few minutes and blow on my cold and scratched and bleeding fingers, I soon fell far behind Howard and Margery. But I didn't care. I didn't care about anything except how miserable I was. Two strings of snot kept oozing down onto my upper lip, and I wiped them away on the sleeve of my coat, which soon became glazed with the shiny stuff, but I didn't care about that, either. The icy wind brought tears to my eyes, blurring my vision so I couldn't see the prickles on the cotton bolls, though I could feel them when they pricked my fingers, and pretty soon the tears overflowed my eyes.

I cried. Dropping down on the cold ground between the cotton rows, I covered my face with my bleeding hands and cried. But Howard soon left his cotton sack and came back to find out what was wrong with me, and when I told him I didn't want to pick any more cotton, he got mad. As the oldest kid in the family, he became the boss when no grown-ups were around, and he took the job seriously, expecting to be obeyed without backtalk or rebellion, and when I refused to get up, he gave me a sharp rap across my head with his knuckles. I threw my arms over my head and screamed, "I won't! I won't!"

He grabbed me by the nape of the neck and rubbed my snotty, tear-stained face into the dirt. All he succeeded in doing, however, was to make me kick and scream and cry all the louder, more determined than ever that I would *not* pick cotton. I would *not*.

"I'll tell Papa and you'll get a whipping," he threatened.

"I don't care!" I cried. "I won't do it! I won't!"

Cursing and panting, he kicked me in the ribs. Though it wasn't a hard kick, it was painful enough—not painful enough, however, to make me get up and pick cotton. There was nothing—absolutely nothing—he could have done to diminish my determination one bit. In fact, everything he did only increased my determination, if that was possible.

"I don't care what you do to me!" I yelled. "If you kill me, you'll just have to bury me! But I won't do it! I don't care! I *won't do it!*"

Then Margery called, "What's wrong with him?"

"The crybaby won't work," Howard said in a voice cracking with frustration and rage. "Thinks he's better'n us. Crybaby!"

"Crybaby," Margery echoed.

"Here comes Mama," Howard said then. "Are you gonna let her see you like that, crybaby?"

I didn't care. It could have been Jesus Christ Himself returning to earth again for the sole purpose of shaming me into going back to picking cotton, but I wouldn't have done it.

They stood by and waited for Mama, Howard muttering curses, Margery tisk-tisking with the shame of it, and this respite from Howard's attacks softened my hysteria. I continued to cry, but by the time Mama arrived, my screaming and wailing had subsided into sporadic sobs and whimpers.

"What's the matter?" Mama asked, and Howard, in a contemptuous voice, told her that the only thing the matter with me was that I was feeling sorry for myself—neglecting to tell her that he had kicked and cuffed me and rubbed my face in the dirt.

Mama got down on her knees beside me. "What's the matter with you, Whit?"

"I won't!" I cried again in a new spasm of hysteria. "I won't do it!"

"Look at me," Mama ordered. But I wouldn't do that, either, until she put her hands on my shoulders and jerked me toward her, saying, "I told you to look at me!"

And when I finally did look at her, her eyes blinked as if the sight of my face was shocking. And quite a sight I must have been, too, with the dirt turned to mud in the snot and tears that were smeared across my face. She was kneeling on her cotton sack, her huge belly bulging under the faded and frayed bib overalls she wore.

"Whit," she said, "I know it must be hard, but it's the only way we can get some money for Christmas. Don't you want to have a nice Christmas?"

"To hell with Christmas!" I cried, working myself up to another fit of hysteria. "I won't do it!"

She flinched.

When I saw that I had hurt her, I cried, "Mama, I'm cold! And my fingers hurt! Look at my fingers, Mama, they hurt! I won't do it!"

It was then that I saw tears form in Mama's eyes. The tears trembled for a second on her eyelashes, and then fell and trickled slowly down her stolid, expressionless face. And the sight of those tears caused me more pain than all of Howard's kicks and cuffs.

I didn't know what to do. I could feel Howard and Margery's eyes flashing at me with contempt for having done this to Mama. Then Margery put a comforting hand on Mama's shoulder.

"Don't cry, Mama," she said.

Mama reached out to gather Margery and me into her arms.

Then Margery was crying, too, though she said over and over, "Don't cry, Mama. Don't cry."

"I wish there was something I could do," Mama said. "I only pray that when you grow up and have kids of your own, times won't be so hard, they won't have to . . . have to . . ." But she couldn't finish. She hugged us to her and the three of us all cried together.

Howard remained apart. He stood back and glowered at me as if I were some sort of contemptible worm.

In a little while, Mama made an effort to get hold of herself. "All right," she said, "I won't cry no more. Let's all stop crying, all right? Crying won't help none. Here, Whit, blow your nose." She pulled a handkerchief from her sweater pocket and held it to my nose and I honked into it. "Now, maybe Whit's right," she said to Howard. "Maybe he's too young to do this work. Is it all right with you two if he goes on back to the house and does some chores instead?"

"I'll do it," I said—heard myself say, for I didn't know I was going to say it, and could hardly believe that it was my own voice. "It's all right, I'll do it."

And I did. I had no idea why, but I was suddenly seized by something like rage, some compelling need to defy the damned cotton and the damned cold and my own damned pain. Maybe it was because I had suddenly realized, in whatever way a child realizes anything, that I wasn't the only one who hated and resented this task. Not the only one who was cold and miserable and full of pain. Mama was, too.

But for whatever reason, I turned to the task with a vengeance. I picked cotton. I couldn't keep up with Mama or the others, but I did the best I could, and hated every minute of it. And never stopped hating it. I never again rebelled against the galling drudgery of the work, but never a day went by that I didn't renew my determination to get out of those accursed cotton fields someday. But how?

Schooling might have proved the answer, but Papa didn't put any truck in that. He himself had never got beyond the sixth grade, and he figured that what was good enough for him was good enough for his kids. So he kept us out of school every year until the cotton crop had been gathered, which was usually in late October or early November, and by then I was so far behind the other students in school that I could never hope to catch up. Not having learned the rudiments of arithmetic or verbal conjugations, I could only sit at my desk and burn with humiliation when asked to answer a question that I couldn't even comprehend. And soon I learned that no answer at all was better than a wild guess that might make me the butt of the other students' derisive giggles. So finally I refused to answer at all, with the result that the other students—and the teacher, too, if the truth be told—soon decided that I was stupid. And there were even times when I suspected that they were right.

For the same reasons, both Howard and Margery had quit school by the time they reached the eighth grade. What hope had I of doing any better? Was I not my father's child? The child of a failed and defeated man whose only source of moral ascendency was to deny his children a chance to do better than he had done?

Music seemed the only answer. As long as I could remember, people had been telling me that I was a good singer. Even in school, where they thought I was stupid, it was me they called upon when they needed a singer in a school program. But I really didn't begin to consider music as a way out of the cotton fields until Uncle Red's first visit, when he told me that I had talent. Coming from him, it was a benediction, a blessing that held the promise of salvation. And from that moment on, I had dreamed of following in Uncle Red's footsteps. When he sent the postcard from California, the one with the picture of the Dream Bowl on it, I tacked it to the wall beside my bed, and often I would look at it before blowing out the lamp and going to sleep to dream that I, too, might someday appear at the Dream Bowl. Maybe even stand on the stage in the very spot where Uncle Red had stood. . . .

I knew, however, that if Papa had his way, I wouldn't go to Nashville. To him I was merely being uppity, getting too big for my britches. So I went to bed that night without much hope of leaving with Uncle Red the next day. I lay in bed and tried to hear what Mama and Papa were saying about it in the kitchen, but they kept their voices down so low that I couldn't make out the words. I considered sneaking to the kitchen door and listening at the keyhole, but I knew if they caught me I would lose whatever small chance I might have of going, so I stayed in bed and prayed.

When Grandpa came to bed, I couldn't resist asking him if they were going to let me go. But he only said, "I don't know, boy," and sighed, settling his bony body into the lumpy mattress.

"If it was you, Grandpa, would you let me go?"

After a long reflective pause, he said, "I don't know, boy. Go to sleep now. You'll find out soon enough, I reckon."

But it would come soon enough only if it were bad news, so I figured that was his way of answering my question. I was condemned, then—condemned to those damned cotton fields forever.

Still, I nursed enough desperate hope through the long night to make me wake up the next morning at the very first sounds of Mama building a fire in the kitchen stove. She always got up before everybody else to begin cooking breakfast, and I knew that this was my chance to catch her alone. I jerked my clothes on and quietly went into the kitchen.

She turned from the stove and glared at me. "There's no wood in the box," she said accusingly. "Nobody got their chores done yesterday on account a you. Go out and bring me in some wood, so I can fix breakfast."

"All right," I said, "but, Mama, what did—"

"Go do what I told you," she snapped, turning back to the stove. "Get the wood."

I hurried out the back door and went to the outhouse first, then to the woodpile. Chunks of wood flew under my furious ax, and between the sounds of the cleaving oak rounds, I could hear the dawn coming up: the rooster crowing, the cow mooing from her morning hay, a wild fluttering and twittering of sparrows as they swirled from the trees to the house to the barn and back again. I could feel the morning sun on my back. It was going to be a hot day.

Mama came out of the house just as I was about to pick up the chunks of wood, and I had the feeling that she had been standing in the window watching me. She moved slowly, looking down at her hands, making small automatic gestures of smoothing her apron. And still without looking at me, she sat down on the chopping block and smoothed her apron some more.

"Please, Mama," I begged. "Please let me go."

"I don't want you to go," she said.

My heart sank.

"But..."

My heart leaped.

"I don't want him to go alone." She leaned forward, resting her elbows on her knees, clasping her rough red hands together. "Your papa says you shouldn't go. Says we'll need all the hands we can get, picking cotton in California."

I hated Papa at that moment. "Sure," I said. "He don't want me ever to be anything but a cotton picker."

"Don't be too hard on him. Your papa, he was never blessed with...well, he can't help the way he is. Never knew how to do anything but farm."

"Is that any sign *I* got to be a farmer, too? Mama you heard Uncle Red. I got *talent*. He said I got *talent,* Mama, and I can maybe be a real singer someday, and...and make lots a money, and drive around in a big car, and wear fancy clothes, and—"

"I know," she said. "I know you got talent. I always said

you was the gifted one in the family. But you're too young to go gallivanting all over the country."

"I can take care of myself."

"Can you?" she said. "And can you take care of him, too?"

"Uncle Red?"

"You know he's very sick, don't you? He shouldn't be going anywhere by himself. There might not even be anybody around to call a doctor for him."

"I can take care of him," I said.

"I hope so, 'cause you're all he's got. I know it's a lot to ask of a boy your age, but it seems like you're the best friend he's got. But do you have any idea what it'd be like if he . . . if he . . ." Then, as if suddenly exasperated, she slapped her thighs. "All right, then. But only if you promise me two things. That you won't drink no more, not till you're old enough, least ways."

"I promise."

"And that you'll come home as soon's we get settled out in California. Soon's we find us a place, you come home and start your schooling again. Promise?"

"Cross my heart and hope to die," I said.

"And try to bring Hassle back with you?"

"Yessum," I said. "I sure will."

She pushed herself up. "All right, then. Bring the wood in. Breakfast be ready in a minute."

I was never so happy to do a chore in all my life, but I did it as if walking on eggshells, not wanting to call attention to myself. Though happy to the point of delirium, I kept my wits about me, knowing I couldn't let Papa see how happy I was, or he might say I couldn't go.

Uncle Red didn't come to breakfast. I was anxious to see him, so I could at least let *him* know how glad I was to be going. But it was at least ten o'clock before I saw him, and he didn't seem to care. He didn't even seem to notice me, in fact, when he came out of his room. I was all packed and ready to go. A brown paper bag containing everything I had, including Uncle Red's postcard from California, was sitting by the door, alongside Grandpa's old rope-tied straw suitcase. The extent of Uncle Red's luggage was a package that contained his fancy performing suit, washed and ironed, which Mama had taken from the car that morning.

"How'd that chicken doo get in the car?" she asked.

Thinking fast, I stammered, "Uh, I must've left the windows open last night and some chickens roosted in there, I reckon." Uncle Red would have been proud of me, the way I was learning to lie.

We were in the kitchen. Mama was standing at the stove, frying chicken, and I was by the washbasin, wetting my hair and trying to plaster it down on my head, but without much luck. No matter how much water I put on it, or how many times I combed it, my cowlicks just wouldn't stay down.

"You need a haircut," she said.

"I'll get one in Nashville," I bragged. "A real one, in a barbershop."

I had never before had my hair cut by a barber. Mama had always done it, and it always looked as if she had merely put a bowl over my head and hacked off the hair that stuck out. No wonder my cowlicks wouldn't stay down.

"And where you gonna get the money for that, mister big-britches?"

"Uncle Red's gonna be rich," I said.

She sighed. "You and your Uncle Red. Two peas in a pod, I swear." She turned from the stove to inspect me, and obviously didn't like what she saw. She grabbed me and buttoned the collar of my shirt, nearly choking me in the process. "Stand still. How'm I gonna get you ready to go if you don't stand still?" She seemed very irritable. "When's the last time you changed your shorts?"

"Oh, Mama," I said.

"You make sure you always got on clean shorts, y'hear? What if you had an accident or something, and had to go to a hospital? Think how ashamed you'd be if you had on dirty shorts."

"Oh, Mama, gol-*lee*," I complained, having heard that a dozen times before. While she didn't seem to care how ugly our haircuts were, she always wanted us kids to be neat and clean.

Then she almost broke down. With sudden tears in her eyes, she grabbed me to her in a convulsive sort of way, and hugged me, and said, "I don't want you to go."

I felt a flutter of apprehension. "It'll be all right, Mama," I said hastily. "And I'll take care of Uncle Red, too."

She turned back to the stove, using the corner of her apron to dab at her eyes; then, as she turned the pieces of chicken that sizzled in the deep fat, she said, "It's just that you'll be the first one to leave. I always tried to hold the family together. It ain't been easy sometimes, God knows. . . ." She was probably thinking about Papa's drinking sprees, maybe remembering how he beat her that time and gave her a black eye. "But I never thought *you'd* be the first one to leave."

"It ain't like I was going away forever," I said. "I'll be back."

She turned to look at me for a moment, the fork suspended over the frying pan. "Will you?"

"Sure," I said. Come right down to it, though, I wasn't so sure. Once I got away from cotton fields, I wasn't going to be in any hurry to get back to them, no matter if they were in California.

"And you be sure and write us at Bud and Dora's, let us know where you are and how you're doing, you and him, y'hear?" And after I promised I would, she added, "Go on, now. Put your things in the car."

Uncle Red and Grandpa already had their things in the trunk of the car, and as soon as Mama brought the basket of fried chicken and buttermilk biscuits out to us, we were ready to go.

Everybody came out to see us off. Mama held baby sister Penny in one arm and used the other to hug me, then Uncle Red, then Grandpa. The hug made Grandpa uncomfortable, especially since Mama was in tears by the time she got to him. Papa shook hands with all three of us, which surprised me because he had never before shaken hands with me, and when he shook hands with Grandpa, they both looked uncomfortable. Howard hung back. He was seventeen years old then, and was already bigger than Papa. Margery's eyes filled with tears, but she didn't cry. She was fifteen, and looked more and more like Mama every day. My younger brother, Willie, who was ten, chewed on his bottom lip and looked blank. Baby sister Penny whimpered. Tige wagged his tail.

Uncle Red crawled into the back of the car and lay down on the seat. Grandpa got into the passenger's seat, I got into the driver's. With a last flurry of waves and calls of "Bye, now," and "Take care of y'selves," and "Be sure to write, now," I eased the car into low gear and slowly moved away.

Once out of the yard, I speeded up, and we were soon being followed by a long cloud of dust. Through the rearview mirror I caught one last glimpse of the family as they stood in the front yard and began to be lost in the swirling dust.

By the time we had gained the caliche road leading toward Roscoe, I could no longer contain myself. I began to sing "There's a Long Long Trail A-Winding," and pretty soon Grandpa pulled his harmonica from his pocket, tapped it a few times on his leg, and began to play. I had to change keys because the harmonica was in D and I was in something else, but that was all right, it sounded good. And pretty soon we began to hear Uncle Red joining in. His tone was lethargic and coarse, a sort of hum-growl, but at least he growled on key.

> *"There's a long, long trail a-winding,*
> *Into the land of my dreams,*
> *Where the nightingale is singing,*
> *And the white moon beams . . ."*

We were off to Nashville.

12

Uncle Red told me not to drive through the center of Roscoe, and I didn't need to ask why, though Grandpa did.

"I want to stop at a store and get a couple of things," he said.

"We'll stop in Enid," Uncle Red said. He leaned over the front seat and took a map from the glove compartment.

"Enid?" Grandpa said, his craggy brows knitting. "Ain't we going through Tallapoosa? Why go that far outa the way?"

"I got something to do in Enid," Uncle Red lied. "Now, you just hang on there, Mr. Wagoner. We'll be in Tulsa 'fore midnight."

After we had skirted Roscoe, Uncle Red showed me our route on the map, then lay back down on the back seat and went to sleep with his cowboy hat over his face and his boots sticking out the window. But Grandpa's puzzlement about why we had to avoid Roscoe put him off his stroke on the harmonica, so he quit playing and I quit singing. I turned on the car's radio instead, and got station KVOO out of Tulsa in time to hear Bob Wills and the Playboys do most of "Dust Bowl Blues." Tommy Duncan sang it, and I sang along with him. Bob Wills a-haaaaaed now and then.

*"I'm leaving this morning, gonna bid my pals goodbye,
I can't live here no longer under this old dusty sky,*

Honey, hand me down my walking shoes,
Lord, I've got 'em, the mean old dust bowl blues."

Actually, though, the sky wasn't all that dusty at the moment. Hazy, yes, and tonight the sun would drop from a sky ablaze with fiery red dust, but for now, as we drove along the two-lane blacktop toward Enid, the sun beat straight down on us, its glowing brightness and heat only slightly softened by the haze.

"We're getting close," Grandpa said.

We were entering a landscape of low rolling brown hills and parched grassland, and Grandpa had been acting sort of strange for the last few miles, his hawk's eye darting here and there, searching for something.

"Getting close to what?" I said, but he didn't answer me— apparently didn't even hear me. He kept looking around, growing more and more tense as he grew surer of his ground.

"It's up here a ways," he said after a long pause.

"What is?"

"Stop when I tell you to," he said, and kept searching the dry brown hills for a landmark.

I had no idea what he was talking about, but I could see he didn't want to be questioned, so I kept silent and drove on down the heat-shimmered highway, hearing now and then the squishy sound the tires made on the heat-softened blacktop.

About ten miles farther on down the road, as we were driving along the side of a gently sloping hill, Grandpa said, "Here. Pull over and stop."

I didn't ask him why. I could see that it was important to him. In fact, I couldn't ever remember having seen him so tense, so portentous. His aloofness I had always associated with his advanced age, but now he seemed as intense as a bridegroom at a shotgun wedding.

"Up there by the windmill," he said, and that was where I pulled the car off onto the graveled shoulder of the highway.

Running alongside the road on our left, in the direction where Grandpa was staring, was a barbed-wire fence, and beyond that, maybe a hundred yards down the gentle slope of the hill, was a windmill with a watering trough for cattle. The trough was made from an old enameled cast-iron bathtub. The windmill turned shakily in the feeble hot breeze that now and then stirred the yellowed tufts of dead grass along the slope

When the windmill turned, a thin stream of water pulsed gurgling from a pipe and spilled into the old mossy bathtub, then overflowed into a muddy bog made by cattle that had come there to drink.

"You want to get a drink?" But I realized immediately that it wasn't water Grandpa was after. He was acting too strangely for that. He got out and walked around to stand in front of the car for a moment, gazing down the slope toward a rolling plain beyond.

"That's where it happened," he said, as if to himself.

"Where what happened?" I asked. I switched off the motor and got out to join him.

"The Hennessy Line," he said, his eyes slightly glazed, as if his sight had turned inward and he was seeing something in himself. "Stretching from horizon to horizon. . . . It was here. Right here. The Hennessy Line. . . ." Like a man dreaming, he crossed the weed-choked ditch and crawled carefully through the barbed-wire fence.

"Where you going?" I called, but he didn't answer. He started down the slope of the hill, at a slight diagonal from the windmill, and I followed him, leaving Uncle Red to snooze in the back seat of the car. As we walked through the dry grass, grasshoppers flew out of our path, making dry clicking sounds.

When Grandpa got just below the watermill, he stopped. I stopped behind him and asked, "What is it? What d'you see?"

He pointed directly before him to the low rolling hills. "All the way to the horizon, wagons and horses, buckboards, mules, and people, people. . . . It was the Run, boy! It was the Run!"

So that's what he was talking about. The Run. I hadn't realized sooner because he had always refused to tell me about it, thinking I wasn't old enough to hear it, to understand it, and I wasn't even sure that it was me he was talking to now. It didn't matter, though. He was talking to someone, at least, and I was listening, as he stared out across the heat-shimmered land with those dreamy, inward-looking eyes, the eyes that once again had a vision of what it was like that day along the Hennessy Line.

"As far as the eye could see . . . people . . . people of all ages, men and women and kids. All kinds a people—hicks and dandies, cowboys and hoboes, whores and housewives. I was just down there, near midway of the line. See? See that blackjack tree down there? That's where I was, nearabouts. . . . I was

eighteen years old then, straddling an old mule without a saddle.
Rode that mule all the way from Tennessee, I did, and got
here three days 'fore the Run, so I could get a place on the
starting line." He fell silent for a moment, tilting his head as
if straining to hear sounds that were just out of range. "Noise
like you never heard before. People shouting, cussing, hawking
maps and claim forms and suchlike, babies crying, horses snorting and neighing and stamping the ground. Thousands of horses,
boy! Thousands of riders and drivers! A cloud of dust hanging
over us. . . ." He shook his head at the wonder of it. "Boy, that
was some sight!"

He was silent again, and remained silent this time for so
long that I began to wonder if he was finished, so I said, "Tell
me about it, Grandpa. What was it like, the Run?"

He snorted. "It was the biggest horse race there ever was,
boy, and for the biggest prize." With his good right arm, he
made a wide, expansive gesture that took in all the prairie
horizon to the north. "The Cherokee Strip! Hundreds of thousands of acres, some of the best land God ever put on this
earth. Was then, anyway. And all for the taking. . . ."

"You didn't have to pay any money for it?" I prompted.

He shook his head. "No. All a man needed was a registration
permit from one of the booths that was set up along the line
here, and the permit was just to keep the sooners out."

"Sooners?"

"Men who tried to sneak in before the starting gun. They'd
sneak in and camp in the blackjack thickets, hide out in the
ravines and gullies, then ride out when the first honest settlers
showed up, claim a prize quarter section, just like they'd made
the run and beat the others to it. Over yonder, other side of
Turkey Creek, over that rise there, a troop of cavalry was
camped. Patrolled the line, trying to keep the sooners from
sneaking in, and details of troopers went on regular patrols
deep into the Strip, trying to flush 'em out."

When he faltered again, I asked, "And the Indians? What
happened to the Cherokees?"

After a moment of sad reflection, he said in a husky whisper.
"All gone. Moved out to what was left of their nation, over
east there. But I reckon they was used to it by then. They'd
had their lands taken away from 'em back in Georgia and
Alabama, and forced to march all the way out here to Okla
homa. Government give 'em this land here for as long as th

grass grew and the rivers flowed." He snorted again. "But there was too many white men who wanted the land. . . . Oh, there was a few raggedy bands of Indians, Cherokees mostly, who rode out to see the Run, but they stayed out a the way. Was a few of 'em on the hills over there, where they wouldn't get run over. Just sitting there on them mangy ponies, watching the flood of white people pouring into their land." He shook his head. "Well, weren't nothing they could do about it, poor halfstarved buggers, 'cept sit up there on them black hills and watch."

"Black?" I said. "The hills?"

"Burned over. Troops done it, mainly to make the section markers more visible, but I reckon they were trying to smoke out the sooners, too. Set too late, though, them fires. In some places they were still burning on the day of the Run, and for a right smart while afterwards, too. Black, smoky land, far as you could see. Made it terrible when the Run stared. Black dust." He paused again, but I no longer felt the need to prompt him. His excitement was growing, not lessening, his speech was becoming more intense, his vision more vivid. And soon I realized that I wasn't watching Grandpa—not the taciturn and grumpy Grandpa I knew. Who I was seeing was the young man he must have been on the day of the Run: eager and excited, a young man with a vision of the future, rather than an old man with only sad memories of the past.

"September 16th, 1893. . . . The line was supposed to break at twelve o'clock. High noon. Something happened, though. Some crazy fool fired a gun off by accident, I reckon, and a whole section of the line broke away, just over yonder a ways. That was at eleven-fifty-five—five minutes before the official gun. Troopers tried to hold 'em back, but they just about got trampled for their troubles. And soon's I seen there was no turning back the tide, I whopped that mule across the ass, boy, and I headed out into the Cherokee Strip, damned and determined to get me my hundred and sixty acres.

"The dust cloud that was raised . . . blinding black dust . . . only the riders on the fast horses out in front could see where they was going. Rest of us banged into each other, yelling and screaming. Rigs locked wheels, overturned. Wagons ran into gullies, broke down, stalled, turned over. No roads, you see. No bridges. No trails, even, 'cept the Old Chisholm Trail, and that was away over yonder a few miles, and it was so crowded with wagons and rigs that they just about come to a standstill before they got a mile.

"But I was on my mule, so I didn't have no trouble crossing ravines and gullies and suchlike. Wasn't very fast, that old mule, but he was steady, and I paced him so's he'd be able to make the eighteen miles to Enid without slowing down. Idea was to get to Enid and get one of the choice claims nearby. Oh, he was a good un, that old mule. Rode him all the way from Tennessee, and he still had enough in him to make the Run. His bones rattled a right smart, and his guts was always agrumbling, but, by God, he went on. And pretty soon we began to overtake people who'd got a faster start. After six or seven miles, the fast horses were beginning to give out, some of 'em crippled in gopher holes. And the dust was thinning out, too, so I knew I was getting closer to the lead.

"But the smoke . . . the fires . . . sometimes you had to ride right through the flames, running through droves of rabbits and coyotes and snakes that were trying to get away from the fires. Hellfires—that's what they was, boy, hellfires! There was a woman, had a rig that got stuck in a ravine, was trying to save her team 'fore the fire got to 'em. She begged me to help her. But I didn't. Didn't have the time. I was getting near the lead. Later, I heard she got burned up, her and her team. . . ."

He paused briefly, pensive and sad, as if remembering the woman that he could have saved so long ago. Maybe he was remembering her face, how she looked there in that ravine that day as she tried desperately to unhitch the plunging and whinnying team of horses. How she looked when she screamed for him to help her. . . .

"I just couldn't," he said, and now a new tone had entered his voice, a tone of mingled regret and frustration. "I was too close, you see. I was within five-six miles of Enid, and of the twenty thousand people who'd started the Run, maybe a hundred held the lead, and, by God, I was one of 'em. I had rode thirteen miles as fast as that mule could go and still hold out. Rode through dust and smoke and the fires of hell, with my face blacker'n any nigger's you ever saw, my throat parched, every bone in my body aching. . . . I couldn't stop. It wasn't just the land, not just the dirt and the grass, I mean. It was the Promised Land."

He cleared his throat. "What you have to understand about the people who made the Run . . . like most settlers, I reckon, we was the have-nots of this country, the ones who'd always lost out in other places, or been run out, or escaped. It was the last chance for us, the last land rush in the history of the world."

He was silent for so long that I said, "Did you get your land?"

He nodded. With no sound of pride or excitement left in his voice now, he said, "Yeah, I got it." He spat. "I lost it later. But, hell, that don't matter. Wasn't just the land. . . . That's what you got to understand, Whit. That's what I try to make people understand. I try to tell 'em that it wasn't just the land, it was the dream. The dream. Twenty thousand people made that Run, and every one of 'em had the dream—a dream of a new country, rich and unspoiled, where the land was for the taking. Dreams of new towns springing up overnight on the prairies. Of new homes and farms and schools. A place where everybody could start out on an even footing. A new land where every man had a chance. . . . That's what I try to tell 'em," he said in an urgent and pleading voice, and suddenly his eyes were filmed with tears. "We wasn't just land chasers, Whit, we was dream chasers."

After another brief pause, he sighed. "And look at it now. All turned to dust . . . all turned to dust. We ruined it, Whit." He slowly shook his head. "We ruined it."

During the long silence that followed, I could hear the windmill behind me creaking as it caught a soft breeze and spun around a few times. Then I became aware that there was someone behind us, and turned to see Uncle Red. He was squatting on his haunches a few yards up the slope, smoking a cigarette, staring at Grandpa, studying him with his brooding deep-set blue-gray eyes. I had no idea how long he had been squatting there.

"Turned to dust," Grandpa said again.

"But there's other places," I said, searching for something to say that might comfort him. "California, now. They say that's the Promised Land, too."

"They'll ruin it," Grandpa said with sour confidence. "If it ain't already ruined. Anyway," he continued in a milder tone, "I'm too old for that. Just one dream left now, of going home."

"But I thought this . . ." I wasn't sure what I wanted to ask him, but I was curious to know why a man who had spent maybe forty-five years of his life in a place, who had married and buried a wife there, who had children and grandchildren there—why didn't he consider that place his home?

"I don't know," he said, as if he had intuited my unfinished question. "I reckon I was just here looking for some-thing . . . something I never found."

It sounded like a line from one of his poems, and it was sad, the way he said it.

"Reckon it's about time I quit looking." Abruptly he turned away from the scene. When he saw Uncle Red, he seemed a little surprised, but not enough to break stride. He went on up the slope toward the car. I followed.

"Well, if you two don't mind," Uncle Red said as we passed him, "I'm gonna take a bath." He got up and ambled toward the windmill. "I ain't seen that much water in one place since I been back to Oklahoma."

I followed Grandpa up the slope. It was too hot to stay out in the sun any longer, and besides, I felt I ought to stay near Grandpa in case he wasn't through talking yet. He had spoken more words to me in the last fifteen minutes than he had ever before spoken to me in my whole life. And I felt honored to hear them, particularly when he called me Whit. As far as I could remember, it was the first time he had ever called me by my name. It made me feel strangely close to him, so I stayed close.

But he had finished talking. That much was obvious when we got into the car and, exhausted and withdrawn, he settled down on the seat and pulled his hat down over his eyes as if he intended to sleep.

Uncle Red pulled his clothes off and hung them on a lower rung of the ladder that went up the windmill. Then, naked as a jaybird except for that cowboy hat and a cigarette that dangled from his mouth, he tiptoed through the mud and slipped down into the water in the mossy old bathtub. He stretched out in the tub, tipped his hat over his eyes, and lay there in that water and smoked his cigarette as though he were perfectly at home in some posh hotel.

I closed my eyes for a couple of minutes, hoping I might get a catnap, too, but pretty soon I heard Uncle Red's alarmed voice suddenly saying. "Hey! Hey, what the hell! Get out of here!"

I looked up to see some cattle approaching the bathtub. They were coming to water at the trough, four or five Brahma cows following a mean-looking, humpbacked bull, and they apparently didn't see Uncle Red in the tub until he yelled at them. They stopped then, wide-eyed with wonder, and stared at him.

"Shoo!" Uncle Red said. "Get the hell outa here!"

But the Brahma bull's look of wonder quickly turned to one of fierce disapproval. He obviously didn't like seeing a man stretched out in his drinking water. He tossed his head, flashing his horns, snorted, lowered his head, and bellowed a furious warning, pawing the ground, kicking up long arcs of dust over his back and onto the cows behind him. When he moved, it looked as if he was going to charge the bathtub, but he lunged to within a few feet of the tub, then abruptly halted, sniffing the air as if he hadn't as yet figured out what it was that he saw in his watering trough.

Uncle Red seemed to vacillate between being frightened and being offended. "Get outa here, you sonofabitch!" he yelled, and flicked his cigarette into the bull's face.

The glowing end of the cigarette hit the bull between his eyes, sending out a little explosion of sparks. The bull snorted and jumped backward. And then he *really* got mad. He pawed the mud furiously, lowering his horns and bellowing. Then he charged the bathtub. He slammed his horns against the side of the tub, *bam!* The bathtub rocked sideways, spilling out some water, and the bull, stunned, stepped back to shake off the impact, and then charged again, *bam!*

"Help!" Uncle Red cried. "Get him away from here! Hey! Hey! Look out!"

Grandpa and I got out of the car, but we stayed on our side of the barbed-wire fence. There didn't seem to be anything we could do to help Uncle Red except go down there and get that bull to chase *us,* and neither of us was in a hurry to do that.

"Help!" Uncle Red cried again. "Get him away from here! Do something! Holy shit!"

Bam! The bull hit the side of the bathtub again. This time Uncle Red had ducked. He went all the way under the water for a moment, leaving his cowboy hat to float on the surface, then he came up under the hat, so that it was still perched on his head when he spurted water out of his mouth. "Come on, goddammit, do something! For Christ's sake, this sonofabitch's gonna kill me!"

But what could we do? We still couldn't think of anything

to do except attract the bull's attention to ourselves, which might give Uncle Red a chance to get out of the tub. But then what would *he* do, with the bull between him and the car? Still, it was something, anyway, so I finally screwed up my courage and asked Grandpa if he would stand on this side of the barbed-wire fence and hold the bottom strand up for me in case I had to run and dive under it. He gave me a doubtful look, but said he would do it, and so I crawled through the fence and began cautiously edging my way down the slope. I yelled at the bull a couple of times, but he didn't see me until I got the idea to take my shirt off and use it as a cape.

He saw me then. He snorted and tossed his horns, which must have been sore by now from banging into that cast-iron tub. He roared out a challenge, lunged around the bathtub, and headed straight for me. I whirled and ran like blue blazes back toward the fence, which suddenly seemed much farther away than I had thought it was. I could hear the bull's rumbling hoofbeats behind me, rapidly gaining on me, and for a second or two I thought I was a goner. But I got to the fence and dived through, rolling over the weeds and thistles, and Grandpa let the bottom strand of wire spring back in place just as the bull came to a skidding, dust-billowing stop. Then the bull pawed furiously at the ground, slinging dust up over his back, and bellowed with such rage that the mere sound of it sent shivers up my spine.

"Keep him there for a minute," Uncle Red shouted as he climbed out of the bathtub. "Let me get my clothes on."

I was willing to wave my shirt some more and hope the bull wouldn't charge straight through the fence, but it was too late, anyway. As Uncle Red sloshed out of the tub, one of the cows that had been watching everything with dumb bewilderment suddenly bellowed, as if to inform the bull that his quarry was escaping, and the bull did one of the most amazing things I had ever seen: he sprang into the air, and, with all four feet off the ground, whirled completely around before he hit the ground again, so that now his dung-smeared rump was toward us and his wild eyes were fixed on Uncle Red again. With another bellow, he cut the air with his horns, and then he was suddenly running again, already at top speed the moment he left his starting place, and he was headed for Uncle Red.

"Look out!" I yelled. "Here he comes!"

Uncle Red grabbed his shirt and pants off the ladder and

scrambled up the rungs as fast as his skinny legs could take him.

The bull came to a skidding stop directly at the foot of the ladder. Uncle Red, up there just out of range of the bull's tossing horns, looked down, terrified and indignant, yelling, "Shoo! Get away from here!" He had thrown his shirt and pants over his shoulder when he had leaped for the ladder, and now the pants and shirt slipped off and fell onto the bull's head.

That bewildered the bull. He let out another bellow and hooked wildly at the clothes. The pants were shaken off, but the shirt had fallen in such a way that the two sleeves were slipping down over the bull's horns, and the shirttail was flapping over the bull's face, blinding him.

He panicked. He went crazy. No longer paying any attention to Uncle Red, the bull ran, farted, bucked, bawled, twisted, flung his horns about, rammed them into the ground and plowed the dust with them.

"Hey!" Uncle Red shouted as the bull bucked and floundered away from the windmill. "Hey, come back here with my shirt, you sonofabitch!"

But the bull was mindless of everything except the shirt on his head. He bucked and twisted his way across the prairie. He fell once with earthshaking force, but was immediately on his feet again. And his cows followed him, keeping a safe distance from his horns and hooves, mooing their solicitude.

Uncle Red, naked except for his hat, leaned outward from the ladder at arm's length to shake his fist at the retreating bull. "You sonofabitch!" he yelled. "Come back here with my shirt!"

Followed by his cows, the bull went loping headlong over a prairie knoll, still blinded by the flapping shirt, flicking his hind hooves into the air as if kicking at yellowjackets.

"God*damn,*" Uncle Red said. He came down off the windmill and picked up his trampled pants, shook the dust out of them, and pulled them on. After getting into his boots, he retrieved a pack of Lucky Strikes that had fallen from his shirt pocket and been trampled by the bull, and then he came toward the car.

I began to hear a peculiar sound from Grandpa's direction, a sound that seemed to be coming from deep down in him somewhere, and as it worked up to his throat, I realized it was the sound of suppressed laughter.

Uncle Red was bent over, half through the barbed-wire

fence, when Grandpa's laughter finally erupted, and the sound caused Uncle Red to hesitate for a second and give Grandpa a puzzled look.

It was the first time I had ever heard Grandpa laugh like that. I had heard him chuckle, of course, and had even heard him guffaw a time or two, but this was deep rich yolky laughter, and it was contagious. I found myself beginning to chuckle.

"What's so damned funny?" Uncle Red demanded, staring at us with puzzled and reproachful eyes, his skin-and-bone chest heaving. "That was my new khaki shirt."

That brought another burst of laughter from us, but finally Grandpa got control of himself enough to say, "When you was going up that ladder, that bull's horn missed your asshole about that far." His old knobby fingers indicated a distance of about an inch.

"Well, what's so funny about that?" But now the laughter was beginning to get to him, too. He tried hard to keep from smiling at first, and his first chuckle was sort of tentative, as if he still wasn't sure he was going to laugh. Finally, though, he couldn't help himself. He laughed too. We all did.

Grandpa and I were wiping tears from our eyes as our laughter became more sporadic and finally tapered off into an exhausted, hiccoughy silence. Then Uncle Red said, "Come on, let's get out a here."

He got into the back seat and put on his fancy fringed cowboy shirt that Mama had washed and ironed for him.

I was feeling good as I drove on down the highway toward Enid, mainly because I'd had a good laugh, but also because the three of us seemed, at least for a little while, closer than we had ever been before. Certainly I had never felt closer to Grandpa. I had never seen him shed tears before, and today I had seen his eyes film over with tears of lost dreams, and then, a little while later, spill over with tears of laughter. And not only had he finally told me the story of the Run, he had also called me by my name, instead of calling me *boy*. So now it felt as if we were three grown-up buddies, three good ole boys, going down the road together, having an adventure.

13

We got to Enid about four o'clock that afternoon. Grandpa said it was a far cry from the raw frontier town that had sprung up after the Run, a town of tents and wooden sidewalks and dirt streets. Now there were not only paved streets, but streetlights, too, and brick sidewalks. Even so, it wasn't much of a town: dusty and withered in the hot afternoon sun, with dusty withered farmers loitering along the sidewalks and in the doorways of boarded-up buildings.

When we stopped at a service station, we found that almost two quarts of oil had leaked from the bent oil pan. But we didn't have enough money to fix it.

"Till we get to Tulsa, at least," Uncle Red said, "and I find Mr. Durwood Arnspriger."

"Mr. *Who?*" I said.

"Feller owes me some money," Uncle Red said.

We stopped at a few places in downtown Enid so that Uncle Red could look for a bootlegger. He said he wanted to get a bottle, and Grandpa, when asked, said he wouldn't mind having a little nip himself. But though Uncle Red went into a couple of seedy poolhalls and a barbershop, he couldn't locate anybody who was selling whiskey. The men he talked to, sour and suspicious, said that the sheriff had recently run all the bootleggers out of town. Tulsa, they told him, would probably be the nearest place he could get any booze.

It was while we were parked in front of the last poolhall that a bum approached the car. Grandpa and I had been sitting in the car, waiting for Uncle Red to return, and we had been watching the bum—a one-armed man—rummaging through a trash can a few yards down the street. And when Uncle Red came out of the poolhall and got into the car, the one-armed bum noticed him and came shuffling up to the car. He leaned down to look in the window at Uncle Red.

"Say, friend," he said, "any chance to bum a cigarette offa you?" The cuff of his right sleeve was safety-pinned to the shoulder of his ragged shirt. He was a fairly young man, maybe not much older than Uncle Red.

Uncle Red tugged his pack of Lucky Strikes from his shirt pocket. The bum hesitated for a moment, his hand hovering above the pack.

"Say," he said, "ain't you . . . ?" He tried to remember. "Ain't you . . . ?"

"Red Stovall," Uncle Red suggested.

"Yeah. That's right." The bum's face brightened. "Red Stovall. I saw you play once. Down in Lawton a few years ago, at a Rotary picnic. 'Member that? I sat in with your band for a while. Played the fiddle."

He was obviously hoping that Uncle Red would remember him, and though Uncle Red obviously didn't, he was quick to say, "Oh, sure. I 'member now. A fiddler. . . ."

The bum leaned forward to light the cigarette from the match that Uncle Red struck for him, and he noticed the uneasy glance that Uncle Red shot at his right sleeve. After his first drag on the cigarette, he flapped the stump of his arm, and said, "Was then. Before this happened. Was pretty good, too." He smiled, "'Least, you said I was."

"Sure," Uncle Red said. "I 'member that. What happened?"

"Lost it working in the jute mill there at Lawton," he said, without any apparent self-pity or even any remorse. "Got it tangled up in a machine."

"Ah," Uncle Red grunted, at a loss for something to say. "Well. Sorry to hear that. So what're you doing now?"

"Looking for work," the bum said. "Heard there was some WPA jobs opening up here in Enid, but . . ." He shrugged. "They got more two-armed men than they can use, what d'they want with me?"

After a moment's hesitation, Uncle Red dug into his pocket

and took a five-dollar bill from the thirty dollars that Grandpa had given him. "Here. Maybe this'll help out a little."

"Oh, I wasn't putting the touch on you for any money, Red," he said, though he obviously wanted it very much.

"Take it. Call it payment for the time you played fiddle with us."

The bum didn't have to be told twice. His eyes sparkled greedily as he took the bill. "Well... well, much obliged, Red."

Uncle Red tapped me on the shoulder, and I started the car. "Sure, sure. Forget it. And take care of y'self, y'hear? See you around."

The bum kept up with the car for a few feet, saying, "Well, it's mighty nice of you, Red. Hell, now I can go back to Lawton in style, huh? I was figuring I'd have to catch a freight, but now..." And when we were on our way, the bum shouted, "Hey! You playing here in Enid somewhere?"

Uncle Red stuck his head out the window to shout back, "Just passing through."

We stopped once more in Enid, this time to go to a grocery store, where Uncle Red bought some cigarettes and soda pop and cookies. And while we were walking back to the car, we passed an old storefront church with a crudely lettered sign painted on the window, *Tabernacle of the True God*. On the door was a sign that said, "Ye who are poor in spirit and pocketbook, come ye in for a repast. FREE SOUP before sermon." There were quite a few people waiting their turn in the soupline: hoboes and jobless farm workers, men and women with the pinched look of hunger and humiliation. From within the store came the voice of a damnation-and-punishment preacher haranguing his soup-bribed congregation with threats of everlasting agonies.

Uncle Red stopped in front of the place for a few minutes. I thought at first that he was considering getting into the soupline, but then I realized he was listening to the preacher, who was saying in his hellfire voice "... and if we turn to chapter six, verse eight in Revelations, what do we read? What do we hear? The voice of doom, oh, brothers and sisters, the voice of doom, saying, 'I looked, and beheld a pale horse; and his name that sat on him was Death, and hell followed after him.' Yeah, the Pale Rider himself, astride that big pale horse, coming to get us!"

Uncle Red listened with his head tilted and his eyes squinted, and there was a peculiar look of peaceful abstraction on his face. In years to come I would try to remember that look. I would try to remember if there had been a clue in his face as to what he was thinking at the moment, since it later proved to be the moment of conception for "Pale Horse, Pale Rider," which is generally considered to be among the best songs he ever wrote. And not only was I there when he got the idea, I was there when he wrote it.

It happened while we were on our way to Tulsa. First Uncle Red passed around the basket of fried chicken and biscuits that Mama had made for us, and Grandpa opened each of us a Nehi soda pop, and we drove on down the highway in a silence broken only by the sounds of soda pop swilled, chicken bones gnawed, fingers licked. Then, after we finished eating, Uncle Red told me to stop so he could get his guitar from the trunk. He also got a pencil and a piece of crumpled dirty paper from the glove compartment. Then he sat in the back seat and experimented with chord progressions as we drove along. I listened intently, filled with the same wonder that I had felt when I first watched a baby chick peep and peck its way out of an eggshell. And as the song slowly took shape, I began to understand what he was doing. I began to anticipate the particular sound he was searching for, and I always felt a mysterious sense of mingled elation and relief when he found it.

He finally settled down to a chord structure that was much more complex than any I had ever heard him use before, and then he started searching for the words that would become the chorus of the song, mumble-singing,

> *"Pale Horse, Pale Rider,*
> *Where do you come from?*
> *Where do you go?*
> *Pale as the sunshine,*
> *Cold as snow. . . ."*

He hesitated indecisively over only a few of the words before he found the right ones, and then he hastily scribbled them down, using one of the jump seats as a table. It was clear from the chorus that he was writing a song about death, but it wasn't until he got into writing the first verse that I began to see that he was also writing a song about Grandpa—about what he had heard Grandpa say at the windmill.

> *"With your bag of broken dreams,*
> *You ride on through the sky,*
> *Gathering up the broken dreams*
> *Of those who had to die."*

Those lines made up a musical movement in themselves, and brought Uncle Red to a long plateau of high musical intensity, as he sang, with only a few stumbles and alterations, the rest of the first verse.

> *"You took one from a pioneer*
> *Who searched for the Promised Land.*
> *You took one from a little boy*
> *Who dreamed of being a man.*
> *You took one from a prisoner*
> *Who dreamed of being free,*
> *And great Godamighty now one of these days,*
> *You'll take mine from me. . . .*
> *My dream of going home."*

While Uncle Red was finding the words for the second verse, I stole a few sidelong glances at Grandpa, but he was just staring straight ahead, giving no indication that he was even hearing the song, let alone being affected by it.

> *"With dreams so alive within us,*
> *We think it will never end,*
> *But someday our dreams will turn to dust,*
> *And be gone with the wind.*
> *But there's one place I dream of*
> *And pray to God I see*
> *Just one more time before I go*
> *Into eternity.*
> *I dream of going home."*

With a repeat of the chorus, Uncle Red struck one last triumphant chord on his guitar and let it fade away into silence, and then said, "Well? What d'you think a that, Mr. Wagoner?"

"Pretty song," Grandpa said, and that was all.

"Pretty, my foot," Uncle Red said, scorning such lukewarm praise. "It's a beautiful song—that's what it is, bee-you-tee-ful. How 'bout you, Hoss? What d'you think?"

"I think it's *great*," I said, not only flattered that he asked my opinion, but also filled with pride over witnessing the song's creation.

"Well, I don't know 'bout it being *great*," he said with a sort of mock modesty. "But it's a good un, ain't it? A real high-class tearjerker. Make them people cry in their beers." He put his guitar away and, with it, his strangely abstracted mood of creative intensity. A little lighthearted now, he said, "And speaking of beer, when the hell we gonna get to Tulsa? I'm dry as a popcorn fart."

14

We got into Tulsa shortly after ten o'clock that night, and went searching for Mr. Durwood Arnspriger, the shady gambler and promoter who owed Uncle Red a hundred dollars. But the dilapidated old building where Arnspriger had once had an office was now boarded up, abandoned, and his name wasn't in the telephone book. We cruised the shadier parts of town until almost midnight, looking for card parlors, hoping to find one of Arnspriger's cardshark compatriots who might tell us where he was, but all the card parlors that Uncle Red remembered from a few years ago had been closed down, or had moved someplace else, so we finally gave up.

We spent the night in the car. We parked on a side street, ate the last of Mama's fried chicken, threw the bones to an old mangy dog on the street, and then tried to get some sleep. But Uncle Red tossed and turned on the back seat, kept awake most of the night by a small hacking cough, and since there wasn't room on the front seat for both Grandpa and me to lie down, we tried to sleep while sitting up. Grandpa was too old for that sort of thing, however, his bones too brittle, his joints too stiff. He leaned his head against the window and succeeded in falling asleep now and then, only to be awakened in a little while by the need to rearrange his old bones, and every time he moved, he disturbed my sleep, or woke me up entirely. And every time

I woke up, I seemed to recall that five dollars Uncle Red had given to the one-armed man in Enid. I felt ashamed for being so begrudging about it, but I couldn't help thinking that that money would have bought us all warm beds in a tourist cabin somewhere. Of course, we wouldn't have spent it for that, even if he hadn't given it away; we would have saved it to help us get to Nashville. But now we not only had to sleep in the car, we had five dollars less with which to buy gasoline, and what were we going to do if we didn't find this man with the funny name of Arnspriger?

But we did. We found him the next morning. And we did it with the help of a man whose name held even more fascination for me than did Durwood Arnspriger's. It was Bob Wills. Though I knew that Uncle Red and his band had once opened a show for Bob Wills and his Texas Playboys at the Dream Bowl out in California, I didn't know until that day in Tulsa that Uncle Red and Bob Wills were actually friends. I found out when I turned the car radio to KVOO, Tulsa's radio station, in time to hear the announcer say, "Bob Wills and his Texas Playboys are on the air!" And Uncle Red, who had by then almost given up hope of finding Durwood Arnspriger, said in a voice of suddenly renewed hope, "Hey! *He* might know. Let's go over to that radio station. Take a right up here on Fifth Street."

He directed me to the station, which was in downtown Tulsa in a monstrously tall building, maybe the tallest I had ever seen. I found a parking place about a half a block from it, and Grandpa stayed in the car, hoping, he grumped, to get a little shut-eye now that the sun was warm and he could have the back seat to lie down on.

We had to take an elevator up to the twenty-first floor. It was the first time I had ever ridden in an elevator in my life, and it scared me a little. Uncle Red and I stopped in the lobby of the radio station, where there were chairs and a sofa and two big loudspeakers that blared the music that was being played by the band inside the studio. There was a big plate-glass partition that separated the lobby from both the studio and the control room, and another one separated the control room from the studio. Over the door leading off the lobby into the studio was a big red-lighted sign that said ON THE AIR.

Since the band was going to be on the air for another thirty minutes, Uncle Red, after waving at Bob Wills through the soundproof glass partition, settled down on the sofa in the lobby. But I couldn't sit still, I was so excited. I had heard Bob Wills and his band on the radio many times, but this was the first time I had ever *seen* them. It was like magic for me, seeing the music produced that I had only heard before. There they were, the Texas Playboys, with fiddle-playing, cigar-chomping, pint-sized, potbellied, cowboy-costumed Bob Wills strutting around the studio like a bantam rooster, pausing long enough now and then to holler his famous *Ah-hah!* into a microphone.

Smack up against the plate-glass partition, mashing my nose flat against it, I stared, awestruck, at a legend in the making. I even got to hear him introduce Leon McAuliffe, "playing his own composition"—this last word said in an ironic tone of snooty refinement—"'The Steel Guitar Rag.' Take it away, Leon! Take it away!"

And Leon did. I knew the tune and could play along with it in my head. I knew that Bob Wills called his music Western Swing, a sort of country version of big-band jazz, and that no other country band except his used horns and drums and played syncopated rhythms; but it wasn't until I saw him and the Playboys in the radio station that day that I finally figured out what made Bob Wills's music so much more exciting than most country music. It was in the solos. In country music, the in-strumental solos always seemed to be woven around the melody line. In Bob Wills's band, however, when the guitar or sax-ophone or piano took a solo, the solo was always improvised. The players composed their own music as they played, and the only concession to the melody was to keep within the scales. It was very exciting for me, this revelation of how free music could be, this thing called jazz.

When the broadcast was finished, the ON THE AIR sign went off. The man in the control booth began reading a commercial for Playboy Flour, and while the other band members were packing up their instruments, Bob Wills came out into the lobby to greet Uncle Red.

"Well, damn my hide, if it ain't Red Stovall," Bob Wills said as they shook hands. "What're you doing back in this neck of the woods?"

"Just passing through, on my way to Nashville, try out for the Opry."

"No shit! Well, hell, that ought to do it for you, Red! Son

of a gun. That's all you need, a spot on the Opry. Put you right up on top, boy, see if it don't. By God, it's good to see you again, you old boozer, you! How the hell you been?"

I sidled up to them and sort of stood around, hoping to get introduced. Bob Wills was still hanging onto Uncle Red's hand, and didn't release it until Uncle Red nodded at me and said, "Bob, I'd like you to meet my nephew here. Name's Whit— Whit Wagoner. Gonna be a picker-and-grinner someday, for sure. He's going to Nashville with me."

Bob turned toward me then, full-faced. His eyes, attentive and alert, about on the same level with mine, were crinkled in the corners by a wide smile that never seemed to leave his face for more than a second or two. He seemed to be giving me all the attention and courtesy that he would have given an old friend. And his short body seemed to throb—literally throb— with energy and enthusiasm.

"Young man, I'm pleased to make your acquaintance," he said in a courtly way as we shook hands—though he didn't really shake my hand, he trembled it. Touching him was like touching a dynamo. He smelled of whiskey and cigar smoke. "And I'll tell you what, when you get good enough, you just look me up. I may need a guitar picker by then. Boys I got in there'll probably be wore out by then."

I was speechless. I had a "thank you" right on the tip of my tongue, but I couldn't get it out, even though my mouth was hanging wide open.

Bob glanced up at Uncle Red. "Don't talk much, does he?" He still held my hand, trembling it.

"No," Uncle Red said, "but he sings a right smart. Pretty good, too—'least he will be, I 'spect, when his voice gets through changing."

"Well, young man, I tell you what. If you sing anything like your ole Uncle Red here, why, by God, son, you gonna tear it up." With an emphatic wink, he released my hand and turned back to Uncle Red.

I hadn't been able to say one single word to him. Not one. I felt like an idiot.

"Well, goddamn, Red!" He put a hand on Uncle Red's shoulder and gave him a friendly shake. "How you been doing, son? Skinny as ever, I see. Hellfire, boy, when you gonna get married and settle down, put some meat on your bones?"

Uncle Red patted Bob's paunch. "That how you got that? Home cooking?"

"Shiiiit, no," Bob said, smiling broadly. He jammed his cigar between his teeth so he could have both hands free to slap his paunch. "That ain't home cooking, Red. That's good beer. Comes from hanging out in honkytonks, keep from having to go home to the wife's home cooking." He laughed. "And speaking of toddy for the body, I got a bottle. . . ." He gestured toward the studio.

"Sure," Uncle Red said. "Beats home cooking any day."

"Wait here, I'll get it," Bob said, and hurried back into the studio.

The other musicians were coming out now, most of them carrying instruments. Some of them recognized Uncle Red, and a few of them stopped to shake hands with him and ask him how the hell he was doing. One of them was Tommy Duncan, the band's singer, who seemed particularly glad to see Uncle Red. This time, however, I didn't step forward and try to get myself introduced. I was afraid I wouldn't be able to speak again, and it was bad enough that Bob Wills probably thought I was an idiot, I didn't want Tommy Duncan to think so, too.

When Bob returned from the studio with the pint bottle of bourbon, he ushered Uncle Red down the hall to a restroom. I followed them. I wasn't going to let Bob Wills out of sight for a minute, hoping I might get a chance to say something to him that would redeem me.

He took two small paper cups from a dispenser over the washbasin, poured the cups full of bourbon, and then touched his cup to Uncle Red's.

"Here's to the Opry. Hope you make it big."

After they tossed the bourbon down, Uncle Red coughed lightly a couple of times, then cleared his throat. "Well, I might not make it at all. Depends on whether or not I find a man named Durwood Arnspriger, used to promote shows in this part of the country. Figured you might know 'im."

"Shiiiit, yeah, I know old Durwood—'bout as well as I want to. He owe you money?"

"Yeah. Gave me a rubber check for a show me and the boys done here a few years ago. Said he'd make it good, but we had to leave for a date in Dallas the next day, and I ain't heard from the sonofabitch since."

"Sounds like old Durwood, all right. Let's see, now. Last time I heard of him, he had a card game going some place 'round town." He thought for a moment, pursing his lips around his big cigar "Choo-Choo! That's it, the Choo-Choo Cafe. Down by the freightyards. He's got a card game in the back room."

One of the Playboys poked his head in the door. "Bob? Herman wants to see you a minute 'fore you get away."

"Be right there," Bob said. He filled his and Uncle Red's paper cups once more from the bottle. "One more for the road. Long way to Nashville. Wish I was going with you, but them damn Opry people still won't allow drums or horns on the stage. What're you gonna do for rhythm?"

"I'll just stomp my foot real loud," Uncle Red said.

Bob laughed. I laughed, too, but I don't think they heard me. And I had just about screwed up my courage to say something to them when Bob corked the pint bottle and shoved it into his hip pocket. "Listen," he said. "You hear the one 'bout the farmer who . . ." He put his hand on Uncle Red's elbow and ushered him out of the restroom and back toward the lobby. He rode down in the elevator with us, he and Uncle Red chuckling over the story about the farmer. I didn't catch the whole story, but it had something to do with a man who crossed a turkey with a cat and got a pussy gobbler. Uncle Red thought it was awfully funny.

On the front steps of the building, Bob stopped and shook hands with Uncle Red again, and said hesitantly, "Listen, now, Red, if Arnspriger don't come through for you, and you need some money . . ."

"Oh, he'll come through, I reckon. But thanks, anyway, I 'preciate it."

They said their goodbyes, promising to keep in touch, and Uncle Red started for the car. I followed him for only a few steps, and then turned around to make one last effort to say something to Bob. But the look on his face stopped me. He was watching Uncle Red walk away, and all the vitality and mirth was gone out of his face, replaced by a sort of last-look gravity, a sort of calmly accepted grief.

"Mr. Wills," I forced myself to say.

All the vitality was instantly back in his face. Smiling broadly again, he said, "Ah, you *can* talk!"

I probably blushed. This time, however, I wasn't struck dumb by his attention, by the way he looked at me as if I were somebody important. He probably talked to everybody that way. Even so, I hardly knew how to deal with it, especially coming from him, who really *was* somebody. But I managed to tell him, without having my tongue cleave to the roof of my mouth, that I was very glad to have met him.

He held out his hand. "My pleasure, young man, my pleasure." He trembled my hand once more, and then glanced in Uncle Red's direction. "But looky here, Whit, looky here. How long's Red been like this?" And once again he had that grave, worried look in his eyes.

"Well, I guess I really don't know. I just been with him for a few days now."

"He should be in a sanitarium."

I didn't know what to say to that. His somber expression stirred up my own apprehensions about Uncle Red's health and made me wonder if I was doing the right thing by helping him get to Nashville. "But he says he has to get to Nashville."

Bob nodded. "Reckon so. Soon's it's over, though, you think you might be able to talk him into getting his skinny ass into a sanitarium somewhere?"

"I'll do my damnedest," I said, putting it strong so he would think I was strong enough to do it.

He smiled again. It was as if a light were suddenly turned on behind his face. "Well, nobody could ask more'n that, could they?" He clapped his hand on my shoulder and gave me a friendly shake. "And you take care of yourself, too, y'hear?" he said, and after I told him I would, he turned to skip lightly back into the building.

In a daze of mingled awe and apprehension, I hurried back to the car to get a look at Uncle Red. From the way Bob had talked, I thought Uncle Red might be in danger of falling dead at any moment. But he looked all right to me—no worse than usual, that is. And he seemed lively enough. He sat in the front seat now, on the passenger's side, his legs crossed, drumming his fingers impatiently on his boot. Grandpa was still lying down on the back seat, a quilt pulled up over his face, snoring.

"Come on, let's go," Uncle Red snapped, impatient to get to the Choo-Choo Cafe.

We found it in a sooty, rundown section of town across from the railyards. The sidewalks in the vicinity of the cafe were crowded with hoboes and panhandlers, with bindle stiffs and railroad workers, with the loose women and out-of-town salesmen who stayed in the cheap hotels in the area. The Choo-Choo Cafe was in an old wooden building next to a back alley.

The card room in the back of the cafe had a separate entrance off the alley.

Uncle Red told me to stay in the car, but since I had promised both Mama and Bob Wills that I would look after him, I figured I would be remiss in my responsibilities if I let him go into such a dangerous-looking place alone. Besides, my curiosity about this Durwood Arnspriger had become so acute that I would have been miserable if I'd had to sit in that hot car with nothing to do but listen to Grandpa snore, so I decided to tag along with Uncle Red, who really didn't seem to care, one way or the other.

The only person in the card room was a girl who looked to be about sixteen. She was cleaning up the place, absentmindedly humming some tuneless ditty, and she dropped a dustpan when we came in. "Yes?" she asked timorously. Her tangled mass of hair was about the same color and texture as one of those copper pads used to scour pots and pans. Her eyes were cornflower blue. Her toes protruded from holes in her worn gym shoes, and the gingham dress she wore had obviously been made for someone much bigger. She was skinny as a greyhound and just as skittish.

"I'm looking for Durwood Arnspriger," Uncle Red told her.

"He's . . . Mr. Arnspriger? He's upstairs, taking a nap," she said in a breathy voice, gesturing toward a curtained doorway that presumably led to the living quarters upstairs.

Uncle Red sat down in one of the straightback chairs, propped one boot on the edge of the felt-covered table and pushed himself backward to balance precariously on the chair's hind legs. "You go tell him Red Stovall's here to see 'im."

"Oh?" she said, and then changed the question to a statement. "Oh." She blinked a couple of times. "Who?"

"Red Stovall."

"Oh, yes, of course," she said, as if she ought to have known that. Then she seemed to make about three different moves at the same time. She took a step toward the curtained stairway while reaching down to pick up the fallen dustpan and simultaneously attempting to lean the broom against the round card table. The broom clattered to the floor. "I'll go get him," she said. Leaving the things exactly as they lay, she made a clumsy exit through the curtain. We heard her stumble on the stairway with a cry of "Oof!" and then there was the sound of something clattering to the floor at the head of the stairs.

"What in the name of hell is going on around here?"—this said by a furious man somewhere upstairs. A short whispered conversation issued from that direction, and in a few moments a man's heavy footsteps on the stairs presaged the entrance of Mr. Durwood Arnspriger.

He was a huge man—*huge*. A big blubbery man with straight black hair that lay along the contours of his skull as if it had been plastered down with axle grease. He wore a collarless peppermint-striped shirt that fell voluminously over his elephantine paunch, and the beribboned sleeve garters he wore on his ham-sized biceps were the same fire-engine red as his suspenders. His pants, on the other hand, had a color and sheen that I had never seen anywhere before except on the iridescent belly of a bluebottle fly.

"Well, as I live and breathe!" His voice was surprisingly small and high-pitched for a man his size. "Red Stovall! Red Stovall, of all people! I've had occasion to wonder what'd happened to you, Red. It's been *years*."

"I've thought about you a couple of times, too," Uncle Red said dryly. With an almost insulting languor, he let his hand fall into Arnspriger's huge outstretched palm for a couple of perfunctory shakes. Uncle Red didn't get up or even take his boot off the table.

The girl with the scouring-pad hair entered the room behind the vast bulk of Durwood Arnspriger to remain unseen there until Arnspriger, with a sudden vicious kick, sent the fallen broom clattering across the floor and barked, "Get this shit out of here. You should've been done in here an hour ago. Get it out!"

The girl scrambled for the broom and dustpan. She banged into a couple of things before she fled through the curtained door with the broom and dustpan clenched in her small fists.

Arnspriger shook his huge head with dismay over the girl and lowered his bulk carefully into a chair. The chair creaked and groaned in protest whenever Arnspriger shifted his weight or made the slightest movement.

"So!" Arnspriger said. "So! Here you are, eh, Red? So what's happened to you, boy? You don't look like you're doing too well. Working you to death, are they? Eh?"

Lighting a cigarette, Uncle Red explained that he was on his way to Nashville for a shot at the Opry. "And I need that hundred bucks you owe me."

Arnspriger wouldn't meet Uncle Red's gaze. He picked up some of the loose poker chips on the green felt table and poured them nervously from one huge hand to the other. "Well, Red! Boy, I sure wish I could help you out. Truth is, though, I haven't got it at the moment. I've had it any number of times since I last saw you, but you didn't leave me any address to send it to, did you, eh? Oh, I made inquiries, all right. I asked around and found out you were somewhere out in California, but I couldn't just send it to 'Red Stovall, California,' could I? Eh? Eh, Red?"

Uncle Red blew a long plume of smoke toward the ceiling. "How much you got?"

"Now? Right now, you mean?"

"Right this minute."

The sound Arnspriger made was a sort of half-snort, half-chuckle, a sound meant to express an embarrassed self-loathing. "Oh, a few dollars. Only a few dollars." And because he had no neck to speak of, but only a fat head sitting upon a fat body, his shrug lifted his huge shoulders almost to the the level of his huge earlobes. "Hey, Red, I'm sorry. I'm really sorry, but . . . well, the Depression, you know. No money anywhere. If somebody would only kill that goddamned Roosevelt . . ." But he saw that line of thought was irrelevant. "How about a drink, Red? Eh? I'll get the girl to bring us—"

"I want the hundred now," Uncle Red said, and there was something in his voice that made me a little wary, even a little afraid.

Arnspriger's voice went up another octave to falsetto. "But, Red! I told you I haven't *got* it."

"Get it."

Sputtering with baffled innocence, Arnspriger said, "But . . . but . . . just like *that?*" He tried to snap his fingers, but they wouldn't snap. "Nobody's got any money these days. A hundred dollars? Ha! Just like *that?*"

"Yeah," Uncle Red said. "Just like that."

Arnspriger became indignant. "Well, I ain't! And I'm surprised at you, Red, questioning my honesty! Is that what you're doing? Eh? Calling me a liar and a cheat?" He seemed to be pushing for an opportunity to get angry, looking for an excuse to throw Uncle Red out without paying him.

But Uncle Red surprised him—surprised me, too, for that matter, although I ought to have known by now not to be surprised at anything Uncle Red did. And what he did was, he slowly took his boot off the table, lowered his chair onto all four legs, dropped his cigarette butt to the floor and mashed it under his boot, and then leaned forward to stare straight into Arnspriger's offended eyes. In that tone of deadly indifference, he said, "Yeah. That's what I'm calling you, Arnspriger, a liar and a cheat. And I can think of a few more things to call you, too. Like a lowdown rotten scumbag sonofabitch. Like a big fat slob of a pigfucking fool. That enough for you? If not, I can think of a few more things."

There was a moment of thunderous silence in the room. And now I knew for sure that Uncle Red was crazy. That man could have picked him up and crushed him with one hand. He could have torn him limb from limb in a matter of minutes. And yet Uncle Red showed not a sign of fear, not the smallest indication that he was anything but totally and contemptuously indifferent to any danger Arnspriger's bulk and strength might pose. It was the audacity of a crazy man. And it was apparently this very craziness, this deadly indifference to violence or its consequences, this audacity of a lunatic, that once again caused his antagonist to back down.

After a moment of totally suspended animation, Arnspriger chuckled nervously. "Oh, come on, Red! You don't mean that! Hell, boy, I'm just trying to get along in this world, same as you are. I'm not out to cheat anybody. Hell, things are bad enough without that, eh? No use getting at each other's throat because times are so hard. That's what I say. What do you say, Red?"

"I say I want the hundred dollars."

Arnspriger seemed amazed that Uncle Red could be so dense. "But, goddammit, Red, don't you understand, boy? I haven't *got* it."

"Get it."

Arnspriger threw up his hands in despair. But in midgesture his hands stopped, and an idea brightened his face. "Wait a minute," he said. "I think I've got it. I think I know how to square it." He made flabby gestures toward the curtained doorway. "That girl? The one that was just in here? I'll tell you what I'll do, Red, I'll let you have her, and we'll call it even. What do you say? Eh?"

Uncle Red obviously didn't know what to say. Like me, he was dumbfounded by what he thought he had just heard. Finally, he cleared his throat and said, "Let me get this straight. You're offering to . . . to *sell* me that girl for the hundred dollars you owe me?"

"You'd be getting a bargain," Arnspriger said. "Hell, I paid a hundred and fifty for her."

After another brief pause, Uncle Red said, "What's the penalty for slavery these days?"

"Oh, slavery!" Arnspriger said disparagingly in his falsetto voice. "What's slavery? Which one of us isn't a slave, eh? In one way or another? Look, I got the kid the same way I'd be giving her to you, to settle a debt. She's an orphan, see? Parents deserted her when she was a little kid, she got sent to live with an uncle who already had six kids of his own and didn't want another mouth to feed. Well, he happened to owe me a hundred and fifty bucks, that uncle did, but he couldn't pay up, so he gave me the girl instead. What's slavery about that? Eh? You'd be doing her a favor, Red, just like I did when I took her out of her uncle's house, where they didn't have anything to eat, day in and day out, except grits and greens, greens and grits. No shoes. Never had a new dress. Would you believe that? Hand-me-downs and leftovers, that's all she ever had. Now, what kind of life is that for a good-looking kid like that? Eh? I ask you."

It bothered me that Uncle Red was beginning to show some interest in the proposition. The cold crazy fury had begun to leave his face, giving way to a sort of sardonic bemusement. The idea seemed to tickle his fancy. "And just what in the hell would I do with her?" he said at last.

"Whatever you want to," Arnspriger said, as if that should be perfectly obvious. "Well, for one thing, you could resell her, if you wanted to. Probably make a tidy profit, too. For a hundred, you're getting a bargain. Oh, I know," he added hastily, "she's not what you'd call really bright, but she's not bad when it comes to cooking and cleaning up. A little clumsy now and then, sure, but . . . talent! Listen, Red, that kid's got talent—musical talent. Plays guitar and sings. Wants to be a star. You could maybe work her into your show, eh? Pretty girl like that? Eh? What do you say?"

Uncle Red said nothing.

"Look, I'll call her down. Let you talk to her yourself. All right?" But seeing that he already had Uncle Red at least half hooked, he didn't wait for an answer. Turning in the creaking chair, he yelled toward the stairway, "Marlene! Get yourself down here!"

And suddenly she was there. She had been standing behind the curtain that covered the doorway, and so she must have overheard everything. It didn't seem to bother her, though. Still as skittish and timorous as a greyhound, she came into the room and stood with her hands clasped behind her back, waiting to see what trick Arnspriger wanted her to perform.

"Marlene, this here's Red Stovall. You ever heard of him? Well, you will. He's a singer, and a damned good one," he added for Uncle Red's benefit. "One of the best."

Marlene's cornflower-blue eyes blinked with sudden excitement, and from that moment on she stared at Uncle Red with awe. That must have been exactly the way I had looked when Uncle Red introduced me to Bob Wills.

"He's on his way to Nashville right now," Arnspriger continued in an unctuous and coddling voice. "How'd you like to go with him? Eh? You'd be a good girl, wouldn't you? If he took you along?"

Marlene was overwhelmed. Unlike me when I met Bob Wills, however, she soon found her voice. "Oh, my goodness!" she said, and pressed her hands against her cheeks as though physically trying to contain the ecstasy that was bursting from her face. "Nashville! That is my heart's dream! Oh, I would do *any*thing to go!"

She talked like that, as if she were reading from a script, or as if she had not only learned the phrases by rote, but had practiced them in front of a mirror. But there was no doubting her sincerity. I had never met anyone in my life who seemed so painfully sincere.

"Well, there you are, then." Arnspriger assumed that the matter had been settled to everyone's satisfaction. "She can have her things packed in a few minutes. Can't you, honey?"

"Oh, yes, I can have my things packed in a few minutes," she parroted. Unlike Arnspriger, however, she hadn't as yet jumped to any conclusions. She was looking intently at Uncle Red for the smallest sign of his assent, and she trembled with hope as she waited.

And what of Uncle Red? How was he responding to all this? I couldn't really tell. He sat there with a look of brooding amusement on his gaunt face, so I knew that this outrageous idea had some sort of cynical appeal for him. Still, I couldn't believe that he would actually, seriously consider taking this girl to Nashville with us. He would have to be crazy to do a thing like that—but, of course, that was precisely what bothered me about it. Maybe he really was just crazy enough to do it.

But when he spoke, after a long and suspenseful pause, he took a load off my mind and revived my faith in his sanity somewhat by saying matter-of-factly, "It won't do, Arnspriger."

Marlene was crestfallen. Crushed. Arnspriger sighed. I sighed, too, but not for the same reason that Arnspriger did.

"Oh, *please,*" Marlene said then, and clasped her hands in front of her like a supplicant. I half expected her to go down on her knees at any second. "Oh, *please* take me with you, Mr. Stovall. I won't be any trouble, I promise you. It would mean *so* much to me. And God will bless you if you do. Oh, you don't know how I've dreamed of going to Nashville and becoming a singing star." Then her blue eyes flashed with a new idea, a new approach. "And I'm good, too," she said with absolute confidence, with an assurance that held not a trace of modesty or humility. But it wasn't vanity, either. It was a sort of astounding innocence. "The Lord has given me a great talent. Just ask anybody who's heard me. They'll tell you. Lots of them say I'm great."

Arnspriger nodded his head in solemn agreement, and with each nod, the folds of fat under his chin squished outward. "She's a great little singer, all right."

Marlene clapped her hands, perhaps applauding herself. "Maybe you'd like to hear me. If you've got your guitar with you, maybe I could borrow it, and, oh, I'd be glad to do it. I'd love for you to hear me sing, Mr. Stovall, for then you'd let me go to Nashville with you. I *know* you would."

"Oh, that won't be necessary, I'm sure," Arnspriger said to her. "He doesn't want to *audition* you, do you, Red?"

But Uncle Red only repeated his former phrase, "It won't do, Arnspriger," and this time his tone was emphatic and final.

Arnspriger conceded defeat with another twist of his massive shoulders.

"Oh, *please!*" Marlene cried. "Please, Mr. Stovall, I beg you, let me go with you."

I was sympathetic to her pleas, of course, because I, too, had had to beg in order to be allowed to go with Uncle Red. But Marlene's begging nearly went beyond the bounds of decency. It was almost shameless, the way she was laying it on.

"Oh, go on, get out of here," Arnspriger said to her, thoroughly disgusted. "He doesn't want you. Isn't that obvious? Maybe now you'll be more grateful that *I* put up with you. Go on, now. Go get us some coffee and doughnuts. You want coffee and doughnuts, Red?"

"All I want from you, Arnspriger, is that hundred dollars."

Arnspriger didn't ask *me* if I wanted any coffee. In fact, he didn't even seem to be aware of my existence. I didn't want any of his coffee anyway, but it made me feel bad that he could simply ignore me as though I were nothing more than an old coat hanging against the wall.

Marlene—cast down, hopelessly despondent—put her hand over her small left breast and said in words that rang with thespic splendor, "My heart is broken."

"Well, your ass is going to be broken, too, if you don't go get that coffee," Arnspriger snapped.

Like an actress making a grand exit from a stage, Marlene crossed to a door in a far corner of the room, a door that led into the kitchen of the Choo-Choo Cafe. She fumbled with the bolt lock for a moment before she got the door open. Sounds of clinking dishes and the heavy smells of frying food came from the cafe.

Arnspriger seemed badgered beyond endurance. He puffed out his cheeks, looked searchingly around the room. "Well, Red, what can I tell you? Eh? I've told you a dozen times I haven't got the money. You don't expect me to shit it, do you?"

"If shit was money, Arnspriger, you'd be a millionaire."

"Now, see here, Red, I'm getting a little tired of this lack of cooperation on your part. I've tried to do right by you, haven't I? Eh? Hell, it's not my fault I don't have the money. I wish I did! And I might have it, too, if only somebody would kill that damned Roosevelt. Hah!" he snorted, as if deriding himself for entertaining such a hopeless dream. "But I'll tell you what I'll do. I'll show you how white I am. I'll fix it so you can make yourself a hundred dollars, maybe more, in no time at all. But that's the best I can do, Red. The very best. Take it or leave it."

After a brief pause, Uncle Red said in a coolly noncommittal voice, "I'm listening."

"Well, the deal is this. I do a little service once in a while for some of my business friends around town, see? Insurance stuff, mostly. If they want something stolen, I make sure it gets stolen. If they have insurance and want to cash in on it, I see that their place gets burned." He shrugged modestly. "Simple. Nothing to it. And I get a small percentage for my troubles, see?"

"You want me to burn somebody out?"

"No, no, no. This job I've got lined up is even easier than that. All you have to do is walk in and pick up some money. It's a setup." He hesitated, searching Uncle Red's face for signs of interest. "Well, what do you say? Interested?"

"Robbery?"

"Well, not *really*, of course. Sure, you have to make it *look* like that, in case there're any witnesses around. The insurance company has to believe it's the real thing, see? But it's a setup. All you got to do is walk into this place and tell the woman that it's a stickup, and she gives you what she's got—maybe a hundred bucks, maybe more—and it's all yours to keep."

Marlene returned from the cafe, empty-handed.

"Well?" Arnspriger asked her. "Where's my coffee and doughnuts?"

"Junior's bringing them," she said in her breathy way, and just before she ducked through the curtain to go upstairs, she turned to give me a forceful stare, and I saw that her eyes were brimming with tears. I couldn't remember her having really looked at me since I came in, but now that oversight was corrected with compensation. The strength of the stare seemed to imply that we understood each other. She seemed to assume that something—our closeness in years, maybe—formed a bond between us, and that I was therefore obligated to help her. To help her do what? Get to Nashville—what else? That was what she was asking me with her teary blue eyes that sparkled like cornflowers splashed with rain: to urge Uncle Red to let her come along with us.

I shook my head, and she understood. She clamped a hand over her mouth and rushed up the stairs, a mournful whine seeping through her fingers.

"What the hell's the matter with you *now?*" Arnspriger shouted after her. "Damn that dingbat girl," he groused to himself. "Sometimes I swear I'd sell her for fifty, I swear I would. Well," he said to Uncle Red, "what d'you say? Is it a deal?"

If Uncle Red wasn't actually interested, he was at least mildly curious. "So what's the woman get out of it?"

"Ah, that's the trick, you see? The robber gets about a hundred dollars, but she tells the insurance company it was *two* hundred. She sometimes has that much on hand after a good weekend, so they'll believe her. And, well, she'll report a few other things missing, too. But that doesn't concern you. As for me, I get my cut when the insurance company pays off. Simple?"

A young man in a wet, greasy apron came through the cafe door, carrying a cup in one hand and a stack of glazed doughnuts in the other. He had a mean, puffy, acne-scarred face and dark, greased-down hair. He dumped the coffee and doughnuts down on the table in front of Arnspriger.

"What kinda place?" Uncle Red asked.

"A cafe. Belongs to a friend of mine, Myrtle Cross." Arnspriger tore a doughnut apart and dunked a chunk of it up and down in his coffee. "Owns Myrtle's Diner, a cafe on the highway west of town." He lowered his head to suck in the soggy part of the doughnut before it dropped into his coffee. It was the first time I had ever seen anyone slurp a doughnut.

The waiter didn't go away. He stood by the table, glancing back and forth from Arnspriger to Uncle Red, nervously wiping his hands on his wet apron, resentful and sullen. His lips moved for a few seconds, as if he were rehearsing something, and then he said, "Myrtle's? But you said I could. You said . . ."

Arnspriger slurped another piece of doughnut. "I know, I know, I know! I said you could do it, but . . ." He turned to Uncle Red. "You see? You see what I'm doing for you, Red? I told Junior here he could have the job. You see what I'm doing for you?" Some coffee spilled over his lip and trickled down his three chins. As he wiped it away with his sleeve, he turned back to Junior. "Look, something's come up and I got to give the job to Red here. But don't worry, now, you'll get the next one."

Junior had been wiping his hands on his apron, but now he was twisting it. "But you said, you said."

"I *know* what I said, Junior, goddammit, and I know what I'm saying now. Do *you*? Now just go back to your work. I'll tell you when I want you again."

Junior gave Uncle Red one last dirty look, turned on his heel, and strode back into the cafe, slamming the door behind him.

Arnspriger cast his eyes toward the ceiling, as if asking God why he had forsaken him. But he quickly found solace in another piece of coffee-dunked doughnut. "The things I have to put up with," he muttered to no one in particular, and then said to Uncle Red in the tone of an ultimatum, "Well, Red?"

"She got a phone?"

Arnspriger looked puzzled. "No. Why?"

"Thought I might phone her, find out if it's on the level."

"Oh, for pity's sake, Red! Why do you think I'd lie to you? I've already incriminated myself, and *I* sure as hell don't want to go to jail. Come on, now, give me a break."

"What if I drove out there and asked her?"

Arnspriger sighed. "If you *must,* then go ahead. But it'd be a dumb thing to do. What if somebody sees you? The cook, for instance. He's not supposed to know it's a setup. What if he sees you, and is able to give the cops a description of you? Come on, now, Red, be reasonable. Trust me a little, like I'm trusting you. I tell you, it's safe all the way around. Everybody gains but the insurance company."

I didn't want to believe that Uncle Red was actually getting serious about robbing somebody. Though "serious" wasn't the right word. He seemed amused by the idea. It tickled his fancy.

"What about a gun?" he asked. "You said it had to look real."

"Don't worry about that," Arnspriger said, reeling him in fast. "I got an old sawed-off shotgun you can use. No shells for it, but, hell, you don't want shells anyway. Don't want any gunplay in this, do we? Just a nice, safe operation. Nobody gets hurt and everybody gets a little something for their troubles. I got the shotgun upstairs. Marlene!" he shouted over his shoulder, the folds of fat under his chin wobbling. "Bring that old shotgun down here. It's on the top shelf of my closet. And don't take all day about it."

"Arnspriger," Uncle Red said, "you 'member that feller I cut up in Claremore that time?"

Arnspriger chuckled nervously. "That rowdy you had the fight with? Do I! Hadn't ever seen a fellow get worked over like that before in my whole life." He hesitated, frowning, "Why?"

"Well," Uncle Red said, "if you're shitting me . . ."

"Oh, for Christ's sake, Red, you think I'm crazy?"

Marlene made her entrance with the shotgun. She held it at

arm's length, cringing from it as if it were a dangerous snake. Arnspriger started to take it from her, but Uncle Red beat him to it. He deftly snatched the shotgun out of her hands and settled back in his chair to look it over.

Marlene looked at me again, this time with a soft, forgiving gaze, and for a moment I thought that hers were the most trusting eyes I had ever seen on a human being.

"Well, what're you standing around for?" Arnspriger asked her.

She hurried away.

Uncle Red broke the shotgun and looked inside it, presumably checking the firing pins, and then he closed the gun on the empty barrels, cocked both hammers and snapped them off. It worked, all right, if that was what he had been wondering about.

"Well, what do you say? Eh?" Arnspriger wanted to know. "I'll get in touch with her and tell her you're coming tonight. Right before closing time, twelve midnight. Wait till the last customers leave, then go in, and she'll give you the money. Right?"

With the sawed-off shotgun lying carelessly across his lap, Uncle Red slowly lifted his foot, put his boot on the edge of the table, and pushed himself backward to balance once again on the chair's back legs. Then he took a long drag from his cigarette and slowly blew the smoke out of his nostrils. "Right," he said.

15

Uncle Red wrapped the shotgun in an old newspaper and carried it out to the trunk of the car. Grandpa was still asleep in the back seat.

"No use for the old man to know 'bout this," Uncle Red said. "We'll go get us a tourist cabin, and he can stay there while we do the job. Then we'll pick him up on the way out of town."

"While *we* do the job?" I said.

"You don't expect *me* to drive the getaway car, do you? I'd probably run into the back of a cop car 'fore I got two blocks."

"Getaway car?" I said, feeling the hairs at the base of my skull begin to prickle. "Uncle Red, you're not really going to go through with this, are you?"

"Why not? You heard the man. It's a setup. Nothing to it."

"You *believe* him?"

Uncle Red scratched his unshaven chin, reflective and cautious. "Yeah. I think so."

"You *think* so!"

"He's too scared of me to be lying now."

When we got into the car, I said, "Uncle Red?"—remembering how he had called Arnspriger, a man at least three times his size, every name in the book and got away with it. *"Why* is he so scared of you?"

"He saw me carve a man up once," he answered, the corners of his lips curling into that sinister little grin.

"Carve a man up? With a . . . a *knife?*"

He shook his head. "Broken bottle. Let's go."

I didn't ask him any more about it. I didn't want to hear about it. I didn't want to imagine Uncle Red carving somebody up with a broken bottle. But as we drove toward the outskirts of town, he volunteered a few more details.

"Happened in a honkytonk in Claremore. Me and the boys was playing there one night. Arnspriger had him a card game going in the back room. Well, there was this drunk come in. Oil-field worker, he was, a roughneck, big bastard, too, spoiling for a fight. I got a hunch Arnspriger give the ole boy a couple of dollars if he'd bust me up a little. Reckon Arnspriger thought I was a wise-ass, wanted to see me get a good drubbing." He chuckled. "Never laid a hand on me."

We found a dusty little rundown tourist court on the eastern outskirts of town and rented a cabin with twin beds. Uncle Red got one of the beds, Grandpa the other, and I made a pallet on the floor. Uncle Red said we were going to be on our way shortly after midnight, so we had better get some sleep.

But I didn't get much, worried as I was. I lay awake on the pallet in the hot still room, listening to a couple of blowflies bumping and buzzing against the dusty windowpanes, brooding over my predicament, panicked with the feeling of being sucked farther and farther into a life of crime and outlawry. Thinking that if Mama knew what I was doing, my God, she would just have a hissy. But what could I do? There was no way I could talk Uncle Red out of it, and I certainly couldn't tie him down hand and foot. And since I had promised Mama I would look after him, I couldn't let him go rob somebody alone. So I finally resigned myself to it, hoping to God that he knew what he was doing.

Late that afternoon, Uncle Red roused me from the pallet and had me drive him downtown so he could buy us some hamburgers and milkshakes for dinner.

"First, though," he said after we got downtown, "let's try to rustle up a bootlegger. I need a bottle."

In what was at least a token attempt to honor my promise to Mama, I tried to think of some way to talk Uncle Red out of getting the whiskey. But how to appeal to him? I couldn't nag, plead, demand, preach, or wheedle, of course, because his most likely response to such tactics would be a dirty look, if not something worse. So I decided that the only thing to do was to approach the subject on a sort of intelligent man-to-man basis.

"Uncle Red," I said, trying to sound thoughtful, "you ever think that maybe you got a drinking problem?"

"Sure do," he said. "I'm thirsty as a hound dog in hell."

"Hmmmmm. Well, I mean, don't you think you might need some help with your drinking?"

"Hell, no. I do just fine by myself."

"Hmmmmm. I mean, ain't there doctors who—"

"Look, Hoss, let's get one thing straight. If you wanna be my driver and sidekick, we got us a deal. But you got to knock off that nursemaid stuff. When I want a nursemaid, I'll get one a lot prettier'n you are, one that wears skirts and has tits out to here."

When we located a bootlegger in the back of a poolroom, Uncle Red bought two pint bottles of whiskey. "Now let's go out and take a look at Myrtle's Diner. Just drive by, is all," he added after I gave him a disapproving glance.

We found the place on the western outskirts of town. It was a tourists' and truckers' cafe, set off by itself, a place with big bay windows and a parking lot. We drove by slowly a couple of times, and then Uncle Red said, "Okay, let's go get them hamburgers."

We didn't get them at Myrtle's Diner. That's what I feared Uncle Red was going to suggest, since it would appeal to his sense of humor, but apparently the idea didn't occur to him. We got the hamburgers and milkshakes at a small cafe downtown and took them back to the tourist cabin.

Uncle Red had told Grandpa earlier that he was going to play and sing at some honkytonk in Tulsa that night, which was the reason that we couldn't get on the road until about midnight.

"We'll pick you up here soon's the gig's done," he told Grandpa. And even though he was lying to Grandpa, he was respectful and polite to him, calling him "Mr. Wagoner," and never playing him for a fool. "You be ready to go as soon as we get here, all right? And then we'll be on our way to Tennessee 'fore you can say Jack Robinson."

Grandpa apparently had no suspicions that Uncle Red was lying. In fact, he seemed a little hurt that he hadn't been asked to go along and listen to the music. But he had too much pride to invite himself along, so we left him there in the tourist cabin reading a Gideon Bible.

To make Uncle Red's lie plausible, however, we had to leave the cabin about eight o'clock, and that left us with four hours to kill—although I certainly would not have used that expression at the time.

"Tell you what," Uncle Red suggested. He was feeling pretty good from the drinks he had. "Let's make this *your* night, Hoss. As a token of my appreciation for your grit, I'll treat you to anything you want to do tonight. Big steak? It's on me. A movie? Name it. Or what about a whorehouse?" He chuckled. "You ever had a piece of ass? I mean, besides cows and sheep and that sorta thing?" He reached over and gave me a comradely punch on the shoulder. "Hell, don't I know? I was a farm boy myself." He took another shot from the bottle. "How 'bout that, Hoss? Get you a big fat whore, turn you every which way but loose. Whoooo-eee! Hell, come on. And while we're there, I might see something I like, too. Hell, I'm hot to trot. Look out, girls, here we come!" He sang, "Two ding-dong daddies from Dumas, honey, and you gonna see us do our stuff!"

I could feel myself blushing, feel my head spinning, feel my mouth getting cottony dry. My throat was constricted, my heart was pounding, and I was conscious of having a silly grin plastered on my face that I couldn't make go away. A whorehouse? The idea scared the living daylights out of me. And on top of that, Uncle Red's remarks were very embarrassing. But what embarrassed me more was that big silly grin that wouldn't leave my face.

"Up here 'bout three blocks, you take a right turn," Uncle Red said. "Couple miles outa town. Best cathouse in Oklahoma."

"Oh, no, I couldn't . . . I mean, I could never—"

"The hell you can't," he declared. "Got to be a first time for everything, and your time for a woman has come, Hoss. Make a man outa you. Tomorrow you'll wake up with hair on your chest. Turn right here."

In addition to all my other symptoms of panic, I had broken out into a cold sweat by the time we got to the whorehouse. It was an old farmhouse hidden in a grove of mulberry trees. Every light in the house seemed to be on, including a very bright porch light, and there were a few cars and pickups parked in the yard.

"Uncle Red," I pleaded, "I . . . I can't . . ."

"Bullshit. Come on."

My legs wobbled a little as I followed Uncle Red up to the front door of the whorehouse. *Whorehouse*. Was I really there, getting ready to go into a real, honest-to-God *whorehouse?* Where there were women—grown-up women, with tits and everything—who, for a sum of money, would let you *do it* to them? Actually *do it?* A queasy, fainting feeling was beginning to radiate out from my belly, and I must have been running a temperature of a hundred and two.

I was standing half hidden behind Uncle Red when the door suddenly opened and there she was, the first real live whore I had ever seen. She was dressed in some sort of fluffy gown, and from the room behind her wafted the most thrilling effluvium of fleshy musk and exotic perfume that I had ever smelled in my life, the cloying odor of crushed magnolia blossoms, of sweet desires now decayed.

Uncle Red said, "Howdy. Glad to see you're still open. I used to come here a few years ago. Was a big red-headed gal here then, name of Sylvia, I think. She still here?"

"Nobody here by that name," the woman said, looking Uncle Red over. "But they come and go, the girls do." She darted a couple of curious glances at me, but she kept going back to Uncle Red with crafty, probing eyes. She was an overripe middle-aged woman with wrinkles and graying hair. She was the whorehouse madam, but I didn't know that at the time. I didn't even know what a madam was. I knew for a dead certain fact, however, that I wasn't going to *do it* with *her*.

"Well, the thing is, you see," Uncle Red said in a confidential undertone, as if trying not to be overheard by eavesdroppers who might be lurking about. "The thing is, this boy here . . . my son . . . well, I brought him here to get him bred. He's sixteen years old and still a virgin, and I'm getting worried 'bout him. Figured it was high time he had a woman, 'stead of all them . . . well, he's a farm boy, you see? You know what they do, I reckon? And this Sylvia, now, was just what he needs."

"We don't take no kids here, cowboy," she said. "Got enough trouble with the law as it is. Can't afford to get charged with contributing to the delinquency of a minor."

But her tone wasn't adamant, so Uncle Red said, "Oh, come on. Hell, I'm the kid's father, ain't I? I'll take full responsibility."

"Well . . ." She still wasn't persuaded, not by a long shot, but she relented enough to step aside and let us come in.

We stepped into a small parlor crowded with overstuffed chairs and coffee tables and fringed lamps. There were reproductions of naughty paintings on the walls. One was a picture of beautiful naked girls trailing long gossamer scarves in the breeze as they gamboled lightly through a scene of bright flowers and dark brooding trees, pursued by a gang of lewdly grinning, goat-legged little satyrs. Somebody was playing a piano in the next room.

Once the door was closed behind us, a sound that had the ring of a fatal thud, the madam took a good look at me. "Why, this boy's not sixteen."

"Sure he is. Just a little short for his age, is all."

"And you're not old enough to have a sixteen-year-old son."

"I was a child groom," Uncle Red said. "Anyway, what difference does it make? Hell, if he's old enough to diddle farm animals, he's old enough to do it to a woman, ain't he?"

In a desperate effort to find some distraction from this terrible conversation, which was near to making me faint, I turned toward the piano. The sliding double doors between the parlor and the piano room were about half open, and when I looked through the space between the doors and into that room, I saw something that stunned me.

I saw a woman sitting at the piano. She was wearing black fluffy open-heeled house shoes. Her sleek legs—one crossed over the other, with the dangled foot languidly keeping time to the music, the open-heeled shoe flopping around on her dainty foot—were encased in black mesh stockings. She wore a black chiffon nightie, a garment so thin that I could see her lacy black brassiere and panties. Her hair, dark and straight, was cut in a pageboy bob. Her eyebrows were two thin penciled lines. The white powder she wore on her face made it seem carved from alabaster, all except for her lips, which were a luscious red, a thick sticky red, like waxen rose petals.

She was the most beautiful woman I had ever seen. As Uncle Red and the madam talked on, I stood and stared at this lovely phantomlike lady playing languidly upon the piano— hitting a few false notes now and then, it was true, but always quick to correct them. A cigarette dangled from one corner of her mouth, causing her to squint one eye against the upcurling smoke.

"No," the madam was saying to Uncle Red. "He's just too young. None of the girls would take him."

"Hell, I said I'd take full responsibility, didn't I?"

Then the woman at the piano looked at me. "What're you staring at, kid?" she asked me, taking the cigarette from her red lips and dropping it onto an ashtray on top of the piano. The question had been asked as a reminder to me that it was rude to stare at people. She resumed playing, but she kept looking at me, waiting for an answer.

"You," I finally croaked.

"Why you staring at me?"

I hesitated for a moment. "'Cause you're beautiful," I whispered.

The last note she played was an off-key one, but she held the note as long as its resonance could be heard, and she looked at me. She kept looking into my eyes as the plaintive note faded into silence, and now there was in her dark eyes a glimmer of something sad and remote. Then her red lips curled into a soft smile and she said, "You're kinda cute, too."

I was in love. There was no other word for it, no other word that would even come close to describing the tender emotion that burst from my heart at that moment. No other word but *love*.

"But it wouldn't be you or the boy that'd get arrested if the cops come," the madam was saying to Uncle Red. "It's the girl with him, that's who'd get arrested. Besides me, of course. And that's why won't none of 'em take him."

The woman slowly got up from the piano stool and walked toward me. She stopped within arm's reach of me and looked at me for another few seconds before she said, "Miss Maude?"

The madam turned toward her. "Yes, Belle?"

"I'll take him."

"Well, it's your risk, I guess," the madam said skeptically, as if it were still against her better judgment. "That'll be two dollars, then, if you want a girl, too," she said to Uncle Red.

"Hell, yes," Uncle Red said. "You got any good-looking girls 'round here that's built for comfort?"

The woman—*Belle!* The name rang like a bell in my heart— reached out and brushed a strand of hair from my forehead. "Hi," she said.

I started to say "Hi," but that didn't sound quite grown-up enough, so I decided to substitute "Hello," but before I quite got it out of my mouth, it occurred to me that a more formal "How do you do?" would probably be better still—with the result that all the words got tangled up together, and came out as a greeting that was more unrecognizable than an Eskimo's: "Hilodedo." I could have cut my tongue off.

But Belle didn't laugh at me. I wouldn't have blamed her if she had, but she only smiled, obviously aware of how nervous I was. "Want to come with me?"

"Go on, Hoss," Uncle Red brayed. "Get your ashes hauled."

I wasn't quite sure of everything that happened after that. I was aware that Belle took me by the hand and led me down a dim hallway. I was aware (because I searched desperately for something on which to focus, so that I would stop staring at the hypnotic undulations of her hips as she walked) of a primrose pattern in the hallway rug. I was aware that we met a man and woman coming out of a room, and the woman said, "What're you doing, Belle?—robbing the cradle?"

"Shut up," Belle said in a harsh but unbelligerent voice.

There was a room that smelled of perfume and decay. There was a bed with a wrought-iron bedstead. Belle helped me undress. She got down on her knees to untie my shoes. I wanted to touch her dark sleek hair as she knelt there in front of me, but I didn't.

"Now we'll just wash you a little," she said. "All right? Little warm soapy water, is all."

There was a washbasin in one corner of the room. From its spigot she drew a pan of warm water, stirred some soap into it, picked up a towel from a stack of neatly folded towels on her dresser, and brought them to me. I was only dimly aware of her washing me, bending over and holding the pan below my groin to catch the warm streams of water.

"Oh, my goodness," she said, tenderly, admiringly. "It sticks right up there, don't it? Well, we'll just dry you off a little now, and I'll hurry and get undressed." And when the drying was done, she tossed the towel into a receptacle next to the dresser. "Now, honey, you just go on over there and lay down, and I'll be right with you."

I was aware of lying down on the bed. I was aware that every muscle in my body, from my curled-up toes to my tingling scalp, was as stiff and as throbbing as a lightning rod in an electrical storm. But it was her body, not mine, that I was most aware of. As I watched her slip the gauzy frock from off her shoulders, as I saw her reach back to unhook the black lacy brassiere and take it off, revealing her huge purple-nippled breasts, and then watched her bend over to slip her black panties off—as I watched these movements, I felt that ecstasy within me bust like a shuddering volcano, spewing out the hot lava of my love. . . . Well, it didn't really *spew* out. Actually, it just sort of dribbled out. But it sure *felt* like a volcano.

"Oh, my goodness," Belle said again. "Oh, my goodness, it just couldn't wait, could it?" She got another towel and wiped me off.

I was mortified. My first opportunity to *do it* with a woman— and not just any woman, either, but a beautiful woman whom I loved!—and I flubbed it. If I hadn't enjoyed it so much, I would have sulked.

All was not lost, however. Belle, beautiful Belle, knew what to do. She washed me again, and then pulled me onto the bed. "That's right," she coaxed. "Come on. Come right up here. That's it. Oh, my goodness," she said, reaching down to help me, and then I was *doing it* to her. I! Whit Wagoner! *Doing it* to a real live beautiful willing soft coaxing gushy warm sweet-smelling tender woman!

"Oooooh, slow down a little, honey," she coaxed, gazing up at me with those beautiful dark eyes. "It's like an ice-cream cone, you want to make it last as long as you can."

Ice cream, hell! It was better than any ice cream *I* had ever had! Better than a thousand ice-cream cones! A million! She was right about one thing, though: it didn't take very long. But I didn't care about that. I was so overloaded with feeling that I would have blown out like an overloaded fuse in another minute. In fact, I *did* blow out, with a sizzling feeling that began at the very tips of my toes and slowly worked its way up my legs, straining every fiber of my body to the point of convulsion, and then exploding in my groin like fireworks. And with a squeal like that of a stuck pig, I collapsed.

"Oh, my goodness, you do have strong ones, don't you?" Belle said, hugging my spent and rag-limp body to hers, and I lay there savoring the realization that this was the happiest day of my life.

"We have to go now, honey," Belle said. While we were dressing, she came over to brush the strand of hair off my forehead again. "Well, honey, how'd you like it?"

I couldn't answer.

"What's the matter? Cat got your tongue?"

No. It was because there was something in me that didn't want to talk about it in ordinary words. The only words I could speak to her were those that described the profoundest feeling my heart had ever felt.

"I love you," I said.

I saw her fight back a smile, and then she looked at me for a long moment with eyes that had gone a little out of focus. Placing the palm of her hand feather-soft against my cheek, she said, "You're a sweet boy."

She said it sweetly, but I wished she hadn't called me a boy. Not after what I had just done to her. However, she obviously meant it as a term of endearment, not of derision, so it was all right.

"Come on, now, 'fore Miss Maude charges you overtime."

We went down the hallway this time without holding hands, and she left me in the lobby with only a small, quick smile and a wink. "Come back and see me sometime, honey," she said to me, and then to the madam, "Gonna get a bite to eat now, Miss Maude. Tell any customers who want me, they'll just have to wait."

"All right, but don't take too long," Miss Maude said. She was standing with a big florid-faced man in a business suit.

I stood and watched Belle disappear down the hallway, and I might have stood there until she appeared again, but I soon felt Miss Maude's eyes boring into me. I darted a sheepish glance at her.

"Well, boy?" she jibed. "Was it better'n them farm animals?"

She and the man with her laughed. I blushed furiously and rushed out the door. I didn't want my feeling for Belle besmirched by such comments. I wanted to keep the wonderful feeling I had of being in love. I wanted to romp in the moonlight, swing from a limb, roll around in deep green grass, sing a song to the stars. I was in love! And she had asked me to come back and see her, and I knew I would. I would come back here someday and ask her to marry me, that's what I would do! I would marry her and take her away from here and she wouldn't be a whore anymore and we'd have babies.

Well, why not? Stranger things had happened. I had once heard of an eighty-year-old woman marrying a twenty-year-old man. And I had heard about lots of old men who married young girls. And I was probably at least half Belle's age. So why not?

When Uncle Red came out and got into the car, he said, "Well, Hoss, how'd you like it?"

I busied myself with starting the car and getting it turned around in the yard so I wouldn't have to answer him. But he soon asked me again, and I was feeling so good that I had to say something, make some sound, or burst, so I said, "Hee hee hee."

"Yeah," he said. "That's the way I felt when I got laid the first time, too. Big old homely girl, she was, built like a brick shithouse. Lived down the road a ways from our place. Get you in a haystack quicker'n you could blink an eye, and whooooo doggies, but that homely gal could shake that thing! Shake a whole haystack right down around your ears."

I started to ask him if he had loved her, but that didn't seem quite right somehow, so I asked him instead if she had been his girl.

"She was anybody's girl who wanted her. If she'd had as many pricks sticking *out* a her as she'd had stuck *in,* she woulda looked like a porcupine. Married an old boy down El Reno, and he shot her six months later. Caught her in the haystack with the hired hand once too often, I reckon. Pull into the first gas station you come to. Let's fill this sucker up."

I missed two gas stations because I wasn't watching where I was going. I pulled into the third one, though, because Uncle Red called my attention to it. After we'd filled up with gas and oil, Uncle Red offered to buy me a hamburger.

"You must be famished after all that exercise you got tonight," he said.

"Hee hee," I said.

But for the first time in my life, I ate a whole hamburger without tasting a bite of it. I hardly knew I was eating it, my head was still so full of Belle, beautiful Belle, and every time I thought of her I became goosebumpy and a little giddy.

"What's the matter with you?" Uncle Red said, snapping his fingers in front of my unfocused eyes. "You been mooning around like a lovesick puppy ever since you got outa that whorehouse. What'd you do, fall in love with that whore?"

I crammed my mouth full of hamburger so I wouldn't have to answer him. He really didn't expect an answer, though. He was just kidding.

"Uncle Red," I said, gulping down the last of the hamburger, "have you ever . . ." I faltered. I was going to ask him if he had ever been in love, but I couldn't do it.

"Have I ever what?"

"Nothing."

"Look here, Hoss, you better snap out of it. You got some driving to do tonight."

And that little reminder was all I needed to snap me out of it. In the throes of first love, I had nearly forgotten about what we had to do tonight down at Myrtle's Diner. So I switched from giddiness to glumness in a matter of seconds, and the glumness got progressively worse as midnight neared, until finally, as we were approaching Myrtle's Diner, I was downright depressed. Not to say scared.

16

"Uncle Red, are you sure you—"

"Go up and make a U-turn, come back and park on the other side of the street."

We parked in some shadows across the street from the diner. Now and then a car whizzed by on the highway, and there were a few customers still left in the diner, but other than that, the whole area seemed quietly asleep. Scattered houses loomed as dark shadows in weedy lots set back from the highway, but there were no lights in any of them. And there were only a few cars parked along the curb—all parked parallel, for which I was thankful, since it meant that we wouldn't have to back the car out of a parking place before we took off.

We sat in the dark car for a few minutes and looked across the highway at the diner, watching to see the last customers leave. The diner's big bay windows and interior lights allowed us to see everyone in the dining room, including the lone waitress, presumably Myrtle herself, a big pursy-gut woman who looked as if she was more used to giving orders than taking them. She seemed to be hurrying the last two customers out of the place, but they—two men in grease-smeared clothes, maybe oil-field workers—were in no hurry to go. Finally, though, they left, and after they got into a pickup and drove away, Uncle Red said, "Well, I reckon now's the time. Keep the motor running."

"Be careful," I whispered.

"Don't worry. It'll be easy as falling off a log."

He got out and went around to the trunk and took the shotgun out, and, looking both ways to make sure no cars were coming along the highway, he hurried across to the diner. I started the engine and let it idle.

He held the shotgun hidden behind his right leg as he flung the door open like some cocky cowboy out of a movie and stood there in the doorway, waiting for her to notice him. Myrtle was busy wiping the counter and tidying up, and apparently didn't notice the shotgun at first. I saw her look up and say something to him, something short and snappy, like "We're closed." Then Uncle Red, as friendly as you please, walked on into the place, leaving the door open, and said, "Howdy," as he lifted the shotgun to show Myrtle why he was there.

Myrtle's mouth dropped open, her eyes widened, and she froze for a moment, as if she were suddenly staring death itself in the face. But only for a moment; before Uncle Red could even approach her, she panicked. She threw up her hands and screamed as she whirled and made a mad dash for the kitchen. She knocked a whole tray of glasses off a counter as she shot through the kitchen door, leaving behind her the sound of breaking glass.

"Hey!" I heard Uncle Red shout. "Wait a minute! It's me! I'm the man who's supposed to . . ." But he couldn't stand there and yell that he was the man who was supposed to rob her, so he walked over to the counter and pushed the service bell. "Hello?" *Ding ding.* "Hey, it's me!" But that got no response either. "Oh, for Christ's sake, it's me!" he finally shouted. "Arnspriger sent me!"

But by then Myrtle wasn't even in the building. From where I sat, I could see the side of the building that bordered a vacant lot, and from it, through a back door, Myrtle and two other figures suddenly emerged. The two figures following her were both men, one in a white cook's uniform, the other in a dishwasher's apron, and they were apparently even more frightened than Myrtle was. One of them—the dishwasher—took off fast across the dark vacant lot, and the cook started to follow, but he was an old man and didn't even get started before Myrtle reached out and grabbed him. She gestured for him to follow her. It was then that I saw that she was carrying a big pistol.

Uncle Red, at a loss as to what to do, turned and looked in my direction. Since I was in deep shadows inside the car, I wasn't sure that he could see me, but I waved frantically for him to come back, while Myrtle, with that big pistol in her hand and the cook following close behind her, tiptoed along the side of the building toward the front of the place.

Meanwhile, Uncle Red ambled toward the open front door, stopped, looked across the street at me and shrugged elaborately, as if to say, "What the hell do I do now?"

Now I was motioning wildly toward the corner of the building, stupidly and desperately making a pistol of my hand, trying to warn him, but my signals only seemed to puzzle him more. However, he did get the idea that something was going on around the side of the building, so he sidled cautiously over to the corner.

"Oh, my God," I moaned aloud. I wanted to honk the horn, or yell, or do something to warn Uncle Red, not just about Myrtle's approach, but about the pistol she carried. Before I could think of anything, however, Myrtle had reached the corner, and maybe Uncle Red finally sensed the danger, for, approaching the corner, he raised the shotgun. He raised it so that the shotgun's double-barreled muzzle was exactly at eye level and flush with the corner of the building, and when Myrtle leaned forward to take a cautious peek around the corner, she found herself looking straight down the two black barrels of the shotgun.

She jumped back, screamed, fired the pistol, and threw up her hands, all simultaneously. The bullet made a long *whang* as it splattered into the gravel of the parking lot, kicking up a little spurt of dust, and ricocheted off into the distance. The pistol flew out of her upflung hand with such force that it landed in the vacant lot maybe twenty feet behind her. And she *screamed*. I had never heard anything like it. She evidently assumed that she had been shot. With her hands wildly flapping above her head, she began a sort of St. Vitus's dance, and she kept screaming.

The cook had turned and fled across the vacant lot as soon as Myrtle screamed and fired the pistol. And as soon as I recovered from the sound of the shot and the sight of the flames spurting from the pistol, I leaped from the car and started to dash across the highway to see if Uncle Red had been hit. But I stopped when I saw him examining himself for wounds.

"You dumb bitch!" he shouted. "You almost shot me!"

But Myrtle *didn't* seem to hear him—probably didn't even see him. She just screamed on and on, flapping her hands above her head.

"For Christ's sake, shut up, will you?" Uncle Red shouted. "I'm the guy that's supposed to . . . Look! Arnspriger sent me! You hear me? Arnspriger! Shut up, will you? You gonna wake up the whole neighborhood. Look," he said, breaking the breech of the shotgun to show her there were no shells in it. "For Christ's sake, I'm not gonna shoot you! It's not even loaded!"

But the only time the screaming stopped was when she had to suck in a breath.

"Come on!" I yelled to Uncle Red from the edge of the highway. I could see lights going on in houses all over the neighborhood. "Let's go!"

"Good God!" Uncle Red said in disgust. He started shambling back toward the car, leaving Myrtle to stand there and scream her head off.

"Hurry!" I shouted.

He trotted the rest of the way to the car, and as soon as he was in, I released the clutch and stamped on the accelerator and the car leaped onto the highway, the spinning rear tires squealing so loudly that they almost obscured Myrtle's continuing screams.

"You ever heard anything like that in your life?" Uncle Red asked as we zoomed off down the highway. He was still speaking in a voice of profound disgust, but now there was amazement, too. "Good God! They ought to tie her on the front of a train to scream when it comes to railroad crossings. That shriek would put a train whistle to shame."

In order not to attract attention from any passing cop cars, I slowed down to a normal speed when we were out of sight of the diner. After a while I took a deep breath and said in a surprisingly angry voice, "You almost got yourself killed!"

"Just about," he conceded. "I could feel the wind from that bullet. Wheeee-ew! Wonder what went wrong? That sonofabitch Arnspriger . . ."

"So *now* what're we going to do?" I said. I meant it more as a reproach than a question. I wanted him to realize what a terrible predicament Arnspriger's "setup" had gotten us into. Not only were we without the hundred dollars or more that he was supposed to get from Myrtle's Diner, we had spent most of Grandpa's remaining money on a tourist cabin, booze, whores and hamburgers. Not that I begrudged the dollar that Belle had cost. But it didn't change the fact that we had been left without enough money to get us to the Arkansas line, let alone Nashville. And while that was bad enough, Uncle Red had almost got himself killed in the bargain. "Some setup!" I sneered.

"Yeah," he said. "Let's go see Arnspriger, that sonofabitch. . . ."

"What? What're you gonna do?"

"Gonna get that money he owes me."

"But that'll just mean more trouble, won't it? Why don't we just—"

"Goddammit," he snapped, "do what I tell you! If you're with me, you're with me, goddammit, and if you ain't, get out and walk!" He was feverish and angry, frustrated and full of fight, and I was more afraid of his wrath than I was of Arnspriger's treachery, so I drove to Arnspriger's place. I parked in the back alley near the door of the card room. I was going to wait in the car and sulk, but when Uncle Red got out of the car with the shotgun, he said, "Come on. I 'spect he's got a poker game going on in there, and I might need you."

So I followed him. I didn't stop sulking, however. As I hung behind him, we could hear voices coming from inside the card room—mumbled bits of conversation and laughter— but we couldn't go in because the door was locked. Uncle Red knocked, and in a moment a voice asked from the other side, "Who's there?" It was a male voice, but not Arnspriger's.

Uncle Red leaned down and whispered to me, "Tell 'im it's Western Union, a telegram."

I said, "West . . ." but my voice caught in my throat and I had to start over. "Western Union telegram for . . . for Arnspriger."

It was Junior who opened the door, and he seemed rather startled to find a double-barreled shotgun sticking in his belly. He threw up his hands, and when Uncle Red nudged him back into the room, he quickly complied. Then Uncle Red, holding the shotgun at hip level, turned the muzzle on the men who sat around the card table.

There were four of them, including Arnspriger. They had cards in their hands and piles of poker chips in front of them, and they had been a jolly bunch until they saw the shotgun leveled at them. Then they froze. One had been in the act of counting his chips, another had been lighting a cigar, another sipping a drink, but they all froze like a group of ground squirrels who have just seen the shadow of a hawk.

"Sit still, gentlemen," Uncle Red said in what seemed to be a casual and almost carefree voice. "Keep your hands on the table in front of you. You," he said to Junior, "go over there and sit down." He jerked his head toward a stool near the curtained door to the stairway. Again Junior complied readily enough, but he kept nervously glancing toward Arnspriger as if looking for a signal of some sort.

And Arnspriger, bug-eyed with wonder, sputtered in his nervous falsetto, "What . . . what is it Red? Eh? What the hell . . . ?"

Without looking at me, Uncle Red said, "Lock the doors, Hoss," and I hurriedly fumbled the bolt lock into place on the side door. The door leading to the cafe was already bolted.

"You sonofabitch, you almost got me killed tonight," Uncle Red said to Arnspriger.

"What?" Bubbles of spittle formed at the corners of Arnspriger's flabby mouth. "Red, I . . . I . . ."

"You didn't tell her I was coming," Uncle Red said. "That crazy bitch almost shot me."

"But . . . but . . . but of course I did!" Arnspriger protested. "Well, I mean, I didn't personally. I had this game going, couldn't leave, but I sent word. That's a fact. I sent word. Told her to expect you." He fell silent and sort of nodded toward the other card players, as if to say that he didn't want to be too specific in front of them. "For Christ's sake, Red, use your head. What would I get out of doublecrossing you?"

"Oh, I don't think you doublecrossed me. I think you just fucked up and almost got me killed. How'd you send word to her?"

Arnspriger turned to look at Junior. "I sent . . . didn't you do it?"

Shifty-eyed and obviously lying, Junior said, "I . . . I sent somebody else."

"I sent Junior to tell her. I swear I did," Arnspriger said to Uncle Red.

"Did you now?" Uncle Red said. "Well, I tell you what, I believe you. I believe you're an honest man, wouldn't cheat anybody—"

"That's right, Red. That's right. You know me, Red."

"So I tell you what you gonna do," Uncle Red said, pointing

the muzzle of the shotgun directly at Arnspriger's face. "You gonna pay me that hundred dollars you owe me, and since you're a fair and honest man, I'm gonna collect another hundred for the trouble I went through tonight of almost getting myself killed on account of your boy here. So that'll be two hundred dollars altogether. Now. Right now."

Three or four *hah hah hah* sounds escaped from Arnspriger's mouth, but they could hardly be called a chuckle. "Well, in the first place, Red, I haven't got it. Like I told you. And in the second place . . . *hah hah* . . . I don't think you got any shells in that shotgun."

Uncle Red stared at Arnspriger for a long moment in utter silence. You could hear Arnspriger breathing. Then Uncle Red said in a small, frigid, goading voice, "Wanna bet?"

And the wonder of it was, he seemed to be amused— *amused*—by the fact that the gun didn't have any shells in it. For a moment that small vicious smile flickered over his lips as he continued staring at Arnspriger, that smug smile of someone who has a secret that he isn't going to tell.

"Hah hah . . . oh, well," Arnspriger said then, as if he would just as soon pass up that bet. "But the fact is, I don't have two hundred dollars. Don't even have a hundred. See?" He gestured toward the poker chips in front of him on the table. There was a cigar box on his left that he was trying to conceal with his forearm.

"How much you figure you got there?"

Arnspriger nervously ran his huge fingers over the chips. "Oh . . . fifty-sixty dollars, maybe."

"Open the cigar box," Uncle Red ordered.

Arnspriger was appalled. "What? Listen, Red, that's not all my money, that's the bank."

Uncle Red moved around behind Arnspriger's chair. He put the muzzle of the shotgun against the base of Arnspriger's skull. "Hand the box to the boy there," he said. "Hoss, see if it's got two hundred in it."

I couldn't move. I couldn't speak, either, or I would have warned Uncle Red that Junior looked as if he was getting ready to jump him. Probably the only reason he didn't was that Uncle Red had that shotgun to Arnspriger's head and Junior was aware that any violent movement on his part might cause Uncle Red to pull the trigger.

"You'll never get away with this, cowboy," one of the ca

players warned. He was a man in his middle forties, wearing a white Stetson hat and an expensive suit. He looked as though he might be a prosperous rancher, or something like that, tough and half drunk and full of authority.

Ignoring the rancher's remark, Uncle Red announced to the card players that he wasn't taking their money. "Arnspriger is," he said. "He's gonna borrow some money from each of you, and he's gonna give you his IOU for every penny he borrows. Ain't you, Arnspriger?" He nudged Arnspriger's head with the shotgun.

"Red, this is robbery," Arnspriger sputtered. "You know that, don't you?"

"Might be worse than robbery if you don't hand that box to my boy there."

Arnspriger jerked the box off the table and thrust it toward me.

"Hoss," Uncle Red said quietly, and I moved—or at least I was aware that I was moving. There seemed no conscious will in the movement, however, and I was jerky and stiff, as if I were a puppet. I snatched the box from Arnspriger's outstretched hand and jumped back.

"Now take out . . . what'd you say you had there, Arnspriger? Sixty? Take out sixty dollars for Arnspriger."

I set the cigar box on the seat of an empty chair, flipped it open, and stared at the money. There must have been at least three or four hundred dollars in it.

After I counted out sixty dollars, Uncle Red pulled the shotgun away from Arnspriger's head, and the moment he did, Junior bunched his muscles as if to spring. But Uncle Red stepped away from him, out of reach, and Junior aborted the spring. He chewed his lip, rubbed his palms against his thighs and glared at Uncle Red.

Uncle Red began sort of stalking around the table, giving appraising looks at the piles of chips on the table in front of each player. The first player he stopped behind was the one who, with the possible exception of Arnspriger, was the most frightened. He looked like a grocery-store owner.

"Take out fifty dollars for this man," Uncle Red told me. "And you," he said to Arnspriger, "you take that pencil and pad there and write him out an IOU for fifty dollars."

Arnspriger reached for the scratch pad and pencil at his elbow, but suddenly flared up with a sort of last-ditch defiance.

"See here, Red, this's going too far! You may not realize it, but I pay protection to the cops in this town, and—"

"Do it!" snapped the grocery-store owner. His bumpy face was hotly flushed and his rimless eyeglasses had begun to fog over. "Don't be a damned fool! Do it!" His bottom lip trembled as if he were about to cry.

Arnspriger did it. And while he was doing it, Uncle Red stalked around the table some more. Once he came dangerously close to Junior, who once again leaned forward on the stool and tensed his muscles as if preparing to spring, but once again Uncle Red stopped just out of striking distance and reversed his direction around the table, leaving Junior to sit there on that stool and quiver like a coiled snake.

This time Uncle Red stopped behind the third card player, an old man who looked as if he were gambling with his pension money.

"This's all the money I got," the old man said, and slapped his palms down on his chips as though to keep Uncle Red from snatching them away.

"You come to a hell of a place to spend it, Pops," Uncle Red said.

The rancher spoke again, his voice a little cocky, even a little disdainful. "You'll never get away with this, cowboy. You know who I am?"

"Yeah," Arnspriger said. "You know who he is? Eh?"

"Sure," Uncle Red said. "You're the man with all the chips." He stalked around the table to stand beside the rancher, and once again he stopped just out of Junior's striking distance. He must have been aware of the danger. It was as if he were teasing a coiled rattlesnake.

He put the muzzle of the gun to the back of the rancher's head and, in an insolent little gesture, used the gun to tip the rancher's Stetson forward so that it was almost over his eyes. It seemed to me to be a needless humiliation. The man was close enough to an explosion as it was, and he would be dangerous if he did explode. But Uncle Red didn't seem too worried.

"Take the other ninety out of this man's money," he said. "Write him an IOU, Arnspriger."

As the rancher was swallowing his pride and I was counting out the money and Arnspriger was writing out the IOU, we suddenly heard footsteps descending the stairs. Marlene jerked the curtain back.

"Did you...?" She faltered when she saw the shotgun. Gargling a few *ah ah ah* sounds of panic, she whirled and dashed back up the stairs.

"Ah," Arnspriger said. "She'll go get the cops now. There's a back stairs to the living quarters. She'll get the cops. Too bad for you, Red. It's not too late, though, to back out of this. We won't prosecute, if you stop now—will we, men? Eh? No, sir. We'll forget all about it."

Uncle Red seemed curious to push back the curtain and take a peek up the stairs, so he held the shotgun high and wide to his body in his right hand, and started to push the curtain back with his left, and that's when Junior braced his feet on the bottom rung of the stool, tensed his muscles and finally leaped.

Whuck! The barrel of the shotgun caught him alongside his head with the sickening sound of metal against bone. And since Junior was caught without footing, the force of the blow almost made him turn a somersault in midair. He slammed against the wall, rebounded, and crashed facedown on the floor. Blood spurted from a long gash along the side of his head.

Uncle Red quickly shifted the shotgun's aim back toward the cardplayers, but he wasn't through with Junior yet. He put his boot on Junior's neck and ground his face into the floor, saying, "You ain't very bright, are you, boy? You shouldn't be allowed to walk around by yourself. You just stay there, now, y'hear? Keep your face to the floor."

We heard footsteps clopping fast down a stairway somewhere behind the building.

"Ah! You see?" Arnspriger said. "She's gone for the cops, Red. Best thing for you to do is—"

"Shut up," Uncle Red said. "Well, Hoss? You got the two hundred? And you men got your IOUs. So we'll let you get back to your poker game now."

A car door slammed in the alleyway just outside the card-room. It was too soon for Marlene to have brought the cops, so it was probably somebody else coming to take a hand in the poker game. As Uncle Red and I backed toward the door, I expected to hear the door handle rattle at any moment. That's all it would have taken to make me faint.

When I unbolted the door and flung it open, however, nobody was there. The Packard was the only car near the place. Still, I was sure that I had heard a car door slam.

Uncle Red stopped long enough to say, "Now, the first one of you that sticks his head out this door 'fore I'm gone'll be the one who finds out for sure whether or not this shotgun's got any shells in it."

I dashed for the car. Uncle Red closed the door to the card room and followed me. I was already in the car and had it started before he jumped into the passenger's seat. I shoved the two hundred dollars into his hand, released the clutch and got away from there in a hurry. Turning out of the alley with the tires squealing, I almost collided with a couple of cars.

"Take it easy," Uncle Red said. "We're in the clear."

I got the car into the normal flow of traffic, but that didn't mean we were in the clear. I kept glancing into the rearview mirror, expecting any second to see a cop car behind us with its red lights flashing, and I knew this time there would be no escape. And strangely enough, I was just too numb and weary to care. If it came to that, a year or two in reform school might be just what I needed to recover from four days of being with Uncle Red.

"Look at that," he said, fanning the two hundred dollars out and shaking them. "That's enough to get us to Nashville in style, Hoss."

"It's sure a lot of money," I said. But while Uncle Red thought my remark was one of admiration, all I actually felt was dread. Two hundred dollars to me was so much money that I thought the cops would tear up half the state of Oklahoma to get it back.

"Ah, this ain't nothing," Uncle Red said scornfully. "Stick with me, Hoss, and you'll be shitting in high cotton."

Sure, I thought. On a prison farm somewhere.

"Now let's go pick up the old man and head out for the Arkansas line," Uncle Red said. "First, though, I want to get rid of this thing." He meant the shotgun. "When you get on the outskirts a town, slow down and I'll throw it out."

We found a likely spot along the highway just before we got to the tourist cabin. I slowed the car down and Uncle Red flung the shotgun out into a weedy field, and I was never so glad to see anything go since I got rid of the chickenpox.

There was no light on in the tourist cabin. Grandpa was supposed to have been ready to go when we got back, but it didn't look as if he was. He had probably fallen asleep.

"Stay in the car," Uncle Red said. "I'll get him."

As soon as he was gone, I felt a peculiar movement in the car. It made the hairs on the back of my neck prickle, because it was clearly a movement made by something that was alive. That knowledge should have prepared me for what happened next, but it didn't, and I almost cried out with astonishment when I suddenly felt fingers tapping me on the shoulder.

"Psssst," she said.

I jerked around in the seat and found myself staring into her eyes, our faces only a few inches apart. She was kneeling on the floor and peeking over the top of the seat.

"Holy shit!" I heard myself say. "How'd *you* get here?"

"Will you help me? Please?" Marlene said in an urgent, breathy voice. "I *have* to go with you to Nashville. Won't you help me talk him into letting me go?"

"Are you crazy?" I said. "You know what he's gonna do when he comes out here and finds you?"

"But I can't go back to Arnspriger's. I *can't*. I didn't run out and get the cops, did I? And Arnspriger knows I didn't run and get 'em, and he'll skin me alive. Oh, please, say you'll ask him to let me go with you."

Her pleas were so desperate that I couldn't help sympathizing with her. But what could I do? "Are you kidding?" I said. "He'd never...Look, we got enough trouble without you." I glanced toward the cabin. The lights were on. "Look, you'd better take off. He'll be back in a minute, and he won't like it if he finds you here."

"No!" she said. "I'm going with you, and that's that." She grabbed my shoulder. "Put me in the trunk, then! Please? I'll ride there as far as I can without being discovered, and by then maybe we'll be far enough away so he won't..." She faltered, fighting back tears. "I *can't* go back *there*."

I sighed. "I guess you're right. But he'll probably send us both packing when he finds out."

She gripped my shoulder harder. "Oh, thank you! From the bottom of my heart, I thank you. And God will bless you for it."

"Hurry up." My annoyed voice was calculated to cut down her enthusiasm. If she'd had any idea of what she was letting herself in for...

There wasn't much room in the trunk, what with Uncle Red's guitar and our belongings there, but with a desperately hurried rearrangement of things, we managed to hollow out a place big enough for Marlene to curl up in.

"You gonna be able to stand being shut up in a place that

small?" I asked, knowing that it would be like being buried alive, having visions of her becoming hysterical in a little while.

"I can stand anything," she said as she snuggled down, "as long as I get to go to Nashville with him."

With him—those words caught in my mind like a burr.

"Listen, though, maybe we'd better have a signal or something," she suggested when I was about to close the lid. "If I have to get out for any reason, I'll rap on the lid of the trunk, one-two-three, one-two-three. Like that. Okay?"

"Get down!" I whispered. I had heard the cabin door open. I pushed the lid down fast but gently, dashed back around the car and got into the driver's seat just as Uncle Red and Grandpa came out of the cabin. Then I saw that something was wrong with Grandpa. He was staggering, and Uncle Red had to steady him by the arm. The first thing that occurred to me was that maybe Grandpa had been hurt, or had maybe suffered a heart attack. I jumped out of the car to run and help, but stopped when I saw that Grandpa had recovered his balance and was pushing Uncle Red's hand away. He pulled himself up, tall and proud, carefully set his hat straight on his head, and started for the car. His legs were wobbly—in fact, his whole body was wobbly in spite of his efforts to stand tall.

"What's the matter?" I called, trying to keep my voice down so I wouldn't wake the people in the other cabins.

"He's drunk," Uncle Red said.

"I, sir, am *not* drunk," Grandpa said. "You, sir, rudely woke me."

He was drunk, all right. I had never seen him really plastered before. I had seen him take a few drinks with Papa now and then, and I had learned to recognize the effect it had on him. The more he drank, the more courtly he became. It was as if he knew that liquor took something away from his dignity, so he made a special effort to compensate for it, with the result that each drink seemed to make him a little more dignified. And now he had apparently drunk so much that he was as pompous as a lord.

"I left one of them bottles in there, and he drunk over half of it," Uncle Red lamented.

Grandpa halted and gave Uncle Red a haughty look. "I assumed, sir, that the bottle was left there for me."

Uncle Red opened the back door and motioned Grandpa in. "Ride back here, Mr. Wagoner, so you can sleep it off. I'll ride up front."

Grandpa wouldn't hear of it. He pulled himself up straight and proud. "No, sir," he said with an air of obliging nobility. "The back seat is yours. It's your car, sir, and you need to sleep more'n I do."

"Oh, come on, now—"

"No, sir, I tell you, sir, I won't have it."

"Well, shit, I'm not gonna stand here and argue with you," Uncle Red said, and got into the back seat.

Grandpa got up front with me.

We were off.

17

The country got greener and more thickly wooded as we drove east from Tulsa. We were getting farther away from the prairie part of Oklahoma, which had suffered from the drought and the dust storms more than the eastern hill country had. Here the prairie blackjack and live oak trees were gradually giving way to maples and cottonwoods, and there were more creeks and streams cutting through rocky gorges and wooded ravines. In the cooling night air, the big car purred along with miles of two-lane blacktop slipping beneath us like dark smooth water.

The hum and gentle rocking of the car soon lulled Grandpa into a fitful sleep. Now and then his chin would droop down onto his chest, but then he would jerk his head up again, as if reminded of his dignity. Soon, however, his heavy-lidded eyes would begin to close again, followed shortly by his chin drooping once again onto his chest.

Uncle Red was awake for the first hour or so. He had scooted down in the seat, with his feet propped up on the jump seats, and was taking frequent drinks from the whiskey that Grandpa had left in the bottle. He smoked cigarettes and hummed or half-sang snatches of a dozen songs and spoke to me once in a while.

"Soon's we get to Arkansas, let's stop and get us a hotel," he said. "Hell, we can afford it now. And if you get tired a driving 'fore then, you just let me know, and I'll take over for a spell."

Sure. And get us all killed. But though I was already tired, I liked driving at night. Other cars were very rare, a bright moon bathed the countryside in its pale glow, and the air had turned cool enough to be comfortable. It was very peaceful, driving along like that, passing through little towns like Broken Arrow, Coweta, Redbird, and even a small town called Okay. All the towns were closed down for the night, empty and peaceful.

It was just past Okay that I heard the first thumps on the lid of the trunk. Uncle Red had just gone to sleep and was now snoring away on the back seat, so he didn't hear the thumps, and Grandpa seemed too drowsy to notice them. I pulled over to the side of the road and stopped.

"Humph? Humph?" Grandpa muttered under his mustache, coming awake because of the sudden absence of movement. "What? What's going on?"

"Shhhh, you'll wake Uncle Red," I whispered. "Just gonna get out and stretch my legs a little. Get something out of the trunk. Go back to sleep."

He already was. A little wheezing sound from his nose accompanied the descent of his chin toward his chest.

When I quietly opened the lid of the trunk, Marlene whispered, "Oh, I have to go pee. I've held it as long as I can. Is he—?"

I put my fingers to my lips. "Sleeping. Here, I'll help."

Though stiff and awkward, she managed to get quietly untangled from the rest of the stuff in the trunk, and once outside the car, she whispered, "Now you have to turn your head."

"What?"

"I got to go pee. Turn your head."

"Oh, hell," I said below my breath, "I got a sister the same age as you." I didn't know what I meant by that exactly, but it was the disdain in my tone that carried the message: after seeing Belle—beautiful, voluptuous, sweet-smelling Belle!— what could any gangly, clumsy teenage girl possibly have that I would want to see?

I did turn my back, though, but only because I also had to pee. Marlene walked down the road a ways, I walked across the road. The night was alive with soft sounds. Crickets chirped nearby, and I could hear, farther away, the frogs in a pond or creek croaking contentedly through the night, and, still farther away, from the foothills of the Ozark Mountains, I could hear the faint bell-resonant voice of a lonely hound dog baying at the moon.

When I was through peeing, I turned to see Marlene emerging into the moonlight. I went to meet her far enough away from the car so we could talk without having to whisper.

"You all right back there?" I asked.

She sighed. "It's a trial. It's a sore trial, I can tell you, but if that's what I have to do to be with him, it's not for me to complain."

There were those words again. I felt a vague sense of alarm. "What d'you mean about being *with him*? Uncle Red, you mean?"

Her eyes sparkled in the moonlight. "Yes. Him. Red Stovall." She spoke his name as though announcing a cosmic event.

"What's your being here got to do with him? I thought you was just trying to get to Nashville."

"Oh, yes. My heart is set on Nashville. That's where I wanted to go before I met *him*. But now I *have* to go."

"What d'you mean, you *have* to?"

She was silent, thoughtful and slightly self-conscious. The moonlight made a sort of nimbus in the fringes of her frizzy hair. "Well," she said finally, "the truth is, at first I only wanted to get to Nashville so I could become a singing star. And I still do. But now I feel I *have* to go. I have to be with *him*."

"With *him*?" I felt the hairs on the nape of my neck prickle with my growing suspicion that I was in the presence of someone who wasn't quite right in the head.

She nodded.

"Why?" I asked.

She frowned. "I don't know, it's just a feeling I have that . . . that somehow our destinies will be intertwined, his and mine, like vines."

"Intertwined?" I said. "You and Uncle Red?" I said. "Like vines?" I said.

She smiled self-consciously, gave her coppery hair a shake, and looked down to scuff at the pavement. "Oh, I don't expect you can understand what I mean. You'd have to be older and be a girl to know what I mean, I reckon. It's just that when I saw him, something happened, and I *knew*."

"Look," I said, "if I was you, I don't think I'd mention anything about that intertwined destinies stuff to Uncle Red. I don't think it'd make your chance of getting to Nashville any better." I was sorry now that I had let her come with us. She was crazy.

She nodded. "Thank you," she said. "I do 'preciate what you're doing for me. What's your name?"

I told her. "But Uncle Red calls me Hoss."

"Oh," she breathed. "Well, do you mind very much if I call you Hoss, too? Hoss . . ." She seemed to contemplate the name for a moment. "Mine's Marlene. Marlene Moonglow."

"Moonglow?"

"Oh, well, it's not my *real* name, of course. Real name's Mooney, but Marlene Mooney . . . that's just too common for a singing star, don't you think? But Moonglow . . . Marlene Moonglow . . ." She said the name caressingly. "Don't you think that's a wonderful stage name?"

"I think we better get on back, 'fore they wake up."

"Oh, dear, back to the dungeon," she said, sighing with a desperate effort to renew her determination. "Oh, well, if that's what I have to do . . ."

I got her into the trunk again, and I thought we had gone undetected, but as I was pulling the car back into the highway, Grandpa abruptly cleared his throat. I glanced at him. He was regarding me steadily with one opened eye. "What's the girl in the trunk?"

With a quick glance toward the back seat to make sure Uncle Red was asleep, I whispered, "She's trying to get to Nashville."

"Who is she?"

"Girl we met in Tulsa. Name's Marlene."

"He know she's there?"

"Not yet," I whispered.

Grandpa studied me for another moment in silence before he cleared his throat again. "You know what you're doing, boy?"

"No," I said. "No, I don't." And more truthful than that I could not be. Though I had been with Uncle Red for only a few days now, I had been scared out of my wits so often with gunfire and getaways, holdups and whorehouses, alarms and altercations, that I now wondered if I had any wits left at all. I felt as if I had been on a four-day roller-coaster ride, and, numbed and reeling, my nerves shot, I no longer knew what to expect from moment to moment, let alone what I was doing.

"Humph," Grandpa grunted, as if to say that it was none of his business. He closed his eyes and drowsed off again.

By the time we got through a town called Tahlequah, I realized that I, too, was very tired and sleepy. In fact, there was one place where the highway ran straight for a mile or two that I found myself nodding off. I jerked awake with a stab of panic, rubbed my burning eyes, tried to shake the cobwebby sleep from my head, and rolled the little wing window out so that a stream of cool air blew into my face. I was trying to make it to Fayetteville, Arkansas, where we could maybe get a hotel room, but it was getting too late for that, and, besides, I was just too sleepy to go on. So as soon as we crossed the Arkansas state line, I drove the car off the highway and into a grove of cottonwood trees and went to sleep. I half expected to be awakened at any moment by a sudden rapping on the trunk lid, but I didn't let the dread of that keep me from falling asleep immediately. As soon as I was asleep, I began to dream of Belle. I had a hard-on all the time I slept.

The sun was already up and the birds were twittering noisily in the canopy of limbs overhead when I woke up. Had I heard a thumping in the trunk? No, it was only Grandpa getting out of the car to pee. I got out for the same purpose, but went off by myself and made sure that my back was to Grandpa because I still had a terrible hard-on. What I really wanted to do was jerk off, but I couldn't do it right there in front of God and everybody, and if I went off into the woods by myself, Grandpa might get suspicious, wise old codger that he was, so I had to settle for simply peeing.

A little mossy creek ran through the cottonwood grove, and after Grandpa and I got through peeing, we went down to the creek and washed our faces and hands in the tepid water.

Uncle Red was sluggishly coming awake when we got back to the car. "Where are we?" he wanted to know, and when I told him we were just over the Arkansas line, he said, "Stop at the first cafe you come to, let's get some coffee." He made a horselike blowing sound with his tongue and lips. "Feels like a dirty bird's been nesting in my mouth all night. How you doing, Hoss?"

"All right."

"'Bout seven-eight hours to Memphis," he said. "Think you can make it that far 'fore we get us a hotel? Be nice if we could get there by tonight, see old Flossie King." He said the name in a tone of nostalgic delight.

"Reckon so," I said, but I wasn't so sure. Whenever I blinked, my eyelids seemed to rake and scratch my burning eyeballs, and I had that light-headed feeling that comes with exhaustion. But I was willing to try.

Down the road about ten miles we stopped at a little combined cafe and service station. As we were going in, I wondered about Marlene. I hadn't heard a tap out of her, and it occurred to me, in my light-headed fatigue, that she might be dead back there in the trunk. Suffocated or something.

But I didn't let that thought keep me from eating. I wolfed down a stack of flapjacks, three strips of bacon, three eggs, two cups of coffee, and a slice of cantaloupe. That perked me up a little. And I felt even better after I had gone to the toilet—felt so good, in fact, that I got to thinking about Belle again, and got another hard-on. I found myself wanting to jerk off, but I didn't want to sully my love for Belle by thinking about her while jerking off in the dirty old toilet bowl. Besides, somebody rattled the door.

It was Grandpa. "I's beginning to think you'd fell in and drowned," he said.

While Uncle Red was paying the check, I hurried out to the car and got down on my hands and knees in the gravel, pretending to be inspecting something under the back of the car. "Psssst! Hey!" I said. "Are you all right in there?"

She moaned. "I'm still alive, anyway, praise the Lord," she said weakly, her voice muffled. "Where we at?"

"Arkansas. Be in Fayetteville in a little while. We just stopped and had some breakfast."

She moaned again. "Oh, I'm so hungry I could eat a horse! Can't you bring me something? Please?"

"You kidding? You want Uncle Red to see me putting a sandwich in the trunk?" As a matter of fact, however, I had thought of sneaking some food out for her, but had been dissuaded, not by the danger of Uncle Red seeing me, but by an impulse to let her go hungry. I was curious to know just how much she was willing to suffer to get to Nashville; curious to know how much of a loony she was. "Want me to let you out here? Get it over with?"

"No. I can stand it a little while longer yet, and the farther we get, the better it'll be."

"Okay. But that trunk's going to get hotter'n blazes in a little while."

She moaned.

Uncle Red and Grandpa came out of the cafe. "Shhhhh," I said, and started to crawl out from under the car. And it was then I noticed oil leaking out of the car's rear-end housing. I wondered how long that had been going on.

"What's the matter?" Uncle Red asked.

"Rear end's leaking oil."

Uncle Red squatted down to peek under the car. "Something serious?"

"Could be. We better get it checked."

"Well, we can do it in Fayetteville. Come on, let's go. I'm antsy to get to Memphis tonight."

I drove on. The oil leak worried me, though, and soon I began to fancy I could hear a soft whining sound coming from the direction of the rear-end housing. And it sounded as if it were getting louder and louder. But then, suddenly, I heard a loud wailing noise behind us, a sound so loud that it completely drowned out the soft whining of the cogs in the rear end. It was a siren. I looked into the mirror, and there it was: a sheriff's patrol car right on my tail, with its red lights flashing and siren wailing.

It would have been impossible for me to describe the peculiar feeling I had at that moment, the moment I saw the patrol car behind us. I couldn't have been more sickened and frightened and helpless if it had been death itself that hugged our bumper and screamed for us to stop.

"Oh, Jesus," I moaned.

"Just take it easy, Hoss," Uncle Red said, suddenly cool and in command. "Take your time. Pull over and stop when you can, and don't get rattled. Let me handle it."

That's what I was afraid of.

"Wonder what they want?" Grandpa said. "You wasn't speeding."

If he only knew, he would no doubt have been as sick and frightened as I was. I knew they were going to cart us off to prison and probably keep us there forever for all those things we had done in Oklahoma. In fact, once I got the car stopped on the shoulder of the pavement and the patrol car had stopped behind us, I expected to see the cop get out with his gun drawn. I expected him to make us get out and lean against the car for a frisk and put handcuffs on us. Or maybe he would just shoot us the way they had shot Bonnie and Clyde.

Instead, he walked from his car to ours in a shambling way, his hands on his hips, looking at the Packard as if it were some kind of weird monster unearthed by a bulldozer.

He gave us a cursory glance as he walked on to the front of the car, where he stopped to contemplate the crumpled left fender.

My heart began hammering with desperate hope. If the cop had known about all those things we did in Oklahoma, he probably would have shot us already, so it began to seem possible that he had only stopped us for a traffic violation, or maybe just because the Packard was so conspicuous.

The cop came to stand by my window. He chewed his mustache in a reflective way. "'Gainst the law to drive with only one headlight in this state. Lemme see your driver's license."

I gave him a sick little smile and a palms-up gesture.

"'Gainst the law to drive in this state without a license." His eyes squinted behind the dark glasses. "How old you, boy?"

"Sixteen," Uncle Red and I said at the exact same instant.

Uncle Red was leaning forward on the seat. He reached out and tousled my hair. "This here's my nephew, officer. I'm learning him how to drive. This here's his grandpa, Mr. Wagoner. My name's Red Stovall, and I'm on my way to Nashville to—"

"You got a driver's license?" the cop asked him.

Uncle Red chuckled sheepishly. "Well, as a matter of fact, officer, I lost my wallet two-three days ago, ain't had a chance to get another license yet, 'cause I'm in a hurry to get to Nashville, where I'm gonna sing on—"

"You own this car?"

"Sure do."

"Lemme see your registration."

Uncle Red chuckled again. "Well, there you are. I had it in my wallet, 'long with my license and everything else. I'm always losing things like that. My old daddy used to tell me I'd lose my ass if it wasn't tied on."

"'Gainst the law to drive a car in this state without a registration slip."

"Sorry 'bout that, officer. I'll get it all fixed up once I get to Nashville."

I could hardly believe what I was hearing. With suspense that was wrenching my guts, I had been expecting Uncle Red to start smarting off at the cop at any moment and get us shot or dragged into the slammer for sure, but here he was, being as polite and charming as you please. And he had that same bubbly enthusiasm and sincerity that he'd had that night at the Grange Hall when he told the people about the wonders of California. The same willingness and concern to please that he'd had while singing before an audience. So there simply seemed no way of predicting what he would do in any given situation. One cop he would goad, another he would charm.

The cop chewed his mustache. "How 'bout you?" he asked, leaning down to look at Grandpa. "You got no ID, either?"

Grandpa pulled out his wallet and held it between his legs as he used his one good hand to take from it a few scraps of paper and his Social Security card. The cop glanced at them all, then lingered for a moment over what appeared to be the oldest and most ragged scrap of paper in the bunch. "What's this?" he said, frowning with his effort to decipher it.

"My registration slip for the Run," Grandpa said. "Issued to me on the Hennessy Line three days before the Run into the Cherokee Strip."

"No fooling?" the cop said, impressed. "You was there? I be durn. My kids was just learning 'bout that in school a while back. But you're from Oklahoma. The car's from California."

"That's me," Uncle Red said. "Had a band out there for a few years. On my way to Nashville now to appear on the Grand Ole Opry. I picked these two up at my sister's house in Oklahoma. Was learning my nephew here how to drive."

After leaning down and handing Grandpa's papers back to him, the cop switched his reflective gaze to Uncle Red. "Grand Ole Opry? You a musician?"

"Play guitar and sing some. Red Stovall's the name. Maybe you heard of me? Used to sing on the Louisiana Hayride, out of Shreveport."

"Nope," the cop said, and looked around inside the car. "Where's your guitar?"

"In the trunk," Uncle Red said. "Be glad to get it for you, if you wanna see it." And he didn't wait for the cop to answer, but started getting out of the car.

Oh, Jesus, I moaned to myself.

The cop and Uncle Red went on back to the trunk, and I clutched the steering wheel and steeled myself. And when the

get stopped by some other lawman who wouldn't be so easy to get along with as me."

"We'll do that," Uncle Red said. "Do it soon's we get to Fayetteville."

"I'd rather you didn't do it in Fayetteville. Do it after you're out of Washington County. Okay? County line's only 'bout twenty miles from here, straight ahead." He was telling us to get out of his county, but saying it in a nice way. Then he looked at me and said, "You're a pretty good driver, boy. Better get y'self a license, though, soon's you can."

He didn't wait for me to assure him that I would. Leisurely, he got into his car, and we hurriedly got into ours. I took the driver's seat again, and Marlene, without waiting for an invitation, leaped into the back seat with Uncle Red. He glowered at her, and Marlene, intimidated, scooted as far away from him as she could, cowering in a corner.

The cop followed us. He kept back about two hundred yards, but he stayed on us, and his hovering presence kept everybody in the Packard quiet for a while. The only sound that impinged upon the ominous silence inside the car was the ominous sound of grinding cogs coming from the rear-end housing.

After we had gone two or three miles, and got used to the cop being behind us, Uncle Red slowly lit a cigarette, blew a plume of smoke toward the ceiling, and said, "Well?" That was all. He waited. "I'm waiting," he announced. I could see him in the rearview mirror glancing back and forth from me to Marlene.

Marlene was evidently waiting for me to take the lead, and I figured I might as well get it over with, so I told him how she had come to be in the trunk. I made a feeble attempt at justification by saying, "Well, we couldn't send her back to Arnspriger, could we? After all, she didn't go get . . ." I started to mention the cops, but remembered that Grandpa wasn't supposed to know about what we had done back there in Tulsa. Actually, though, he didn't seem to care. He just sat there, staring straight ahead, as if to say that it was none of his business what we had done in Tulsa or anywhere else.

Uncle Red suddenly turned to Marlene. "How old're you?" he demanded.

"Eighteen," she whispered.

"You're a liar," he said.

She hung her head. "Yes, I am. I'm really only seventeen."

"And you're still lying," he snapped. "You're sixteen, at the most."

She didn't respond.

"And just what the hell you think's gonna happen to a sixteen-year-old girl in Nashville? You got any money? Any place to stay? What d'you plan to do, live on the streets?"

"The Lord will provide."

"Oh, yeah?" Uncle Red sneered. "Well, maybe He'll provide you with a way to get there, too, 'cause you sure as hell ain't going with us. Next town we come to that's big enough to have a bus depot, you're getting out, y'hear? I'll give you the money to get back to Tulsa, but that's it."

Marlene moaned. "Oh, please, Mr. Stovall, don't send me back! Let me go with you. I won't be no trouble. Honest, I won't."

"No!" he thundered, maybe hoping to frighten her into silence. But it didn't work.

"*Please?* Oh, *please,* let me go with you! I'd just do *any*thing if I could, Mr. Stovall. I *beg* you—"

"And don't start that begging shit, either," he yelled, "or I'll throw your ass out right here!"

That was the first time I had ever heard Uncle Red yell in anger. Always before when he got mad, he got quiet and deadly mean, but now he was loud and rattled and downright huffy. When it became apparent, however, that Marlene had shut up, Uncle Red simmered down a little. He lit another cigarette, blew a long plume of smoke, and said, "Well, Hoss, you can sure pick'em, can't you?"

"I didn't pick her," I protested. And although I felt a twinge of guilt, as if I were betraying Marlene in some way, abandoning her, I felt even more strongly that I had already stuck my neck out for her, and I wasn't going to stick it out any farther. From now on she was on her own.

Nobody said anything for a long time. The most irritating sound I heard for the next few miles was the grinding noise in the rear end. It seemed to be getting louder. I wanted to stop in Fayetteville and get it checked, but the cop car kept on us all the way to Fayetteville, and then through it. He finally pulled over to the side of the road on the eastern outskirts of Fayetteville and watched as we disappeared down the twisting highway.

We were deep in the Ozarks now, and the country was a marvel to me. I had never seen anything like it. There were

green trees and corn fields and heavily wooded creeks. Log
cabins on hillsides, thin ribbons of smoke curling from their
chimneys into the hazy sky. Smells of grapes mingled with
hickory smoke, with watermelons ripening on the vines. Red
squirrels darted across the highway, flocks of sparrows swirled
through the trees, crows flapped across the fields, and black-
birds dotted the telephone wires along the road. We passed
through small settlements full of hillbillies and hound dogs and
old cars and mule-drawn wagons. In one of the wagons, sitting
on the seat next to his father, was a boy playing a banjo. I
waved at him, but he didn't wave back. He just stared at us,
goggle-eyed and gape-mouthed, as we whizzed on down the
highway.

Cass was the first town we came to that had a garage. We
had a mechanic check the rear end. He told us that it was going
out. "Have to get a new un," he told us. "This un won't last
much longer."

"How long'd it take to fix it?" Uncle Red wanted to know.

Wiping his greasy hands on a rag that was even greasier
than his hands, the mechanic said, "Two-three days. Have to
send to Li'l Rock fer hit."

But Uncle Red wasn't having any of that. "Will it get us
to Memphis like it is?"

"Mought," the mechanic said. "Mought not."

Uncle Red said, "Hell, let's chance it. Who the hell wants
to spend two days in *this* town?" He glanced at some men who
were pitching horseshoes beside a feed-and-grain store, then
turned his attention to an old hound dog that was sleeping in
the middle of the street. "Hell, I'd rather be in Philadelphia,"
he said.

After we filled the car with gas and oil, we stopped at a
grocery store and Uncle Red bought some bread and bologna,
cheese, potato chips, soft drinks, and beer. We drove until we
saw a small roadside park just across a wide wooden bridge
that spanned a river. The Mulberry River. The park was one
of those make-work WPA projects. It had a paved parking
area, a few concrete picnic tables and benches, and a privy.
Huge maples shaded the park, their branches overlapping, their
leaves shimmering silvery in the slightest breeze. The park was
empty except for us.

Marlene ate about four sandwiches, and much more than
her share of the potato chips.

"If you ain't gonna eat that," she said, pointing to the half-

Not as good as I sing, but . . ." She giggled and gestured as if
to say that we couldn't have everything.

Uncle Red looked at me. "Get the guitar."

I got the guitar from the trunk and took it from its case and
gave it to Marlene, who was so excited she could hardly contain
herself. She almost dropped the guitar before she got the fancy
strap around her shoulders. She strummed it a few times, shuffling in the gravel with her scruffy gym shoes, as if trying to
get a solid footing. "Well, let's see. First—"

"No, no," Uncle Red said. "Up there"—indicating one of
the unused picnic tables. "That'll be the stage. And, Hoss, you
be the announcer. We have to give Miss Moonbeam here every
professional advantage."

"Moonglow," she corrected him, and stepped up on the
concrete bench and then onto the table.

"Whatever," Uncle Red said.

She stood on the table, strummed a C chord a couple of
times, and giggled. "Gosh, I'm sort of nervous. Well, the
first—"

"Announce her," Uncle Red told me.

It had become obvious to me by now that Uncle Red was
playing with her, the same way he had played with the men
in the cardroom during the holdup. He was angling for a chance
to make her look foolish, and I was reluctant to take part in
the game. On the other hand, however, I myself was very
curious to hear Marlene sing, and since she was so anxious to
do it, I went over to the table and turned to face Uncle Red
and Grandpa.

"Here she is, ladies and . . . I mean, here she is, gentlemen,"
I announced. "The one and only, Miss Marlene Moonglow!"

Nobody clapped.

"Well, the first song I'd like to sing," she said to a vast
imaginary audience, "is 'My Bonnie Lies over the Ocean.'"
She strummed another C chord, hummed to get her voice in
tune, and then began singing.

> "My Bonnie lies over the ocean,
> My Bonnie lies over the sea,
> My Bonnie lies over the ocean,
> Oh, bring back my Bonnie to me!"

I hadn't expected her to be as good as she said she was,
but at least I was hoping she wouldn't be bad. Well, she wasn't

bad, she was *awful*. Her thin breathy voice didn't have a trace
of resonance or vibrato. In fact, she had no singing voice at
all. Instead of singing, she sounded as if she were trying to
carry on a breathy conversation in the middle of a loud party.
She did manage to keep in tune, and that was something to be
thankful for, but her phrasing was atrocious, her rhythm was
shaky, and her guitar playing was adequate for a rank amateur.

> *"Bring back, bring back,*
>   *Oh, bring back my Bonnie to me, to me . . ."*

I glanced at Uncle Red. He looked pained and shocked, as
if someone had just dropped a piece of ice down the back of
his shirt. But then something happened to make him change
his expression. Marlene, having finished the chorus and apparently unable to remember the second verse, substituted a
verse from a children's version of the song, a verse that could
only have come from the innocently cruel imagination of a
child.

> *"My Bonnie has tu-bur-cu-losis,"*

Uncle Red blanched.

> *"My Bonnie has only one lung,"*

His eyelids closed to slits and his jaw muscles flexed with
rage.

> *"My Bonnie spits blood and corruption,*
>   *And—"*

Uncle Red leaped to his feet and grabbed the guitar from
Marlene with such force that he almost pulled her off the table.
"You stupid little bitch!" he said with cold-blooded fury.
Dumbfounded, and with her hands in the position of playing
a guitar, she stammered, "What's the matter? You didn't like
it?"
"Like it!" Uncle Red answered. "It stunk. Sing? Shit! You
couldn't sing a note if your life depended on it. In an amateur
contest with a braying jackass, honey, you might stand a chance.
Other than that, you'd best give up any idea you got of ever
being a *singer*."

Uncle Red walked away in disgust. This was the first time I had ever seen him completely at a loss about how to handle someone. Obviously he didn't know what to do with this freaky girl.

"But... but I hadn't even got warmed up," Marlene said. "I was coming to 'Red River Valley' next, and I do that a lot better."

Uncle Red put the guitar back in the case and put the case in the trunk. Grandpa and I cleaned off the picnic table. Uncle Red got into the car, Grandpa and I walked toward it, and Marlene was still standing there on the table, holding a nonexistent guitar.

"You coming?" I called to her.

She sprang to life. "Yes! Oh, yes! Don't leave me!" She jumped off the table and leaped once again into the back seat. Uncle Red turned on her like a bear.

"There!" he growled, kicking a jump seat. "That's where you'll sit till we get to a bus depot. And if I hear one peep outa you 'fore then, I'll put you back in the goddamned trunk."

With her hand over her mouth, Marlene unfolded the jump-seat behind Grandpa and sat sideways, hunched over. Uncle Red reclined the full length of the back seat, as if it were a chaise longue, and opened himself another beer. It must have been deliberate, the way he opened it, because beer sprayed all over Marlene. She cried out and threw up her hands, as if to ward off a violent attack.

"Sorry 'bout that," Uncle Red said sarcastically.

We zoomed on down the road.

18

Clarksville was the first town we came to that was big enough to have a bus depot, but Uncle Red was asleep, so I just drove on through town. Grandpa didn't say anything. He just sat there and stared straight ahead, as if to say that it wasn't any of *his* business.

Marlene, hunched on the jump seat, her elbows on her knees, rocked back and forth and stared at the floor with unfocused blue eyes. When she became aware that Clarksville was coming up, she became very still, very apprehensive, and when she saw that I wasn't going to stop or wake up Uncle Red, she touched my shoulder. Being careful not to whisper loudly enough to disturb Uncle Red, she said, "Thank you," and then added, "Hoss."

For some reason, I blushed a little when she called me that name.

Uncle Red didn't wake up until we were about twenty miles past Clarksville. We were leaving the Ozarks then, going down into the Arkansas River basin. The river coiled through the corn and cotton fields like a sluggish snake. The air had become steamy, and the smells, too, had changed. The muddy odor from the river mingled with the sticky-sweet smells of flowers and greenery, a smell that reminded me of Belle. And when I thought of her, I got a hard-on, so I tried to concentrate on the countryside. I had never seen anything like it. Delta country for me was something strange and exotic. And my first sight of a bayou was a moment to remember. Actually, it didn't look much different than a big old mossy creek, but the name of it was what I remembered: Choctaw Bayou. What a wonderful combination of words they were: *Choc-taw Bi-yew.*

I said the name a number of times, until I realized I was chanting it, and then I added some other words and it became a little tune.

> *"Going up Choctaw Bayou,*
> *Gonna see my beautiful Belle,*
> *She lives on Choctaw Bayou,*
> *Something, something I . . . fell*
> *In love . . ."*

It didn't scan very well, but I kept at it, and pretty soon I began to hear Uncle Red grunting along with me. He was still half asleep and the hat over his face muffled his voice, but I could hear him beginning to get more and more caught up in the song. And when he understood what the scanning problem was, he said, "That's all right, Hoss. Keep it like that. Just put your subdominant chord on that *in love.* Like this." He pushed his hat off his face, and sang the first verse in a low, tentative voice, and when he came to the *in love,* he said, "Right there, see?" And sang,

> *"In love with that woman,"*

and then he supplied a line of his own,

> *"One night when the moon was shining bright."*

He sat up. "Why don't we make it a real shitkicker?" he said. "Somebody gimme a piece of paper and a pencil."

Grandpa emptied out one of the grocery bags and handed it back to Uncle Red, who smoothed it out on his knee, spit-wetted the end of a pencil, and said, "So what's the next line gonna be, Hoss? Got anything that'll rhyme with *night?* Or we could put a couplet in there, if you wanna."

I couldn't believe it. The idea of me and Uncle Red writing a song together frightened me into a dumbfounded silence.

Here was a man who was on his way to becoming famous, mind you, and I was just a nobody kid, a cotton picker who didn't know a subdominant chord from a couplet, let alone how to make up words for a song. So I froze up, afraid to try, and even more afraid not to.

"Uh," I grunted, trying hard to think of another line for the song, but only succeeded in saying, "Uh...uh...uh..."

"Come on," Uncle Red said, chiding and encouraging. "You was doing great. Gimme a couple of rhyming lines to take us into the bridge."

"Bridge?" I said. I thought he meant the bridge over the bayou. "We passed the bridge already."

"Did we?" he said, and looked down at the notes he had scribbled on the paper. "Yeah, by God, maybe you right. Them last two lines ought to be the bridge." He hum-sung the two lines, and then said, "Yeah, you right. Well, but we still need a couplet there. Throw a line or two at me."

My heart was pounding like a kettledrum, and it—or a lump, or a frog, or something—was lodged in my throat, blocking all the sounds except a sort of croaky "Uh...uh...uh..."

"Goddamn, Hoss," he said. "You sound like a lovesick bullfrog."

"Uh?" I said.

He stared at me, and I knew that I would have to come up with something quick, no matter how bad, just to keep from looking stupid. But the only way I could do it was to sound like a smart aleck and pass it off as a joke, in case he didn't like it. "Well, how 'bout...uh...

> *"She was always swinging through the trees.*
> *Had hands hanging down to her knees...."*

Uncle Red, to my surprise, considered the lines for a moment, and wrote them down. "All right, then, what d'you say we make her an alligator wrestler?"

Then it happened. It was almost a sort of magic, the way the lines started coming, the way we bounced ideas off each other, chuckling over the good ones, pretending to puke over the bad ones. We strung together the ones we liked, made experimental variations on the tune and bars as we went, and pretty soon we had written a song, a crazy up-tempo shitkicker we called "The Belle of Choctaw Bayou." It was about a guy going up the bayou to see his sweetheart, Belle, who was an alligator wrestler, which was

> . . . *quite a sight to see.*
> *But that wasn't nearly half as much fun*
> *As when she was wrestling me.*

When it looked as if we had it just about done, Uncle Red said, "Stop somewhere I can take a leak—roadhouse, gas station, or something—and I'll get the guitar out. We'll put some chords to this sucker and see how it sounds."

I stopped at the first place I came to, a roadside bar and grill, and while Uncle Red and Grandpa went to use the toilet, I got Uncle Red's guitar out of the trunk. I even took it from its case and laid it on the back seat for him, I was so anxious to hear him play our song.

As soon as Uncle Red was out of earshot, Marlene said, "Oh, that was a swell song you and him just wrote. A beautiful shitkicker," she added, as if trying the word for the first time. "I didn't know *you* was a singer! And a songwriter, too!"

"Well," I said in an offhanded way, "I reckon Uncle Red done most of it. Wasn't for him, there wouldn't a been any song."

"Yes, isn't he wonderful!"

I looked at her askance. Could she really think he was wonderful, after the way he had treated her?

"Oh, I wish he liked me a little!" she said, and pounded her knees with her fists.

"Marlene," I said. "Marlene, he has TB."

She looked as if I had just set a date for the end of the world. "Oh, my God. Oh, of course! *That's* why he's so skinny! And I thought it was just 'cause he didn't take care of himself, and I thought maybe if he had someone to take care of him, get him healthy, see that he eats the right things, and gets plenty of . . ." She faltered. "Oh, my God! That song! Oh, I'm so *stupid!*" But suddenly a glimmer of joy broke through. "Of course!" she cried. *"That's* why! That's why he made me stop singing. It wasn't my singing, it was the *song!* Oh, I *knew* he liked my singing!"

"Don't count on it," I said.

"Oh, I could tell," she said. "I could tell by the way he

looked. He was very impressed, I could tell."

"We all were," I said.

"There! You see? Oh, I'm *so* glad to hear it!" But suddenly her face collapsed into a frown of sorrow. "Oh, but of course I'm not glad to hear he's... Hoss? Is he *very* sick?"

"Shhhhh," I said. "Here they come."

Uncle Red had a bottle of whiskey wrapped in a brown paper bag. As soon as he got into the car, he took a drink from the bottle without removing it from the bag. But as soon as we were under way again, he corked the whiskey with a flourish and then picked up the guitar. "Well, come on, Hoss, let's see how this sucker sounds."

We faltered only a couple of times in the beginning, when Uncle Red experimentally altered the chord structure a little, but by the time we got through the first verse, we had it down pat, and we sang it. And soon Grandpa started patting his foot and reached into his pocket for his harmonica. He played along with us, and he played good. He even took a solo.

And Marlene couldn't keep from clapping her hands. But at least she, in obedience to Uncle Red's order to keep her mouth shut, didn't try to join us on the singing. What she did, almost from the moment Uncle Red opened his mouth to sing, was to stare at him. And when the song was over, she could contain herself no longer. She applauded wildly. "Oh, that was wonderful! Wonderful! Oh, I just *knew* you'd be a great singer! I just *knew* it!" She paused briefly, and then, with the startled look of having been plugged into an electric socket, she cried, "Of course! That's how our destinies are going to be intertwined—as singers!"

There was a sudden silence inside the car. All I could hear was the grinding sound in the rear end, and the *pat pat pat* of Grandpa knocking his harmonica against his thigh to clear it of spit. Uncle Red was staring at Marlene, and it didn't take her long to realize that she had done it again. She cringed on the jump seat and darted a couple of pleading glances at me.

"Hey, that's a pretty good song, ain't it?" I said lamely, trying to deflect Uncle Red's attention from Marlene. Without success, however.

"Pass that by me again." Uncle Red seemed to be making an effort to be calm and collected. "That part about our 'destinies' being—what'd you call it?—'intertwined'?"

Marlene was hesitant now, but she seemed so happy to be

of any interest to him that she just kept rattling on. "Oh, it was just a feeling I had, about me and you. . . ."

"A feeling?" Uncle Red prompted, staring at her with the frown of a man examining a pitiful carnival freak.

"Well, it was more than just a . . . a *feeling*," she said. Her every move had a jerky, awkward quality to it, as if it had been rehearsed in front of a mirror, and yet there was no doubt that she was as guileless as a child. "I mean, sometimes I'm what you call clar-voyant. It means I can see into the future, sort of." She took a deep breath. Like a person floundering in a quagmire, she apparently decided that she had gone too far to turn back now, so she plunged on. "And it came to me, while you were there at Arnspriger's, that our futures, yours and mine, would be . . ."

Uncle Red supplied the word. "Intertwined?"

She nodded.

Uncle Red didn't know what to do. He started to groan with weary disbelief, but the groan turned into a snort of contempt, and he shook his head. "Well, if you can predict the future, I guess you can predict what's gonna happen when we get to the next bus depot. I'm putting your ass on the first bus back to Oklahoma, and if you can't foresee that, you better polish up your crystal ball. Clar-voyant, my ass!" he snorted. "You better watch out, or one of these days they're liable to haul you away in a butterfly net."

Marlene sniffled. "Oh, why is your heart so hardened to me?" she whispered. It sounded like a line from a tearjerker. "I'd just do anything if you'd let me go with you. Just *any*thing."

Uncle Red took a deep breath, as if preparing to lambast her, but then changed his mind. In a low, insinuating voice, he goaded, "*Any*thing?"

Shamefaced, Marlene bowed her head.

"*Any*thing?" Uncle Red repeated.

Marlene nodded.

We zoomed on down the road.

19

We weren't zooming very well now, though, because the rear end was getting so loud at high speeds that I half expected it to disintegrate. So I kept the car down around forty, hoping to make it to Memphis before the rear end went out, but judging by the rate at which the pitch and volume of the grinding whine were increasing, we obviously weren't going to reach Memphis.

In the interest of traveling the shortest possible distance to Memphis, Uncle Red, while sipping from his whiskey bottle, mapped out a new route that took us back into the foothills of the Ozarks. We passed through little towns like Jerusalem and Quitman, none of which was big enough to have a bus depot, and by the time we got to Latona, which did have a bus depot, Uncle Red was asleep again, so I just drove on through again. By then, however, it had begun to sound as if all of us might be needing the services of a Greyhound bus soon. The rear end had begun to sound like a bucket of bolts being run through a cement mixer. I felt as if the car was in agony, and I was in agony with it.

We were just leaving the foothills, dropping down into the Mississippi Delta country, when we came to a little town called Noxpater.

"Well, that's it for us," I said, heartsick for the poor car. "We can't go any farther."

Uncle Red, who might not have been fully asleep after all, sat up and said, "Where are we?"

"Place called Noxpater," I said.

"Good God," he groaned. *This* is where it gives out on us! Noxpater!"

I steered the clanking car into the driveway of an old two-story building whose faded sign said GARAGE BLACKSMITH LIVERY. The building's tin roof had long ago rusted to a golden brown, while its paint-peeled sides were cluttered with signs advertising soft drinks, cigarettes, syrup, motor oil. There were two old gas pumps in front of the building and a haystack behind it.

The mechanic, a hairy, big-bellied man in a blacksmith's apron, was standing in the doorway idly talking to a couple of squatting hillbillies. When I got out to explain what the trouble was with the car, the mechanic showed the black rotted stumps of his teeth in a canine grin and said, "Don't have to tell me, boy. I got ears. Yo rear end's plumb shot to hell." He sauntered idly out to the car. "Naw suh, nary another mile will ye git out a that. Sho is a fancy car, though, ain't it? Don't see many lak thet 'round chere these days. People too po."

"How long'll it take to fix it?" Uncle Red asked.

The mechanic rubbed his balding pate absently, tenderly. "Two days."

Uncle Red groaned.

"Have to send to Li'l Rock fer parts. Take one day ta git 'em. Fix hit in another day. Two days."

Grandpa got out of the car. "Is there a bus somewhere that a feller could catch to Memphis?"

"Sholy," the mechanic said. "Ozark Stage. Leaves from rat chere at six o'clock shop."

"*Ratchere?*" Uncle Red said. He was about half drunk, and a little irritable. "Where's *Ratchere?*"

The mechanic stamped on the ground with his heavy shoe. "Rat chere," he said. "Stops rat where we standing."

Grandpa cleared his throat. He glanced around at Uncle Red. "If you fellers don't mind, I think I'll just go on by bus. No sense in me sitting 'round here for two days. If I take a bus, I'll be in Murfreesboro 'fore you get the car fixed. Don't see no sense in me sitting 'round here."

Uncle Red looked up and down the main street, which was merely a highway that bisected the town, and it looked to be the only paved street the town had. Standing in front of the garage, you could see from one end of the town to the other. There was a cafe directly across the street. Men in bib overalls and floppy hats slouched on the benches and sidewalks in front of the cafe. Their whittling and talking had been interrupted by our arrival, and now they were all staring across the street at our car. An old black man wearing a frayed straw hat creaked by in a wagon pulled by two languid mules, while an old mongrel dog ambled along in the shade underneath the wagon.

After clearing his throat again, Grandpa said to Uncle Red, "Red, I'd be much obliged if I could have some of the money back. Seeing as how we come only 'bout halfway."

Uncle Red held up his hands as if to tell Grandpa that it was all right, he needn't explain. Then he once again addressed the mechanic, who was now busy examining all the dents and scratches and crumpled fenders on the car. "How far's it to Memphis, anyway?"

"Frum where?" the mechanic wanted to know.

"From rat chere, of course," Uncle Red said irritably.

"Eighty mile, thereabouts."

"Does that Ozark Stage go all the way there?"

"Sholy do, the good Lord willing and the creeks don't rise."

Uncle Red turned to me, hemming and hawing. "Uh . . . looky here, Hoss. There . . . uh . . . don't seem much sense in me and your grandpa sitting 'round here for two days. You the only one can drive, after all. What d'you need us for? So I was thinking maybe I'd just get on that bus, too, and go on to Memphis, if you don't mind. I'll leave you enough money to get the car fixed up, of course, and when it's done, why, you could pick me up in Memphis. How's that sound?"

"Well," I said, and shrugged. It disappointed me to hear that I was going to be deserted here in this strange little town for two whole days, but I figured they were right, there was no use in all of us having to stay. Even so, all I could do was shrug and say, "Well . . ."

"By God, I knew you'd be a sport about it, Hoss," Uncle Red said admiringly.

"But . . . but what'll I . . . where'll I stay?"

Uncle Red asked the mechanic, "Any hotels in this town?"

"Nope," the mechanic said, giving us that rotten-toothe

grin. "Hotel burned down four-five years ago. Some tourist set hit afar. Smokin' in bed, he was. Burned hisself up, too. Durn fool."

"Well, is there any other place in town my nephew here can get a room for a couple of days?"

"Mought be."

After it became clear that the mechanic wasn't going to volunteer any further information, Uncle Red snapped, "Well, where?"

"Rat chere," the mechanic said, jerking his begrimed sausage-sized thumb toward his building. "One room. Upstairs. Old woman'll put some sheets on the bed, if ye want hit. Dollar a day rent."

"Well, there you are, Hoss, you got y'self a room. And when I get to Memphis, I'll send you a telegram, let you know where to find me. How's that sound?" But without waiting for an answer, he said to the mechanic, "When'd you say that bus leaves?"

"Two a day," he said, holding up two fingers. "Six tonight, eight o'clock in the morning."

"Damn," Uncle Red said. "More'n two hours." He glanced forlornly up and down the street, squinting his eyes for distance, scratching his unshaven chin. "Wonder what a man could find to do in this town for two hours? Any place to get a drink 'round here?"

The mechanic jerked his thumb down the road in the direction from which we had come. "Roadhouse back 'bout half mile."

"Well, Mr. Wagoner," Uncle Red said to Grandpa, "you feel like walking on down there and getting us a drink?"

Actually Uncle Red didn't look as if he could walk that far. He was pretty drunk already, he was in his cowboy boots, which made his walking even wobblier, and the sun was roaring in the hazy Ozark sky. But I knew there was no stopping him if he wanted to go.

Grandpa was at least politely willing. "Don't mind if I do. Stretch my legs a little."

Uncle Red gave the mechanic some money for the room, and they haggled for a minute over the estimated cost of fixing the rear end. Uncle Red said fifty dollars was too damn much, and the mechanic, giving us another look at his rotten teeth, allowed as how it might not cost over forty-five. And when they finished haggling, the mechanic said, "I'll see the old woman gits the room ready."

Uncle Red said to me, "Might's well go on up to the room, Hoss, get settled in. Me and Mr. Wagoner'll be back 'fore the bus leaves."

"What d'you want me to do with her?" I asked in an undertone, nodding toward the car, in which Marlene still sat, hunched over on the jump seat, sulking.

"I don't give a good goddamn what you do with her. Keep her here with you if you wanna, keep you company. You two can have a rip-roaring time here in old Noxpater for two days. But when you get to Memphis, I don't want her to be in the car. Understand me? I'll leave enough money for her bus ticket back to Tulsa."

And as he and Grandpa shambled back down the highway toward the roadhouse, Uncle Red staggering a little now and then, I walked over to the car. "Marlene?" She didn't look at me. "What're you gonna do?"

"I think I'll kill myself," she said.

"There's a room here," I said. "I have to stay here for a couple of days. Till the car gets fixed." My tone implied that she could maybe hang around until then if she wanted to.

She gave me a quick, searching look, and seeing that all hope wasn't yet lost, she leaped out of the car.

The mechanic had called a young black man from the interior of the building and sent him shuffling off down the street. "He gonna git the old woman. She'll put some sheets on the bed," he said as Marlene and I approached. He looked at her. "Two staying?" he asked, and held up two fingers to make sure of his numbers.

"I don't . . ." Then I understood why he was asking. "This's my sister," I said.

"Only one bed," he said.

"That's all right," I said. "I'll make a pallet."

"No no no, *I'll* make a pallet," Marlene protested exuberantly.

I didn't want to argue with her there in front of the mechanic, who was looking at us suspiciously. "You smoke?"

I didn't know what to make of the question. I couldn't tell if he was trying to mooch a cigarette or catch us in a crime.

"No smoking in bed," he said, clarifying the matter. "Mough burn the durn place down 'round mah ears."

He showed us the stairway leading to the room above. The place smelled of dust and mold and disuse. There was one old wrought-iron bedstead in the room, with a lumpy, stained mattress and rusty coiled bedsprings and a couple of soiled pillows. The only other furniture in the room was a chest of drawers and an old frayed cushion chair. There was one window, dusty and cobwebby, that looked out over the gas pumps and the street below. The windowshade was tattered and patched with black tape. The linoleum on the floor was worn and cracked and curled at the edges. There was no shower in the toilet, only a flush bowl and an enamel washbasin, and the hot-water spigot didn't work.

But there was one good feature about the room: a big closet. The closet door hung loose on its hinges and wouldn't close all the way, but the floor of the closet was more than big enough for me to make a pallet on it. It would be almost like having a room of my own. Marlene protested that she didn't want to take the bed, that she would actually prefer to sleep on a pallet in the closet, but I had already made up my mind that I would prefer the small physical discomfort of sleeping on the floor to the guilty discomfort that would be mine if *I* slept on the bed and *she* slept in the closet. Between being a martyr or a cad, I would have been a martyr any day.

While I got the quilts from the car, Marlene tried to tidy up the place a bit. But when the aged, snuff-dipping woman came in to put the sheets on the bed, Marlene and I became so discomfited by her malicious stares that we left the room and went across the street to the cafe. I still had two dollars left, so we feasted on hamburgers and cokes and potato chips. Marlene was shocked to see me spending money so recklessly, and urged me not to, but seeing how impressed she was, I became even more reckless. I bought us each a dish of strawberry ice cream. Marlene was overjoyed. I felt like a big shot.

"Thank you, Hoss," she said, as we were leaving the cafe. "I wish I really did have a brother just half as swell as you are."

I was distracted by the sight of Grandpa, who was standing on the other side of the street in front of the gas pumps. He was alone, standing there with his frayed straw suitcase beside him, waiting for the bus. Uncle Red was nowhere to be seen.

"I left him at the roadhouse," Grandpa answered in his it's-none-of-my business tone. "Met a woman there. Waitress. He said he'd be back in time to catch the bus." A drop of sweat rolled down his nose and he flicked it away with a jerk of his head. The underarms of his shirt were half-moons of sweat. He had his coat hung across his good arm.

"Bus due in a li'l while," the mechanic said from the big doorway of his garage. He had already driven the Packard in and begun working on it. "Where the cowboy?"

"Don't know if he's gonna make it," Grandpa said.

"Well, he better hurry iffen he is," the mechanic said, grinning, and jerked his head toward the highway.

The Ozark Stage was coming. It was an ancient battered green bus that chugged along the heat-shimmered highway toward town like a daunted but very determined turtle. Its roof was piled high with boxes and milk cans and chicken coops. As it slowed to a laborious stop in front of the gas pumps, the engine expired with a death rattle, and the bus shook with one last quivering motion before it came to rest. The back of the bus was filled with Negroes.

"Leaving in five minutes," the driver announced as he stepped down from the bus. "Howdy, Pooch," he called to the mechanic. "How you be? Got somethin' here fer you from Li'l Rock." He climbed up on the roof of the bus and began rummaging through the freight.

Grandpa pulled his snap-case gold watch from his pocket. After glancing down the highway for some sign of Uncle Red, he looked at his watch. "Never make it," he said. "I might's well get aboard." He turned to face me then. "Well, Whit," he said, stiffly self-conscious, and it wasn't until then that I fully realized we were saying goodbye. I didn't know what to do or say. "Well, Whit," he said again, and held out his right hand. I probably blushed a little. It was the first time I had ever shaken hands with him. "You be good, now, y'hear? And come see me while you're in Nashville, if you can."

"Where'll I find you?"

"Cainsville. Little town twelve-fourteen miles north of Murfreesboro. Ask anybody 'round town for the Wagoner place. They'll tell you."

"I will, Grandpa. I'll come see you."

"And, Whit . . ." He hesitated. "Stay with him, Whit." His voice had a sad, resigned quality to it. "Take care a him as best you can." There seemed to be something else he wanted to say as he stood gazing down the highway in the direction of the roadhouse, but finally he just gave my shoulder an affectionate pat, picked up his suitcase and got on the bus. He found a seat among the white passengers in the front of the bus. It was on my side of the bus but not a window seat, so there was somebody between us, and, mindful of his dignity, Grandpa wouldn't talk across the passenger in the window seat. So he sat there and stared straight ahead while the driver finished his business with the mechanic. Grandpa's hawk-fierce profile had the unyielding quality of a face stamped on a coin. I stared at him, wondering if I would ever see him again.

"Let's go!" the bus driver said, climbing into the bus.

"Goodbye, Grandpa," I called.

He looked at me, nodded his head gravely. The door closed, the engine rattled into life, and the bus started pulling away.

"Goodbye, Grandpa," I called again, and waved. He returned the wave in a gesture vaguely similar to a salute.

As the bus pulled into the street and started grinding its way toward Memphis, I thought I heard something, a sound just below hearing, like the sound from a dog whistle. I looked back to see something coming from the direction of the roadhouse. It was a vehicle of some sort, but its features were so blurred by the heat waves rising from the blacktop that I couldn't tell for a moment whether it was a car or a truck. The shimmering distortion of the heat waves made the vehicle seem to be a black bug trying to work its way through a substance as palpable as water. Then I saw that it was an old truck, and that Uncle Red was standing on the bed of the truck behind the cab, waving his hat. Then I could faintly hear him calling, "Stop that bus! Stop that bus!"

I turned and dashed a few yards after the bus, a yell already beginning to emerge from my throat, but I saw it was hopeless. The bus was going out the other end of town, gaining speed, its outlines beginning to be blurred by the heat waves.

The truck Uncle Red was riding in was driven by a boy about my age. His father, a farmer, sat in the cab on the passenger's side. The truck pulled to a brake-squealing stop in front of the gas pumps to let Uncle Red jump off, then immediately pulled away again, with the driver and his father stealing one last glance at Uncle Red as they might have stolen a glance at someone who was deformed, aware that it was impolite to stare, but too fascinated not to.

Uncle Red staggered up to me, sweating and panting, drunk

again. "Well, shit fire and save matches," he said, gazing
wistfully down the highway after the bus. Then, still with a
philosophical air, he put his hands on his hips, cocked one
cowboy boot forward, and drawled, "My mama always told
me never to run after a bus or a woman. Said there was always
another one coming. Well, looks like I managed to do both
today. I was running after that big ass-shaking waitress so
much, I ended up running for the bus. Didn't catch either one
of 'em." He took off his hat, wiped the sweat from his forehead
with the sleeve of his shirt. *"Now* what'm I gonna do? Stuck
in Noxpater, Arkansas, for..." He turned to the mechanic,
Pooch of the rotten teeth, who was standing in the doorway of
his garage, watching us. "When'd you say that next bus leaves
for Memphis?"

"Eight o'clock tomorrow mornin'," Pooch said. "Shop."

Uncle Red looked at me. He was just getting his breath
back. He dug some bills out of his pocket and handed me two
dollars. "Here. Get y'self a dinner or something. See if you
can find y'self something to do 'round this burg. Me, I figure
I might's well go on back down to that roadhouse and try to
finish what I started there." Speaking out of the side of his
mouth in an undertone so that Marlene couldn't hear him, he
said, "There's this waitress down there, fattest woman I ever
seen. Well, Hoss, you know me—if there's one thing I wanna
be able to say when I die, it's that I fucked a fat woman." He
winked. "Tell you the truth, I 'spect she's something of a
prickteaser. But if she ain't..." He nudged me with his elbow.
"Don't wait up for me," he said, and turned to leave, never
having given me a chance to say a word. He dashed out into
the street.

A model B Ford coupe was passing at that moment, headed
in the direction of the roadhouse, and Uncle Red staggered out
into the street and waved the car down. "Hey! You going past
the roadhouse? Gimme a lift, will you?" And as soon as the
startled driver slowed down, Uncle Red, with an audacity that
would have shamed a politician, jumped up on the car's running
board.

"I'll just hang on here," he said, taking it for granted that
the driver had consented. And the driver, though he kept darting
startled glances at Uncle Red, probably trying to figure out
whether or not this madman was harmless, drove on down the
highway. They disappeared into the blurring heat waves with

Uncle Red standing on the running board, one hand holding his hat on, and the other holding onto the car.

Pooch stood and watched the scene from the doorway of his garage. With him now were two other men who also watched. In fact, now that I noticed it, there seemed to be a growing number of people emerging from the stores and shops along the street to watch Uncle Red. Word was evidently getting around that a fancy cowboy had arrived in town in a fancy car. They didn't gawk or giggle—in fact, most of them pretended indifference—but there could be little doubt that they were all trying to get a glimpse of Uncle Red and the car.

Marlene and I didn't know quite how to pass the time. We walked around town for a while, but since there was no movie theater, we didn't find much to do. We finally went back to the cafe, where we each had a piece of blackberry pie à la mode, and then went up to the room above the garage. I was so tired and sleepy by nightfall that I crawled into my closet and settled down for a night's rest on my pallet. Marlene, however, wanted to talk—that is, she wanted *me* to talk, especially about Uncle Red. I had already told her everything I knew about him, which really wasn't much. I didn't even know his birthday.

"I got a feeling he's gonna be famous someday. I *know* he is," she said. "It's one of them clar-voyant feelings." She was lying on the bed, her hands clasped behind her head, staring at the dim overhead light. She had taken off her gym shoes, but still had her dress on, and was lying on top of the covers. I could see her through the crack in the closet door. I tried to close the door a number of times, but it kept creaking open on its loose hinges, and Marlene kept talking.

"Has he ever been in love, do you think?"

I yawned loud enough for her to hear me. It wasn't that I had no interest in the question—indeed, I had recently considered putting the same question to Uncle Red—but I wanted nothing more at the moment than to go to sleep, and it didn't take me long to do it, tired as I was.

I woke up only once during the night. That was when Uncle Red came in. I had been dreaming of Belle. It had been a beautiful sensual dream of cuddling up to her purple-nippled breasts, and at first I thought I was still dreaming when I began to hear drunken mutterings and sounds of stumbling, curses, groans. I couldn't reconcile such irritable sounds with the pleasurable comforts of my dreams, so I struggled to block them out. I pulled a pillow tightly over my head, and sank, once again, into a deep, deep dream of warm sweet love.

eaten sandwich that Uncle Red had dropped on the table, "I'll finish it for you."

"Leave it alone," he said warningly. It was obvious that he wasn't going to finish it himself, and I assumed that the refusal to let Marlene eat it wasn't from spite or meanness, but from a routine concern that the sandwich carried his germs. But of course Marlene didn't know that, and Uncle Red certainly wasn't going to explain himself to *her*.

She was crushed. This was the first time she had spoken to him since he had threatened to throw her out of the car, and to have her simple request rebuffed so curtly and unreasonably caused her eyes to film over with tears. "Mr. Stovall," she murmured, hanging her coppery head, "I wish there was something I could do to make you like me a little."

This was said so poignantly that even Uncle Red couldn't keep from being affected. He flushed, glanced guiltily at me and Grandpa, and turned his back on us all to gaze toward the tree-shaded waters on the Mulberry River.

"If you only knew..." Marlene faltered, her head bowed over the table as if in prayer. "If you would only let me..."

Uncle Red turned to look at her, his expression sarcastic, his voice goading and harsh. "If I'd only let you what?"

Sensing an opening, Marlene jerked her head up and tried to think of something fast. The birds in the maples overhead might have given her the idea. "Sing!" she said, her face brightening with enthusiasm. "If you'd only let me sing for you, you'd...maybe you'd..." But her words trailed off and died in a sort of hopeless silence.

"Sing?" Uncle Red said. "Here? Now?"

Marlene nodded, suddenly hopeful again. "Sure! I'd be glad to! More than glad! Oh, I'm sure you'll like me. Everybody does. They say all I need is a chance and I'm sure to be a star."

Uncle Red stared at her, apparently wondering if this girl could possibly be real. He too seemed to have noticed that there was no vanity in her amazing statements, but only a sort of brassy innocence.

"All right," he said at last. "Sing."

Flustered at having her wish so unexpectedly granted, she said, "Oh! You *really* want to hear me? Well, would it be okay to borrow your guitar?"

"You play the guitar?"

"Oh, yes," she said, nodding vigorously. "I play it good

20

"I have conceived."

"Uh?" Uncle Red grunted, struggling to come awake. He had raised up on one elbow and managed to get one skinny shank over the side of the bed. His eyes were puffy and blood-shot, his hair wildly tangled, his mouth hanging open. "What . . . what's zat?"

"I have conceived," Marlene repeated.

"Uh," Uncle Red grunted again, oblivious to her meaning, perhaps not even aware that she was there in bed with him. He continued his pained and laborious efforts to get out of the bed, and finally succeeded in heaving himself to his feet. He swayed precariously for a moment, rubbed his face, scratched his head, smacked his lips, and then seemed to become aware that he was naked. "Uh?" he grunted, looking down at himself.

We had been awakened a few minutes earlier by a loud rapping on the door. Pooch had come to tell Uncle Red that the morning bus for Memphis was leaving in five minutes. Marlene had said, "Okay, okay," obviously hoping Pooch would go away without waking Uncle Red. But Pooch hollered through the door, "Tell 'at cowboy, if he's going to Memphis, he best shake a leg."

I had come awake with a start when Pooch knocked on the door, but I didn't get up because I saw, through the crack in the closet door, that Uncle Red and Marlene were in bed together, and I didn't know what to make of it. I didn't want to embarrass them by letting them know that I saw them, so I stayed on my pallet and watched them through the crack in the warped door.

"Five minutes," Pooch shouted.

"I'll tell him," Marlene said in an annoyed whisper. But she didn't. She let Uncle Red sleep on.

But Pooch's mention of Memphis apparently sank slowly, deeper and deeper, into Uncle Red's sleep- and booze-befuddled brain, for soon he began struggling to free himself from the rumpled bed. That was when Marlene told him that she had conceived. She announced it as though she expected it to change any plans Uncle Red might have about leaving on the bus. He, however, seemed far more surprised by his nakedness than he was by her announcement. In fact, he didn't seem to have heard her.

"I have conceived," she said again, sitting up and holding the sheet under her chin.

Uncle Red looked around for his clothes, saw them scattered over the floor, and frowned as if he couldn't recall how they came to be there.

"Didn't you hear me?" Marlene asked.

"Uh?" he grunted, staggering into one leg of his pants and shorts, the shorts already inside the pants. "What're you talking . . . ?" He was about halfway into the left leg of his pants when Marlene made herself understood.

"I am," she said, "in the family way."

Uncle Red froze. Bent over, his left leg half in his pants, he looked up at her, frowning horribly, and seemed to see her for the first time. He seemed totally baffled by her presence there in the bed he had just crawled out of.

"What're you . . . ? Family way? What're you . . . ?" Then he seemed to make some connection between his nakedness and Marlene's presence in the bed. "Holy shit," he muttered, jerking on his pants as fast as possible, staggering and reaching out to brace himself on the bedstead.

She seemed to think she knew just what would make it all comprehensible and delightful for him. "And guess what, Red," she said. "Now I know how our destinies were meant to be intertwined. It's this," she said, bringing one hand out to place it against the sheet over her abdomen. "I'm going to bear your child. I have conceived. I *know* I have. I can *tell*. Isn't it wonderful, Red? You're going to be a father."

"Ohhhhh," Uncle Red moaned with mounting panic.

Someone shouted from the street below, "Hey, up there! Best hurry! Bus ready to go!"

In a sudden flurry of movement, Uncle Red grabbed his shirt off the floor and ran to the window. He was trying to put his shirt on and open the window at the same time. He waved frantically to somebody below, and when the window finally came open with a bang, he leaned his head out and shouted, "Wait! Hold that bus! I'll be right down! Hold it!"

"Well, you best come on," said the voice from below. "We ready to roll."

Marlene cried, "But you're not going *now,* are you? After last night? After what you said last night?"

Uncle Red came tearing back across the room, his shirttail flying, fumbling at the buttons, but he stopped abruptly at the foot of the bed and gave Marlene a horrified glance. "What d'you mean? What'd I say? Never mind!" And he came tearing on across the room to the closet where I lay on my pallet. He jerked the door open. "Get up, Hoss! Quick! Put your pants on and run down and get my guitar out of the trunk. Take it to the bus for me, tell 'em I'm hurrying fast as I can, I'll be right there. Holy shit!"

"But, *Red,*" Marlene pleaded. "Ain't you heard anything I said? 'Bout me being in the family way, and you saying last night how—"

"I've heard enough!" he shouted. "I don't wanna hear no more! Not another word! You're crazy, you know that? You're *crazy!*"

Marlene's eyes filled with tears.

Uncle Red went scurrying about the room, grabbing his hat and boots. I slipped into my pants and came out of the closet with my shoes and shirt in hand, but Uncle Red, bouncing around like a Mexican jumping bean as he tried to get into one of his boots, shouted, "Never mind the shoes. Go on down, get the guitar, tell 'em not to go without me."

The bus horn honked. U.. Red dashed to the window and yelled, "For Christ's sake, I'm hurrying fast as I can! Can't you wait a minute?"

I dashed down the stairs barefooted, jerking on my shirt as I ran. I dashed into the garage and got Uncle Red's guitar out of the trunk of the car. When I came out, I noticed that quite a few people had gathered in front of the garage, presumably to get a look at Uncle Red. The bus was waiting, the driver already in his seat, the motor running.

Uncle Red came bounding down the stairs, tucking in his shirttail. "Hold it!" he shouted to the bus driver. "I'm coming!" But he stopped in front of me and dug a handful of crinkled bills from his pocket. "Listen, Hoss," he said in a frantic voice, "here's sixty dollars. That's enough to pay for the car and get you to Memphis, easy. I'll send you a telegram soon's I get there, let you know where to find me."

"What about her?" I glanced up at the window. Marlene, dressed now, stood in the window, watching us wistfully.

"Her! I don't care!"

"Come on!" the bus driver called. "I'm leaving."

"All right, all right, I'm coming!" He had already picked up his guitar and started for the bus, but now he turned back, sat the guitar down, and dug another twenty-dollar bill from his pocket. "Here. Get rid of her. I don't care how. Put her on a bus to somewhere, anywhere, I don't care. Just don't have her with you when you pick me up in Memphis, y'hear? If you're a friend of mine, Hoss, don't do it. 'Cause if you do, we're not gonna be friends any longer. You understand?"

I nodded. I had never seen him so rattled. He was the same man who had looked down the barrel of a pistol and said, "Boom, boom, big man," wasn't he? And yet here he was, totally unable to deal with a slip of a girl who had said she would do *any*thing for him.

"Listen," he said out of the corner of his mouth, "was you . . . I mean, did you hear anything last night? I mean, did me and her . . . *do* anything?"

"I'm leaving!" the bus driver called, and eased the bus a few feet forward to show he meant it.

"I'm coming!" Uncle Red shouted. "See you in Memphis, Hoss," he called over his shoulder, and once he was inside the bus, he turned to shout, *"Alone!"*

The bus pulled out. I watched it go, not knowing quite how I felt, uncertain of what I should do—especially what I should do about Marlene. I dreaded the thought of having to get rid of her. How could I do it without hurting her feelings? Where would she go? And what if she really *was* pregnant? I was still too young then to realize how improbable that would be unde the circumstances, and yet old enough to know that such things did happen. Old enough, too, to feel the terrible guilt of dumping her somewhere, a half-grown girl with a fatherless child, with no money, no relatives, nowhere to go.

"I'm sorry," I said when I went back upstairs and told her what Uncle Red had said. I figured I had better tell her immediately and keep her from building up any false hopes of seeing him again.

"He has scarred my heart forever," she said. She was lying on the bed, her hands clasped behind her head, staring at the ceiling, her eyes misted with tears. And though her words sounded as if they had been rehearsed, the hurt and disappointment she felt were obviously genuine.

"What'll you do?" I asked, wanting to get it settled.

"I'll go to Nashville."

"But I just told you, I—"

"Not with you and him. I'll go by myself. I'll get a job, and have my baby, and make a career for myself, and someday he'll want me. I *know* he will. Someday I'll be a star, and he'll come and see me, and I'll show him the baby, and he'll be sorry he . . ." The vision was too poignant for her to go on with it. She bit her bottom lip to keep from crying. Tears overflowed her eyes and trickled down her face.

I sighed. "Well, I guess I can leave you off at the bus depot in Memphis 'fore I go pick him up. If you buy a bus ticket to Nashville, I guess it's none of my business. Just don't tell *me* where you're going and then I won't have to tell *him*."

That perked her up a little, and when I handed her the twenty dollars that Uncle Red had given me for her bus ticket, she was so grateful she kissed the back of my hand. I blushed and pulled by hand away. I wasn't used to gratitude being expressed so dramatically.

"Oh, thank you, Hoss!" she said in that whispery voice. "You're the best brother any girl ever had."

I blushed again, and busied myself putting on my shoes. "I'm gonna go across the street and get some breakfast. You want some?"

She sighed and said she wasn't hungry. After a moment's reflection, though, she said, "But I reckon I ought to eat for the baby, huh?"

If she wasn't hungry, the baby sure was. She downed a stack of flapjacks, two eggs, a side order of bacon, and a cup of hot chocolate. By the end of the meal, however, her gusto gave way to a look of slight nausea, as though, with hunger appeased, she suddenly remembered that she was broken-hearted. She stared with steady but unfocused eyes at the dregs in her empty cup for a moment, and then she looked up at me. Her eyes were brimming with tears.

I probably did something—squirmed, or frowned, or became shifty-eyed—to betray the discomfort she was causing me, for she quickly wiped her eyes, tried to compose herself, and said, "I'm sorry. It's just that I was wondering what kind of life the little tyke'll have, without a daddy or a home."

It sounded so woebegone and pitiful, the way she said it, that I found myself fighting back tears. I was disgusted with myself, of course, for doing such a sissy thing, but it sure was pitiful, the way she said it. But then she said something that really made me sympathetic, not because it was pitiful, but because it wasn't. In a matter-of-fact tone, she said, "What's it like to have a home, Hoss?"

And what could I say to that? How could I tell her what a home was like? "Well, gee," I said, and sort of shrugged. "I don't know. You never had one?"

"No," she said. "Most of my life I lived with my Uncle Carl and Aunt Ellie, but, boy, I sure wouldn't call *that* a home."

"Why not?"

"Why not?" she parroted, as if making sure she understood the question, maybe even a little surprised that I could ask it. "Shoot, how would *you* feel if you was someplace where you wasn't wanted?"

"Well, how'd you come to be there?"

She hesitated for a moment, fidgeting, and then raised her shoulders and her eyebrows in a simultaneous shrug. "Daddy left me there. Aunt Ellie was my daddy's sister, see, and when Mama ran away from home, Daddy started drinking real bad, and pretty soon he lost his job—he was a fireman for the B&O—and then he took me to Aunt Ellie's. I was six then. Haven't seen Daddy since. He said he was going to come back and get me when he got a job and got on his feet again, but I knew he wouldn't. I just knew it. He didn't want me, and that's the plain fact of it. Neither him or Mama.

"Trouble was," she added after a short silence, "Aunt Ellie and Uncle Carl didn't want me, either. To them, I was just another mouth to feed."

"Gee," I said, "I'm sorry," and that was all I could think to say. I didn't want to encourage her to go on talking about the past, since it was obviously painful for her. On the other hand, though, she seemed to want to talk about it. She seemed grateful for any word or question from me that showed any interest, so I said in a tentative way, as if I didn't really expect her to answer, "Were they mean to you?"

She nodded. "Oh, Aunt Ellie was all right, I guess, 'cept she couldn't stand up to Uncle Carl when he was mean, and he was always mean, seemed like. Not just to me, either. Mean to his own kids, too. Used to beat us with a rubber hose sometimes, when he got drunk, or when we'd do something that made him mad."

"A rubber hose?" I searched her face for signs of exaggeration, but she was either telling the truth or was doing the best job of acting I had ever seen.

"A piece of garden hose," she said, and her face puckered for a moment as if she was about to cry. She didn't, though. By an almost visible effort of will, she fought back her tears. Then she cleared her throat, and said, "Anyway, I sure never considered *that* place a home."

"And he's the one—your uncle—was he the one that sold you to Arnspriger?"

"Well, yeah, but he didn't actually *sell* me. Not really. I mean he just sent me there to work for Arnspriger till I paid off a gambling debt that Uncle Carl owed him." She paused. "Of course, I knew they was hoping they'd seen the last of me. I knew they didn't ever want me to come back.

"Trouble is," she said after another brief silence, "Arnspriger didn't want me, either—leastways, not after he found out I wasn't going to do everything he wanted me to. But I guess he was afraid to throw me out. Probably afraid I'd get picked up by the cops, or something like that, and maybe spill the beans about a few things he'd done."

"What . . . ?" I was on the verge of asking her what was the "everything" that Arnspriger had wanted her to do, but that seemed too prying, too tactless, so I changed the question. "Was he bad to you?"

She tilted her head in a gesture of grudging dismissal. "Oh, not really, I guess. I mean, he never tried to whup me like Uncle Carl did, anyway, and he didn't even take to hollering and cussing at me till Madam Zora died."

"Madam Zora?"

"An old woman who used to live in the front apartment over the cafe. Called herself Madam Zora. An old Indian woman who went around in fancy gowns and boas and things like that, and always had about a dozen cats hanging around. She'd once been a fortune-teller in a carnival, till she got too old. She's the one who told me I was clar-voyant. She was like that, too—clar-voyant, I mean. And she could read palms, too, and cards, and everything like that, and some folks said she could even cast hoodoo spells."

"Gol-*lee*," I said. "Really?"

"Yeah," Marlene said, pleased to see that I was impressed. "That's what some folks said, anyway. Arnspriger, though, he said it was just a lot of bull, but I think he was scared of her anyway, 'cause she told him she'd put a spell on him if he didn't treat me decent." After another brief pause, she said, "But then she died, and since then . . ."

It seemed once again that she was edging toward tears, so I quickly diverted her by asking if Madam Zora could really tell fortunes.

"Oh, sure," she said with absolute conviction. "She could tell all sorts of things. When Arnspriger lost a ring once, for instance, she went into a trance and told him where he could find it, and that's where he found it, too, just where she told him to look. And she was the one that told me I was going to be a star someday. She said she saw me on a stage in a spotlight, all dressed up in feathers and things, and the audience was just applauding like crazy."

That made me suspect Madam Zora's abilities somewhat, but I said, "Gol-*lee*," anyway, because my supply of responses was about used up.

"But of course, *I* knew that all the time. Ever since I first picked up Cousin Buddy's guitar, I just *knew* I was going to be a star someday, 'cause I'm clar-voyant, too. Madam Zora told me I had the gift, and that's how . . ." She faltered and frowned as if she had stubbed her toe, and then continued in a more intense tone, "That's how I knew that me and Red . . . that our destinies were going to be intertwined, somehow. I just didn't . . ." She floundered again, fighting back tears. "I just didn't know we were going to be intertwined like *this*—with me going to have his baby, and him done run off somewhere, and now the poor little tyke won't have a home or a daddy."

And finally two big tears did dribble off her eyelashes and trickle down her cheeks, and that was when I made motions to go. We had long since finished eating, anyway, and people in the cafe were beginning to stare at us. So I got up to pay the check. I asked the old woman at the cash register where the post office was, and she said it was in the general store a few doors down the street. All Marlene's talk about never having had a home had got me to thinking about my own, and then I realized that I was sort of homesick for the first time in my life. I got to wondering where the family was, and what they were doing. Still in Roscoe, no doubt, packing up, getting ready to leave for Bud and Dora's place out in the Panhandle, and that's where I decided to send the postcard that I wrote to them.

Marlene tagged along. We went into the general store, which, like every other general store I had ever been in, smelled of new leather harnesses and cheese and dried beans and crinkly new clothes. There was a room in the back of the store that served as Noxpater's General P.O., and the store's salesclerk doubled as the postal clerk. She sold me a penny postcard and let me borrow a stubby pencil to write with. Marlene looked over my shoulder as I put the postcard on a glass candy case and tried to think of something to write. I found that I didn't have a thing to say except that I was okay, Uncle Red was okay, Grandpa was okay, and I hoped that they were all okay. I signed it, "Your son, Whit," as if they might not know who it was unless I told them.

"Are they a nice family?" Marlene asked when we were back on the street again, walking back to the garage.

"Oh, well," I said, a little flustered by the question. I had never thought about it before. "Yeah, I guess so. 'Bout like any other family, I reckon."

When we got back to the garage, Marlene dragged herself up to the room, where she spent most of the day lying on the bed and staring up at the ceiling with an expression that varied between self-pity and a sort of heartbroken beatitude.

I spent the rest of the day in the garage, watching Pooch fix the car. I felt sorry for Marlene, but there was nothing I could do to help her, and, anyway, I was getting a little tired of being around her when she was so teary and emotional. It was much more interesting to watch Pooch work on the car. The parts for the rear end had arrived from Little Rock that morning—on the same bus that had taken Uncle Red away, in fact—and so Pooch, who hadn't expected the parts until the evening bus, was able to finish the job ahead of schedule. He even bolted a headlight on the front bumper to take the place of the one that had been smashed. And the car was ready to go that night. I couldn't leave, though, until I got the telegram from Uncle Red, telling me where to find him in Memphis.

21

The telegram came the next morning. Marlene got out of the squeaky bed and took the telegram and brought it to my closet. She held the closet door open and waited with a sort of wistful longing to see if the telegram carried some mention of her. It didn't. It only gave me the name and address of the hotel where Uncle Red was staying, and I was careful to hold the telegram so Marlene couldn't read it.

"He didn't say something 'bout me?" she asked.

I shook my head. Her wistful look faded, and once more she assumed that odd expression of someone experiencing a beatific bellyache. And that was the expression she wore when, as we were leaving Noxpater, she looked back at the town and murmured, "I shall always remember this place." It was impossible to tell whether she would do so in joy or in sorrow.

Leaving Noxpater, we dropped quickly into the lush Mississippi Delta country, the richest farming country I had ever seen. Head-high corn and waist-high cotton grew in long green rows, and there were rice paddies, too, the first I had ever seen. Also, I got my first look at some swamps, where huge oak and cypress trees towered in tangled profusion, their limbs festooned with long strands of Spanish moss, where white long-legged birds stalked daintily through the scummy water in search of frogs and fish, where colossal white-columned mansions lorded over nearby Negro shacks, where poor black men and toiling mules plowed the rich black earth.

And the smells of these Mississippi bottomlands were as different from those of the Oklahoma prairie as red clay dust is different from silty black mud. I had grown up with the dry creosote smells of jimsonweed and scrub-cedar trees; here were the pungent smells of cantaloupes ripening in the sun, the mud-cooled scents of oleander and honeysuckle, the sharp heady smell of woodsmoke from fetid cypress swamps, the ripe sweetness of watermelons bedded in hay on a farmer's wagon on their way to the markets of Memphis.

And then Memphis itself, on the banks of the Mississippi River. My first sight of the Mississippi almost took my breath away. I had not thought that all the rivers of America combined would have so much water. It was the biggest body of water I had ever seen, spanned by the biggest bridge, which led into the biggest city. And on the Memphis side, the river teemed with activity, with heavy-laden boats and barges, cranes and piers, with overflowing warehouses and swarms of shirtless black stevedores.

I was so busy gawking at the sights that I almost collided with other vehicles on two different occasions, and I also got lost a couple of times before I finally found, with the directional help of several gas-station attendants, the Greyhound bus depot in downtown Memphis.

"Well," I said to Marlene after I parked near the depot. "Well, I guess..."

"Yeah," she said, but she didn't get out. "Seems like all my life everybody's been trying to get rid of me."

"I'm sorry," I said, "I wish there was something..."

She shook her head and gave me a sad smile. "You got no reason to be sorry for anything. You been a good friend to me. And I'll see you in Nashville, someday, just you wait and see. And I'll be sure and see Red, too, when he sings on the Grand Ole Opry. I'll be there clapping my hands off. And some-day..." Her misty eyes became unfocused and dreamy for a moment, but then she sighed and shook off the reverie. She unlatched the door, but before getting out, she gave me a quick kiss on the cheek.

She stood on the sidewalk and watched me drive away. In her scruffy gym shoes and wrinkled flour-sack dress, holding her frayed denim jacket in her folded arms, she looked like a refugee, a waif, a victim, lonely and lost. I felt terrible leaving her there like that. I worried about what might become of her. But I was powerless to do any more for her without being in outright defiance of Uncle Red.

I got lost a couple more times before I finally found the Exeter Arms, the seedy hotel in the tenderloin section where Uncle Red was staying. The clerk at the desk, smoking a chewed and slobbered cigar and reading a racing form, looked at me disapprovingly over the tops of his bifocals when I asked for Uncle Red, and the look didn't change even after he had phoned Uncle Red's room and found that I was expected.

"Room 206," he said, returning his cigar to his mouth and his attention to the racing form. "Second floor, fourth door on yo left."

Uncle Red was lying on his bed when I came in. He had on a new pair of black pants and a new rose-colored shirt, but he had been sleeping and he looked feverish, haggard, exhausted. There was a half-empty bottle of whiskey on the bedside table, and an ashtray overflowing with ashes and cigarette butts. He tried to work up some enthusiasm when I came in, but he soon gave it up and sank back into a sour sickliness.

"You had anything to eat today?" I asked him.

He thought for a moment. "Had a couple of doughnuts for breakfast. You hungry? I could have the bellboy bring us something. Hamburger?"

He also had the bellboy bring a cot into the room for me to sleep on.

"We don't have to stay here tonight if you don't want to," I told him. "We could go on to Nashville. I'm not too tired."

"No, no," he said. "I found out Flossie King's gonna be in town tonight, the Top Hat Club, and I wanna see that big black bitch 'fore I go. Last time I seen her was in Baton Rouge, oh, four-five years ago. She's made a big name for herself since then. Probably sells more records than Jimmie Rodgers, if you can believe that. Race records. You ever hear her? Well, sonny, you got a treat in store for you. Best goddamn gut-bucket blues singer that ever lived, Flossie is, and whoooo-eeee, what a woman! 'Bout six foot one in her stocking feet. Got shoulders like that. Packs a wallop like Jack Johnson. Stand toe to toe and fight any man in the place, and she'll only go to bed with the bucks she can't whup." He wagged his head admiringly, and took a drink from the whiskey bottle. He was very pale and his cavernous eyes were bright with fever.

"And speaking a songbirds," he said then, "what'd you do with *that* one?"

"Left her at the bus depot, like you told me," I said, without mentioning which bus depot. "Gave her that twenty dollars for a bus ticket to somewhere."

"Did she say where she might be going?"

"She mentioned Nashville."

"I thought maybe that'd be it." After a sigh, he said, "Loony little bitch. She'll probably be turning tricks in a whorehouse within a month."

That left me feeling slightly sick. I hadn't realized until then just how much I had come to like Marlene, and I wondered why she rattled Uncle Red so much, especially since nothing else seemed to rattle him at all. The situation had a light resemblance to the story of the woman who was capable of chasing a bear with a broom, but would run shrieking from a mouse. Why was he so defenseless against her? Could it be because she loved him?

I gave this some thought as I ate my hamburger, and finally I got up enough courage to wonder aloud why he should think so badly of her since she obviously . . . uh . . . loved him.

"Loves me?" he huffed. "Loves me? You gotta be kidding. What makes you think she loves me?" He was sitting on the side of the bed now, trying to force a bit of masticated hamburger down his uncooperative throat.

"Well," I said, "she . . . I mean, she . . ." I searched for a tactful way to remind him that she had given herself to him, after all, and wasn't that proof of her love?

When he understood what I was driving at, he smiled dryly, probing his tongue into his cheek. "Look, Hoss, lemme explain something to you. Marlene's a star-fucker. You know what that is? Well, I'll tell you. There's a special breed of women that likes to hang around performers and fuck 'em when they get the chance. And the bigger the star you get to be, the more star-fuckers you get. Seems like the only way women like that can feel important is to fuck somebody that's important. Know what I mean? Okay. But you gotta be careful with 'em, 'cause anybody who'd do something like that is crazy to begin with, and they're liable to get you into a whole lotta trouble. Might yell rape at any minute, or hit you with a paternity suit, just so they can show everybody that they got fucked by a star. So don't say I didn't warn you, 'cause if you're playing some dance hall someday and some little ole gal comes up and starts blinking her eyes at you and wiggling her ass and telling you how she likes you and how she'd do just *any*thing for you . . . look out."

After a while, I said, "You really believe she'd do something like that to you?"

"Hell, yes. What d'you think all that 'I'm in the family way' stuff was about? She was laying the groundwork for a paternity suit against me, that's what, sure as God made little green apples. She's probably knocked up already, see, maybe by Arnspriger or somebody like that, and she gets a chance to blame it on me. And if it comes down to that in a court of law, Hoss, I'm gonna ask you to be a witness that nothing happened between me and her that night. You'll have to swear I wasn't in bed with her. Understand? It'll be our word against hers."

It baffled me that his view of her could be so different from my own. Was she really capable of such monstrous duplicity? I couldn't believe it. Not that I thought she was incapable of lying. She had lied readily enough, both to the deputy sheriff and to Pooch about being my sister. Even so, there had been something about her, even when she was lying, that made me doubt she could ever be as treacherous and untrustworthy as Uncle Red seemed to think; something like a guilelessness so remarkable that it made her seem simpleminded, even dim-witted sometimes. It wasn't that she seemed unsullied by sin, but as if she could sin and still be unsullied. And I wondered then (it would be years later before I became fairly sure of it) if it was *this* about her that rattled Uncle Red so much. Was he so far gone in debauchery that he could do nothing but flee in panic from that inviolable innocence?

"To hell with her," he said, tossing the remains of his hamburger onto the bedside table. He wiped his fingers on the bedspread and took a swig of whiskey from the bottle. "I'm gonna try to get some more shut-eye 'fore we go down to Beale Street. You do what you want to. If I'm asleep around five, wake me up."

Stretching out on the bed, he groaned with infinite weariness. His breathing was shallow and phlegmy, his face clawed with pain.

"If you're not feeling good, maybe we should call a doctor?"

I suggested, trying to be offhand about it, trying not to seem like a nagging nursemaid.

He waved me away. "I'll be all right. Just need a little rest, is all. Went out last night trying to find Flossie, got drunk as a hoot owl, and ended up in bed with a big black whore. Whoooooo-eeee," he added softly, wheezingly, and closed his feverish eyes.

I lay down on the cot for a while and tried to nap, but everything inside of me seemed in such turmoil that all I could do was stare at the flaking paint on the ceiling and listen to the noises from the street below and wonder who I was, and what I was doing here, in this place, in this time, in this body. It wasn't a siege of profound introspection, for I wasn't capable of that, but a great worry, a feeling that the very structure of my life—all that I had ever been taught and become accustomed to—was falling down around my head. A black whore . . . Uncle Red had gone to bed with a black whore. And he had not merely admitted it, but bragged about it. And only a little while ago, he had assumed, in the most casual way, that I would perjure myself in a court of law if Marlene brought a paternity suit against him. He had assumed that I would put my hand on a Bible and swear that he hadn't slept with her that night in Noxpater. The mere thought of it terrified me. Lying was one thing, but perjury! That would be inviting eternal damnation. That was something even more frightening than going to a black whore. Could it mean so little to him? Would there come a time when it would mean so little to me that I could actually do it?

That was a fitful afternoon for me. It was a fitful afternoon for Uncle Red, too, but for a different reason. He was sick. Feverish, and with an ashen tinge on his face, he tossed and turned on the bed. Like a man struggling in water, he fought his way to the surface now and then for a few quick strangling gulps of air, then sank again into an exhaustion that seemed to carry him farther away than sleep.

Once, when I went into the bathroom to take advantage of the hotel's full-length bathtub, I found one of Uncle Red's handkerchiefs in the wastebasket under the sink. It was spotted with blood. The sight of the blood caused my bowels to constrict with dread, with pity and horror, and I didn't feel like lying in the tub after all.

When I went back into the room, Uncle Red was awake.

He was sitting on the side of the bed, taking a drink from the whiskey bottle. "What's the matter with you?" he asked. "You look like somebody who's just lost his last friend."

"Nothing," I lied. "I was just wondering if you, if we, should go out tonight. Maybe we oughta just stay here."

"And miss Flossie? Shit," he said. "I'd rather drink muddy water and sleep in a hollow log than miss ole Flossie."

It was nearly evening, and he said we might as well go down to the Top Hat Club and see if Flossie was there yet. She and her band were supposed to arrive early at the club to go over some of their material before they began their nine o'clock set. He wanted to catch her before she went on.

"And if you never thank me for anything else in your life, you'll someday thank me for taking you to hear Flossie King," Uncle Red repeated as we left the hotel and started walking toward Beale Street. "Best goddamn gut-bucket blues singer in the world."

Beale Street was in the heart of the city's Negro district. I accompanied Uncle Red into the area, but with the forebodings and misgivings of a child being led into an enchanted forest. It was a place beyond my wildest imaginings, threatening in its strangeness, exciting in its novelty, forbidding in the blackness of its teeming people.

At first I stuck very close to Uncle Red, hoping and praying that he knew what he was doing, where he was going. But after we were a block or two into the heart of Beale Street, I began to hang back and gawk at the myriad scenes that filled me with wonder and excitement. The street was in a turmoil of life, teeming with cars and trucks and wagons, and the sidewalks teemed with people, some of them wearing the fanciest clothes I had ever seen. There were men in shiny apple-green suits, men in charcoal-gray pinstripes, men who wore black shirts with yellow ties and big wide-brimmed yellow hats. And they all wore mustaches. There were women in high-heeled, open-toed patent-leather shoes who sashayed up the street swinging their red patent-leather purses, their high saucy asses moving with feline lassitude under the rustling silk and satin of their tight bright dresses. They had straightened hair and glossy red lipstick and deep matte tints of rouge on their ebony cheekbones.

I slowed down to watch a huge black man unloading blocks of ice from an ice wagon. Shirtless and sweating profusely, his rippling muscles glistened as he hooked his tongs into a hundred-pound block of ice and slung it over his leather-padded shoulder. He took the ice into a butcher shop. In the butcher shop's awning-shaded display window, catfish and bass and bluegills lay gutted on beds of ice. An enameled tray overflowed with oysters. Chickens lay upon their beds of ice, plucked and gutted, but with their feet and feather-fringed heads still on them.

An old toothless black woman with a rag tied around her head sold vegetables from a cart: spring potatoes, crisp carrots in bundles, buckets of okra, small ears of spring corn. Another cart on another streetcorner carried hot smoky chitlings and pickled pig's feet and hot link sausages in greasy buns.

Music and squealing laughter spilled from doorways. Bands of barefooted black boys played games on the sidewalk and shot dice in alleyways amid cries and curses and squeals of laughter. An old blind man, with a guitar slung over his shoulder and a harmonica held in front of his mouth on a wire frame, sang as he played his guitar, all the while keeping an eye tuned to the jingle of coins falling in the tin cup held by a shy young black boy hovering at his side. Radios blared from open windows, horns honked, vendors called, sirens wailed, and the smells that pervaded the muggy river-bottom air were as rich and varied and funky as the sights and sounds themselves— the mingled smells of grease and turnip greens and automobile exhaust and horse turds flattened in the street, of sweat and perfume, of pomade and cigars and shoeshine wax.

The assault on my senses almost made me dizzy. I reeled with the wonder of it all, the flamboyant vitality of the place, so unlike anything I had ever experienced before. These were not the nappy-headed Negroes of Oklahoma, who were as dry and dusty and sullen as the land they worked and the white people they aloofly lived among. These were people whose laughter and music and flashy clothes reflected the fecundity of the black river-bottom land they sprang from.

And then the Top Hat Club. Uncle Red and I had to stop for a moment after we entered to allow our eyes to get used to the sudden dimness, and when my eyes did, I began to see an opulence that was in keeping with everything else on Beale Street. It was a huge place, with a bar and a bandstand and a dance floor and many booths upholstered in red imitation leather. There were large gilt-framed mirrors and fancy lamps with cut-glass globes. There were polished brass cuspidors and tuxedoed bartenders. From the four corners of the ceiling to the center of the room hung multicolored crepe-paper streamers, stirred by the huge overhead fans. And directly in the center of the festooned ceiling hung a multifaceted mirror ball, which, rotating slowly, cast a confetti of colored lights over the walls and the bar and the bandstand. The garish splendor of it all was almost unbelievable to a boy who was used to nothing more than dusty Grange Halls and seedy honkytonks.

A small tuxedo-suited black man came up and asked politely what he could do for us, and Uncle Red said that he had come to see Flossie King. The musicians were at their places on the bandstand, but at the moment they weren't making music. They were talking among themselves, and on the edge of the dance floor, by the bandstand, stood a big black woman in a silver lamé gown. She had been talking to a bald-headed man in shirtsleeves, but when she caught sight of Uncle Red, she suddenly ceased talking and shoved the man aside, and an enormous smile of recognition flashed over her face, revealing gleaming gold teeth set among the very white ones. Pointing a finger accusingly at Uncle Red, she shrieked, "Red Stovall! You . . . son . . . of . . . a . . . *bitch!*"

This had to be Flossie King. She was as tall as Uncle Red, but about four times thicker. She wasn't fat, she was just big, and she moved with all the sleek, ponderous grace of a high-stepping Clydesdale horse. She had a wide, flat, pecan-colored face and a carefully combed mass of straightened black hair, held in place by a pearl headband. She wore rings on every finger and garlands of pearls around her dusky neck, and bracelets and bangles of silver and gold dangled all along her arms.

She threw out her bespangled arms and rushed to meet Uncle Red. I thought she was going to hug him. Instead, she picked him up. With an arm at his back and the other behind his knees, she picked him up as a groom picks up his bride to carry her over the threshold.

"Look who's heah!" she squealed as she carried Uncle Red to the bandstand to show the musicians what she had. "You skinny devil, you! You get any skinnier, goddammit, Red Stovall," she laughed, "I can use you for a toothpick!"

"Hell, Flossie, I been trying to get the girls to use me for a toothpick for years now," Uncle Red said, grinning slyly, "only they say I ain't stiff enough."

Flossie laughed again, long peals of rich laughter, flinging her head back, baring her gold-gleaming teeth. It wasn't the laughter of amusement, but of sheer gutsy delight.

She dumped Uncle Red back onto his feet. "Maybe what they need is the prick of a he-coon," and the musicians up on the bandstand all laughed.

Uncle Red reached up and shook hands with a couple of them. They were dressed in tuxedoes, and they were drinking and talking and passing around what looked to be a handrolled cigarette, each taking a drag off of it and passing it on to somebody else. It struck me as odd that they should look so prosperous and yet have to share one hand-rolled cigarette among them all. But then I noticed that they were smoking ready-rolled cigarettes, too, though not sharing them. It was only the hand-rolled cigarette that they passed from hand to hand.

Flossie and Uncle Red jabbered for a minute or two about how they were doing these days. He told her that he was on his way to do the Grand Ole Opry, and she told him that she had been booked into the Apollo Theatre in Harlem. So they were both doing all right. They congratulated each other, and she slapped his shoulder with such unwitting force that she staggered him. Abruptly, her laughter died and she looked at him with pitying concern. Uncle Red was visibly weak. He was managing to smile and banter with Flossie and the members of the band, but it was obviously costing him great effort. His skin was ashen, and his face, even when he was smiling, had a look of profound weariness and dread.

"What's a matter, Red? Ain't you feeling good?" Flossie asked, with good-natured gruffness. "Ain't as frisky as you was down in Baton Rouge, when you 'most got the Klan down on us, is you?" She laughed. "Here, you, Ruf! Give Red one of 'em sticks, see can we perk 'im up a little. Make 'im sing a song. We ain't gonna get bothered by no Klan while we on Beale Street, honey."

Uncle Red jerked his head toward me. "This here's my nephew. Name's Whit Wagoner. Whit, this here's Flossie King, I was telling you 'bout." To her, he said, "He's dying to hear you sing. Think it's all right if he stays 'round for a little while?"

After flashing me a hello smile, Flossie passed Uncled Red' question to the bald-headed black man in shirtsleeves, wh said, "A white boy? Tell you what. Have 'im stay ovah by the back do. That way, if the po-lice come, we'll say he our delivery boy."

That brought laughter from everybody, I didn't know why, but I grinned to show them I could take a joke. And I moved over by the back door, which opened onto an alley behind the club. I sat down on a stack of beer cases and tried to be inconspicuous as I feasted my eyes on the glittering scene. Black people in flashy clothes and costumes were coming in the front door and being ushered to booths or tables by the headwaiter. I could smell hot spicy meat—barbecued ribs?—cooking in the kitchen behind the bar.

"You loose yet, Flossie?" the piano player asked.

"Loose!" she said. "Sheeee-yeet! If I was any looser, I'd be illegal!" Chuckling softly, she stepped up on the bandstand and stood behind the microphone, swaying her hips. "Aw right, le's do 'Long Old Road' again. In D this time. And see can we git some more bottom in it. Clarence," she suggested to the piano player, "put a lotta sustain on them bass notes."

"Wait a minute," the trombone player said, offering a butt of one of the hand-rolled cigarettes to the piano player. "Maybe some of this'd accentuate your armbuster, Clarence."

Clarence shook his head. He was probably the oldest member of the band. Strands of gray could be seen in his straightened, slicked-down hair, and he had a wizened, puckish face. "Not me," he drawled. "I start smoking that stuff, I start chasing women, and that'd be like a dog chasing a car. What he gonna do wid it when he catch it?"

"What's a matter?" Flossie teased. "You got no mo git up and go?"

Musingly tickling the ivory keys with long black spidery fingers, Clarence said, "Oh, I don't know 'bout that. Sometimes I needs a little help getting it up, but after that, I can still go."

And this exchange of waggery didn't end until Flossie gave them a count-off. They came in exactly on time with a sound as dense and smooth as a huge body of softly flowing water, a sound with the fullness and funky richness of the Mississippi River itself. And when Flossie started singing, my toes curled with excitement. Hers was a voice such as I had never heard before, a strange, lovely, forlorn voice crying out of darkness, plaintive with a sweet longing.

"It's a long old road, but I'm gonna find the end."

She sang the line again, with a slight shift in harmonies, her voice cracking with its burden of sorrow, and brought the verse to a climax.

> *"And when I get there,*
> *I'm gonna shake hands with a friend."*

All the sweet longing felt by everyone who ever lived seemed to converge in her harsh and beautiful voice.

> *"Weepin' and cryin', tears fallin' on the ground.*
> *Weepin' and cryin', tears fallin' on the ground.*
> *When I got to the end, I was so worried down."*

"Ain't she something?" Uncle Red said. He had come over to stand beside me. He brought with him one of the thin, handrolled cigarettes the band members had been passing around. "Want this?"

"A cigarette?" I asked, uncertain of my desire for it. I had tried smoking a few times before, and while it made me feel grown-up and rather rakehelly, it also made me dizzy and slighty queasy.

"Not tobacco," he said. "It's tea."

"Tea?"

He smiled. "Not really *tea*. That's just what they call it. It's marijuana."

I had absolutely no idea what that was. In fact, I thought he had said Mary Wanna, a girl's name.

"Gets you high," Uncle Red said. "Something like booze does, only a lot better. Don't leave you with a hangover. Makes you feel kinda dreamy. Kinda pleasantly pickled."

"Don't you want it?" I said, afraid to accept it.

"I'll get another from Ruf, if you want this un." The tone of his voice made it clear that he was merely offering, no suggesting.

I took it. I had no intention of smoking it then and there As a matter of fact, I had no intention of smoking it at all, an might never have, except that he struck a match and lit it fo me. I coughed a couple of times with the first puff, but Uncl Red told he how to smoke it, and then it was all right. It didn taste as bad as tobacco, and as long as I didn't suck in to much smoke at one time, the harshness was bearable. It didn't seem to be any big deal.

When Flossie finished her second song, she called Uncle Red to the bandstand. She didn't announce or introduce him to the audience. Uncle Red had been getting curious glances from many of the customers and waiters, and I could feel a slight diminution of the conversational sound level when Uncle Red stepped up on the bandstand. The diminution seemed to bespeak curiosity, however, and maybe a sort of challenging suspension of judgment, but not hostility. The fact that he was obviously a friend of Flossie's no doubt gained him a certain amount of acceptance from everybody in the club, patrons and employees alike.

A guitar came from behind the bandstand, and Uncle Red strapped it on. It was an electric guitar, a Gibson, the same kind that was used in Bob Wills's band.

The first song Flossie and Uncle Red sang together was an up-tempo bouncer, a sort of Dixieland thing called "Just Because," and they tore it up. They obviously loved performing with each other, and their singing styles were surprisingly complementary: his a high lonesome sound, hers a black bottomland sound, each voice remaining very distinct even when they were singing really close harmony.

> *"Just because you think you're so pretty,*
> *Just because you think that you're so hot,*
> *Just because you think you got something*
> *That nobody else has got."*

I was so absorbed in their teasing, bantering interchange that I forgot all about my stick—that's what Uncle Red had called it, a stick—and it went out before it was half-finished. But I didn't want any more of it anyway. I was feeling sort of woozy. It was a pleasant but spooky feeling, and it seemed to me that I could hear and see much more clearly than I ever had before. Flossie's dress sparkled and shimmered as her body shook to the music, and Uncle Red's rose-colored shirt, in the multicolored lights from the mirrored ball on the ceiling, looked like a rainbow.

> *"Just because you spend all my money,*
> *You laugh and call me old Santa Claus,*

I'm telling you, honey, I'm through with you,
Because, just because."

And now some of the patrons had begun to dance. The
couples whirled and undulated, their ass-shaking, tit-bouncing,
groin-thrusting movements so wild and abandoned as to be
shocking. I loved it.

And when the song ended, the dancers and patrons broke
into applause that was more than merely polite or approving.
They really liked Uncle Red. They loved Flossie King, of
course, but much of their applause seemed to be for Uncle
Red, letting him know that he had passed some crucial test.
There were scattered calls of "Awright! Awright!"

"Red Stovall!" Flossie announced over the microphone, and
there followed another burst of applause.

Swollen with pride and flushed with pleasure, I clapped
wildly for Uncle Red and Flossie. I loved them, and I loved
everybody because everybody loved them, and everybody loved
everybody, and I felt dizzily wonderful and loving.

I was cockeyed, of course. The tea had begun to have its
full effect. And during the next song, a bawdy blues in which
Uncle Red and Flossie traded verses, I closed my eyes for a
moment to concentrate on the music, and made one of the most
astonishing discoveries of my life: I discovered that I could *see*
sounds—actually *see* them in shapes and colors projected onto
the backs of my eyelids. At first the discovery frightened me.
I thought maybe the tea had taken me so deeply into a fantasy
world that I might never come back, but the experience soon
proved so sensational and beguiling that I no longer cared if I
came back. Like the shifting shapes and colors in a kaleido-
scope, the musical notes and sounds constantly whirled and
scattered and dissolved and took new shapes and colors, right
on the back of my closed eyelids. The sharp, stinging notes of
a guitar solo became little silver arrows that tore through the
throbbing red gelatinous background of drum and bass and
piano. A trombone riff made blue notes that ascended like a
stairway to a sudden sunburst of yolky yellow cymbal crashes,
while Flossie and Uncle Red's singing voices took the shapes
and colors of clustered opalescent bubbles in a pool of greens
and oranges.

"Hoss?" Uncle Red said.

I didn't know how long ago they had stopped singing.

"Red Stovall," Flossie said, rebuking him affectionately, "has you been letting that boy smoke dope?"

Somebody said there was a taxi out front. I couldn't walk very well. Uncle Red walked on one side of me, Flossie on the other, each holding an arm. Everybody was looking at me. I smiled at them. They smiled back. They loved me. I loved them. Everybody loved everybody.

And then I noticed that I could not only *see* sounds, I could also *feel* colors. My cheek brushed against Uncle Red's rose-colored shirt, and the color—not the cloth, but the color itself—felt like a warm non-wet liquid. And when they were putting me in the taxi, I reached out to touch Flossie King's face, and found that her light-brown color had the feel of a baby rabbit's fur.

Flossie laughed, chucked me under the chin, and said I was as cute as a bug's ear, and Uncle Red took me back to the hotel, and sleep came suddenly.

22

Uncle Red was right, tea didn't leave me with a hangover. I felt a little fuzzy and limp the next morning, but the feeling wasn't painful or even unpleasant—nothing like the busthead hangover I'd had from the booze I drank that time at the Grange Hall. In fact, I felt good.

It was Uncle Red who felt bad. He had spent a restless and feverish night, coughing more than usual, and was so lethargic the next morning that he didn't even seem to care whether or not we went on to Nashville. Despairing and miserable, he had to be coaxed into getting out of bed and into a bathtub of hot water that I had drawn for him. He felt a little better after the bath, or at least his disposition improved a little, and after he had nibbled on a breakfast of flapjacks and eggs, he even regained some interest in going on to Nashville.

For more than two hours after we left Memphis, as we drove out of the Mississippi Delta country, and through the lush rolling cotton and corn and cane fields of western Tennessee, Uncle Red huddled against the door, brooding and taciturn, taking an occasional sip from a bottle of whiskey. We had country music coming over the car radio most of the time, but he didn't seem to hear it. I tried a few times to draw him out. Searching for subjects, I mentioned that the tea had caused me to see sounds, and I wondered if it had that effect on everybody.

"If you get high enough on tea," he mumbled, "you can see

'bout anything you wanna see. The stick I gave you was that strong, huh?"

I asked him a few questions about it, but he answered with grunts or slight shrugs, hardly rousing himself from his stupor of despair. It was only when I mentioned Flossie King that he showed any real interest in my questions. And his first smile of the morning came when I haltingly asked him, "Well, I was wondering if you had ever . . . well, you know, if you'd ever *done it* with her."

"Shit," he drawled. "You kidding? I told you, she only goes to bed with guys she can't whup. What chance you think I'd have? Shit. She could break me in two with one hand." He smiled faintly. "Ain't she something, though? Whoooo-eeee! Big flashy funky nigger bitch, I love every inch of her."

That was the first time I had ever heard him say he loved someone. I knew he didn't mean it in a conventional sense— that is, he obviously didn't love Flossie the way I loved Belle. She wasn't someone he would marry. But it started me wondering again if he had every loved anybody in that way.

"Didn't you ever . . ." I faltered, trying to find the best way to phrase the question. "Didn't you ever meet a girl you wanted to marry?"

"You kidding?" he said scornfully. In spite of that, however, he seemed to think about it for a moment. "Well, actually, there was a girl once. . . ."

"You loved her?" I prompted.

He looked at me. He seemed to be wondering about my motive for asking, and when he saw that it wasn't just idle curiosity on my part, he told me the story of him and Mary Simms. He told it sporadically and out of sequence, and I had to keep prompting him with questions to keep him going. He seemed to get lost in reverie very often, leaving a sentence in the middle and gazing absently out the window for a long time. But he told it.

"I met her in California, eight or nine years ago," he said, and then he was silent, as if that were all of it. I prompted him by saying I was surprised to hear that he had been in California eight or nine years ago. I was under the impression, I said, that his first trip to California had been four years ago, the time he stopped to visit us for a few days in Oklahoma. Mama must not have known about the earlier trip, I said, or I surely would have heard about it.

"There's a lotta things your mama don't know 'bout me," he said, and that was certainly true. If she knew only half the things I knew about him, she would not have idolized her baby brother the way she did, and certainly she would never have allowed me to go to Nashville with him.

"Me and some boys from Shreveport put a band together, back in the summer of 1930, I guess it was. Figured to make our way out to California by stopping and playing in honky-tonks along the way, one-night stands here and there. But we didn't always get jobs playing, and when we got broke and stranded, we'd just take farm jobs for a few days—chopping cotton, heading maize, picking beans—and then be on our way again, looking for places where we could play our music. We was all nineteen and twenty and twenty-one then, and was like ducks, we didn't give a quack. If it didn't rain, we'd walk."

They ended up in a farming town in the Imperial Valley. "Town called Brawley. Played at the Dew Drop Inn on Friday and Saturday nights, and during the week we worked on a farm owned by a man named Simms. Tough old bastard. Barrel-chested. Had a big bull neck. And had two sons just like him, only bigger.

"One of the sons—the youngest one—was married to a girl named Mary, and they had two kids, both boys, about six and eight years old. Mary had married him when she was fourteen years old, and she was a year or two older'n me when I met her. A rawboned Okie girl, she was. Not much to look at, really. Thin and sinewy, I guess you'd call her, with straight brown hair and a few freckles across her nose. But decent . . . know what I mean? Decent, hard-working girl, good mother, faithful wife—all that stuff—and you knew it just by looking at her. So she had her own kinda beauty. . . ."

He met her when he went to work on Simms's farm, picking tomatoes by the lug. Old man Simms and his two spit-'n'-image sons worked in the fields, too, driving the wagons that picked up the lugs of tomatoes, or overseeing the work, while Mary Simms often worked right alongside the hired hands, bending over the tomato vines, picking and lugging tomatoes with the best of them.

"And most of the time, I'd sing while I worked. I was in much better health then, the work had toughened me up, and I was brown all over. Anyway, I'd sing a right smart while I worked, and when I did, I nearly always found that Mary just happened to be working somewhere nearby. Reckon it was could I say then? 'Hey, honey, I didn't mean it. I was just saying that to get in your pants'? And, anyway, I thought maybe I really did love her. I respected her a lot, and I liked her a lot, too, so what the hell is love anyway, if it ain't that?"

He was silent for a moment then, and when I asked him what happened next, he said, "The band broke up. Was getting on toward the end of the summer by then, and the field hands were starting to move north to work in the orchards and vineyards in the Central Valley. So the Dew Drop Inn lost a lot of its customers, and pretty soon the place could no longer afford a band. We could of moved, like I wanted to do, but the boys in the band was tired of being on the road all the time. The fun had gone out of it. Fiddle player was homesick, the bass player had a sweetheart in Shreveport that he wanted to go see, and the dobro player'd been offered a steady job with a well-established band in Dallas.

"So there I was, left in Brawley with my guitar and a raw-boned Okie girl who was in love with me. When I told her I had to be leaving soon, she just naturally assumed that she'd be leaving with me. To her way of thinking, that's what people done when they fell in love, they clove to each other. She was like that Ruth in the Bible, you know? 'Wither thou goeth, I will go'—that kinda stuff.

"'What about your kids?' I says. She had two of 'em, two boys. And they were Simms boys, too, chips off the old blocks. And she knew that the old blocks, old man Simms and his sons, would die and go to hell 'fore they'd let her take them two boys gallivanting 'round the country with a two-bit troubadour like me, living in hotels and honkytonks, broke half the time, not always sure where my next meal was coming from. What kinda life would that be for a couple of kids?"

So Uncle Red figured he'd be moving on by himself. But along about then the Simmses found out about Mary's parking-lot love affair with Uncle Red. And she didn't try to deny it. She told them she was in love with Uncle Red and wanted to go away with him, and that night—the last night that Uncle Red was to play at the Dew Drop Inn—Old Man Simms and his two sons paid him a little visit. Uncle Red was ready for trouble, of course, as soon as he saw them. The two sons—Mary's husband and his brother, big bruisers, both of them—obviously would have liked nothing better than to tear Uncle Red limb from limb, but the old man held them in check. He could I say then? 'Hey, honey, I didn't mean it. I was just saying that to get in your pants'? And, anyway, I thought maybe I really did love her. I respected her a lot, and I liked her a lot, too, so what the hell is love anyway, if it ain't that?"

He was silent for a moment then, and when I asked him what happened next, he said, "The band broke up. Was getting on toward the end of the summer by then, and the field hands were starting to move north to work in the orchards and vineyards in the Central Valley. So the Dew Drop Inn lost a lot of its customers, and pretty soon the place could no longer afford a band. We could of moved, like I wanted to do, but the boys in the band was tired of being on the road all the time. The fun had gone out of it. Fiddle player was homesick, the bass player had a sweetheart in Shreveport that he wanted to go see, and the dobro player'd been offered a steady job with a well-established band in Dallas.

"So there I was, left in Brawley with my guitar and a raw-boned Okie girl who was in love with me. When I told her I had to be leaving soon, she just naturally assumed that she'd be leaving with me. To her way of thinking, that's what people done when they fell in love, they clove to each other. She was like that Ruth in the Bible, you know? 'Wither thou goeth, I will go'—that kinda stuff.

" 'What about your kids?' I says. She had two of 'em, two boys. And they were Simms boys, too, chips off the old blocks. And she knew that the old blocks, old man Simms and his sons, would die and go to hell 'fore they'd let her take them two boys gallivanting 'round the country with a two-bit troubadour like me, living in hotels and honkytonks, broke half the time, not always sure where my next meal was coming from. What kinda life would that be for a couple of kids?"

So Uncle Red figured he'd be moving on by himself. But along about then the Simmses found out about Mary's parking-lot love affair with Uncle Red. And she didn't try to deny it. She told them she was in love with Uncle Red and wanted to go away with him, and that night—the last night that Uncle Red was to play at the Dew Drop Inn—Old Man Simms and his two sons paid him a little visit. Uncle Red was ready for trouble, of course, as soon as he saw them. The two sons—Mary's husband and his brother, big bruisers, both of them—obviously would have liked nothing better than to tear Uncle Red limb from limb, but the old man held them in check. He had only one thing to say to Uncle Red: "Get outta town. If Mary wants to go with you, we won't stop her. But the children stay here. If she goes, she gives them up forever. But whatever happens, if I ever see your face around here again, cowboy, I'll turn these two boys loose on you, and when they get through, you won't have a face left. You understand me?"

"Hell, yes, I understood him. Hell, I was even sympathetic. Now that I'd done got what I wanted, you see, I was beginning to be sorry I'd caused them so much trouble, busting up their home like that. Hell, they wasn't bad folks, come right down to it, and I figured that after I was gone, Mary and her husband would probably patch things up and go back to living the same dull and I guess peaceful lives they'd been living 'fore I came along.

"What I didn't understand, though, was how much Mary loved me. She simply wouldn't be left behind. Said she was willing to give up everything for me—her kids, family, home, a life of security and comfort, her friends, everything, just to be with me. Can you beat that?" he asked, shaking his head with awe. "Even her kids. . . .

"Well, it was flattering, of course, but I wasn't at all sure I wanted anybody to love me that much. But what could I do? I couldn't just chuck her over, could I? Not after she'd given up everything for me. So I thought, well, what the hell, why not take her along? I had nothing to lose, after all, and she'd done lost everything she had to lose. So I thought, what the hell, let's see how things work out."

Things worked out fine for a while. The two of them started following the harvests up through the San Joaquin Valley, living in migrant shacks and rooming houses, going from town to town on a bus, "just as happy as if we had good sense," Uncle Red said, "'cept that now and then Mary'd get to thinking about her kids, get to missing 'em, and I'd have to do something to cheer her up. Other'n that, though, I reckon we was what you'd call happy. She was a good influence on me, I'll have to say that for her. She worked right alongside me in the fields every day, always looking after me, helping me get my health back, and she even talked me into giving up booze and ciga-rettes. That's right. For two whole months, I didn't have a drink or smoke. And she kept me outta honkytonks, too. We lived a quiet, healthy, lots-a-loving life, working our way up the valley. Picked cotton in Bakersfield, grapes in Delano, almonds in Fresno, pears in Merced, apples in Modesto. . . ."

But when they got to Stockton, things changed. "By then I was getting itchy to play music again. So I went to a honkytonk one night and sat in with a band, and was offered a job on the spot. I could play six nights a week and make enough money to live on. To hell with breaking my back in them damned asparagus fields every day."

Of course, he started drinking and smoking again. "Mary didn't like any of it, but she stuck by me. For a while, she hung around the honkytonks every night while I played. She soon got tired of it, though—tired of the smoke and the noise, tired of being hassled for dances and dates by barroom drunks, and finally even got tired of hearing the same old songs, night after night.

"And by then I was tired, too—tired a having her there every night. She was cramping my style. I got to wondering what the hell I was doing with her, anyway. Why was I with this rawboned Okie girl, when there were all sorts of luscious sluts hanging 'round the bandstand, showing me what I could have anytime I wanted it? And some of them were real pretty, too. Wore perfume and silk stockings and had their hair all piled up on their heads. Real knockouts."

So he suggested to Mary that maybe she ought to get a waitress job or something like that—something to keep her from hanging around the honkytonk every night when he played.

"Well, she had her pride. She knew when she wasn't wanted. So she didn't hang 'round no more. Got herself a job as a nighttime attendant in a convalescent home. And that left me free to diddle them painted-faced floozies in the honkytonk. And I did, too, lemme tell you. Whoooo doggies, but there was some good stuff 'round there!

"But one night Mary caught me at it. It was during intermission. I was out in the car with this ole girl, smooching and panting, with my hand clear up in her crotch, and all of a sudden I look up and see Mary there. She's just standing there, looking in the window at us, and for a few seconds she looks me straight in the eye. Then she turned around and left.

"Well, I knew what I had to do then. I went back to the rooming house, and I told her, I said, 'Look kid, I think we made a mistake.' She'd been crying, but she'd wiped her eyes when she heard me coming, and holy shit, she was mad! I gave her some money and told her I was gonna move out, and she threw the money in my face. Can you beat that? Right in my face! Said she didn't want a damned thing of mine, and she never wanted to see me again. *Never.*

"Well, I was so mad at her for throwing that money in my face like that, I told her, 'Good riddance,' and went out to get drunk as a skunk. Left the money on the floor where it'd fell. Ended up at some ole gal's place, swilling booze and playing grab-ass. But pretty soon, she passed out on the couch, with her stockings hanging down 'round her big ankles, and I got to looking at her—a snoring, boozy slut with henna hair—and wondering what in the name of hell I was doing there. I got to thinking 'bout Mary—'bout what a strong, decent, sweet girl she was, and how much she loved me. And I guess I got to feeling sorry for myself, cussing myself for being a no-good whiskey-swilling cunt-hound fool, wishing I was worthy of Mary's love.

"That's when I first realized that I really did love her," Uncle Red said absently, his thoughts and his feverish eyes focused on something far away. "Sure, she was just a plain, rawboned down-home girl, but, hell, she was worth any number of them painted-pretty barroom floozies. She was...everything them floozies wasn't.... And the more I thought 'bout it, the more I realized how much I cared 'bout her. Loved her. And always had. I hadn't lied to her at all when I told her I loved her. Sure, I had told her that just so's I could get in her pants, but by God, it was true! It was *me* I was lying to when I told myself I didn't love her...."

And after coming to that astonishing realization, he hurried back home at dawn to tell Mary how much he loved her, to ask her to forgive him.

"She was gone. Cleared out. Took all her clothes and vanished. The money was still scattered on the floor.

"Well, sir, I took off after her. Didn't know where I was going, really, but just chased all over town, checking with everybody she knew. But nobody'd heard from her. Nobody knew where she was. I kept going back to the rooming house, hoping maybe she'd changed her mind and come back, or at least had phoned, but no luck. And I was there when the doctor bill came in the mail, to Mrs. Mary Stovall.

"Doctor? Why the hell'd she gone to a doctor? Was something wrong with her that I didn't know about? Well, I had to find out, of course, so I hotfooted it over to the doctor's office, and what I found out was, Mary was pregnant. That's right—pregnant. Well, that done it. That really tore it. I felt lower'n whale shit then, I wanna tell you, so I bought a whiskey and went back to the rooming house to get drunk again. Why not? My life was in ruins. I'd lost the only woman I'd ever loved—and I hadn't even known that I loved her till I'd already lost her."

And as he was lying on the bed, brooding and drinking and feeling sorry for himself, he suddenly became aware of a radio playing in another room. He had been hearing the song without being totally aware of what it was until he heard the last lines,

> *"Going home on the Silver Zephyr,*
> *Going home for the last time."*

He sat up in bed. He knew then, suddenly and without any doubt whatsoever, where Mary had gone. She had gone back to Brawley. He phoned the train depot and learned that, yes, the Silver Zephyr left early that morning on its run south.

Drunk and half crazy, he jumped on the next bus to Brawley. "I had some crazy idea that I could find her and win her back. But the bus ride gave me lots of time to consider my chances of success, and by the time I got to Brawley, I knew with dead certainty that old man Simms and his sons would never let her go again. Never.

"But I hung around town for a few days anyway, hoping I'd get a chance to see her, or that somehow she'd find out I was in town and maybe get a message to me. And, sure enough, old man Simms found me at the Dew Drop Inn one night and told me that somebody was waiting outside to see me. I thought it was Mary," he said, musingly sarcastic. "Or at least I was hoping it was. Actually, though, I reckon I knew what was coming, and, truth to tell, I figured I deserved it. That's why I didn't even fight back when the two Simms boys jumped me in the parking lot.

"They beat the living shit outta me. Whammed me, slammed me, kicked and cuffed me, and left me laying there in the dirt, bleeding and only half conscious. And before they walked away, the old man leans down and says to me, says, 'I told you what'd happen if you ever showed up here again, didn't I?' Says, 'Now, maybe you'll believe me when I tell you what'll happen if you ever show up here again.' Says, 'Next time, we'll break every bone in your hands and fingers so bad you'll never play the guitar again. Think 'bout that,' he says."

Uncle Red snorted, and then was silent again, frowning, his lips pursed.

"What'd you do then?" I prompted.

"What'd I do!" He snorted again. "Laid there and bawled, that's what I done. Laid there between two cars in that parking lot and cried like a baby. Not just 'cause I was hurt, though. I was in plenty of pain, I can tell you, but that wasn't why I laid there and bawled. It was 'cause...oh, I don't know. Everything just seemed so damned *hope*less. I'd been glad to die, right there. Maybe I did, in a way. It was the first time I ever wondered, 'What in God's name are we living for?' Just laid there, crying, wondering, 'What in God's name are we living for?'"

He took another sip from the whiskey bottle, cleared his throat, and turned to gaze at the passing countryside. We were about two hours away from Nashville.

"Did you ever see her again?" I asked.

He shook his head. "Stopped in Brawley once...couple of years ago, it was. Just after I done that gig at the Dream Bowl with Bob Wills. I had one of the boys in the band drive me over to Brawley. I was curious to see her. Curious 'bout the kid. If she'd had it, I mean. Well, it turned out that she did. I met an ole boy I'd worked with that summer out on Simms's place, and he told me that exactly seven and a half months after Mary got home—they kept track of things like that in a small town like Brawley—seven and a half months after she got back to Brawley and was taken in by the Simms family again, she had a baby. A girl. That ole boy didn't know what they named her, but he'd seen her—she was seven years old by then—he'd seen her 'round town a few times. Cutest little red-headed girl you ever saw. That's what he said, 'Cutest little red-headed girl....'"

After a long silence, I said, "You never saw her? The girl?"

"No. Left town soon's I heard 'bout her. Figured, what the hell good would it do for me to see her? Or her, me? Best she never knew 'bout me. Mary'd been right to go back to the Simmses. What the hell did I have to offer her or a kid? Honkytonks and flophouses." He looked at me. "That's the life of a country singer, Hoss. Think you want any part of it?"

It sounded awfully bleak, but I didn't have time to think

about it very long. "Well, it sounds better'n cotton fields and sharecroppers' cabins, anyway."

"Yeah," he said. "Maybe it does, at that. Maybe it does." And once again his words trailed off.

It was so odd to see him so subdued, so timorous and sparing in his expressions and gestures, but attentive, like a man feeling his way through a familiar darkness. And I no longer tried to draw him out. Instead, I was busy trying to figure him out. He never ceased to surprise me. That he had once been in love didn't really surprise me, nor was I even surprised to learn that he had a daughter somewhere out in California. What surprised me was that he had cried. Uncle Red? Lying on the ground in a parking lot, crying like a baby? The only grown man I had ever seen cry was Papa, but he had done it only when sloppy drunk and wallowing in blubbery self-pity, a sight that had always left me disgusted and ashamed. But to imagine Uncle Red, of all people, crying...

Then he made a sound that filled me with sudden fear. His mouth fell open and he made fishlike gulping sounds, fighting for breath, and then came a terrible coughing fit. His sunken eyes grew wide and his ashen face flushed crimson and he roared with long phlegm-rattling coughs. The whiskey bottle fell from his lap, and his bony hand trembled frantically for his handkerchief. Leaning forward, he coughed again and again, choking with terror, holding the handkerchief over his gaping mouth.

I pulled the car off the road and stopped. Roaring and choking, Uncle Red clawed the car door open and stumbled out. He dragged his retching body to a roadside tree and leaned against it, bent over, racked and shaking.

Wanting desperately to help, I ran to him, but of course there was nothing I could do, and he waved me away. He kept his back to me as I, helpless and terrified, stood and watched him, but when the coughing fit reached its tearing and rattling climax, I saw the blood ooze out of his mouth and spill over his lip. He was hemorrhaging.

"Uncle Red!" I cried in panic, and took a few more halting steps toward him. But once again he waved me away. He didn't want me to see it, but I saw him wipe the blood from his mouth, and I saw how his body went on shaking and trembling, and I heard his breath come in shallow, hoarse rattles for a long time after.

"Uncle Red," I pleaded, "there'll be a doctor in Nashville. Come on, I'll take you."

He cleared his throat and spat bloody saliva onto the ground at his feet, threw away his blood-soaked handkerchief, and held his hand out toward me. "Handkerchief?" he said hoarsely.

I jerked my handkerchief from my hip pocket and ran to place it in his bloodstained fingers. He used it to scrub harshly at his mouth and hands.

"Uncle Red?"

He shook his head. "No good. Doctor'd just wanna put me in a sanitarium. Goddamn."

"But if it's getting worse, maybe a sanitarium, just for a while?"

"I been in a sanitarium," he said hoarsely, and spat again. This time the saliva was less crimson. "Ain't never gonna be in another one. They don't let you sing in a sanitarium. Come on, now, let's get on to Nashville. Get us a place to stay 'fore it gets dark."

I caught his trembling arm and helped him into the back seat of the car. I, too, was trembling, unnerved by the pain and bewilderment and terror that I saw in his face. When I saw him stretched out on the back seat, with his feverish eyes closed and his pale skinny hands clasped over his chest, I had my first intimation of how it was going to end.

23

The Ryman Auditorium was built as a tabernacle. Later it became the home of the Grand Ole Opry. But it never lost its awesome, sacred air. On the day that I first visited the Opry House with Uncle Red, the scarred church pews were empty, which made the space in the auditorium seem even more vast. It was the biggest auditorium I had ever seen, with its huge stained-glass windows and balconies and cluttered stage. The enormous canvas backdrop that once was emblazoned with Biblical admonitions for a better life was now covered with signs advertising Prince Albert tobacco, Black Draught cough syrup, and Checkerboard Feeds.

On the huge stage, the Monroe Brothers were going through some new songs that they were going to play next Saturday night on a five-hour Grand Ole Opry show that would be broadcast over radio station WSM. It fascinated me to think that Roy Acuff had often stood on that very stage and sung, and his voice had carried, sweet and clear, over the mountains and rivers and prairies to reach my ears in the little town of Roscoe, Oklahoma. Truly, to be heard so far and wide seemed a power that could only belong to the gods.

"That's it," Uncle Red said, nodding toward the stage. "You sing into *that* microphone, Hoss, and ten million people hear you, all at the same time."

"Ten million?"

"I ain't bird-turding. Every Saturday night. Hear you all the way from Mexico to Canada."

I was there with Uncle Red to hear him audition for the Opry. We had been in Nashville for two days, staying in a rooming house only a few blocks from the Ryman Auditorium. We had rented two rooms in the house, a bedroom and a sitting room. I slept on the sofa in the sitting room, while Uncle Red slept in the bed—and that was mostly what he had done for two days, slept. I brought his food to him from a nearby cafe, and he only went out a couple of times. The first time was to phone the program manager at the Opry, who appointed an hour and a day for him to come to the Opry House for his audition. The second time he went out, it was to get a pint of whiskey. But he didn't get drunk. He took the bottle to bed with him and sipped on it medicinally.

Uncle Red left me by myself in the huge auditorium. He went backstage, carrying his guitar. I took a seat in an aisle pew about ten rows back from the stage. I had the whole auditorium to myself while the Monroe Brothers finished their rehearsal on the huge stage. But when Uncle Red came out of the wings and onto the stage, his guitar strapped on, a man and a woman came out from backstage and sat down in a pew three rows in front of me. I was to learn later that the man— a severely good-looking older man with wavy, iron-gray hair and rimless eyeglasses, the very image of a Baptist deacon— was George Stubbs, the Opry's program manager. The woman with him was his secretary.

Uncle Red shambled up to one of the microphones and pecked on it with the tip of his finger.

"You won't need it," Mr. Stubbs said, his voice so crisp it crackled. "I can hear you all right without it. Well, then, Mr. Stovall—Red—anytime you're ready."

Uncle Red seemed not exactly nervous, but tense and a little disturbed, as if he were worried about something other than the audition. He carelessly strummed his guitar a few times, cleared his throat, and began to sing one of his original compositions, a song called "Boogie Man."

> *"Lock up your daughters fast as you can,*
> *Hide 'em away from the wild Boogie Man.*
> *He's coming to town on the midnight train,*

No girl's safe till he's gone again,
He's the Boogie Man,
The Boogie Woogie Man. . . ."

That was as far as he got before Mr. Stubbs signaled him to stop. "That song's too Nigrah for the Opry, Red," he said, crisply but without any implied criticism. "I'd like to hear you do a more country tune. You have any songs in three-four?"

"Yes, sir," Uncle Red said, strumming carelessly. "Little thing called 'It's All Downhill from Here.'"

"Fine, let's hear that," Mr. Stubbs said. He held his hands together in front of him, the fingers interlaced except for the two index fingers, which stood straight up and were stiffly pressed together to form a spire over the church of his clasped hands.

Uncle Red began his song, one of his humorous songs, sung in a mournful parody of a tearjerker, about a man whose wife has run off with another man—

"A guy she met in a bar.
I don't mind that they took all my money,
But I sure wish they'd left me my car."

He wasn't really putting a lot of energy into it, but he was in good voice, and his lackadaisical delivery fit well with the mocking lament of the song. It turns out that the man in the song doesn't give a damn about losing his wife, it's the loss of his pretty car that he laments.

"'Cause it's all downhill from here,
Yeah, it's all downhill from here.
I might as well sit here and cry in my beer
'Cause it's all downhill from here."

But that was as far as he got. Mr. Stubbs once again raised his hand as a signal to stop. Uncle Red's singing and playing trailed off into puzzled annoyance.

"Sorry to interrupt you, Red," Mr. Stubbs said, "but that song can't be done on the Opry. We don't allow the mention of alcholic beverages on the program."

"Beer?" Uncle Red said, incredulous.

"Even beer. Ours is a clean, wholesome, family show, Red,

clean and wholesome, and we don't allow our artists to mention any alcoholic beverages. Beer included. What else you have that I could hear?"

Uncle Red thought for a moment, strumming on his guitar again. "Got one about death."

"Ah! Good," Mr. Stubbs said, brightening. "Death's always a good subject for a song, 'specially if it's about someone's mother dying. People love to cry, Red. They love to laugh, but they love to cry, too, and there's nothing that'll make 'em cry quicker than a song about Mother dying. Let's hear that one."

"Well, this ain't about Mother," Uncle Red said. "It's about death."

"Oh?" Mr. Stubbs said, earnestly trying to understand. "Well, let's hear it."

"It's called 'Pale Horse, Pale Rider.'"

"Ah!" Mr. Stubbs said approvingly. "A Biblical reference. That's always good. Well, then . . ."

Uncle Red looked blank for a few seconds. I was hoping to God he wasn't going to make some sarcastic remark about dying mothers. But he appeared to be calm and collected— even a little detached. And he didn't look bad physically, either. Even though his gaunt face was still ashy-colored and clawed with fatigue, he was at least clean-shaven and close to being sober. He wore his newly cleaned cowboy performing suit, and he'd had his boots shined earlier that morning.

When he began singing "Pale Horse, Pale Rider," Mr. Stubbs slowly turned to give his secretary a significant look. Her response was an enigmatic lift of her eyebrows. Then they turned their attention back to Uncle Red. As he sang mournfully of death's indifference to dreams, Mr. Stubbs leaned forward a little, with the tips of his spired fingers touching the end of his thin turned-up nose. Then he suddenly leaned toward his secretary and whispered something in her ready ear. And as soon as he finished whispering, she got up and hurriedly tiptoed backstage. She returned in less than a minute with another man, whom she stealthily led to a seat in the pew with Mr. Stubbs. I was to learn later that this man was Pete Clemmens, the Opry's general manager, a nondescript middle-aged man with a half-chewed cigar clenched in his teeth. He and Mr. Stubbs exchanged glances but said nothing.

Uncle Red sang the song flawlessly, as if he had been

playing and singing it for years. He sang it as if it were an incantation, as if it were the only thing in the world that mattered to him at the moment, and the cutting-edge intensity of his voice made everybody else feel the same way.

When he finished, I almost applauded. I caught myself in time, however, the impulse suddenly inhibited by the dead silence of the three people sitting in front of me. They didn't applaud. They only kept staring at Uncle Red as the last faint notes of the song hummed hauntingly into the auditorium's stained-glass gloom.

Then Mr. Stubbs and Mr. Clemmens, like two birds leaving a limb at the exact same instant, leaned toward each other across the front of the plump secretary. They held a brief whispered conference, after which Mr. Stubbs said, "Well," and got up and walked briskly toward the stage. In a tone of guarded and perhaps conditional delight, he said, "Well, that was very nice, Red. Very nice, indeed." He took the short stairway to the stage in two hops, and approached Uncle Red with his hand extended. "Come on up to my office. We'll talk."

Mr. Clemmens and the secretary also got up and went backstage, leaving me once again the only occupant in all the clothes-polished pews, the only seeker in the auditorium's cathedral hush, awaiting Uncle Red's return. I hadn't known quite what to make of Mr. Stubbs's response. It had seemed favorable, but any response to Uncle Red's singing that was less than ecstatic perplexed me. Still, I couldn't imagine them turning him down. Uncle Red? Not a chance. Within a year—no! Six months at the most!—he would be there on that stage, one of the Opry's biggest stars, singing his heart out to ten million listeners, all of whom would worship him. And then maybe someday—who could tell?—I myself might be standing there, front and center, on the very spot where Uncle Red and all the other great Opry stars had stood, dressed in a fancy sequined costume, playing my guitar and singing to the gathered multitudes. I could hear them in the balconies, clapping, stamping their feet, whistling. "More! More!" And all the people in the crowded pews rise as one in a standing ovation, urging one more encore. "More! More!" And my eyes become misted as I raise my hands in benediction to the wildly cheering throng. A heavenly choir of angels makes the tabernacle throb with sweet hosannas, shafts of sunlight stream through the stained-glass windows and, mote-filled, fall like spotlights upon me as I become my dreams.

"Penny for your thoughts?"

It was Uncle Red. I hadn't seen him come from backstage. He shifted his guitar case from one hand to the other.

"A penny?" I shook my head. "They were priceless."

"Good. We may need to hock 'em 'fore we leave Nashville," he said. And as we walked up the aisle toward the main entrance, he told me that Mr. Stubbs had offered him a spot on the Friday-night Opry two weeks hence. "Only the Saturday show is broadcast," he said, explaining the significance. "Friday-night shows are just played to the house audience, and all I get paid is twenty-eight bucks for the show."

"Oh," I said, not knowing quite what to make of it. "They liked you, didn't they?"

He nodded. "Said they did. Said I had a big future ahead of me." He snorted. "But they'd heard I was a drinker, and they want me to prove my reliability 'fore they put me on the Saturday-night hookup, and that won't be for at least a couple of weeks. Means we gonna be mighty poor for the next two weeks, 'less I can rustle up a gig somewhere. You got any money left over from what I give you?"

I had a little over eight dollars left.

"Hang onto it," he said. "We might need it."

I hadn't intended to spend it on anything. Well, actually, the thought—the fantasy—of another visit to a whorehouse had flitted through my mind once or twice lately. I was getting primed to try that again. True, I didn't want to do it with any woman other than Belle. At the same time, however, I realized that it was going to be a long time before I saw her again; meanwhile I had eight dollars in my pocket and I found myself thinking now and then of all the women it would buy. The very thought of being able to buy a woman had given me a hard-on more than once during my nights on the sofa in the rooming house, and I had found myself hoping that maybe Uncle Red might soon feel the need of a whore and once again take me with him.

But he was too sick for that. He didn't seem to be recovering very well from the last coughing fit and hemorrhage. He remained feverish and listless, racked by more frequent and more debilitating coughs, restless and yet exhausted. He stayed in bed most of the time, smoking and drinking and frowning with distaste at the hamburgers and French fries I brought in for him. He forced himself to eat a little, though. It seemed that he was finally beginning to show some concern for his health. Appearing on the Opry had been the dream of his life, a long-nourished desire that overrode all the others, and now that the dream was within grabbing distance, he didn't want to be cheated of it by sickness. So, for two days following his Opry audition, he hardly left his room except to go out and eat or to buy a bottle. He didn't get too drunk and even spent a couple of hours every day with his guitar, working out an arrangement for "Pale Horse, Pale Rider."

In spite of his efforts to eat and get adequate rest, however, Uncle Red's fever and frequent coughing fits didn't subside. Though not as severe as the fit he had suffered on the road, the explosions of coughing that racked his body more and more frequently since our arrival in Nashville soon drove him to an exasperated fury.

"God*damn!*" Striking the butt of his fist on the bed or on his thigh, he would curse and moan, "God*damn!*"

And the night before his scheduled morning rehearsal at the Opry House, he was convulsed by a coughing fit that finally drove him over the edge. Sweating and furious, he slammed out of his hot room, and when I asked him where he was going, he snapped, "Gonna get a drink. Be back after a while."

Three hours later he still hadn't come back. By the end of the first hour I was too worried to lie on the sofa and read my comic books any longer, and by the end of the second hour I was walking the floor and looking out the window, and by the end of the third hour I knew I had better go look for him. Figuring that he had probably gone to the nearest honkytonk on lower Broadway, I went to search for him there. A cooling air drifted up Broadway from the Cumberland River at the low end of the street. It was nearly midnight, and only a few busi-nesses—smoky cafes, saloons and poolrooms—were open along the street. Unlike the loud and festive air of Memphis's Beale Street, Broadway, its white Nashville equivalent, had a mean and stringent air. Though it was the center of Nashville's white nightlife, the only people on the street were hard-faced hillbilly whores with their drunken customers, a few hoboes hanging out in the poolrooms and beaneries, a few bums sleep-ing under newspapers in doorways.

I found Uncle Red in the third saloon I came to, a place called Rosie's Club. Before I even opened the door, I heard a woman screeching from within, "Damn men that can't hold their liquor, anyway!"

It was Uncle Red she was referring to. He was passed out with his face on the table. The woman, overweight and sassy, dressed in an apron and wearing square-framed granny glasses, was standing over Uncle Red's sprawling form, shaking his shoulder. "Come on, you sumbitch, get outta here! Closing time! Out out out! Move it! You hear?" When she caught sight of me, she snapped, "What d'you want, kid?"

"Him," I said, hanging back. I was afraid of her. "He's my uncle."

"Well, get 'im outta here!" she said, as if she had already told me a dozen times. Then she yelled at the few customers who were still at the bar. "All right, it's losing time. Drink up and get the hell out, all of you. Come on, now. Out out out!"

Uncle Red's ashen face lay contorted on the table top, his mouth open, drooling. His hat sat askew on his head. From beneath the hat tumbled his wavy red hair, with wispy strands clinging to the sweat on his high bony forehead. He grunted and mumbled, "Uh? Uh?" when I shook him and called his name.

"Get 'im outta here," the shrill woman said again as she passed the table. "Damn men who can't hold their liquor. Comes in here to see how much he can put away in a couple of hours, the damned fool, but it puts him away, instead. Ha! Out out out!"

"Come on, Uncle Red," I pleaded, shaking him some more. "It's me. Come on, I'll help you back to the rooms. The woman wants to close up here."

"I don't *want* to, sonny, I'm *going* to. Now you got one minute to get 'im outta here, or I'll toss 'im out on his ear. Out out out!"

I finally shook Uncle Red into a semblance of consciousness. Cockeyed and sputtering, he flopped back in his chair. "Wha' . . . wha' you wan'?"

"Let's go home. Come on. I'll help you."

It took us over twenty minutes to walk only about six blocks. Uncle Red staggered along with his bony arm around my shoulders. He mumbled, he hummed, he made hawking noises. He even sang a few snatches from unrecognizable songs, growing maudlin and expansive. "Ole Hoss!" he said once, clasping my shoulder with a heavy, good-natured roughness. "Ole Hoss! My buddy! You my buddy, ain't ya, Hoss?"

"Sure, Uncle Red. Sure. Watch the curb, now. . . ."

It was the first time I had ever seen him the least bit maudlin. There seemed no danger of his beginning to cry, as Papa always did when *he* got on a maudlin drunk. Still, there was a sort of exaggerated rough-hewn tenderness in the way he clapped my shoulder, and mumbled, "Ole Hoss! My good ole buddy!" Then he staggered, sniggered, and said, "Boy, am I shit-faced! Thin' you'n ge' me Opry House in a mornin', Hoss? Ole buddy?"

I did. It took some doing, but I got him there on time. I helped him out of bed at eight, pushed him, still dressed in his shorts, into the shower, then helped him into his clothes, and then guided him down to a cafe and filled him up with black coffee and doughnuts. Then he looked almost respectable. His hands were shaking, it's true, and his eyes were bloodshot, not to mention that he hadn't shaved since yesterday, but he had at least begun to look alert and could walk without staggering.

When we got to the Opry House, the backup band had already assembled on stage. There was a bass, a dobro, a piano, a fiddle, and an acoustic guitar. Mr. Stubbs introduced Uncle Red to each of the musicians, and then he told him, "Go ahead and line it out to them. I'll take a seat down front here, and listen for a while, it it's all right with you. There'll be some more people joining me in a minute, if you don't mind. Well, go ahead. . . ."

Mr. Stubbs stepped off the stage and sat down in the same pew that he had occupied on the day of the audition, and because I, too, sat down in the same seat I'd had that other day, Mr. Stubbs was again three rows in front of me. And soon he was joined by four other men. As Uncle Red was carefully lining out the complex chord changes of his song, the four men ambled into the auditorium from backstage and took seats close to Mr. Stubbs. And just as Uncle Red was about to count off the beat for the first run-through of the song, Mr. Stubbs raised his hand.

"Pardon me, Red," he said in his crisp Baptist-preacher voice. "Before you begin, let me introduce you to these men here. They want to hear you sing. This here's Pete Clemmens, the Opry's general manager. Next is WSM's advertising director, Jim Thornsby. And these two gentlemen here are visitors from New York. Henry Axle and Charlie Jones, with Burnside Records, down here to see if we got any talent worth recording."

Uncle Red merely exchanged casual nods with the men and

grunted greetings as their names were called.

"Well, then," Mr. Stubbs said, as if they could now get on with the music.

The public-address system was being used today, and as Uncle Red began singing into the microphone, the four men in front of me became still and alert, each one staring at Uncle Red with the rapt attention of a cat staring into a mousehole. It was very exciting for me to watch their reactions, because I sensed that these men had the power to make Uncle Red one of the biggest country stars in the land. They could do it. All they had to do was like him, and they obviously liked him. In fact, when he finished, they applauded. It was only a sort of token applause, of course, but it was sincere, not just polite applause, and it was obvious that *any* kind of applause from these men was an accolade of the highest order. Then they smiled at each other and exchanged significant glances, as if congratulating themselves on making an exciting discovery.

"That was fine, Red, just fine," Mr. Stubbs said. "But it occurred to me while you were singing that maybe we ought to put a church choir in the background. How'd you like that? A whole choir? We could make it the program's big production number. What do you think of that?"

Uncle Red was flattered. Grinning, he said, "Sure," and then added sardonically, "As long as *I* don't have to pay for it."

Mr. Stubbs and his associates chuckled, and Mr. Stubbs said, "Don't worry. It'll be the choir from my church, and I think they'll be glad to do it for nothing. Well, then, with that in mind, how about running through it again? And listen, boys," he said to the musicians, "when you come to those minor chords, I'd like to hear the fiddle and debro really bear down in complementary registers. Maybe with the fiddle on the high register. Squeeze all the darkness you can out of those minor notes." He paused briefly to see if he had been understood. "Well, then . . ."

All the men stayed to hear the song again, and I knew then that if nothing went wrong—if Uncle Red didn't stagger into the microphone, or didn't strain his whiskey-raw voice beyond its breaking point—then he was on his way to fame and fortune.

But something did go wrong, the worst possible thing. As he was just finishing the third verse—

"Come close to me, my darling,
And hear the midnight cry
Of Death that steals away our dreams
As he rides on through the sky—"

and was about to begin the last chorus, a terrible coughing fit suddenly exploded from his gaping mouth. He grabbed frantically for his handkerchief, his eyes widened with horror, his pale face flushed crimson, and the gagging coughs spewed from his mouth with the harsh rasping sound of gravel being rattled in a tin bucket. The song collapsed into shambles. The musicians, shocked by the suddenness and fury of the coughing fit, stopped playing one by one, and as the last whining sound of the dobro dribbled away into the vastness of the auditorium, Uncle Red, with his handkerchief clasped over his mouth, strode off the stage and disappeared into the wings, trailing behind the loathsome sound of his lungs tearing apart.

There was a long moment of stunned silence in the auditorium. Mr. Stubbs and the other men began to exchange slow, pitying glances.

"A lunger," Mr. Clemmens murmured at last.

"I should've known," Mr. Stubbs said, shaking his head sorrowfully. "The poor man." He sighed. "What a rotten shame. . . . Well, it's in God's hands," he added as he got to his feet. To the abashed and silent musicians on the stage, he said, "You boys might as well pack it up and go home." Then to Mr. Clemmens, "Well, I better go tell him."

All of them filed sadly out of the auditorium, going backstage, and the musicians put away their instruments, talking among themselves in hushed voices.

"Jesus, the poor bastard."

"So damned good, too."

"Helluva singer, all right."

After they left the stage, I was once again alone in the tabernacle's gloomy silence. I sat and wondered what was going to happen now. From what I had overheard Mr. Stubbs and the others say, I gathered that Uncle Red's coughing fit was more than merely an embarrassment. To them it appeared to be a fatal flaw, as if the revelation of his being a "lunger" changed everything for them, and doomed Uncle Red's chances of ever becoming a star. Could it possibly be that serious? Was as hopeless as that?

"It's all over," Uncle Red said, confirming my worst fears. He had come from backstage with his guitar in his hand. Shaken and gloomy and pale, he walked with the trembling gait of an exhausted old man. "We made the trip for nothing."

"They're not going to let you sing on the Opry?" I asked, and took the guitar from his hand.

He leaned against a pew and rested for a moment, his breathing shallow and rapid. "Not 'less a doctor says it's all right." He snorted. "They're sending a doctor 'round to check me out this afternoon. Bastards." His voice was bitterly hopeless, his face pinched with pain, his body limp with fatigue and despair. "All this way for nothing. . . ."

But I couldn't believe that it was so—couldn't let myself believe it. I didn't say anything to Uncle Red for fear that he would ridicule my hopes and leave me nothing, but in my silence I nursed the desperate hope that the doctor would let Uncle Red have his chance to sing on the Opry. I refused to believe that the dream of a lifetime could be destroyed by a cough. Had he come so far, surviving car wrecks and jailbreaks and armed robberies, only to be defeated by an ill-timed cough? Was fate as capricious as *that?*

"What'll we do now?" I asked, as we were driving back to the rooming house.

"Don't know 'bout you," he said, "but I'm gonna get shit-faced drunk. Maybe tomorrow I'll figure out a way to get us back to California. Or to get you out there, anyway. Maybe I won't even go back. What the hell? One place is as good as another, ain't it?"

"I want to stay with you," I said.

He looked at me reflectively for a moment, and then said matter-of-factly, "I may not be around much longer."

"Don't say that," I pleaded, believing then, as a child or a savage believes, that words spoken aloud have the power to make themselves come true.

"What the hell," he said. "Everybody's gotta die sometime. Even you, Hoss. Anyway, if you're around when I go, I want you to have my guitar."

My eyes flooded with tears.

"That's with the understanding that you never hock it or sell it," he added hastily. "You can give it away, if you wanna, but that's all." Seeing that I was all choked up, he said in a bantering tone, "Meantime, how 'bout giving me some of that money you got? I wanna get a bottle."

When we parked at the rooming house, I offered him all the money I had, the whole eight dollars. He took only half of it and started off for the bottle, a gangling, shambling, withered man in black pants, rose-colored shirt and cowboy hat, stoop-shouldered and scowling, hollow eyes haunted by death and dreams.

When I got up to the rooms, I took the guitar from its case and fondled it. It was a lovely instrument, so sensitive that you had only to breathe on the strings to make them hum. I strummed it gently and found myself searching for the chord progression for "Pale Horse, Pale Rider." The verses proved too complicated, but I soon found the chords to the chorus, and sang it softly in my alternating baritone-soprano voice.

"Trying it on for size, are you?" Uncle Red said in his familiar bantering tone as he came in, carrying a bottle in a brown paper bag. He went on into the bedroom and closed the door before I could say anything.

The doctor came about two o'clock that afternoon. He was mopping his florid face with a handkerchief when I opened the door to his knock. He was dressed in a white linen suit with a black string tie, and wore a floppy straw hat over his flowing white hair. He carried a small brown medical kit.

When I knocked at Uncle Red's door and told him the doctor was here, Uncle Red said, "Tell 'im to go away."

The doctor shrugged and promptly turned to leave. I put a hand on his arm. "Please," I said. "He's just grouchy, he's . . ."

He seemed to understand. He stepped to the bedroom door and rapped smartly on it. "See here, young man," he said in an authoritative voice, "I'm Doctor Hines. I've been sent here by the folks at the Opry to do a job, and I intend to do it. I'm coming in." And without waiting for a response, he went into the bedroom and closed the door behind him.

He stayed in the room for about fifteen minutes. I heard frequent mumbles coming from the room, and toward the end there were a few sharp exchanges, but I couldn't make out clearly what was said. I heard "sanitarium" mentioned a few times, which was usually followed by mumbled curses from Uncle Red, and when Dr. Hines came out, he was visibly chagrined. Mopping his face with the huge handkerchief, he strode out the door without once glancing at me.

I dashed down the hallway after him. "Doctor? Will he be able to sing on the Opry?"

He stopped and turned. "Who're you?"

"I'm his nephew. Name's Whit . . . Hoss, Hoss Wagoner. I'm . . . I'm sort of taking care of him."

"Well, if you're taking care of him, son, you'd better get him into a sanitarium. That's where he belongs. He's badly in need of medical attention. Now, here's my card"—flicking a business card from his vest pocket and handing it to me. "If you can talk him into going into a tubercular sanitarium, and if he can get the money to pay for it, you give me a call. Otherwise . . ." He shrugged.

"And the Opry? Will he be able to sing?"

"Son," he said warningly, "you don't appear to realize how sick your uncle is. The Opry? Lordy mercy, boy, you think they want to run the risk of him coughing his lungs out on a national hookup? Be serious. That man shouldn't even be singing in a shower. He should be absolutely quiet and lay off the liquor and do nothing but sleep and eat for at least six months. Give the lesions on his lungs time to heal. If he doesn't . . . well, it's his life. I wouldn't want to be responsible for what happens." He turned and went down the stairs.

I prowled the hot room for a while, and then went out and got a hamburger and ordered one to go for Uncle Red. Confused and apprehensive about what I should do, I hurried back to the rooming house with the idea that I would try to talk some sense into Uncle Red. Even if it meant making him angry, I would try to talk him into going into a sanitarium. I even rehearsed a few of the arguments I would make, such as, "Now, goddammit, Uncle Red, you got no right to throw your life away." Or, "What about the people who love you? Don't you owe them something?" And such like.

Maybe it was just as well I never got to say them. When I got back to the rooming house, I found a man standing in the hallway, knocking on our door. It was the man called Henry Axle, whom I had seen at the Opry House, one of the men from the New York recording company. He was dressed in two-tone perforated shoes, a seersucker suit, and a snap-brim hat. He was carrying his suit coat over his forearm, his tie was loosened, and his armpits were soaked with sweat.

"I'm trying to find Red Stovall," he told me. "People at the Opry said I'd find him here, but nobody seems to be in."

"He ain't feeling too good."

"Ah," he said. "Sorry to hear that. Think he'd be up to talking to me for a few minutes?" He had a strange accent.

I invited him in and knocked on Uncle Red's door. "There's a man here from a recording company to see you."

"Henry Axle," the man shouted through the door. "Met you this morning at the Opry. I'd like to talk to you for a few minutes, if it's all right."

Uncle Red grunted and came to the door. He stood in the doorway, leaning against the jamb, disguising his weakness behind a sort of sloppy insolence. "What d'you want?" Hatless now, with his red hair in wild disarray and his shirttail tumbling out of his pants, he leaned against the doorjamb, lit a cigarette, and dropped the spent match to the floor.

"Well, first I'd like to tell you how much I enjoyed your singing this morning."

"The coughing, too?"

"I'm sorry about your...your illness, Red. All right if I call you Red? But that won't stand in the way of a deal that I've got to offer you. Can we sit down and talk about it?"

Uncle Red nodded. He wasn't at all enthusiastic, but he was at least curious. He was also drunk. He staggered to a straight-back chair, turned it around, and sat down on it backward, folding his arms over the back of it and resting his chin on his arms. Henry Axle dropped his hat on the sofa beside him. He kicked his feet out and simltaneously gave his pants legs a tug.

"Well, my partner and I, Charlie Jones, you met him this morning, too, I believe? He's my sound engineer. By the way, maybe I didn't mention that I'm head of A&R at Burnside Records?"

Uncle Red nodded.

"Well," Henry Axle went on, "so Charlie and I are down here from New York, looking for talent. And I don't mind telling you, Red, you've got one of the best country singing voices I've ever heard." He paused for a moment to give Uncle Red a chance to respond to the compliment. But Uncle Red didn't. He just kept staring at Henry Axle, blinking now and then to refocus his booze-blurred eyes.

"Well, as soon as we heard you this morning, we knew we wanted to record you. I got right on the phone to New York and the upshot is, I've been authorized to make you an offer to record for Burnside."

After another moment of silence, Uncle Red said, "Yeah?" That was all.

"We've set up a temporary recording studio in a warehouse

over on Sixteenth Street. We'll supply the backup band and make a few masters. If we like them, we'll pay you twenty dollars for each song you record. How many originals you got?"

"Hundred," Uncle Red said, slurring the word so that it was actually "hunnerd." "Maybe more. How many you want?"

Henry Axle smiled. "Well, we wouldn't want quite *that* many. Not at first, anyway. Just a few of your best ones. That one you sang today, of course. That's great. Then we'll go from there. Okay? Of course, the company expects to buy all ownership rights to the songs we release. That's included in the twenty dollars per song."

"A flat fee? No royalties?"

Henry Axle tipped his head, a gesture of regret and sympathy. "Afraid not. The people in the front office insist on that. But it'll be a chance for you to find a mass audience, and that's what you want, isn't it? You get one hit record out of this, you can write your own ticket."

Uncle Red nodded his acceptance of the offer. "When we start?" He flicked the ashes from his cigarette onto the floor.

Henry Axle was delighted. "Tomorrow, if you feel up to it. I'll have the legal papers at the studio tomorrow, and a backup band, too, if you want to start then."

"I want a hundred in advance."

Henry hesitated for a moment, doubtful, but then nodded. "I think I can get you that, as long as we see that you have at least five songs we can use. Twenty dollars apiece."

"And drums," Uncle Red said. "I want drums and a steel guitar in the band."

"I was thinking along the same lines," Henry Axle said. "And if it's all right with you, we'll use the boys you worked with at the Opry."

When Uncle Red agreed, Henry Axle gave him the address of the warehouse, and offered him his hand, which Uncle Red shook limply without getting up.

As soon as Henry Axle was gone, I screwed up my courage and said in a voice that betrayed incipient panic, "But, Uncle Red! The doctor said you shouldn't sing at all. He said—"

"Oh, shit," he interrupted, "they been telling me that for years."

"Well, maybe they been right for years, too," I snapped, surprised at my own audacity.

He ignored me. He gazed reflectively for a moment at the business card that Henry Axle had given him, and said, "Never mind. Think how lucky we are. Twenty bucks a record? Hell, I'll make enough money in a couple of days to get back to California."

When he got up to stagger back to his room, I handed him the sack with the cold hamburger in it.

"What's this?" he asked. "Another hamburger? Holy shit, is that all you ever eat? You gonna turn into a hamburger, that's what's gonna happen to you, Hoss, if you don't watch it. Tell you what, since we gonna be rich soon, I'll take us out for a good steak dinner tonight. If," he added, tottering toward his rumpled bed, "I can get up, I mean. You might gimme a call later, see what happens."

Nothing happened. He drank himself into a stupor, and I ended up going out and having a hamburger for dinner. Afterward, I prowled the streets for a while, wondering what to do. I happened by a theater where a cowboy movie was showing, and was tempted to go in, but I didn't want to leave Uncle Red alone for very long for fear he would burn himself up. He had the habit of rousing himself to addled consciousness now and then to take a nip from his bottle and light a cigarette. Then he would promptly fall asleep again, with the burning cigarette between his fingers. Only that evening, when I went in to see if he wanted to go out to dinner, I found him asleep with a cigarette burning between his fingers, and the fire had already begun to sear his withered, nicotine-stained flesh. He was so drunk he hadn't even felt it.

So I didn't go to the movie—which was just as well, because I was almost out of money anyway. Instead, I roamed the streets for a while, and found myself peering into faces in hopes that I might recognize someone. I felt very lost and alone. I found myself wishing there was some way I could get in touch with Mama, so she could tell me what to do about Uncle Red. I even thought about trying to find Grandpa. I had once found Cainsville on a road map. It was only a couple of hours' drive from Nashville. But even if I found him, what good would it do? He would probably only tell me that it was none of his business. Still, it would sure be good to talk to someone.

I even found myself hoping I would run into Marlene somewhere in the streets of this city in which we were strangers. Not that I thought she would be of any help, but at least she would be someone to talk to. Someone to keep me from feeling so alone. Where was she now? Somewhere in Nashville? I had expected to see her when Uncle Red made his appearance at the Opry, but now that he wasn't going to appear what would she do? Would she manage to find us somehow? In the meantime, how was she living? The twenty dollars I had given her was probably gone by now. What would she do by herself, broke and alone, in a strange city? Might she be walking the streets of Nashville this very moment, looking for me and Uncle Red? Poking her coppery head into saloons and honkytonks, asking the bartenders if they knew a singer named Red Stovall. But of course if she was really clairvoyant, she would find us sooner or later, with or without the help of bartenders.

I went back to the rooming house to check on Uncle Red. He was asleep, sprawled on his rumpled bed, fully clothed except for boots, in the flatulent and boozy stench of the hot room. I stood over him for a while, watching him sleep, watching his sunken and unshaven cheeks flutter as he breathed.

An empty whiskey bottle was on the floor beside the bed. I picked it up to put it in the trash, but I found myself staring at it for a moment. Then I looked at Uncle Red, and realized that the only time I had ever seen him at rest was when he was dead drunk. It was as if he had a demon inside him that tore him apart, and the only way he could have any peace was to drink himself—and the demon—into oblivion.

24

During the next four days, Uncle Red recorded twenty-two songs. In the hot mote-swarming silence of an old half-filled warehouse on Sixteenth Street, sitting on a high stool in front of a microphone, backed up by some of the best musicians in Nashville, Uncle Red left his legacy of twenty-two songs on acetate discs. These were the songs that would finally result in his being one of the first singers elected to the Country Music Hall of Fame. The songs that would be recorded for many years to come by singing stars such as Ernest Tubb, Hank Snow, Johnny Cash, Merle Haggard, Ray Charles, Waylon Jennings, and Elvis Presley. Songs that you could still hear played on honkytonk jukeboxes in places like Medford, Oregon, or Abilene, Texas, thirty and forty years after the man who wrote and sang them was dead.

He was dying when he sang them. Maybe that's what gave them their agonized beauty: each was sung as though it would be his last. He gave them everything he had, and the toll on his ebbing strength was devastating. By the end of the first day he and the band had rehearsed and recorded six songs, starting with the simplest and gradually working up to the more complicated ones. At first there were difficulties with the acoustics in the old warehouse, but Charlie Jones shifted microphones around on booms and hung blankets as baffles around one side

of the band area, and, finally, by the time the band had done
their third take of "It's All Downhill from Here" and listened
to the playback a couple of times, everyone seemed satisfied
with the balance.

"I love the echo effect in this old place," Charlie Jones said
as he made adjustments on the mixing board, "but the resolution
is the shits."

"Well, let's go with it," Henry Axle said. "We've got Red's
voice clear, and that's the important thing. We're paying these
other guys by the hour."

We were inside the recording booth, a small makeshift but
nearly soundproof room in one corner of the warehouse. We
could watch Uncle Red and the band through a thick window,
but we couldn't hear them except through the microphones. I
stayed in the booth with Henry Axle and Charlie Jones. When
I first went in the booth, I had the urge to ask, "What's this?"
and "What's that for?" But Charlie Jones, scurrying between
the mixing board and the microphones, obviously didn't want
to be bothered with any dumb-kid questions. So I sat out of
the way in the back of the booth, and watched Uncle Red
through the window, and I could see, as the day wore on, what
a terrible effort the recordings were costing him. By the time
they had got to the fourth song, "Boogie Man," he was flushed
and feverish, and was beginning to forget the words to the song
and making mistakes on the guitar.

But it was only after his voice got husky and raspy that
Henry Axle decided to call it quits. He left the booth and told
the musicians they could pack up for the day. To Uncle Red,
he said, "How you doing, pal? Think you'll be okay for tomorrow?"

"Oh, sure," Uncle Red said. "A night's rest and I'll be as
good as new." He was still sitting on the stool in front of the
microphone, breathing very heavily and hugging his guitar to
him, almost trembling with exhaustion. And when he stepped
off the stool, he almost fell. Henry Axle and I both reached
out to help him, but he waved us away and steadied himself
against the stool. "Damn leg went to sleep a little, is all," he
said. The back and underarms of his shirt were drenched with
sweat, and he was so tired he could hardly stand.

I carried his guitar out to the car for him, and I had to help
him up the stairs to our rooms. It was the first time he had
ever accepted any physical support from me, and the need of
it seemed to embarrass him a little.

"Maybe you ought not go back tomorrow," I said. "Maybe you oughta rest for—"

"I'll be okay," he insisted. "Hell, all they have to do is prop me up and put my guitar in my hands, I'll be fine."

And that's exactly what they did the next day, they propped him up. Henry Axle had a straightback chair brought in for Uncle Red to sit on, and they put a pillow behind him so that he would sit up straight and relieve the pressure on his aching lungs. And Uncle Red, in spite of his pain and fatigue and fever, seemed to be in fairly good spirits and fine form. In fact, he almost seemed to be having a rollicking good time as he and the band cut the first three or four records. But he had a small coughing fit during the recording of the fifth song, "Honkytonk Heaven," and from then on until the end of the session, the coughing fits became more frequent and severe.

The coughing ruined only a few takes during the remainder of the session, and as soon as each seizure ended and Uncle Red cleared his throat with a drink of whiskey, Henry Axle and Charlie Jones would do a retake of the ruined song on a new disc. Late in the afternoon, however, Uncle Red was suddenly racked by a coughing fit so severe and debilitating that they had to stop recording for the day.

No hemorrhaging accompanied the coughing at the ware-house, but after we got back to our rooms that evening, Uncle Red had a coughing fit that brought on a hemorrhage. He was lying down in the bedroom when it began. I was in the sitting room, listening, waiting to see if it would subside. When it became obvious that the attack was going to be another severe one, I got up and went into the bedroom.

He was bending over a washbasin in one corner of the room, shaking like a palsied old man, and his throat rattled loudly with the sounds of strangulation. He fumbled for a towel on a nearby rack, dropped it, and couldn't pick it up. I picked it up and handed it to him, but he suddenly clasped his hands against his chest and staggered sideways, as if struck by a blow.

I cried his name, and reached out to support him, but he reeled away from me, his face flushed with the panic of stran-gulation, his hands clawing at his chest. He was making a desperate, wobble-legged effort to stay on his feet. I reached him just as he stumbled into the bedside table and knocked it over and fell to his knees on the cluttered floor. His fall carried us both down.

I had my arms around him, supporting him as he leaned

forward, when I saw the blood begin to trickle out of his gaping mouth. It poured out in a steady stream as he broke loose from me and thrashed about on the floor.

I told him that I would get a doctor, and rushed out of the room and into the hallway, digging into my pocket for the card that Dr. Hines had left with me. I met the landlady in the hallway. She was a fussy little woman with a few bristles growing from a dark wart on her talcumed chin.

"What is it, boy?" she said. "What's that noise I heard?"

"Please," I said, shoving the doctor's card into her gnarled fingers. "Call the doctor, will you? It's Uncle Red."

"What's that blood?" she asked, pointing to a smear on my arm. "What's going on in there?"

"Phone the doctor," I begged, and dashed back into our rooms. I found Uncle Red on his hands and knees, thrashing around on the floor. His coughing had subsided a little, but blood still trickled from his mouth and spattered on the linoleum floor. I fell on my knees beside him and put my arms around his quaking body. "She'll get the doctor," I cried. "What can I do? Is there anything . . . ?"

In a strangling voice, he croaked, "Tow—Tow—" and groped for the towel that had fallen on the floor out of his reach. I snatched the towel and handed it to him and held his shoulders while he pressed the towel over his mouth. Slowly, the hemorrhaging ceased, but not before the white towel was soaked with blood. It might not have been any more blood than he would have lost with a severe nosebleed, but because it had come from his lungs, it carried with it a horror far beyond its quantity.

Suddenly I became aware of the landlady standing in the open doorway. She was staring at Uncle Red with undisguised revulsion, as if his sickness were a personal affront to her.

"I phoned the doctor," she said. "I want to talk to you, boy."

I managed to tug and haul Uncle Red into a sitting position on the floor. I left him leaning back against the bed and followed the old woman out into the hallway, where she turned accusing eyes on me and whispered, "I'm sorry, but I'll have to ask you all to leave. I don't allow no lungers here. What'd the other roomers do, if they found out? They'd leave. I got a business to run, boy. You got to get him out of here."

"But he's sick," I protested. "We can't go looking . . . I can't go find . . ."

with a spoon, but he pushed himself up in the bed to a half-reclining position. "Hell, I can feed myself," he said. "I ain't no damned invalid yet." He spooned the soup slowly into his mouth with a trembling hand, and each swallow was performed with a look of determination and slight distaste. "Not bad soup," he said, forcing himself to act as if nothing untoward had happened. "Nice of the old gal to bring it."

I didn't tell him that the nice old gal had given us three days to move out. Three days seemed much too far away to worry about at the moment. But I did tell him what Dr. Hines had said.

"Oh, shit," he said, short-tempered, feverish, disdainful. "I know what he said. He's got part interest in a TB sanitarium somewhere, and he's recruiting patients, that's what he's doing. Well, in the first place, I ain't got the money to go to a sanitarium. And in the second place, I wouldn't go even if I had it."

"Well," I said, a little offended by his tone, "it's your life."

"Damn right it is," he said, sloshing a few drops of soup out of his bowl onto his shirtfront. "And I'm gonna live it on my terms, or I ain't gonna live it at all. And my terms don't include wasting away in some goddamned sanitarium somewhere." He paused for a breath, and to let his temper cool. "You ain't never seen how people die in them places. I have. They finally get so weak they can't feed themselves, or get up to go to the damned toilet. Some crabby old nurse has to feed 'em and change their shitty clothes. In the last stages, they get delirious. Toss 'round in bed with oxygen tubes stuck in their noses, feeding tubes stuck in their arms, piss tubes stuck up their peckers. That how you want to see me go?"

"All I want to see you do is get well."

Without speaking, he gazed at me for a long while, a look of surprise and profound pity on his face, and that look said as plainly as words would have, "You poor dumb kid."

I still had hope. That's what amazed him. I hadn't yet given up hope that he would get well, if he would only try. It wasn't until the next day, after I had talked to Henry Axle, that I realized I had better try to resign myself.

Uncle Red had just finished listening to the playback of "Wasted in Waycross" and the band was working out an arrangement for the next song, when I decided to step outside the stuffy sweltering warehouse for a breath of air. I went out and leaned against one of the loading platforms and gazed absently out across the weedy, trash-strewn yard at the cars whizzing by on Sixteenth Street.

Henry Axle followed me out. "He's worse today, isn't he?" he asked. "He have a bad night?"

I gave him a straight look. "He had a hemorrhage."

Henry Axle took off his small city-slicker hat and wiped the sweatband with his handkerchief. "He seeing a doctor?"

I kept staring at him accusingly. "A doctor came yesterday. He said Uncle Red might die if he didn't stop singing and get himself to a sanitarium." My stare and words clearly implied that Henry Axle would have his share of the blame if the doctor's orders were ignored.

Chafing at that, but unable to meet my eyes, he murmured, "Well, I suppose he knows what he's doing."

I turned back to watch the traffic. Now and then a slight breeze rustled the old newspapers and sun-scorched weeds in the warehouse yard. The day was hot and sultry and ripe with smells of melting asphalt and ragweed.

Henry Axle wiped the sweatband of his hat again and ran the damp handkerchief around his neck. "You don't think he should be doing these recordings, do you?"

I had to give that a moment's thought, and all I could say was, "Do you? Knowing it might kill him?"

He sighed. "You want me to level with you, pal?"

I nodded.

"He's going to die anyway," Henry Axle said, as if simply pointing out the obvious. "And he knows it. Why do you think he's doing these recordings?"

"He needs the money," I said, sulky and bitter.

"Sure. There's that. But there's a more important reason. It's his last chance, and he knows it."

"Last chance? For what?"

"To be somebody," he said, without hesitation. Replacing his hat, he took his shirtfront in his fingers, pulled it away from his sweating body, and flapped it for ventilation. "Did you ever feel like you wanted to be somebody?"

"Sure," I said, remembering vividly the plea that I had made to Mama to let me accompany Uncle Red.

"Well, of course these recordings may not do it for him, but they're the last chance he has. In twenty years, without these recordings, what'll he be? Another forgotten man in a

forgotten grave somewhere. But if he makes these recordings . . . well, who knows?" He gave me a little cheer-up smile.
"If he's as good as we think he is, he might just become
immortal. Right?"

Once again I found myself trying to figure out Henry Axle's
angle in all this. Sometimes I wondered if he was so greedy
that he would rob a dying man of his last breath of life and
sell it for a profit, or if he was someone who really loved Uncle
Red's songs and was desperately trying, for the sake of posterity
and Uncle Red's posthumous fame, to squeeze as many of
them out of him as he could before he died.

Well, it really didn't matter. The result would be the same,
whatever the motive. And Henry Axle had no doubt been right
about one thing, anyway: these recordings were the last chance
Uncle Red would ever have to leave something of himself this
side of the grave. And it wasn't until then that I began to
appreciate the heroic proportions of Uncle Red's efforts, and
to resign myself to his impending doom.

On the afternoon of the third day, Henry Axle had a cot
brought to the warehouse for Uncle Red. While they were
listening to playbacks, or while the band was working out an
arrangement for the next song, Uncle Red would lie down on
the cot to rest. There was an electric fan on an orange crate
beside the cot, and Uncle Red, sweat-drenched and exhausted
to the point of stupefaction, would lie down on the cot in the
cooling breeze from the fan and gasp for breath. More and
more, as the third and fourth days wore on, his breath failed
him during recording sessions. Conversely, his voice, when
not entangled in a phlegmy throat-rattle, had a crystalline fine-
ness about it, a mournful and agonized beauty.

By the end of the fourth day, he had recorded a total of
twenty-two songs, and he couldn't go on. The last song he and
the band recorded was a ballad called "Dreams of a Midnight
Man," a song that I had never heard before.

> *"The dreams of a midnight man,*
> *Walking these streets all alone.*
> *Dreaming of things I never had,*
> *A wife, a child, a home."*

He put everything he had into the song, every nuance of pain
and loss, and because he himself felt it so deeply, we who

listened to him—even the musicians—felt it deeply, too. By the time he had finished the first verse, there were tears in his eyes, and by the time he finished the second chorus, there were tears in my own.

> *"I've lived my life in honkytonks,*
> *Playing for handouts and beers,*
> *And before I go*
> *I'd like to know*
> *What did I get for all those years?*
> *Oh . . . I'm so alone . . .*
> *Dreaming of sweethearts and home."*

And when the last sad note of the song died in the vastness of the old warehouse, Henry Axle turned the recording console off, Charlie Jones shut down the mixing board, and all of us, including the musicians, applauded.

As I was driving Uncle Red back to the rooming house, I very much wanted to ask him about "Dreams of a Midnight Man," remembering the tears that had come into his eyes as he sang it, and remembering, too, the story he had told me about Mary Simms. I had been slightly incredulous when he first told me how, after receiving the beating from the Simms boys, he had lain in the parking lot and cried, asking himself again and again, "What in God's name are we living for?" But now I thought maybe I could understand.

"That song," I said. "The last one. Did it have anything to do with Mary Simms?"

He gave me a sharp look. Though grim-faced with pain and exhaustion, he made a small snorting sound of amusement, and then, as a sort of tribute to my sagacity, he sighed and said, "Yeah. I wrote it not long after I got that beating. I was in a skid-row hotel in Los Angeles at the time, sobering up from a two-week drunk."

"I think it's the best song I've ever heard you sing."

He gave me a small, lopsided grin. "Oh, I got a few more good uns to sing yet. Wait till tomorrow."

But tomorrow would be too late for that. Uncle Red had sung his last song.

25

Early the next morning, after spending a feverish and fitful night, Uncle Red suffered a massive hemorrhage. I had been up with him for most of the night, doing what I could do to make him comfortable: putting cold wet washclothes on his forehead, giving him the last of the laudanum, fanning him when he grew feverish. And just before dawn his fever seemed to abate and he finally seemed to fall into a peaceful sleep.

By then I was almost too tired to sleep. Just before dawn, I lay down on the sofa, fully clothed, hoping that I could at least get a little rest before Uncle Red woke up again. I had no sensation of falling asleep, but then the sun was on my face, and there was a terrible sound coming from Uncle Red's room. I struggled against my body's need for sleep, and finally jerked awake to see Uncle Red standing in the doorway to his room, dressed only in shorts. He had one hand on each side of the door, holding himself up, and his pale, wasted body was convulsed with strangled coughs, blood was spilling from his mouth, and his eyes were desperately beseeching.

I leaped up and ran to him. He reached out for support and toppled forward. I tried to catch him as he fell, but it was like trying to catch a bag of sticks. I broke his fall, but I couldn't hold him up. On his hands and knees, he rocked back and forth, fighting for breath, spewing blood over the floor. I cried his name a few times and tried to keep him from thrashing around, as if I could stop his dying by making him hear and be still.

He tried to get up, toppled sideways, overturned a chair, blood all the while oozing from his mouth and streaming down his scrawny, white, plucked-chicken chest. And all I could do in my helplessness was hold him and cry. "Uncle Red! Uncle Red!"

He finally collapsed, sprawling face down on the rug, his body twitching and shaking. I dashed down the hall and pounded on the landlady's door until she opened it. "Call the doctor!" I shouted. "It's Uncle Red!" And without waiting for her to answer, I dashed back to our rooms.

Uncle Red lay where I had left him. He was still breathing in small strangled gasps, but he was no longer coughing, and the blood from his mouth had slowed to a trickle. It was nothing less than agony, the helplessness I felt, knowing there was nothing I could do to help him live. It seemed that the only thing I could do was try to make his dying easier. I got a wet towel and held his head up with one hand and washed his face with the other. It was some sort of senseless compulsion, this washing his face, probably more for my benefit than his, to keep me from going crazy with helplessness.

The landlady came and stood in the doorway. She was dressed in an old soiled housecoat and had a sleeping net over her thin gray hair. There was distress in her eyes when she saw the blood spattered around the room, and her voice was sharp with asperity when she said, "The doctor says he won't come 'less the man agrees to go to a sanitarium. That's what he said to tell you."

"Maybe it'll be all right," I heard myself say, as if I were in a trance. "I think it's stopped now. Maybe it'll be all right."

The old woman stepped inside the room. "Is he feverish? I could crush some ice in a rag."

"Yessum," I said. "That'd be a good idea. Thanks."

I held his head on my lap while she went to get the ice. The blood had stopped trickling from his mouth now, and he was breathing easier, though his emaciated body was shaking in sporadic jerks. He was beginning to come around a little. He blinked his eyes a few times and moaned.

"Uncle Red?" I said. "Uncle Red?"

He didn't respond.

When the landlady came back with some crushed ice wrapped

in a dishtowel, she asked me if I wanted her to help put Uncle Red back on the bed. I asked Uncle Red if that's what he wanted, and though he didn't answer, he stiffened his body a little to make it easier for the landlady and me, each holding him by a bony arm, to carry him to the bed.

There were bloodstains on the bed and on the floor beside the bed, which brought sighs of distress from the landlady. But she had the tact not to complain aloud about the mess. She jerked the bloodstained sheet off the bed and we laid Uncle Red down on the mattress cover.

"Hold that ice to his forehead," she said. "I'll go see can I get another doctor to come. You got any money to pay him, if he does?"

"He has some money," I assured her, and she went dourly away. I pulled a chair up beside the bed and placed the pack of crushed ice on Uncle Red's hot dry forehead. His eyes were opened, blinking but unfocused, as if he were in a state of shock.

It was the beginning of delirium. For the next few hours he was to have brief periods of consciousness and long periods of delirium, in which he tried to talk or sing, but the sounds that came from his grimacing face were hollow, moaning, wheezing sounds full of fear and desolation.

In about thirty minutes the landlady came back. She had changed from her robe to an old dress and a soiled apron, and she no longer wore the hair net. She brought a fresh pack of crushed ice and an electric fan. She set the fan on the bedside table and directed its cooling breeze down the length of Uncle Red's blood-smeared body.

"You don't look so good yourself," she said, placing the fresh ice pack on Uncle Red's brow. "You get any sleep last night?"

"Not much."

"Then go lay down, try to sleep. I'll sit with him for a while. There's a new doctor coming. Said he'd be here in an hour or so. If anything changes before then, I'll wake you up. Go on now."

"Thank you," I said, feeling a profound sense of relief that somebody else was willing to help. "But why're you . . . ?" I wondered if she expected to be paid.

"My Christian duty," she said self-righteously. But she softened a little, and added in a tone of remembered sorrow, "My

husband was a lunger, too. Took him a long time to die. . . . Go
on now, get some sleep. I'll call you if there's any change."

"Doctor Hines said I could get an oxygen tank at a drugstore.
If you'd stay with him while I go . . . ?"

She mopped the trickle of melting icewater from his face.
"Yes yes yes, go on. I'll stay."

Uncle Red's pants were crumpled in a corner of the room.
I took his new wallet from the pants. He had over seventy
dollars left from the hundred dollars advance he had gotten
from Henry Axle on the first day of the recordings. I started
to take a twenty from the wallet, but then it occurred to me,
with mingled suspicion and shame, that the landlady might
steal the money if I left it. I felt that it was base of me to
suspect her, but in my overwrought and fearful state, it was
difficult for me to believe that this old woman was capable of
an act of pure kindness.

Anyway, I took the wallet and all the money with me. I
hurried to the pharmacy a few blocks away and got a five-
gallon tank of oxygen, leaving a ten-dollar deposit for the return
of the tank. Sweating and tired and miserable, I carried the
tank back to our rooming house.

When I got back, Uncle Red's delirium had diminished. He
seemed to be breathing easier and fighting for consciousness.

"He's a little better," the landlady whispered. "Maybe he's
going to be all right"—but it was said in a tone of Christian
duty, not of real hope. She took the ice pack from his head
and ran a towel over his wet face and hair, then moved away
and began straightening up the room a little.

When I set the tank beside the bed and started to put the
cone over his mouth and nose, Uncle Red suddenly fixed his
bright eyes on me in a grave, puzzled stare; then, with consciousness fluttering in his eyes like a wind-blown candleflame,
he slowly recognized me. A soft smile flickered at the corners
of his fever-dried lips, and he tried to say something. His mouth
moved, but the only sounds that came out were whispery
wheezes.

"What?" I said, bending my ear close to his lips.

"Just . . . hello . . . Hoss," he whispered hollowly in my ear.
"Got . . . hands full this . . . time . . . ain't . . . ?" He fell silent as
if he had expended all his strength.

"I got some oxygen here," I told him. "The doctor said it
would help."

Again I had to put my ear almost against his mouth to hear what he was trying to say: "No...not...what they use in...sanitarium....No."

I didn't argue with him. As long as he was breathing easy, the oxygen didn't seem necessary anyway. But I asked him if there was anything I could do for him, and he seemed to give the question a moment's thought before he winked at me and said something. I put my ear to his mouth again, and he repeated his request: "Sure...a fat woman....Never had a fat...really fat...woman. Ought to 'fore...'fore I..." He expelled little puffs of air from his opened mouth, a voiceless chuckle, soundless as a snake. Then he closed his eyes and slowly sank into a wheezing drowsiness.

"Go on, now, try to get some sleep yourself," the landlady said.

I was so grateful for her take-charge tone, and especially grateful for her willingness, however grudging, to relieve me of my death-watch burden, I no longer wondered or cared about her motives. I went into the other room and flopped down on the sofa, and was asleep as soon as I closed my burning eyes.

Henry Axle arrived about an hour later. I woke up when I heard his knock on the door. The landlady let him in and looked at me for permission when he said he would like to see Uncle Red. Though flattered to think my permission was required, I had no opinion in the matter.

"When he didn't show up today," Henry Axle said, dividing his uncertain attention between me and the landlady, obviously unaware of who she was, "I got to wondering if...How is he?"

"He's barely conscious," the landlady told him. "You shouldn't stay too long." She led him into the room.

I couldn't go back to sleep. All the windows were opened, allowing numerous flies to buzz in and out, but no cooling breeze stirred the cheap curtains. The heat and the noisy traffic in the street below the window and the sound of Henry Axle talking to Uncle Red in a fragmented monologue—all this, in addition to my weariness and stomach-growling hunger, kept me from falling asleep again.

"All right, Red, I'll do that," Henry Axle said in the next room. "Twenty-two, yes. Four hundred and forty, in all....I'll do that....Yes, don't worry about it....Take care of yourself, pal. Get well. I'll be back to see how you're doing....So long, pal."

Henry Axle came out of the bedroom and crossed to the sofa. "How you doing, pal?"

I felt as though I might break down and cry if I said anything at all, so I just shrugged.

"Red has three hundred and forty dollars coming," Henry Axle said. "He told me to give it to you. I'll bring it by tomorrow, if that's all right."

I nodded without looking up at him.

He stood there in front of me for a moment in silence, and then he reached out and put his hand on my shoulder. "I'm sorry, pal."

His sympathy almost broke my resistance. I hid my face in my hands, fighting against the sobs that had begun to shake my body.

Henry Axle patted my shoulder. "I'll be back later to see how he is," he said, and then he was gone.

I cried myself to sleep. In a strenuous effort to keep from being heard, I buried my face in the musty horsehair sofa and sobbed in bitter silence, demanding of life, or of God, or of whatever forces shaped our destinies and sealed our doom, *Why?* Why him? Why take someone who had so much left to give? Why should he be endowed with gifts from the gods and then be broken so soon? *Why? Why? Why?* But soon, too exhausted to cry anymore, I fell asleep.

The next sound I heard was the voice of the landlady. "Boy! Come here! Boy!" And I could hear Uncle Red making panicked, strangling sounds and thrashing in his bed.

I ran into the room. "Hold his hands!" the landlady cried. She was trying to put the oxygen mask over his mouth, but he was struggling with the strength of delirium to keep her away from him. He clawed at the air, turning his head from side to side on the wet pillow, his eyes wild with terror.

I grabbed his wrists and made myself hold onto him while the landlady struggled to put the mask over his gasping mouth.

"No!" he whispered, and focused his eyes on me, the eyes of a terrified child begging not to be sent into a dark room.

I couldn't do it. I couldn't torture him, even if it was for his own good. Crying again, I let go his wrists and stepped back, turning away from those eyes. But then there was somebody else in the room—a man, a young man—who grabbed Uncle Red's arm.

"It's oxygen, Doctor," the landlady answered when the man said something to her.

"I'll give you three days," she warned. "That'll give you time to find another place. I'm sorry, but I can't have him here."

I turned my back on her contemptuously and slammed the hall door behind me. I went into the bedroom and helped Uncle Red to lie down on the bed. I took the bloody towel from his hands, then wetted a washcloth with cold water and washed the dried blood from his face and shaking hands. And all the while he stared up at the ceiling with blurred and unblinking eyes.

"The doctor's coming," I said. "You'll be all right. The doctor'll be here soon."

He didn't respond. He just lay there, laboring for breath, staring blindly at the ceiling. I asked him if there was anything else I could do for him. The shake of his head was barely perceptible.

It was more than an hour before Dr. Hines arrived, and it was plain from the moment he came in that he resented being called back on this hopeless and uncooperative case. He went into the bedroom and closed the door, shutting me out, and soon I heard him castigating Uncle Red for his stubborn refusal to go to a sanitarium. I didn't hear any response from Uncle Red.

When Dr. Hines came out of the room, wiping his florid face with a huge linen handkerchief, he imperiously crooked a finger at me, signaling me to follow him.

"Look here, young feller," he said in the hallway. "There's no use calling me again on this case. As long as he refuses to go into a sanitarium, there's nothing else I can do for him. I left him some laudanum. See that he takes it and gets plenty of rest. If his breathing becomes difficult, you can go to Baxby's Pharmacy—just up Broadway a few blocks—and get him an oxygen tank. Cost you five dollars. But like I said, now, unless he agrees to go into a sanitarium, don't call me again. I won't be responsible." Then he turned and waddled away in his wrinkled white linen suit, mopping his face with the damp linen handkerchief.

The landlady brought a bowl of barley soup to the door. "See that he eats this," she said guiltily. But to make certain her kindness wasn't mistaken for a change of mind, she added, "Three days. That's all. I have to make a living, too, you know. If the other roomers found out he was a lunger . . ."

I took the soup in to Uncle Red. I started to feed it to him

"Never mind," he said. He released Uncle Red's arms and dug into a medical kit. "I'll sedate him first."

I wandered, crying, into the other room. Beyond knowing or caring what I was doing, I took a few aimless turns about the room, and then found myself staring at a picture on the wall, seeing it through a blur of tears. It was a cheap print of a familiar painting, the picture of a lone wolf on a snowy hillside at night, gazing witth a sort of sad, infinite longing toward a snug, window-lit farmhouse in a snowbound valley below.

After a few minutes, the landlady came out of the bedroom. "It's all right now," she said, wrapping her hands in her apron. "Doctor Lawrence gave him a shot to quiet him down. Have you had anything to eat today, boy?"

I shook my head.

"Come on. There's leftover meatloaf in my icebox."

I shook my head. "I'd better stay here."

"I'll bring you a sandwich, then." But she didn't leave. She had something else to say, and it took her a minute to work up the nerve. "Maybe it's a bad time to mention it, but . . . like the feller says, I guess there won't be no good time to mention it, so . . . well, the fact is, I heard that man mention that your uncle has money coming, and I'm going to have to ask for some of it. I mean, the sheets, the rugs, the towels—all ruined. Look." She pointed to the bloodstains on the rug, as if they were something that might have escaped my notice. "Who's got the money to have them replaced? Not me. These are hard times. I'm a widow. I don't have the money to replace these things."

"We'll pay for them," I said.

"I'm sorry to bring it up like this, but . . ." She fell silent, as if to demonstrate her helplessness.

"It's all right," I said.

She was relieved that I didn't make a fuss. "I'll get you that sandwich," she said.

The doctor stayed in the bedroom for about fifteen minutes. When he came out, he was putting his stethoscope into his medical kit. He was a young man with close-cropped hair and rimless spectacles. He gave me a long, appraising look. "I'm Doctor Lawrence. You the next of kin?"

The way he said it made me fear that Uncle Red was already dead. I nodded. "How is he?"

"Resting easy now," he said. "But it's only a matter of time now. You're aware of that?"

"There's nothing more you can do?" I begged. *"Nothing?"*

He shook his head. "There's nothing more anybody can do."

"If we took him to a sanitarium? Like Doctor Hines said?"

"It wouldn't matter." He put his medical kit on the table and was now cleaning his spectacles: blowing his breath on the lenses and rubbing them with his handkerchief. "He's too weak to be moved, and, anyway, it's too late for that."

I was fighting back tears again. "How long has he got?"

The doctor held his spectacles up to check their cleanness against the light from the window. Every move he made seemed to be deliberate and routine, as if he were trying to counterbalance my incipient sobs with an air of exemplary calmness. "Not long," he said. "I'll be back this afternoon to check on him. He has the oxygen mask on now. It'll help him be a little more comfortable. I wish there was more that could be done. Unfortunately . . ."

The doctor had gone and I was still in the sitting room when the landlady returned with a meatloaf sandwich and a glass of cold sweet milk. She went in to stay with Uncle Red while I sat at the table and devoured the sandwich and gulped the milk. With my hunger partially satisfied, I folded my arms on the table, pillowed my head on them, and drowsed fitfully in the hot room until the landlady gently shook me awake.

"Better go in now, boy," she said. "I think he's near the end."

She stayed in the sitting room while I, numbed with physical and emotional exhaustion, staggered into the bedroom to have my last look at Uncle Red alive, though he could hardly be said to be living. Above the black rubber oxygen mask that was held over his mouth and nose with adhesive tape, his eyes were half-opened but unseeing, already blurred with death. The only sign of life left in him was a fluttering of his gauntly ribbed chest, as feeble and fragile as the dying quivers of a butterfly. He no longer struggled in agony for consciousness or breath.

I sat beside his bed in the breeze from the electric fan. I looked at him for a long while, and then took his hand. I felt a feeble tremor of life in his fingers, as if he were reaching out from the far side of death for one last grasp at life. Then there was a faint rattle in his throat, and his blurred, unseeing eyes slowly closed. His body quivered almost imperceptibly, and seemed to become rigid. I said my silent goodbye.

But suddenly, miraculously, his body began to shiver as if from a chill, his eyes popped open, and he drew in one more long, rattling breath. To my horror and amazement, his body convulsed, and he began to rise forward, lifting up from his wet pillows. He sat up. His eyes, above the black oxygen mask, seemed to stare, for one terror-stricken moment, at something at the foot of his bed. Then he collapsed. He fell back upon the bed, never to move again. His eyes closed. He breathed no more. A thread of blood seeped out from beneath the black mask that covered his mouth, and trickled slowly through the stubble on his sunken and unshaven cheek.

"Oh, my God," I said, and no longer struggled to hold back my sobs. I dropped my forehead on Uncle Red's lifeless hand. "Oh, my God," I said.

26

"Hoss!"

Someone was calling my name. I was driving the Packard along one of Nashville's downtown streets, and had just pulled away from a traffic light, when I heard a voice calling me. "Hoss! Hoss!" It was a girl's voice, urgent and high-pitched. I slowed down and glanced in the rearview mirror and saw a figure running along the sidewalk, darting through startled pedestrians, waving and crying, "Hoss! Hoss! Wait!"

It was Marlene. She stumbled and almost knocked an old woman down, but kept coming, waving, and calling, "Hoss! Wait!"

I pulled over to the curb and stopped. She came running up so fast that she banged into the side of the car. She poked her coppery head in the open window on the passenger's side. Sweating and panting, she cried, "Hoss! Oh, Lord, what a sight for sore eyes! I been on the lookout for days and days! Been hanging out in front of the Opry House, looking to see this car. Where you *been?* Can I get in?"

I motioned for her to get in, and she did, smiling and flouncing joyously. She was as unkempt and dirty as any waif, was maybe even skinnier than when I last saw her, but certainly no less talkative.

"Sure am glad to see you, Hoss! Oh, I have finally found

a friend in Nashville! This city! Oh, the dirty old men! I have never seen the like! I swear to goodness, Hoss, it's enough to make a preacher cuss, the way men've been running after me. Sometimes it makes me wish I was fat and ugly, then maybe they wouldn't want me so much. But I have been faithful to Red. Faithful, in my heart and in my body." She leaned toward me and whispered, "Where is he?"

I had begun to drive again. I hadn't said a word so far. I hadn't had a chance. But that was all right, I was in no hurry to tell her about Uncle Red.

"What's the matter?" she asked after a brief silence. "Cat got your tongue?"

"No. It's just that . . ."

Finally sensing that something was very wrong, she said, "What's the matter Hoss? You look kinda green 'round the gills. You been sick?"

"No," I said. "Uncle Red has."

All the joy went out of her face. "The TB?"

I nodded.

"Oh, Lord," she moaned. "How bad?"

I didn't answer.

"Take me to him," she begged, suddenly disturbed by my reluctance to talk about it. "Please? Oh, I know he probably don't want to see me yet, but he will someday, and if he's bad sick now, he might. . . . Where is he?"

"I'm going there now."

I was on my way to the mortuary where Uncle Red's body was. I had been to the recording studio in the old warehouse earlier that morning, and Henry Axle had given me the money— three hundred and forty dollars—that Uncle Red had coming. That money, plus what was left of the hundred dollar advance that Uncle Red had in his wallet, less what I had paid the landlady for rent and for the bloodstain damages to her things, and less the seven dollars I had paid Dr. Lawrence when he came to make out the death certificate, left me with three hundred and ninety-two dollars. And now I was on my way to the mortuary to pay for Uncle Red's burial preparations and buy him a coffin.

When I pulled into the driveway and parked, I nodded toward the sign, GOFF'S FUNERAL PARLOR. Marlene stared at the building for a moment in puzzled silence, but then a shadow of comprehension flickered across her face. She looked at me, desperately searching my face for some sign of denial, and when none was forthcoming, she said, "Dead? He's *dead?*"

I nodded.

She gazed at the funeral parlor for a moment longer, and tears trembled in her eyes. As one big tear spilled over and down her pale, taut face, she said, "When?"

"Yesterday."

"I should've known," she said in a husky whisper. "I should've known! Night before last . . . I was sleeping in an old empty store . . . hadn't been able to find you and him, and I didn't know what to do, and suddenly I had one of those clar-voyant feelings, and I *knew* I'd never see Red again. Never in this world see him again. . . . I thought maybe it was because you and him had left town already, or something like that, but it was this . . . this is what it meant. *Dead.*"

"Wanna go in?"

She brushed a tear from her cheek. "I will try to be brave and strong," she promised.

The funeral parlor was gloomy and rank with the smells of formaldehyde and decayed flowers. The undertaker came out of his office to meet us. He was Mr. Goff, and he looked like an undertaker: tall and stoop-shouldered, slightly cadaverous, moving in a solemn rustle of black garments, unctuous and refined. Here was a man who dealt in finalities, who was aware of the decorous importance of his task. Leaning toward me, he asked in a hushed voice, "You got the money?"

"Yes, sir."

He looked relieved. Solemnly, he said, "Very good. This is," he asked, turning to Marlene with a look of subtle disapproval, "one of the bereaved?"

"Yes, sir," I said. "A relative. My sister."

"Ah, yes. Will you be wanting to see the body?"

"I reckon so. And pick out a coffin, like you said. I got the money."

"Ah," he said, as if congratulating me on my wisdom. "The coffin. Yes. This way, please."

He led us into one of the back rooms, a room of polished dark paneling and waxed floors, where a dozen or more coffins of varying sizes rested on wheeled trestles in an awesome display of lacquered and velvet-lined splendor. In the soft lighting, the brass- and nickel-plated ornaments and handles on the coffins glowed with the promise of a luxurious afterlife.

Mr. Goff led us slowly amid the coffins, saying, "He was a well-known musician, you say? A man of some consequence? Ah, yes. Then you don't want something shoddy. You want something befitting his eminence. Am I correct?"

"Yes, sir," I said, stealing a glance at Marlene. She was entranced by the menacing beauty of the coffins. "I reckon so."

"Ah, yes. Well, then, how about this item? It's not the most expensive item we have, of course, but it will serve quite well. It's solid oak, watertight, comfortable, and the velvet will match his coloring perfectly. What do you think?"

"How much?" I asked.

"Two hundred and twenty dollars, and worth every penny of it," Mr. Goff said in the way of a dignified boast. "Of course, if you want the best for him . . ." He led us to the most ornate coffin in the room. Soft, well-placed spotlights illuminated its rich blue velvet padding and curlicued ornaments. "There are none finer than this item, I assure you. It's expensive, of course, but the best always is, isn't it?"

In response to my question, he cleared his throat decorously and said, "I could let you have it for three hundred and ten. It's the best."

I glanced at Marlene, but she didn't seem to have an opinion, so I nodded and said, "All right, then. That one." It was much more than I thought I would have to pay for a coffin, but I didn't want to bury Uncle Red in anything but the best.

"Ah," Mr. Goff said, impressed by my taste and decisiveness. "Well, then, if that's all settled, you might want to view the body now?" He led us through a door to an adjoining room, a dark room until he switched on an overhead light that reflected harshly off the tiled floors and walls. And there in the center of the room, on a table with wheels, lay Uncle Red's body.

He was dressed in his fancy performing suit. When the body and the suit had first been delivered to the funeral parlor, Mr. Goff had delicately questioned the appropriateness of the suit as a burial garment, implying that something a little less garish might be more suitable for someone who was about to stand in front of his Maker. But I couldn't imagine Uncle Red going to his reward in anything less than the fringed and embroidered finery he had worn during the finest moments of his life. I was only sorry that he couldn't wear the cowboy hat, too.

When Marlene first saw his body on the table, a small cry

escaped from her throat and she clutched my hand.

"As real as in life, isn't he?" Mr. Goff said, encouraging our praise of his handiwork.

Actually, he looked no more real than a wax dummy. He had been closely shaved, and his wavy red hair was fastidiously combed. His skin had a grayish-pink tinge, with a smear of rouge on each gaunt cheekbone. His hollow cheeks had been puffed out with some sort of wadding, and daubs of wax glistened in his nostrils. Wax also glistened along his tightly closed but faintly smiling lips. And fake though it was, the smile was the only feature on his face that seemed at all natural. Mr. Goff had no doubt intended it to be a beatific smile, a happy-in-heaven smile, but it had turned out to be a small vicious smile like the one I had often seen on his face when he had been about to do something devilish and provocative, the smile of a man who has a secret that he isn't ever going to tell.

Marlene, with tears on her face, released my hand and stepped closer to the table. She reached out to touch Uncle Red's withered hands, which were folded across his stomach. At the first touch of his cold embalmed flesh, she pulled away, but then apparently forced herself to place her hand on his. She bowed her head, and in a whisper that was only occasionally audible, murmured a prayer. I heard the words, "Dear Lord . . . meet again in Heaven . . . someday . . ." and then she sighed heavily and turned away.

Mr. Goff led us back through the coffin room and into the parlor. "If you'll step into my office," he said to me, pointedly excluding Marlene from the invitation, and placed a spidery hand on my shoulder to guide me.

"I'll wait outside," Marlene said, stifling sobs.

The walls in Mr. Goff's office were decorated with certificates of graduation from correspondence schools and morticians' colleges. He sat down behind his desk like a huge black moth coming to rest. "Now," he said, "to take care of the petty business details . . ." He did some quick figuring on a scratch pad, and said with precision, "Altogether—the coffin, my fee, the minister's fee, the cost of the burial plot, the gravedigger's fee—oh, and what about a headstone? A person of his eminence, a suitable headstone would certainly seem in order, wouldn't it? I have connections, of course, so I can get you a good one for one-third off."

"I don't know," I said, confused and very lonely. "I didn't

think about that. How much would it be?"

"Everything except the headstone comes to five hundred and ten dollars."

I frowned with shock and embarrassment. "I don't have that much," I confessed.

"Ah," he said. "Well, perhaps we had better start with what you *do* have."

"Three hundred and ninety-two dollars."

That seemed like an awful lot to me, but Mr. Goff wasn't impressed. In fact, he seemed downright disappointed. He sighed gravely and said, "That's all? You can't get any more?"

I shook my head.

"Well," he went on condescendingly, "that's not very much, is it? I'll tell you what, though. You take the first coffin we looked at, the cheaper one, and I'll try to scale everything down, so that perhaps we can do it all for that amount. It won't be easy, but if we can cut out the minister's fee—that means there'll be no service, of course. You realize that, don't you? And if we use only the hearse, not the limousine . . ." He sighed again. "Well, we might be able to do it for three hundred ninety-two."

He held out his hand. I took the money from Uncle Red's wallet and gave it to him. He counted it.

"It's all I got," I said.

With the look of a reluctant public benefactor, he handed me back two dollars. "I'll see what I can do for three-ninety," he said, and shook his head in sorrow at the sacrifices that undertakers were called upon to make in times of trouble and grief. "The deceased will be on display between"—he glanced at his watch—"between two and three o'clock this afternoon, in lieu of services, if anyone wishes to view the remains. And if you want flowers . . . well, perhaps some of his friends would care to supply them?"

I nodded.

"I'll arrange for the best burial plot I can for the money," he said, and stood up to indicate that the transaction was finished.

Marlene was waiting for me in the car. Both of us were hungry, so we drove downtown to find a cafe where we could get a hamburger. She hadn't eaten anything since yesterday. I had hoped to use the two dollars I had left to buy gas and oil for the car, since the tank was almost empty and the pistons were beginning to knock for want of lubrication. But when Marlene mentioned that she hadn't eaten since yesterday, I decided to spend the money on food. I couldn't keep the car much longer anyway. I knew I would never get enough money to keep it operating. I only hoped that it would get us to the graveyard.

"Can I have another one?" Marlene asked after she had devoured the first hamburger in a few wolfish bites. "I have to eat for two these days."

So she had another one, which she ate almost as fast as the first. After I paid the check, I was left with less than a dollar, and it was all the money we had in the world. It hurt me to listen to the low, ominous *thunk thunk thunk* of the pistons in the Packard as we drove back to the funeral parlor, but I couldn't afford to buy oil, so I just had to grit my teeth and let the pistons thunk.

Mr. Goff ushered Marlene and me into the room where Uncle Red's body was on display in the big black coffin with pearl-white velvet padding. The room was cool and dimly lit. Syrupy organ music from a phonograph record filtered softly into the room, but other than that, and an occasional sniffle from Marlene, the room remained profoundly silent. Uncle Red's body lay in rigid repose in the coffin, his head propped up on a velvet cushion, with that faint and joyless smile forever curled on his rouged and wax-sealed lips.

The funeral procession to the graveyard consisted of two vehicles. The long black hearse led the way, with a driver and Mr. Goff in the front seat, while Marlene and I followed in the Packard limousine, the gas gauge of which indicated that the tank was virtually empty. And we were no more than halfway to the graveyard when the oil-pressure gauge finally eased over to zero. The deep thunking heartbeat sounds from the engine's vitals tore a painful compassion from my heart, but there was nothing I could do. I was afraid to spend any of our last ninety-five cents for gas or oil, and I was reconciled to the necessity of abandoning the car soon anyway. I could only hope that it would keep going until we got to the graveyard.

It did. Barely. As we were going through the gates and up the last little knoll, the laboring engine began to sputter and cough, but the car kept lurching until we got to the top of the knoll. Then it thunked and sputtered, lurched and shivered and coughed, and died, as we coasted slowly down to where Uncle

Red's grave had been dug and stopped behind the hearse.

There was no canopy over the grave. No imitation grass had been spread over the raw red earth. No folding chairs had been placed beside the grave for the mourners. There were no mourners, in fact, except for Marlene and me. An old black man in a limp felt hat was listlessly shoveling clods of dirt away from the edge of the grave when we arrived, and he was recruited to help me and Mr. Goff and the hearse driver roll Uncle Red's coffin from the hearse and lower it on straps into the grave.

"There ought to be *some* kind of service," Marlene protested.

"I'm leaving now," Mr. Goff said. He handed me his business card. "If you ever get the money and want him to have a headstone, I'll see that one is placed on his grave. Until then, the city will keep a small metal cross on the grave, with his name on it."

I had noticed that all the graves in this corner of the graveyard had no headstones. All that identified their occupants were little metal crosses with name plates on them. It would be years later before I realized that this was the pauper's section of the graveyard, and that Mr. Goff hadn't paid a penny for the plot in which Uncle Red was buried. And it would be almost ten years to the day—on the tenth anniversary of his death, in fact—that Uncle Red's grave would finally be marked by a huge marble monument, paid for and erected by the Country Music Institute, with a big bronze plaque in the center of the monument commemorating the birth and death of "Red Stovall, one of the all-time great country singers and songwriters, who lives on in his undying music."

After the hearse had pulled away and we were left standing in the hot sunshine beside the open grave, Marlene said, "At least we could sing a song, couldn't we?"

I got Uncle Red's guitar—my guitar now—from the trunk of the Packard and strapped it on, and Marlene and I stood at the foot of the grave, looking down on the black coffin, and sang "Swing Low, Sweet Chariot." The old black gravedigger watched us for a moment, then stuck his shovel into the pile of loose soil and came, hat in hand, to join us in the song. He had a good voice. Marlene's singing voice hadn't improved a bit since I had last heard her, but at least she put her heart into it. Nobody could accuse her of not trying.

But it was my own voice that surprised me. Not once while I was singing did it change timbre. Not once did it shift from baritone to soprano. From now on there would be no more embarrassing high-pitched squeaks in the middle of smooth baritone lines. . . .

> *"Swing low, sweet chariot*
> *Coming for to carry me home . . ."*

I found myself wishing that Uncle Red could hear me now.

When we finished "Swing Low," we stood in the soft hot birdsonged silence, wondering what to do next. With tears in her eyes, Marlene suggested that we sing one of Uncle Red's songs, but I couldn't as yet play "Pale Horse, Pale Rider," and nothing else seemed appropriate for a funeral song, so finally the old black man began to hum a familiar tune, and after a few bars, Marlene and I joined in.

> *"Look down, look down that lonesome road . . ."*

Though I had never played the song before, I missed the chord changes only a couple of times in the beginning. And, again, I sang the whole song without a single break in my voice, which gave me good reason to hope that my voice had completed its changes, and now, in my sorrow and pride, in my ignorance, I felt that maybe I was ready to begin preparing for a career as a country singer like Uncle Red.

> *"Look down, look down that lonesome road*
> *Before you travel on. . . ."*

When we finished the song, the old black man put his crumpled hat back on his head. "Dat was a fine send-off, chillun. He be proud, I bet. Now I best git on wif my work." He looked at me for confirmation, and when I nodded my head, he began to toss shovelfuls of the clayey red earth into the grave, each shovelful making a hollow *plop* sound as it fell on the black coffin.

The Packard wouldn't start. Not only was it out of gas, but the oilless engine had froze up and wouldn't even turn over when I pressed the starter. I took the keys from the ignition and went back to the grave and tossed them down onto Uncle

Red's coffin, and the next shovelful of dirt covered the keys forever.

The only thing I carried away from the car was the guitar. We didn't know where we were going or what we were going to do. We talked about it as we walked along. I told Marlene I would have to get back to Oklahoma somehow, or maybe to California, and find my folks. I asked her if she would like to come along, and she said, "Oh, Lordy, would I ever! Hoss, you're the only family I got now, and with Red's baby coming, and all . . ."

So we left the graveyard and walked on down the heat-shimmered highway, that lonesome road that never seemed to end. It was a road that I was to travel all my life.

27

We spent the night in Nashville's Greyhound bus depot. From the graveyard, we had gone back to the rooming house so I could pick up Uncle Red's cowboy hat and my extra clothes, and when the landlady heard that Marlene—my sister—and I didn't have any money or any place to go, she packed us some sandwiches in a brown bag and escorted us to the Greyhound depot, where she bought us each a bus ticket to Cainsville. Under questioning, I had told her that my grandfather lived in Cainsville, and she decided that the most charitable and yet cheapest way she could get rid of us would be to send us to Grandpa.

We got to Cainsville late the next morning, and we found Grandpa in a weatherbeaten and dilapidated old wood-frame farmhouse about two miles out of town. It was his old family home, the old Wagoner place, though there were no more Wagoners around. The house and land now belonged to a man called Everts, the biggest landowner in Wilson County, who remembered the Wagoners and had given Grandpa permission to live in the old abandoned house as long as he wanted.

Grandpa's two brothers were somewhere out West—Oregon, some people said—and his father and old-maid sister had been the last two Wagoners to live in the house. Both of them were buried in the little graveyard on a knoll behind the house, where Great-Grandmother Wagoner, Grandpa's mother, had been buried for over thirty years. She had died of scarlet fever ten years after her oldest son, Elmo Wagoner, my grandfather, had lit out one night on a bareback mule without telling anyone that he was leaving, heading out West, the way generations of his ancestors had done before him, as though his leaving were not so much a decision as a bloodline compulsion, a move as ordained by instinct as the migration of wild geese, pioneers in search of the Promised Land.

And when he came back to die in the place—the house— where he was born, he found it deserted. The windows were broken, the doors hung loose on their hinges, the planks of the porch and floors were warped, and owls lived on the rafters. Grandpa slept on a pallet in the front room and cooked his food on a small kerosene stove. He sat out on the front porch in the evenings and watched the sun go down.

"It'll be all right for the summer," I said, "but what're you gonna do when winter comes?"

"Oh, I 'spect I'll fix it up a little 'fore then," he said, but he didn't sound like someone who really expected to be around that long.

I tried to persuade him to come back to Oklahoma with Marlene and me, and maybe go from there to California, but he shook his head.

"Too old," he said.

The evening before Marlene and I left, I sat out on the porch with Grandpa and got to wondering what would become of him here, all alone.

"Ahhh," he snarled, dismissing the subject with mild contempt. "We're always alone, Whit. Always. We're born alone, and we die alone. Red knew that. And you'll realize it, too, before your time comes."

It was the first time he had mentioned Uncle Red by name since I had told him how he had died, and even then Grandpa only shook his head and said, "The poor man"—not "Poor Red," as if he had been someone Grandpa knew, but just "The poor man," as if Uncle Red had been a stranger to him, as if all men were strangers to one another.

It bothered me to see how bitter he had become. It wasn't an angry bitterness, but rather a soft sourness, like an overripe melon melting back into the earth. As I sat with him on the porch that evening, I remembered him telling me about the

Run. I remembered him telling me how his dreams of a Promised Land had all turned to dust—literally—and how he had
only one dream left, the dream of going home to Tennessee.
And now that he had found that there was no place to come
back to, what of the dream? Was that why he had grown so
bitter?—because he had no more dreams?

"Dreams?" he said, and after a moment's reflection, "Dreams
are something you wake up from."

I would always remember that phrase, and remember what
he looked like when he said it, with his hawk-fierce profile
silhouetted against the sundown sky. It was the way I would
remember him long after he was dead and buried in the graveyard on the knoll behind the old Wagoner house. And I would
remember the phrase in the years to come, as I chased my own
dreams, and came to terms with their consequences.

Marlene and I left Grandpa's house the next day and went
to Murfreesboro to catch a freight train headed West. Neither
of us had ever hopped a freight train before, but we were given
instructions by friendly hoboes along the way, and within a
few days after we first climbed into an empty boxcar in Murfreesboro's railyard, Marlene and I were seasoned bums. We
knew how to hop the trains, how to hide in them, and how to
get off them. We learned how to live in hobo jungles, and how
to read the hobo signs that told us which towns to avoid, which
houses to approach for easy handouts, and which jungles were
safe for hoboes to sleep in.

When we came to the big towns along the way, where we
were less likely to be arrested for vagrancy, Marlene and I
would make a little money by singing on the streetcorners. I
played the guitar and she beat a tambourine as we sang, with
Uncle Red's cowboy hat turned upside down on the sidewalk
at our feet to catch the nickels and dimes that the passersby
tossed to us. We made almost two dollars doing that in Memphis one day, and we did even better in Little Rock after
Marlene printed a sign on a piece of cardboard, "Expectant
Mother," and hung it around her neck.

That sign virtually doubled our daily take. Marlene wasn't
so dumb after all. In fact, as I learned during the many years
that she and I were to be friends, she wasn't dumb at all. That
"Expectant Mother" sign got her more sympathy and money
than her singing ever did.

What it got *me* was a lot of dirty looks. So when we got to

Oklahoma City, I made myself a sign and hung it around my neck: "It wasn't me." And that not only ended the reproachful looks, it brought smiles to a few faces along the way.

We did all right, Marlene and I. We sang our way across the country. We went hungry a few times, but we also ate steaks a few times, and we kept going, two ragamuffin hoboes toting a guitar and a tambourine, hopping freights and singing in the streets. We made our way to my folks' empty house in Roscoe, Oklahoma, and then followed them on out to California, where we finally found them near Bakersfield in a migrant farmworkers' camp, living in a tent and sleeping on cotton sacks. And just about nine months after the fateful night in Noxpater, Arkansas, Marlene gave birth to a seven-pound baby boy with a shock of frizzy red hair. She named him Wagoner Stovall, and I became . . .

But that's another story. It's one I would like to tell someday, for I finally found out what it was like to stand behind a microphone on the same spot on the same stage where Uncle Red once stood. That was in the Dream Bowl in Redondo Beach, California, sixteen years after Uncle Red's death. My band and I, Hoss Wagoner and the Big Wheels, opened a show there one night for the headliner, Bob Wills and the Texas Playboys.

As I said, though, that's another story. This is Uncle Red's story, and if it can be said to have an end at all, this is it.

ABOUT THE AUTHOR

Clancy Carlile lives in various places in California, and is the author of two previous books.